THE GIRL WHO WALKED IN THE SHADOWS

MARNIE RICHES grew up on a rough estate in Manchester, aptly within sight of the dreaming spires of Strangeways Prison. Able to speak five different languages, she gained a Master's degree in Modern & Medieval Dutch and German from Cambridge University. She has been a punk, a trainee rock star, a pretend artist, a property developer and professional fundraiser.

Marnie is the author of the bestselling George McKenzie series of eBook thrillers, the first of which, *The Girl Who Wouldn't Die*, won The Patricia Highsmith Award for Most Exotic Location in the Dead Good Reader Awards, 2015. In 2016, the series was shortlisted for The Tess Gerritsen Award for Best Series (Dead Good Reader Awards).

Also by Marnie Riches:

George McKenzie eBook series
The Girl Who Wouldn't Die
The Girl Who Broke the Rules
The Girl Who Had No Fear
The Girl Who Got Revenge

Manchester series
Born Bad
The Cover Up

The Girl Who Walked in the Shadows

MARNIE RICHES

avon.

Published by Avon
An imprint of HarperCollins*Publishers Ltd*
1 London Bridge Street
London SE1 9GF

www.harpercollins.co.uk

First published in Great Britain in ebook format by HarperCollins*Publishers* 2016
This paperback edition published by HarperCollins*Publishers* 2018

1

Marnie Riches asserts the moral right to
be identified as the author of this work

A catalogue record for this book
is available from the British Library

ISBN: 9780008271466

This novel is entirely a work of fiction.
The names, characters and incidents portrayed in it are
the work of the author's imagination. Any resemblance to
actual persons, living or dead, events or localities is
entirely coincidental.

Printed and bound in Great Britain by CPI Group (UK)
Ltd, Croydon CR0 4YY

For Weez Maria Owenen, who has grown up to be one
of the kickest-assest women I know

PART 1

CHAPTER 1

London, Belgravia, 16 February

Cold jabbed his raw skin where it was exposed. Hands, wrapped in torn, woollen gloves; the filthy threads had come loose, long ago. Blackened nails, blue fingers, toes on the cusp of being devoured by greedy frostbite. Vulnerable. But his discomfort mattered no longer. Only watching these two men, as he crouched behind a Range Rover, out of view. On this grand Belgravia street in London, double yellow lines – hidden beneath thick, shovelled banks of snow, but there nonetheless – ensured a clear line of sight.

Problem was, a man like him stood out, here. An imperfect grey figure, juxtaposed against flawless white stone; perfectly white snow, too deep to clear with grit, even in the city; icicles hanging from every portico and window frame – deadly diamond daggers.

Move along, sir. Sorry, no spare change. Shift, or I'll call the police.

Always looks of utter disdain, as these wealthy denizens of SW1X picked up the scent of urine and stale alcohol. Especially the women. Clad in real fur, now. Since the Siberian winter of discontent …

Fuck them.

He had eyes only for these two men, standing outside Mosimann's private restaurant. A picture of establishment respectability, posed in their cashmere outer layers before ecclesiastical built-beauty, where now only millionaires could afford to dine. Worshipping at the altar of fine food and business transactions, sealed over bottles of wine that cost thousands. Scum of the earth, these two. Black hearts so easily hidden beneath bespoke Jermyn Street clothing. Lies. Corruption. Evil.

His heart was pounding, as he rehearsed in his mind what he intended to do. Steeling himself, though a man could have no better motivation. Would he miss his chance?

Across the road, the men laughed. Easy in each other's company. Moving aside, to let a blonde beauty pass. Some Russian oligarch's squeeze, walking her lapdog. Trot, trot, trot. Firm buttocks clad in baby-pink Lycra. A show-pony, even in harsh conditions, drawing the men's gaze. Now, he had a good look at them, as they turned to follow the blonde's progress.

His quarry was neither tall nor fat. An average man in physical respects. Forty something. Dark-haired. Ordinary looks compensated for with immaculate grooming and a physique that had been created in an expensive gym. He knew this much. He also knew that this man lived in a mansion block with Chelsea views of the river. Too much security round there. So, the backstreets of Knightsbridge would suffice, providing things went according to plan.

The other – Mephistopheles with a paunch – would wait. Somewhat older. Fifty-two, in fact. That his chicanery had gone undiscovered for decades was barely credible. But different rules applied to the super-rich. Not today, though. Not today. A day of reckoning was nigh.

Pushing thoughts of the pain in his joints out of his mind, he crossed the road in haste. Dodged a black cab, skidding along on the ineffectually gritted asphalt. Slush, seeping through the holes in boots lined with newspaper.

The men were on the move. Ambling along. The older man even made a snowball and hurled it against the wall, just beyond the frontage of Waitrose supermarket. Ha ha. Playful and light-hearted. Apologising, like some charming billionaire bastard who fits right in, here, to the elderly woman it had almost taken out, before it had plopped harmlessly onto the brickwork. Chatting amiably, unhurried, like men who had the entire week diarised satisfactorily by their P.A.s. No unwelcome surprises for these masters of the universe.

Well, that was about to change, just as he had changed.

Crippling fear had turned to adrenalin. A rush. A hunger. His bloodlust was rising, fending off the chill of a Wednesday afternoon. -17°C and falling. Light already failing. He had to act fast.

At the head of the junction with the neighbouring Lowndes Street, the considerable bulk of a brown and cream Rolls Royce Phantom was waiting as close to the snow-bound kerb as was possible. A billionaire's car, heated to perfection, its door held open by a liveried chauffeur for the older of the two men. Designed to ferry him to the next Big Meeting. Mephisto with the paunch bade his companion farewell.

Now, it was time.

His quarry started to walk briskly up through Knightsbridge, towards Harrods. Coat hem spattered with icy mess. Head bent forwards, advancing into the jaws of the Arctic wind.

Take a turn into one of the backstreets, goddamn it!

He had anticipated where this man was going. Had studied his movements well enough. But the idiot was staying on the main drag. Too many people, here. Police, cruising by slowly in a patrol car.

Shit. Turn down an alley! Turn!

Except there were no alleys. The man progressed through Lowndes Square. A green strip in the middle, covered in thick snow; a picture postcard straight from Narnia. Fringed by cars, covered in forgetful white blankets. Here. Maybe he could do it here. The snow sucked the sound out of everything. Except, this spot was completely overlooked by townhouses and mansion blocks. Every window, a potential set of prying eyes.

Not here.

The man hastened along the pavement at a brisk pace, given conditions underfoot. Already some way ahead. The distance between them widening fast. But then, *his* belly was full. *His* body had been warmed by fine wine and brandy. *His* energy hadn't been sapped by biting hunger, sucked dry by spending the harshest winter since records began on the streets. Robbed for breakfast. Moved along at lunch. Beaten up for dinner. Pissed on by other homeless, too drunk to realise what they were doing - the only midnight snack on offer.

Stop feeling sorry for yourself, you piece of shit. Remember why you are here.

He kept going. The moment would present itself. He had faith.

Two women, moving towards him now. Bulked up with Puffa jackets and ridiculous furry hats. Blocking his view. Talking, talking. Espanol. *Muy pericoloso. Muy dramatico.* Hands beating the freezing air in telenovela-exaggerated movements, breath steaming like two pressure cookers on the boil. Tourists, no doubt.

Get out of the way, you fat Spanish cows.

Heart thudding, as they crowded his vision, snuffing out the sight of his target entirely.

They passed him by. Grimacing at the sight and smell of a vagrant.

The target was out of sight. Gone.

Shit.

His face prickled with anxiety. Panic rendered him almost breathless. Peering ahead. No sign of the rich, gutless fucker. Glancing in the doorways of the surrounding buildings. Not there. Glancing in the park. Not there either. Was this all in vain? He should have planned better. Had a plan B. All was lost. But then …

Harriet Street. A sharp left, leading to Sloane Street. There he was. Pausing beneath the Victorian lamppost by the cast iron railings that fringed a 1930s block. An unwitting child, stumbled through the wardrobe wearing seasonal finery into a hard, white world. Waiting to be lured into the shadows by a ragged, destitute Tumnus.

The man struggled to light a cigarette in the wind. Sputter, sputter, the flame died. He advanced to the doorway of this white stone and brick mansion block. Unobservant, as he finally lit his smoke. Opposite, every window had been obscured behind some kind of green builder's gauze, stretched tight over scaffolding. Hiding the view below entirely. It was a gift from an otherwise vengeful and unforgiving god.

Heart fluttering. Determination stiffening his aching spine. From the railing, he snapped one of those giant icicles that hung everywhere since the freak cold spell had descended on Europe. Ten inches. Sharpened by nature to a point. Galvanised by weeks of sub-zero temperatures.

Five paces. Four. Three. Clutching the icy shiv in his frostbitten hand.

The man was facing the other way.

Jab, jab, jab in the sweet spot in his neck before the weapon could melt or weaken. The man's blood gushed, hissing hot on the frozen ground, spattering against the wall. Screams coming out as gurgling. But he was the only human being within earshot.

'That's for Amsterdam, you piece of shit,' he said, as the man bled out, staring glassy-eyed and disbelieving into the abyss.

Running away, now, he tossed the icicle down a storm drain that had been cleared of snow. By the time the police found the body, all traces of the weapon would have been washed away in the dirt-splattered slush of the road. Melted by grit-residue. The only clue left at the scene would be the watery holes in the dead man's neck: the calling card of Jack Frost.

CHAPTER 2

North West England, women's prison, 27 February

'Put a bag over my head, didn't I?' the woman said, biting nails that were already at the quick.

Couldn't have been more than twenty, this one. Looked nearer to forty with a complexion the colour of porridge. Overweight and swollen-faced, George guessed anti-depressants were at work. Dull blue eyes, as though the medication had caused a film to form over her sclera, preventing her from seeing the world in its grim true colours. Another poor cow in a pen full of poor cows.

'What do you mean, you put a bag over your head?' she asked the woman. She was poised to write. Steeling her hand to stop shaking. Unnerving to be back inside the very same prison she had spent three unforgettable months in – now a long time ago. A one-star vacation at Her Majesty's leisure. All meals provided. The beatings had come for free. She had not known then that she would swap these Victorian red-brick walls of a one-time Barnardo's home for the ivory tower of St. John's College, Cambridge. No, she had been a poor cow in a stall full of crap, same as the others.

Her interviewee leaned forward. Cocked her head to one side. Grimaced.

'Are you fucking thick or what?' A spray of spittle accompanied 'thick'.

Issued forth with venom, George knew. Tap, tap on her temple with her chewed index finger.

'Donna.' The prison officer's tone issued warning enough for Donna to back up.

'I said, I put the bag on my head. They didn't know I had it. Tied it tight.' Donna folded her arms. Smiling now. Satisfied. 'It was Sainsbury's. It had fucking holes in the bottom, didn't it?'

'Did you intend to kill yourself?' George asked, a rash unexpectedly starting to itch its way up her neck. She knew Donna wouldn't catch sight of it so easily because darker skin hid a multitude. She disciplined herself not to scratch.

'Yeah. Course I bleedin' did.'

The prison officer, a heavy-set woman in her thirties, by the looks, laughed. 'Come on, Donna. We all know you were doing a Michael Hutchence, weren't you?'

'What?'

Donna was almost certainly too young to have heard of him, George thought.

'Feller from INXS. Offed himself by accident, doing an asphyxi-wank or something.'

Donna tugged at the collar of her standard-issue tracksuit – too tight over her low-hanging, braless breasts. 'You taking the piss?'

'Yes.'

Insane laughter from both of them then. A camaraderie that George was used to seeing, along with the gallows humour. When the mirth subsided, Donna confessed the real reason for her grand polyethylene gesture.

'I had bedbugs, didn't I? They were biting like bastards.' She started to rub her forearms through the jersey material. 'I asked for a new mattress but they wouldn't bloody listen. So, I puts the bag on my head, cos if they think you're going to top yourself in here, you stand a better chance of them actually listening to what you're on about.' She glowered at the prison officer, seated beside her. Switched the glare for a grin like a deft pickpocket. 'I been in here two years, right? Got another six to go.'

George scratched at her scalp with the end of her pen. Got the cap entangled in one of her corkscrew curls. Unrelentingly itchy. Was it the nervous rash? Was this her body telling her brain that she was losing her shit? She couldn't possibly be freaked out, though. Definitely not. Not after all this time. Not a pro, like her.

She shuffled her sheaf of paper straight, as if to demonstrate to herself that she had mastery over everything. In control of herself and her environment at all times. Now that she was qualified, she spent more time inside prisons than out. Except when she was in Amsterdam with Paul. Bastard. Oh, well. Not everything was within her control.

'What did you do, Donna?'

'I didn't do it.'

'No? Okay. But what were you convicted for?'

'GBH. I got my son taken off me, didn't I?' Tears welled in Donna's eyes, replacing the Valium film with something more organic. Sleeve pulled down over her fist, she wiped the burgeoning tears away. 'They said, social services said, that I'd battered him. And I hadn't. They said I was unfit, the fucking lying do-gooding bastards. Just because that old bitch next door grassed me for smoking weed and that. And the dead rabbits in the yard. Wasn't my frigging fault. They shat everywhere. Then, I gets social services and the environmental health come knocking. And school gets involved, saying my Thom was truanting and had bruises and that.'

She pursed her lips. Hers was suddenly a mean face that looked as though its owner could inflict pain happily. George had grown up with the likes of Donna. Not so different from Tonya. A hard-faced calamity queen.

'My Thomas was *not* fucking abused.' Poked herself in the

9

chest, hard, so that George could hear the drumming on her sternum. '*I* was fucking abused. I could tell them how I was bounced round Rochdale. Me an' about ten other girls off the estate in the back of a van. Thirteen-year-old rent-a-slags for all the dirty bastards in the area. Two pimping wankers raking in it like we was stock in a cash and carry. Working for some warped bastard called the Hawk or some shit like that. Our mams didn't give a fuck. They was too busy getting pissed down the pub.'

George nodded. Showed no emotion. Dr McKenzie was a criminologist. Professional detachment was the only way to endure these heart-breaking stories. But it was the same story over and over, told by different women. Abuse, leading to abuse. Young girls playing chicken through the fast lanes of traffick. They never made it to the other side intact.

'So why the GBH?'

Donna snorted noisily. 'Day our Thom was put in care. Went out, didn't I? Got mashed up. Beat some slag to a pulp with a snooker cue. She'd been looking at my fella, so ...' She looked up at George. No longer morose but suddenly hopeful, as if a timid sun was trying to push its way through the storm clouds. 'I'm going to get him back. Our Thomas. When I get out of here. He's coming home to his mam.' A gingivitis grin. Radiant with rotten teeth. Thin hair scraped too high on her head into a tight pony-tail made her look like a ruined child.

George had to get out of there. She'd had enough for one day. Checked her watch. Brought the session to an end.

As she made her way through the facility to the entrance, where she would reclaim her phone and her composure, she noticed the latest issue of *Do What?* – the inmates' magazine she had remembered reading when she had been on remand here. Scattered copies on the table needed organising.

The baffled prison officer paused, giving George a moment to tidy the magazines into a neat fan. Beneath the headline that spoke of Shep, the drugs-dog almost choking to death on a hibernating hedgehog, there was a piece that triggered recognition deep within George's mind. A debate on whether an icicle could actually be used as a shiv and whether it was right that the prison staff should leave these freakish twelve-inchers hanging off the old prison eaves.

'Okay, Dr McKenzie?' The prison officer asked.

George nodded. Tucked her portfolio of notes under her arm and made her way back down to security. Scanned on the way in. Scanned on the way out.

Having failed to find a USB stick at Aunty Sharon's, she had once tried to bring in a CD-ROM she had burned especially in order to show the inmates a simple guide to the study she was doing into women's prisons for the government. Security had confiscated even that, saying a teenage inmate had broken up a CD brought in for her by her sister and committed suicide by swallowing the shards. Everything was a weapon in here. She now made damned sure she never ran out of USB sticks.

Got to get the hell out. This place is bringing me down and down.

Beyond the gates, breath steaming on the sub-zero air, she switched her phone on to check for messages. Hoping that cantankerous old fool, Van den Bergen had been in touch. It was weeks since their argument. Six weeks to be precise. Her refusal to speak to him had been deliberate. Even Aunty Sharon had said she'd done the right thing by dropping the shutters on him.

But the screen yielded nothing. Silence. No abrupt words, saying he was sorry and that she had been right. That he would make amends.

On the train she sat at a dirty, crumb-sullied table, clutching her anorak tightly around her. Broken heating meant the journey would be purgatorial. Shivering at the sight of the snow-covered fields and jagged, naked hedgerows that scudded by. A white world, empty of life except for disappointing humanity and the odd cannibalistic robin. Irritation mounting inside her. Oppressive, like the Siberian freeze that had an entire continent in its grip.

Twenty minutes felt like an hour. Her phone still yielded nothing of note. Only nagging emails from civil servants, asking if she would be handing her study in on time. Pointed correspondence from a fellow criminologist who had it in for her. Professor Dickwad Dobkin at UCL. Complaining that he knew about her additional research into trafficking. Saying that he had started something almost identical, eons ago. Long before her. Of course.

'Get fucked, Dobkin,' George said, as she searched for her train ticket.

'Sorry?' The ticket inspector asked, swaying side to side in the Pendolino carriage, as it pelted through the crystalline hills of Staffordshire.

'Nothing,' George said. 'Talking to myself. Too much work. Not enough play.'

The ticket inspector, a sweaty-looking man, despite the unrelenting cold, gave her a disinterested half-smile.

It was true. Her deadline loomed large. Today's encounter with Donna had been one of her final interviews. She would have to start typing it up tonight. Perhaps even do a little work on her laptop now, on the train back to London.

Discipline yourself, George.

Except her phone pinged. Probably Aunty Sharon.

Fuck discipline.

Peered down at the screen.

Ah, finally.

But it was not the sort of message she was hoping for.

    Come to Amsterdam a.s.a.p. Paul.

CHAPTER 3

Amsterdam, Bijlmer district, later

'What do you want me to do, boss?' Elvis asked, pulling his woollen hat down low over his ears, so that bushy red-brown sideburns were only just visible. His breath steamed on the air. Red nose and streaming eyes made him look peaky. But then, these days, Elvis always looked like he never slept. Experience could do that to a detective, even one as dopey and idiotically optimistic as Elvis.

With his protégé seemingly transfixed by the sight of his mobile phone, Chief Inspector Paul van den Bergen hastily slipped the device back into his pocket. 'Get photos of everything,' he said. Felt like he had been caught doing something forbidden, though texting George in a work capacity was hardly a misdemeanour. Since she had qualified, she worked for the Dutch police on a freelance basis often enough.

He turned to Marie, who looked as though she was wearing every garment her wardrobe held. Some ugly hand-knitted cardigan on top of a coat. Purple clashed with the red colour of her hair poking out beneath two hats, by the looks. Bet she smelled worse than usual beneath all those layers. But today, Marie had abandoned the warmth of the office and her Internet research in favour of dusting for prints. After the best part of a year spent

13

working on missing persons cases, she had been desperate to get out. They all had.

'You called forensics?' he asked her.

'Yep. Marianne said she'll be about half an hour.' Marie blushed. Crouched near the dead man's head. Scowled at his blood-spattered face. 'He looks familiar.'

'They always look familiar round here.'

Gazing down at the cochineal Rorschach pattern that surrounded the dead man, Van den Bergen put his hand on his stomach. Though he could not feel the lumpy scar tissue beneath the thick wadding of his anorak, he pressed his long fingers there, tracing the line of the scarring from sternum to his abdomen. Like this dead man at his feet, he had lost almost his entire life's blood. A good two years ago now. Time heals all scars, right? Bullshit, it did.

Elvis clicked away on a digital camera. Blue plastic overshoes over his snowboots. Behind him, the remaining high-rises of Bijlmer loomed. Once Amsterdam's arsehole, a few colourful panels on the front of the renovated blocks and winter wonder-land conditions made it only marginally more enticing than it had been in the dark days. Better than Van den Bergen remem-bered the area when he was a young cop. But still an armpit of a locale, crushed under the weight of second-rate infrastructure and drug-pushers that came out at night like cockroaches.

His phone rang. He was praying it would be George.

'Van den Bergen. Speak.'

It wasn't her. Fat bastard Olaf Kamphuis was on the line, barking at him for information, though why he was getting his big pants in a twist over a run-of-the-mill Bijlmer stabbing was beyond him. Power had clearly gone to his bulbous head, now he was Commissioner. Hands-on micromanagement also had extended to grabbing Van den Bergen by his balls tightly and squeezing.

'I want you off the missing persons bullshit,' Kamphuis had

said, sitting in his new desk chair, cranked even higher than the last one, in an office, even roomier than the one he had amply occupied before. Sweat had blossomed darkest blue around his armpits through the ceremonial glad rags. 'You've had long enough to recover,' he had insisted, huffing, puffing, trying to blow Van den Bergen's house of cards down. 'Get back on active service or it's early retirement for you, you lanky streak of piss.'

How the hell had it happened? Pushing forty-seven now, though he felt nearer to sixty. Two of the biggest cases the Netherlands Police had ever solved, down to him and his team. But trumped yet again by a nemesis in a high-stakes game he thought he had cleaned up in long ago. Commissioner, for fuck's sake. Olaf Kamphuis was his boss. Again! There was no God. And with his unimpeachable ally, Gus Kosselaar retired and replaced as Chief of Police by that other infernal arse-carbuncle, Jaap Hasselblad, Van den Bergen's life had become even more of a misery.

As Van den Bergen leaned over to scrutinise the dead man's face, stomach acid shot up into his gullet. The flames of digestive purgatory the only source of warmth in that unrelenting cold. He straightened up with a click from his hip. Six feet five of broken man. How he longed for the comfort of his office and those stone cold missing persons files now.

He grimaced. Pointed to the gun by the dead man's hand. The scabs around his mouth and nose. Leather jacket, too flimsy for the cold. Covered in stains. Jeans, yellowing at the knees. Greasy blond hair, plastered to his scalp, now encrusted with blood as was his left hand, where perhaps he'd grabbed at his neck. Bleeding out in arterial spurts across the base of the children's slide. Then, on the ground in a foetal position. Leaking his last into the pretty red Rorschach. Butterfly. Humming birds. Flower.

'Crystal meth head. Or mephedrone, is my guess,' he told Elvis. 'This is just a drugs killing over some two-bit stash or a botched deal. Our guy pulls a gun on some other junkie arsehole. A bit of a fight breaks out. He gets stabbed in the neck, judging by the looks of the wound and the blood loss. Perp runs away.'

Elvis nodded. Continued to take photos, as Marie dusted for prints on the semi-automatic pistol that lay inches away from the dead man's blue-grey right hand.

Van den Bergen looked around at the spectators who had started to gather. Rubber-necking, though the scene had been cordoned off with fluttering police tape. Those residents who didn't stop to watch and pass comment on the body – opinions voiced loudly, scathingly in a variety of languages; dramatic hand gestures and beseeching invocations to Allah - shuffled by in the national dress of their country of origin. Women in full burka. Men in salwaar kameez, wearing overcoats over the top. Indonesian. Ghanaian. Somali. Surinamese. All bundled up in this freakishly bitter northern European climate.

'Did anyone see anything?' Van den Bergen asked the crowd. It was a public enough place, for Christ's sake. Right by a brown monolithic block on Sean MacBridestraat. In the kiddy-park, at that! At the foot of the snow-bound slide. Overlooked by hundreds of people, potentially. 'Anyone?'

Blank faces. Chatter ebbing away, now.

'Please come to me with any information you have. Anonymously.' He started to hand out cards, but not a single resident would take one.

Hands tucked abruptly beneath folds of fabric. Into pockets. No eye contact. The crowd started to disperse, fast.

'Marie! Help me take statements,' he called out to his detective.

By the time Marie had finished lifting the solitary print from the gun, the onlookers had all gone, save for a boy of about eight. Drowned in a shabby Puffa jacket that was clearly an adult's given that his sleeves swept the snow. No hat. Inquisitive brown eyes staring at the dead man.

Van den Bergen and Marie approached the child together,

though it was Marie who crouched on the opposite side to the police tape, so that her eyes were level with his.

'Did you see anything?' Marie asked.

The Chief Inspector pulled the chain that held his glasses from the inside of his anorak. Slid them onto his tingling nose to observe the child's reaction. Knew better than to engage the kid in conversation. Only his own daughter understood that he was child-friendly and Tamara was the wrong side of twenty-five now. Marie had the right touch.

The boy was silent. Staring. Staring at the corpse, surrounded by so much red.

'What's your name?' Marie asked, taking the boy by the outsized sleeve.

'Imran.'

'You know him, don't you, Imran? The dead man.'

For five or six almost frozen heartbeats, Imran looked into Marie's watery blue eyes. Opened and closed his mouth, as though he were about to speak. Van den Bergen stiffened, feeling truth and illumination trying to emerge from deep within the silent boy.

But then, Imran turned on his heel and sprinted into the anonymous vertical warren of the apartment block.

'Shit!' Van den Bergen said.

CHAPTER 4

South East London, 28 February

At 2am, the only sound in the small terraced council house was the clickety-click of George's fingers as they tap-danced back and forth over her laptop's keyboard. A consummate performance, outlining the suffering of women on the inside. Bedbugs. Beatings. Braless and behind bars. Family gone. Copy-sheet well and truly blotted for life. Hope in prescription capsules, containing chemical respite from anger and pain.

George paused typing to examine again her pay slip from the Peterhulme Trust. Sighed heavily at the disappointing sum on which tax would be due. Not enough, by far. Pocket change to fund a life split between London, Cambridge and Amsterdam. It was only the second full-length study she had completed for the civil servants of the Home Office in Westminster since becoming a professional criminologist. A career she had fought for. And yet, her working life was not panning out quite as well as she had hoped, even with the continuing support of the formidable Dr Sally Wright. None of it was panning out as George had hoped.

Reflected in the laptop's shining screen, she observed with some distaste the tears rolling slowly down her cheeks. Wiped them away angrily. *Pull yourself together, you wimp. Don't let it all get to you. Don't take shit personally. You mustn't let Van den*

Bergen bring you down. Her hand shook with emotion. Perhaps she should allow herself a good cry. Just this once. Might be cathartic. If she smothered the nose with her sleeve, Patrice wouldn't wake up.

Key in the lock. Front door opened. At this hour, it could only be one person. No time for tears.

'Wotcha, darling,' Aunty Sharon said, prizing snow-encrusted wellies from her swollen feet and putting them neatly on the shoe rack. Next to them, she placed the Betty-Boop heels that she took out of a Tesco bag. Yawning. Throwing her handbag onto the kitchen table. Snatching up the kettle.

'Here, let me do that,' George said, taking the kettle from her.

'All quiet?' Sharon asked. She started washing her hands with Fairy Liquid and scalding water. 'Jesus! You turned the thermostat up again?' She sucked on her fingers, eyeing George suspiciously.

Hand on hip, George rolled her eyes and jerked her thumb in the direction of the door. 'Who do *you* think cranked the heating up?'

Snoring, coming from the adjacent living room. The thunderous, slumberous roar of a dragon, sleeping.

'I gave the bathroom a good do,' George said. 'Got the nailbrush on the grouting. Looks a treat now.'

'Stressed, by any chance?' Aunty Sharon flung herself down onto the kitchen chair. It groaned beneath the weight of her heavy frame. Her taffeta skirt bunched up around her like an airbag triggered in a car crash. 'Fucking thing is doing my head in.' She stood again, unzipped the skirt and stepped out of the layers of electric blue fabric and netting. Flung it over the back of the adjacent chair. Sat back down, wearing only her generous knickers and a thick jumper. Dimpled thighs. Knees like dark chocolate blancmange. White ankle socks digging into her chubby legs. She rubbed her belly. Twanged the elastic in the waistband of her knickers. 'That's better. That new manager is some corny little rarseclart. He's got me dressing up in 1950s shit and bobby socks, like I've escaped some pensioner's mental home. I'm an experienced barmaid in a Soho titty bar. Not some kid serving chips in a themed bloody chicken shop. Cheeky bastard, he is. It's -20 out there tonight. My toes are like frozen meatballs, man! If my fucking legs fall off with hypothermia, I'm going to sue his skinny white arse. At least Derek didn't take the piss, trying to tell me what to wear. And he could have done! But even though he was my baby-father and long-time boss, he never pulled this kind of shit! Fucking novelty nights and all the girls in sodding bunny costumes like the twenty-first century ain't even here!' She sucked her teeth long and low. Paused for breath. Looked at her niece. 'Well? What you been crying for, puffy eyes? Tell your Aunty Shaz.' She reached out to her with a robust, welcoming arm.

George ignored the gesture. Stood steadfastly by the sink, wearing one of Patrice's hoodies on top of her own. Arms folded tightly with sleeves down over her hands. Couldn't get warm, even with the heating on 27 and the gas meter lifted onto a bucket so that the wheel had stopped turning. Fuse wire through the electricity meter too, so that they could put fan heaters throughout the house without worrying about bills. George had gored a hole through the casing with a hot bodkin herself. A trick Letitia had taught her as a child, passed on to a reluctant, law-abiding Aunty Sharon. Chalk and cheese, those two.

'I haven't been crying,' George said.

'Suit yourself.' Aunty Sharon trotted over to the bread bin. Took out a fruit loaf. Cut herself an ample slice, slathered in butter. Made appreciative noises. 'I make the best fruit loaf in the world,' she said. 'Derek used to love my fruit loaf.' She started to cut herself a second piece and dropped the breadknife. Wracking sobs, suddenly.

'Not you as well,' George said, wrapping Sharon in a bear hug as she heaved with grief.

'So, you *w-was* crying,' Sharon stuttered.

'No. Yes. Never mind me. You let it out, Aunty Shaz.'

Sorrow streamed forth from Sharon's face; tears quickly dripping from her jowls. Speech coming in hiccoughs. 'It's still hard, love. Especially working at that place. Porn King and them girls what have been there a while are always banging on about Derek, like he was some fucking saint or something. Uncle Giuseppe, this. Uncle Giuseppe, that.' She looked up at George with ghoulish mascara-besmirched eyes. 'Derek de Falco managed a titty bar badly. Some claim to fame, right?! He fucked himself up. He fucked me and Tin's life up too. Selfish dickhead.'

'They're all selfish dickheads,' George said, wiping her aunt's second-hand make-up off her jumper with a hot cloth. Knowing Aunty Sharon knew the score and wouldn't take it personally.

'Yeah. Stuff Derek, the stupid bastard!' Sharon grabbed the kitchen roll off the worktop and blew her nose loudly into a clean sheet. Dabbed gingerly at her eyes. Tugged at her elaborate arrangement of platinum blonde extensions and brightly coloured headscarf until it all came away in one cumbersome piece. Short greying hair underneath. Receding hairline. A little too thin in parts from stress-alopecia, where cheap hair extensions over the years had taken their toll.

George touched her own head of thick dark curls reflexively. Curls which Van den Bergen liked to grip when he kissed her passionately.

'Anyway. Uncle Giuseppe's old news. Tell your Aunty Sharon what's eating you,' Sharon said, pulling her sizeable bra from beneath her jumper and hanging it over the taffeta skirt. 'It is laughing gas, in there?' She gestured towards the living room.

George shook her head. 'No. She's the least of it. I keep getting texts from Van den Bergen. We're on. We're off. He loves me. He never says it, the arsehole. Up one minute. Down the next.'

'Thought he was always like that, anyway. Didn't you say he was depressed?'

George nodded. 'He's not been the same since the Butcher.

21

Physically, he's healed. But mentally … They've had him chasing missing persons for two years. Sat on his arse in the office, checking online reports or sat drinking coffee in people's houses while he does interviews. Insisting he's not well enough to face active service. But they've got him working a new murder, Marie's telling me. I haven't spoken to the tosser for weeks because of what happened. Now he wants me over there under the pretence of it being in a professional capacity, I'll bet. Wants me to hold his hand, more like. He's full of shit.'

The beginnings of a smile played on Sharon's chapped lips. 'Your fellers always end up in bits, thanks to you, don't they? You're more high maintenance than that mother of yours.'

A heavy sigh. 'Actually, I'd be lying if I said she wasn't doing my head in, too,' George said, breathing out heavily. Glaring at the door to the living room, behind which her mother slept. 'She was such a pain in the arse while you were at work. I'm trying to write my research up, and she's chatting in my ear, giving it, *I'm dying. I've got pulmonary hypertension* – she can barely bloody pronounce it. *I've got sickle cell anaemia* – she doesn't even know what the fuck that is. *You don't give a monkey's about me.* I can't deal with it.'

'Take no notice of that attention-seeking bitch, love,' Sharon said, frowning and shaking her head. 'My sister will play every last dirty card in her hand to get what she wants. I'll believe that "I'm dying shit" when I see it. She's got some brass neck, threatening to die when she's strong as a horse.'

'She's got some brass neck, kipping on your sofa!'

Sharon was unexpectedly silent. Tremors, rippling across her chin and cheeks, gave the impression that she was about to be sick. Her face crumpled rapidly, the silence giving way to wailing loud enough to wake her sister and her sleeping son. Fleshy hands balled into tight fists.

George was taken aback. Barely knew how to react to this secondary outburst. 'Try to remember Derek the way he was,' she said, turning to tend to the tea. Stirring the cup too briskly. Nice and strong. Three sugars and a healthy wallop of rum. That's how Aunty Shaz liked it after work on a cold night. Set the cup down on a coaster with handle perfectly perpendicular to the edges.

With electric blue nail extensions to match her abandoned dress, Sharon wrapped her hands around the mug, spitting and sputtering her words one by one. 'It ain't Derek,' Sharon said. 'Not really. I'm crying cos of …' She flapped her hand in front of her fact, as though she was wafting away unwanted emotion. 'It's just … it's little Dwayne.' She stared off into the middle distance.

'It's not today, is it?' George asked, glancing at the calendar.

Sharon nodded. Looked suddenly feeble and frail, clutching at the silver locket around her neck. Dimpled chin and down-turned mouth. Streams of glistening, sorrowful tears and snot, lit up by the kitchen lightbulb, looked like strange tinsel, two months too late for Christmas.

'Shit. I'm so sorry,' George said, sitting by her side and hooking her arm around her aunt's shoulders. Suddenly her own problems seemed paltry in comparison. Guilt jabbed at the soft spots that were already raw.

'I told you, didn't I?' Sharon said, snapping the locket open, shut, open, shut, revealing the faded colour photo of a small, smiling boy inside. 'No agony in this world like the pain of losing a child. Ten, twenty years later, them wounds never heal.'

The loud knock on the kitchen window made both of them jump. Nothing to see in the black of the small hours with the light on inside.

'Who the fuck is that at this time of night?' Aunty Sharon asked, lurching out of her seat. Grabbing the kettle, still half full of boiled water. 'I got that back gate padlocked to keep those cheeky little dipshits from down the way out.'

George's heart thudded beneath her layers. She snatched up a meat cleaver from the magnetized knife-holder on the wall. 'Stay back, Aunty Shaz,' she said, switching the light off. 'I got this.'

Still nothing to see in the empty, snowy yard at the back, except for a washing line supporting six inches of snow on top, icicles, hanging beneath, like a neat row of teeth strung along a cannibal's necklace. Against the fence were snow-buried wheelie bins, lit by the nearest streetlamp some twenty feet away.

Reaching for the key lodged in the security door, George turned until the lock clicked. Pushed the handle down gingerly, cleaver in her right hand. Pulled the door open suddenly. Blast of arctic wind sucking the air from her lungs. Arm held high ready to slice.

A hooded figure was standing on the back step.

George screamed.

CHAPTER 5

Amsterdam, mortuary, 28 February

'Well, well, well, if it isn't Amsterdam's prodigal son. Long time, no see,' Marianne de Koninck said, eyeing Van den Bergen with what was almost certainly a degree of suspicion. 'Where the hell have you been for the last god knows how long?'

'Welded to the frost-bitten bottom of my cold case,' Van den Bergen said, eyes smiling with mirth.

Almost ten months had passed since he had last seen the head of forensic pathology. The case he had been working on simply hadn't turned up anything requiring forensic examination beyond the initial couple of weeks.

Today, in her scrubs and rubber sandals, with her normally short hair grown into a sleek blonde bob, Marianne looked younger than her forty something years.

'Have you got a new man in your life?' he asked, finally daring to unbutton his anorak. The chilly mortuary seemed warm in comparison to the white world outside.

'Only this poor chump,' Marianne said. She stared down at the naked corpse of the man who had been found in the Bijlmer play-area. Lit by the harsh, overhead lights, his body was a grim palette of yellow, purple and grey. The red stippling of the sores around his mouth and nose like the brush strokes of an impressionist's nightmare. Marianne snapped a fresh pair of latex gloves onto her sinewy hands. Straight to business as usual.

Van den Bergen had always liked that about her.

'What about you?' she said. 'You still cradle-snatching? I'm surprised the young Dr McKenzie isn't with you. I thought you two were joined at the hip since she saved your life.'

There was nothing Van den Bergen could do to stifle the low growl that escaped his lips. Marianne might as well have gouged at his tired heart with her scalpel.

'Like that, is it?'

The pathologist walked around the dead man, recording her observations into a Dictaphone. She scrutinised the blemished skin of his face.

'Aside from the sores around the deceased's nose and mouth that would suggest drug misuse, I can see tiny lacerations on his face,' she said. She prized open his mouth with her fingers to reveal blackened teeth. 'Jesus. Our man was certainly not a regular at the dentist's.'

'Show me a junkie who is,' Van den Bergen said.

'His lips, gums and tongue show bruising,' she continued. 'I'll check his nasal passages later by microscopy, but I'm guessing it's the same there. I can see significant amounts of mucus and blood at the back of his gullet. Petechial haemorrhages in his skin. Oedema.'

'In layman's terms, please!'

'All in good time, Chief Inspector. You just sit tight and let me do my job.' She took samples from beneath the man's fingernails. Bloods. Swabs. 'Okay. Let's see what's inside,' Marianne said.

Taking up her scalpel, she began to open up the cadaver, cutting from his chest, working her way down to his pubic area.

'Oh, Jesus!' Van den Bergen said. He steadied himself against the built in sink at the end of the stainless steel slab. Flashbacks to waking up on the floor of the Butcher's panic room. Strapped to a chair. Awaiting his fate. Then, walking towards the light, thinking it was the end and that perhaps it wouldn't be so bad, only to find the source of the brightness came from a doctor's light pen, checking for the response of his pupils as he emerged finally from his coma in the Intensive Care Unit. Only later, when his wounds were redressed, realising that he had been zipped open from top to bottom.

Just like the body of the Bijlmer man, now.

Marianne set down her scalpel. Staring at him askance as though he was a lunatic. 'Paul? Are you okay?'

Pull yourself together, you loser. 'I'm fine. It's my middle ear playing up.' He pointed to his ear, as though that made his lie more convincing. She didn't need to know he was so weak-minded. 'Vertigo. You know. A lot of viruses going round in this infernal shitty weather.'

'Have you and Georgina split up?' She narrowed her sharp blue eyes at him.

He pulled up a typing chair close to the action. His height made it easy to observe as Marianne resumed her dissection. Pointedly said nothing in response.

'Suit yourself, tight-lipped sod,' she said.

After the bulk of the examination had been performed, internal organs weighed and measured and the dead man scrutinised for signs of foul play visible to the naked eye, the pathologist scowled.

'Well?' Van den Bergen asked, hoping she had not noticed he had been looking anywhere but at the body for most of the procedure. 'We found a big bag of mephedrone on him. It was odd that his stash hadn't been taken. *Are* we looking at a simple drug-related stabbing?'

Marianne tutted. Looked perplexed. 'This is the weird thing,' she said. Snapping off her gloves in silence. Scrubbing her arms to the elbows. Silent all the while. 'He's clearly lost a lot of blood because he was stabbed with something in the carotid artery. Whoever did it knew what they were doing. The wound is about two inches deep, as though it's been done with those home-made weapons you get in prisons.'

'A shiv.'

'Exactly. The wound is conical, but there's no evidence of a blade. At first I thought he'd been stabbed with a stake or maybe one of those conical stoppers you get for wine bottles.'

Van den Bergen crossed one long leg over the other, bouncing his fur-lined boot on his knee. Finally, he pulled his beanie hat off and ruffled his thick, prematurely white hair. 'It's possible. Don't rule it out at this stage. We haven't found a weapon anywhere near the crime scene.'

Marianne pulled up another chair and sat beside him. 'No, but the thing is, there are traces of water in the wound. I don't get it. And though he lost pints of blood, his actual cause of death was suffocation. That's what I was alluding to when I said there were lacerations and bruising in and around his mouth and nose.'

'What?' Van den Bergen leaned closer to her. Scrutinising the fine lines around her eyes and the hollows beneath her cheekbones, where long-distance running had stripped the fat away.

'Someone shoved snow up his nose and into his mouth. They stabbed him first and then made sure they finished the job by suffocation. When I examined him at the scene, I found slush in his nasal passages and mouth. Almost melted, but not quite.' She touched the tip of her own nose thoughtfully. 'Even with the victim's body temperature being a steady 37 degrees, by the time he'd started to bleed out, and his temperature had begun to drop, with the stupid sub-zero conditions we've got at the moment, his extremities would have taken barely any time at all to cool to freezing point.'

'Hence the slush.'

'Yes. Stay outside for more than ten minutes in this weather in the wrong clothes ... It's not exactly taking a bath in liquid nitrogen, but not far off it!'

Van den Bergen chewed over the information. Rubbing his

brow. He could feel the pinching pain of his scar tissue responding to the mortuary chill, now that his coat hung open. Taking a blister pack out of his anorak pocket, he slipped two ibuprofen onto his tongue. Swallowed with spit. 'What do you think of opportunism? This John Doe had no wallet on him. Could he have been robbed because he was in the wrong place at the wrong time?'

The pathologist stood and stretched. Glanced over at the dead man, baring his innermost secrets beneath the mortuary lights. 'Very public place, though. If I wanted to mug a man, I wouldn't choose that spot. Would you? It's overlooked by scores of apartments.'

Van den Bergen nodded. Wished he was sitting on his sofa at home, savouring a hot coffee, bouncing ideas back and forth with George instead. Watching the winter sunlight that streamed through the French windows of his apartment kiss the tips of her hair.

'The bag of mephedrone on the dead man was worth a fair few Euros,' he said. 'Who the hell would kill a junkie, take his money, but leave the drugs?'

Marianne de Koninck started to print off labels for the samples she had taken, methodically categorising the bits of the dead man that would be sent to toxicology. 'You're the Chief Inspector, Paul. Not me. But I'd be asking what kind of psychopath would commit such a public, brutal but efficient murder if it was just about stealing a wallet?'

CHAPTER 6

St. John's College, Cambridge, later

'You're late,' Sally said, smiling, though her tone was acidic enough to strip the wax from the grand wooden mantel of the fireplace. She clutched what appeared to be a whisky, or brandy maybe, in a cut-crystal tumbler in her right hand.

George could smell the fumes from the strong alcohol. At 2pm, it felt like too early in the day for a drink. But then it was beyond freezing outside. 'Can I have one of those?' she asked.

'No. I'm cross with you.' Sally clacked on the side of her tumbler with the two chunky Perspex rings she wore on her gnarled fingers. Marking time. 'I told you to make sure you got here in a punctual fashion.'

George pulled off her Puffa jacket and released herself from the strangling grip of her scarf. 'Overslept,' she said. 'You wouldn't believe—'

'No, I wouldn't,' the Senior Tutor said. Nicotine-stained gritted teeth. Total sense of humour failure. 'You were notable by your absence, young lady. The Master asked where you were and I had to string him a line about emergency dental surgery. So no fucking drinky for you. If he asks, the anaesthetic still hasn't worn off.'

'Oh, you're harsh!' George took a coffee, poured for her by one of the formal hall waiting staff into a cup embellished with the St. John's College logo. Looked grand. Tasted like crap. She grimaced at the bitter, burnt flavour. 'Better than nothing, I suppose,' she muttered under her breath.

The other fellows were scattered around the drawing room in clusters: black crows in their floor-length gowns. All pleasantly pissed after a formal lunch that had been put on for some major benefactor or other. Accompanied by a minor HRH, whom George clocked on the other side of the room. Red ears and a flushed face, chatting to the Director of Studies for Modern and Medieval Languages.

'I should be over there, rubbing shoulders with the Royal,' Sally said. 'Not chastising you like you're an errant child.'

'Well, don't then, because I'm not one.' George set the poisonous coffee down.

'Get your bloody gown on, for god's sake!' Sally said. Fidgeting with her big chunky beads. Tugging at the blunt fringe of her short bobbed hair. 'Christ, I could murder a cigarette.'

George took her neatly folded gown out of an Asda bag. Pulled it on over her idiotic smart black dress, which she wore only at the grand dinners that constituted the College's formal hall. Not warm enough by a long stretch in this weather, she had concealed her thermal long johns as best she could beneath the skirt by wearing Aunty Sharon's knee-length boots – designed for big women, they swam around her calves.

'I'm in a spot of bother,' George blurted, feeling overwhelmed in the fire-lit fug of the Master's drawing room, her thoughts still on the events at 2am, when the hooded figure had appeared at Aunty Sharon's back door.

Sally fixed her with laser-sharp hooded eyes – no less probing for being behind cat's-eyes glasses. 'Whatever it is, I don't want to hear it.' The lines etched into her pruned mouth grew deeper. 'You're a grown woman, now. You can stand on your own two feet. My time playing nanny for MI6 is over.'

'It's nothing like that,' George said. 'I don't think, anyway. But

I've got this homeless woman who keeps tapping me up for cash.'

Sally stealthily swiped the decanter containing amber alcohol, topped up her glass and sniffed at the contents. Swirled them around the crystal so that jambs dripped in perpendicular lines around the sides. 'A homeless woman?'

'It's a long story,' George said, sighing. 'Second time she's shown up at my Aunty's, asking for a handout. It was gone two in the morning. I nearly stuck a meat cleaver in her head.' She exhaled sharply, remembering how the dishevelled woman had screamed for mercy, then shoved her way inside, once she realised George was not about to attack her.

'What you doing at my house?' Aunty Sharon had said, kettle in hand. 'I told you, I don't want you coming here, pestering my niece.'

The diminutive figure had slid the hood from her head, shedding harsh light on cheeks that were raw from being too long in the cold. She looked far older than her years. Thin, with scabs on her knuckles and stinking like those wheelie bins you get outside restaurants of rotten vegetables and stale cigarettes.

'Please. Just a twenty would do. It's so cold out there. I've got nothing to eat. No money. I'm sleeping in a freezing van. I can't even afford to put the engine on to get the heater going.' Imploring eyes, begging George to help.

Seeing her again in the warmth and light of Aunty Sharon's kitchen, George had wanted to give the poor woman a bed for the night. 'Look, I told you not to bother me again,' she had said, pressing fifty into the woman's hand. 'You can't come round here. It's not my house. There's a kid here.'

'The teenager?' the woman had asked.

Aunty Sharon had got aggressive then. 'You been fucking spying on my boy? You fruitloops or something?' She had waved the kettle at the unwelcome visitor. 'Cos I got boiled water in here and I ain't afraid to cob it on your skanky homeless head. We don't want no trouble here, do you get me? I don't want no raggedy white arse in my house. So, take your cash and put one foot in front of the other, darling. And stop preying on my niece's good nature.'

In the end, the woman had stayed until nearly four in the morning. Talking with George and Sharon over a convivial half bottle of rum. Had a shower, using up some of the excessively hot water. Turns out, Aunty Sharon had been just as prone to being a soft touch as George. No surprises there.

Back in the Master's lodge, Sally dragged George into an adjacent room. Empty in there. Together, they forced the heavy window up and lit their cigarettes. Blowing the smoke into the deep-freeze of the snow-blanketed garden.

'Who's the woman?' Sally asked.

George blew a dragon's plume of smoke out of her nostrils onto the sub-zero air. 'It doesn't matter. It's nothing to do with our work here. Just some other bullshit I've got going on. Nothing to do with skeletons in the closet or anything. Don't worry. I'm cool on that front. I'm not stupid.'

'Far from it, Dr McKenzie,' Sally said, flicking her ash onto the sill. 'Now, I clobbered that benefactor during lunch. Flashed him my wrinkly, ageing senior tutor knees and offered him an honorary doctorate in Criminology in return for some funding to keep us afloat.'

George allowed herself a tired smile. 'Please god, yes! I'm so skint.'

'Not for you, smart arse. We need money for the library and to fund your little field trips to interview survivors. Where are you with our research?'

'I've got qualitative stuff from at least twenty people – about twelve are women who were trafficked domestically as young girls in the 1970s and 1980s. Some are participating witnesses in the Operation Oak Tree case. Paedophiles in the media, obviously. The rest were boys in the 1960s and 1970s who were pimped out to some very prominent men in society. Runaways from children's homes. Abductees. There was a boarding house in Sussex where the boys were taken to be abused. If I could only get that fucking idiot at UCL off my back, once I've finished the Home Office shit we'll have a ground-breaking study on our hands in about a year's time.'

'Bugger a ground-breaking study,' Sally said. 'We'll have a non-fiction hardback that tops the *Sunday Times* bestseller list. Mine and your name on the front.' She grinned a piranha grin, which George did not entirely like, especially since she was doing all the actual work. Sally just opened the doors.

'How are you coping?' Sally asked, breaking into a coughing fit that made her sound as though she was a consumptive war-veteran from the trenches of the First World War. 'Emotionally, I mean.'

Focusing on the Persian rug in the room, George shrugged. 'It's horrific, but then, I'm used to distancing myself from pain. I'm fine.' Lies. She wasn't fine. But George knew she had chosen to pursue criminology as a career so that she could give the silenced a voice, as she had been given a voice.

She was just becoming irritated by the fact that the rug was not in perfect alignment with the skirting boards, when a woman – roughly the same age as George – entered the room, wearing a gown that was still deepest black, denoting her newness, though the gown was stained with what appeared to be gravy. She flicked long, unkempt brown hair out of her well-scrubbed face. Dangling earrings with feathers attached told George much of what she needed to know.

'Can I join you for a smoke, guys?' she said. A heavy West Country accent. She pulled out a tightly rolled joint.

Sally winked at the woman. 'Of course, dear.' Turned to George. 'This is your new partner in trafficking crime, Georgina. I wanted you to get here on time so I could make the introduction. Meet the new Fellow in Social Anthropology and expert in all matters regarding Roma child abduction.'

The newcomer stuck out her hand; her fingernails painted gaily in rainbow-coloured nail varnish belied a grip like an arm-wrestler who hustled and won. 'Wotcha, George. I'm Sophie Bartek.'

CHAPTER 7

Amsterdam, Vinkeles restaurant, 2 March

'What have you got for me?' Kamphuis asked, shovelling a piece of steak into his mouth that was far too large, even for him.

The exclusive eatery, Vinkeles was rammed with the great, the good and the possibly criminal underbelly of Amsterdam's high society. Dressed to kill, as though they were impervious to the weather. Understated ritzy decor. Wide armchairs, serving to accommodate even Kamphuis' fat arse, as he enjoyed his Michelin starred lunch. Chewing with his mouth open, like the moron he was, Van den Bergen mused. Staring out at the Keizersgracht, as though the Chief Inspector sitting to his right was not even worth a cursory glance.

'You summoned me here, Olaf,' Van den Bergen said, stomach growling at the sight of the beautifully arranged food. Snatching a bun from a passing waiter bearing a bowl heaped with golden brown orbs – doling them out with metal tongues to those who were still doing carbs. Half the bun gone, in one bite. The morgue always made him hungry. It was something to do with the formalin, Marianne reckoned.

Finally the Commissioner deigned to turn to him. A half-sneer on his face. Sauce hanging in a blob on the side of his mouth. Threatening to besmirch the pristine white tablecloth, or else the jacket he insisted wearing, even in the overheated salon, because brass buttons on top screamed to the other diners that he was top brass. Fucking idiot.

'It's Commissioner Kamphuis to you,' Kamphuis said.

Van den Bergen defiantly chewed his bun in silence for long enough to be irritating. Kamphuis' trigger-points were big-chested new admin girls, Van den Bergen's silent treatment and inappropriately stylish shoes on older men – all elicited responses of extreme ardour or intense dislike.

'Been stood up on a date?' Van den Bergen asked, bouncing his size thirteen boot on top of his bony knee. Ugg Adirondacks. A birthday present from George before they had had The Argument. Far cooler than anything he ever would have bought for himself. Certainly enough to drive Kamphuis wild with annoyance.

Slamming his cutlery down noisily, Kamphuis' eye started to twitch. Sure enough, he grimaced at Van den Bergen's bouncing foot. Took a swig of his sparkling mineral water. 'I'm a busy man. And a regular here. I don't need an excuse to have a quick bite in an establishment where I don't have to look at ugly bastards like you all day. Now, I asked you here to debrief me on the autopsy of that John Doe.' Shovelled in another oversized medallion of rare flesh. Spoke with his mouth full, of course. 'Well?'

Van den Bergen helped himself to a glass of water. Swallowed down an extra strong iron tablet. 'Don't know why you've got your elasticated pants in a twist over some dead junkie.'

'My city. My reputation. Murder rate's right down, thanks to my vigilance.'

'Except it's not your city, is it? It's Hasselblad's. He's the Chief of Police, not you.' Van den Bergen could see the colour rising in Kamphuis' face. Quickly turning florid. Telltale sweat breaking out.

'We're a team, me and Jaap. And I don't need lessons on leadership from you. Facts, please!'

'Suffocated by snow. Stabbed in the neck. Wallet gone. Looks like a mugging by a mugger who missed the drugs on him. Maybe our killer panicked and ran off. It's a very public spot.'

'ID?'

'Nothing yet. Nothing's come in from missing persons.' Van den Bergen peered over the table and through the multi-paned, tall window to the snowy scene beyond. The canals were all completely frozen solid – now thronging with residents who had bunked the day off to ice-skate along the city's waterways. Wrapped up against the blistering cold, he could even see three women skating along, pushing pushchairs that contained grinning toddlers. A modern day Breughel painting, where wool and fur had been replaced by Goretex.

He imagined for the briefest of moments, skating along the Keizersgracht with George, hand in hand. Losing himself in her soft brown eyes. Skating away from his cares and responsibilities. Just for an hour or so. Remembered doing that with Tamara, when she had been a little girl. One, two, three, wee, suspended between him and Andrea, his ex. Swinging the little four-year-old into the air. Tiny gloved hands. Knitted animals on the end of each finger. Fine times long gone, until George had come into his life and set his heart to thaw.

'Are you smirking at me?' Kamphuis asked, snapping Van den Bergen out of his reverie.

'No.' A silent beat. 'It's a waste of my team's time. They're too experienced. We do the serial killers and criminal networks and high-profile cases. You've got plenty of junior detectives who could be looking into the dead junkie. I want to keep working on the missing persons' operation. We've spent so long looking for—'

'Forget it,' Kamphuis said, belching. 'I'm the boss now. My priority is the murder rate. You tow my line, you streak of piss, or I'll put you out to pasture quicker than you can say, "pensioner discount". Right?'

Early retirement. Arrogant turd. Kamphuis' words resounded like a bad bout of tinnitus, as Van den Bergen stood on the steps of the restaurant, watching the skaters. Retirement. Consigned to the scrap heap. Nice. And Kamphuis had grounds. Everyone knew Van den Bergen had been struggling since the Butcher. He touched his scar tissue beneath his coat, poking where it ached in the cold.

The windows of the beautiful, four-storey townhouses that leaned in on him felt suddenly oppressive. Spying on him. Marking him out as a failure. A man who should have died. A Chief Inspector who had not succeeded in solving his most recent case. An ageing idiot who had pushed his young lover away. He felt utterly alone.

Opting to walk through the streets back to the police HQ, instead of driving in the shitty, slippery conditions, he hammered out a text to George. Intended it to be conciliatory. Wanted to tell her that he loved her and was sorry. That he could commit, after all. That he would go for more therapy.

Despite his best intentions, he found he had sent:

```
Assigned to murder case. Suffocation with
snow. Strange neck wounds. What do you
think, Detective Lacey? P.
```

Shit. Why was he such an emotional cripple?

Feeling the lead-weight of disappointment snuff out any lightness of step, he trudged back towards police headquarters. Passed some makeshift stalls that had sprung up on the icy Prinsengracht, selling mulled wine, stroopwafels and greasy doughnut-like ollieballen to tourists and ice-skaters who had overestimated the length of time they could bear in the cold without libation. The sweet cinnamon smell was intoxicating, but he had no appetite. This lingering smell of Christmas was a false God. It was early March now, and only the remaining dead weeks of winter stretched and stretched ahead of him.

He stood in the glazed portico of the police headquarters when a text pinged back. It was from George.

```
Is that an attempt at romance, arsehole?
```

She had attached to the text a jpeg of an article from *The Times* newspaper. The headline made Van den Bergen draw a sharp breath: An icy end for entrepreneur. Who is Jack Frost?

CHAPTER 8

A village South of Amsterdam, 25 May, the previous year

A glance into the garden confirmed that the children were both playing happily. Clambering onto the small plastic climbing frame. Josh was even helping Lucy to get up the three steps. There they both were, squealing as they slid down the Day-Glo pink slide, then crawled into the space beneath the platform, poking their little heads out of the 'window'. Good. And the play area was still in shadow, as the morning sun had not yet moved round from the front. No need to apply sunscreen just yet. They were safe. Perfectly safe. He could concentrate. Even if it was only for twenty minutes or so, that would be enough.

Peering down at the architectural drawing of the Wagenaar family's poky three-bedroomed house, Piet Deenen could see how he could utilise the dead space to the side. Where a washing line currently hung forlornly, he could create an open plan living area. Bring more light into that horrible galley kitchen. Theirs was another poorly designed boxy house on the outermost fringes of Amsterdam. A garden suburb. A post-war poor-man's utopia, thrown together by shortsighted town-planners in response to a burgeoning population and the need for slum clearance. The Netherlands was now crying out for men like Piet: architects with modest ambitions, an easy-going nature and an affordable rate. Gabi had been so wrong about his earning potential. Fuck London with its cut-throat property- and job-market.

A few clicks on the mouse, and he manipulated his design software to create an extra five feet of usable floor space for Mr and Mrs Wagenaar and their three children. Better.

He drank from his coffee. Scattered crumbs onto his jeans from the appeltaart he had knocked up for him and the kids. Gabi wouldn't touch anything containing carbs, of course. She was still on the corporate treadmill in her head. Sharp-dressing. 8 a.m. starts, though she no longer needed to keep those ridiculous hours. An hour of exercise every day: disciplined body, disciplined mind. Old habits weren't dying hard.

Leaning forward, knocking his coffee all over the plans of the existing front elevation, he opened the window.

'Kids!' he shouted in his native Dutch. 'Ten minutes and I'll bring you out some cake and milk. Okay?'

Delighted squeals from outside. Josh jumping up and down, Lucy not really understanding much beyond cake and milk, no doubt. They waved up at him. All, 'love you, Paps!' Sticky juice hands. Dirty knees. Both with flaxen hair just like he had had as a child. But their curls had come from Gabi's side of the family.

Piet surveyed this perfect domestic scene. Perched atop the Day-Glo pink climbing frame were his very own small people. His family. Here – the middle of nowhere – had to be the safest place in the world to raise children, hadn't it? Here, they had green space. Privacy. You wouldn't even know there was a train line running behind the garden. It was a glorious sight. The relocation had been worthwhile. Gabi would come round without water eventually.

Except Josh ruined the perfect snapshot in time, as usual. He started to dangle Lucy by her ankles over the ladder of the climbing frame. Shrieks of excitement from his tiny sibling, quickly turned to anguished screaming.

'Stop that, Josh! Leave your sister alone. Don't make me come down there!'

Shit. Bloody kids. Coffee spillage or Lucy: which was the more urgent? Suddenly, he found himself flapping, and ran to the bathroom to get toilet roll. At least he could blot the worst of it.

'I'm coming down!' he shouted through the open window.

'Pappie!' Cries from Lucy.

Mischievous laughter trilling on the air from Josh.

But then the phone started ring.

Shit. Shit. Shit. Gabi on the other end.

'Did you put the wash on?' she asked. Sounded harried.

'What? Yes. No. Hang on, darling. The kids are going mad in the garden. There's coffee— I've got to …' Looking out at the precarious scene below, he could see that Josh had released his sister from his tyrannical grip but was now holding the sides of the climbing frame, rocking the plastic tower back and forth. Trying to topple that which was not designed to be toppled.

Gabi's voice, tinny but insistent down the phone-line. 'Piet! I told you to put the bloody washing in. The one time your mother actually comes to babysit overnight and there's no clean bedding.' Her tone had quickly turned from undisguised mistrust to naked fury.

'I'll do it! Darling, I can't—'

'Can't? Can't? Then how come I manage? I'm sick of it, Piet. You promised me we'd have some time for ourselves. That was the whole damned point, wasn't it? Better quality of life, you said!'

'Gab, the kids are—'

'Did you put Josh's assessment on the calendar like I told you?'

Piet tore himself away from the window. He turned to the calendar, pinned to a corkboard in his little office, one ear still on the mayhem in the garden. Feeling torn between answering his wife's demands and monitoring his ebullient charges, he was relieved when it became relatively quiet outside. Little children's voices chatting nicely, not bellowing. Laughter. This meant the kids were finally behaving, leaving him to focus on dealing with Gabi. 'Yes. It's down for 10 a.m. on the 18th.'

'Of June? You got the right month?'

He felt the prickle of irritation on the back of his neck that he always got that when Gabi started to undermine him. He imagined her, snip, snip, snip at his testicles with the big garden shears. 'Yes, I got the right fucking month. It says in capital letters, 'Josh – psychiatric evaluation. 18th of June'. It was all he could do not to shout *June* down the phone.

'Did you pay the credit card bill?'

'No.'

'What do you mean, no?'

'Not enough money in the account. Not after the deposit on the car and the first repayment coming out.'

The argument quickly escalated into a slanging match over whether they were going to be cut off by the utilities company or not. As usual. By the time he slammed the phone down on his wife, Piet was exhausted.

He finished mopping the coffee spillage. The drawing was brown and rippled now, like the waves of the North Sea in winter. Damn.

Throwing the soggy tissue into his wastepaper basket, he peered out of the window. Sod Gabi. He would sit outside for a bit with the kids. If he invoiced a few more customers early, chances are, one would pay up before the thirty-day notice and he could settle the overdue gas bill.

Padding down in bare feet to the kitchen – a sleek luxury he had insisted upon if she was to have that ridiculous car they didn't even need – he sliced up the cake. Piet poured milk into two plastic beakers. One green for Lucy. One yellow for Josh. An orange one for him, so he could join in. Took a tray outside.

The rustle of a late spring breeze in the trees was nothing short of idyllic. A train approached in the distance, although he hardly noticed the sound now, as the Rotterdam to Schiphol service trundled past some several metres below the line of houses – out of view, deep in its purpose-built cutting.

'Come on, babies. Let's take some time out.'

Silence.

Had they answered and he hadn't heard them over the train's rumble? Setting the tray down, he looked at the climbing frame, expecting to see his children. They weren't there. Hide and seek, no doubt. Always a favourite. His heart had started to pound. He could feel the blood draining from his face. But that was fine, because they were hiding.

'Josh! Lucy! Come on out now. Time for a snack.'

No sign of them in the void of the climbing frame. Neither could he see small figures skulking behind the wooden sun-loungers.

'Not funny, kids! Come out!'

Peering at the bases of the holly bushes, he could see no tell-tale feet. Crap. The gate! He ran to check the side gate. Had they walked onto the street? No! The side gate was bolted and padlocked.

'I know where you are, you little rascals!'

It was a simple but mature garden, mainly full of evergreen shrubbery and trees. Holly, laurel, a eucalyptus, cotoneaster, the heavy canopy of three Japanese maples, specimen pine, other stuff he didn't know the names of. All surrounded by a solid, six-foot-tall wooden fence. They were hiding. He had to calm down. It simply wasn't possible for them to have disappeared. Only one place could successfully conceal them.

At the far end of the garden was a small weeping birch that cascaded right to the ground, providing the kids with a curtain of green, behind which they could safely hide from view.

Smiling tentatively, Piet crept forward. Preparing to sweep the whippy branches aside to reveal his collaborating toddlers. Grabbed the branches. Hope fading as he realised he could not hear any delighted, anticipatory giggling. Looked for the sandaled feet, mucky knees and brightly coloured shorts in vain. Lifted the canopy suddenly.

'Gotcha!'

The void by the tree trunk was empty.

In a dizzying vortex of panic, Piet stepped backwards. Tripped on Lucy's Sesamstraat tricycle, Big Bird staring goggle-eyed into the abyss as he was now.

'Josh! Lucy!' he shouted at the top of his voice.

Hands shaking. His breath started to come short. Where was his inhaler? Inside. Maybe they had gone inside.

'Lucy! Josh! Where are you?'

Found his Ventolin on the worktop. Inhaled sharply. Eyes scanning the kitchen. Back into the garden now. Screaming at the top of his lungs. Frightened tears starting to leak from his eyes.

'Joshua! Lucy! Where are you?'

He fell to his knees as the bottom dropped out of his world. The garden was empty. His children were gone.

CHAPTER 9

St. John's College, then, The Bun Shop pub, Cambridge, 3 March, present

'Fucking idiots,' George muttered under her breath. She was eyeing the beefy rugger-buggers in the crowded college bar who had hoisted two blow-up sex dolls aloft and were bashing them together, 'like lesboes'. Then, pretending to hump them, doggy style. Pints all round, boys, to celebrate Rupes' birthday. Empty glasses bearing testament to two hours' solid drinking.

Looking at Charlotte, the mousy third-year student she was supervising on the side, George felt suddenly protective. 'Let's call it a night, shall we?'

Charlotte fingered a twee enamel flower brooch on her jumper nervously. Nodded. She hooked her dark blonde hair behind her ears. Left her diet coke half drunk. 'I always find it too rowdy in here,' she said, barely audible above the raucous laughter and bawdy jokes. 'But thanks for the drink anyway. I'm glad you thought the essay was okay.'

'The essay was great, but this was a bad idea. I'm sorry. Next time, we'll have the supervision at my house, right?'

As she pulled on her coat, one of the boys locked eyes with George. Clearly failed to recognize her as a Fellow. He humped the blow-up sex doll towards her, shouting, 'Fancy a ride, darling?

I've got plenty of love to give when I've finished with this bitch.'

Deftly, George detached the enamel brooch from Charlotte's jumper. Nice long, sharp pin, she noticed with satisfaction. Took long strides to meet the leering idiot. Popped the first sex doll. Swung to her left and popped the second.

'Oh, you total cow!' one of the boys shouted.

'See, boys?' George said. All eyes on her. Stunned silence meant she had their attention. 'An unwanted prick's not much fun, is it?'

Before the pack could round on her, she ushered Charlotte to the door. She only barely registered the fact that a man, too old to be a student, was sitting in an alcove. A man who didn't fit with these surrounds. The wafting stench of more than stale alcohol. Watching her. Someone she didn't recognise. Or did she? It was a shadow of a thought and George didn't have time to form it fully before she was through the door; warm air supplanted by cold, a testosterone-fuelled demi-riot supplanted by silence.

Outside in that frozen cloudless night, the drop in temperature punched the air from her lungs. She struggled to catch her breath as she watched Charlotte scurry off towards Cripps block in safety.

George was preoccupied and unprepared, when a figure wearing too many clothes bundled into her.

'Watch where you're going!' she said, wondering if one of the boys from the bar had come to start something with her. But the figure was too small, she realised.

'George!' A woman's voice. Rich rolling R. She pulled back her hood enough to show her face clearly in the moonlight. Dark hair gathered in a low widow's peak above her brow. Feather earrings just peeping out, though the colours were not visible in this half-light. 'I was looking for you.'

'Sophie!' George said. Chuckling with relief at the sight of the Social Anthropology Fellow.

'Fancy coming for a pint and we can chew over our collaboration some more? The Bun Shop does a good burger if you've not already eaten. My treat.'

George assessed her options. Back to her college house full of untidy idiot undergraduates, where she could never find peace enough to work? Beggars, it turned out, really couldn't be choosers. Or off to the pub for a second stab at sociability with women roughly her own age? Her empty stomach growled long and low. It had already decided on her brain's behalf.

'Perfect!'

As the two women trudged arm-in-arm towards the Porter's Lodge, George was unaware of the man following some twenty paces behind.

That he had got past the Porters and into the college was a miracle. No. Not a miracle. Merely a feat of bluff and self-confidence. Walk like you belong there. Head held high. His time on the streets had taught him this was the best way to move around unnoticed. The moment you started acting like you didn't belong was the moment people took you for an interloper.

Still, his heart was thudding as he followed McKenzie and her friend through the labyrinthine medieval sprawl towards the lodge. Seeing the towers loom large, covered in the claustrophobic white blanket that swallowed sound like the walls of a confessional box, he felt sick. But in the middle of the snow-bound courtyard, where the gritted paths intersected, the women suddenly took a sharp left. They entered a different courtyard on the other side of the chapel. Wider spaces here. The snow glittered like homeless man's diamonds in the moonlight. It looked like they were going through some more discreet exit. Except, downside was, he was exposed here. If they turned around, they would realise, perhaps, that they were being followed.

Get to McKenzie, the email had said. *Get her laptop and the USB stick that has her database on it – by any means necessary. The names are all on there.*

Any means necessary. Yes. He was a committed soldier and this was war. It was his job to obey orders. He removed his glove for thirty seconds – just long enough to reach down through the tear in his pocket into the space between the lining and outer of his coat. Touched the tools hidden along the inner seam. Screwdriver. Hammer. Chisel. Tonight he would not use ice and snow. Tonight, he needed something a little more robust.

George looked into Sophie's startling green eyes. Looked away after a couple of uncomfortable beats. Felt instinctively like there was more than just friendly curiosity at play in her new colleague's exacting gaze. Some kind of chemistry shit going on. She hadn't experienced that with a woman since Tonya …

'I'm going to be honest with you,' George said. 'I don't see how your study into the Roma has any bearing on my trafficking research. I'm all about qualitative and quantitative. Interview transcriptions from victims and perps. Stats. You're presumably coming at it from a cultural heritage angle.' She took a large bite out of her burger. Eyes on the clientele in the pub, feeling like she was being observed. Back to Sophie. Perhaps observed only by her.

All hands flapping and smiles, Sophie's intense expression was suddenly transformed. 'You couldn't be wronger there, my love,' she said in that rolling West Country accent. George wasn't sure about the 'my love'. 'The reason Sally wanted us to work together was that the Roma – my speciality – are at the centre of many a child abduction scandal.'

Drinking deeply from her pint of beer, George started to arrange the condiments in a perfectly straight line along the middle of the table. Separating her and Sophie with a barrier of salt, pepper, vinegar and ketchup. 'There's often stories in the media about blond children allegedly being abducted by the Roma. Usually when northern Europeans are on holiday in countries like Turkey and Greece.'

Chewing slowly, thoroughly, perhaps thoughtfully, on her veggie-burger, Sophie nodded and flicked her long hair over her shoulder. 'Stories like that always engender mass hysteria in the press – especially in the tabloids. White Europeans are up in arms whenever they get wind of some kind of abuse of a blond child by an underclass of minority ethnic people like 'gypsies'. And the Roma have always been vilified as child-abductors. It goes back donkey's years, like the myth of Jews baking their Passover bread with Christian children's blood.'

'Racist propaganda, then?' George asked, pulling her e-cigarette out of her rucksack.

'But the point is, the Roma informally adopt children from families that can't bring their own kids up. Happens a lot. I think in the case of the 'Blonde Angel' back in 2013, for example, the mother was Bulgarian and just couldn't look after her daughter. Lack of paperwork implicates the adoptive parents though, and the media jumps onto a witch hunt.'

George thought about how the case Van den Bergen had been working on had been given the moniker of *Operation Roma* by Kamphuis or Hasselblad or one of those odious bastards above him, and wondered about the prejudices behind the name in light of what Sophie was saying. Missing person equals gypsies, if the bigots were to be believed. Hadn't Hasselblad pointed the finger at Romani travellers, amongst other easily maligned groups? She had thought the *Roma* referred to the Italian capital of Rome – a suspected destination of the missing, at one point, and the frequently used European hub of trans-national trafficking networks. Only now did she make the link. *How the hell did I miss that?*

'You've got a point.' She rubbed her finger along her full bottom lip. Chapped and rough from the cold. 'Roma kids from South Eastern Europe are by far the largest ethnic group preyed on by traffickers,' George said, thinking about what she had read about beggars and child prostitutes in Italy, the Russian Federation and

Turkey. 'So, the truth is actually a world away from media representation.'

Sophie seemed momentarily to be assessing George. Peering at her intently over her beer glass. She looked suddenly thoughtful again. 'Yep. Of the kids trafficked out of Bulgaria, the Czech Republic, Hungary, Romania and Slovakia, Roma kids constitute about seventy per cent. They're disproportionately poor. Maybe someone trusted in the family or village offers to get a child work elsewhere. What the fuck have they got in their little villages at home? Domestic abuse, maybe. Poverty, certainly. Sod all in the way of education or prospects. So they often go willingly. Unwittingly. Factor in corrupt border patrol and police, and you've got movement of children over borders into brothels, sweatshops, begging on the streets.'

George drained her beer glass, feeling suddenly lightheaded in the over-heated warmth of the pub, with a full stomach. Sophie was twirling some of that long, unkempt hair coquettishly around her finger. Her chipped nail varnish made George feel itchy. Inadvertently, she found herself checking her phone for texts from Van den Bergen, as though those would save her from the keen-eyed appraisal of the inexpertly groomed Dr Bartek. Nothing. She found herself looking up at the décolletage of her colleague.

'So, studying human trafficking in Europe...' Sophie said, licking her fingers now that her plate was clean '... is not all stats. There's a social anthropology aspect to it to. Poverty, ethnicity ... Do you fancy a fuck?'

George burst out laughing, and felt the heat suffuse her cheeks with embarrassment though she had not been easily embarrassed in years. 'I only came out to supervise my Sociology finalist!'

'So?!' Sophie reached out, stroked her hand, and started to play footsie with her under the table, which, in snow boots, felt more like a football tackle than flirtation.

The sight of ketchup under Sophie's fingernails made George pull her hand away. She pressed her lips together and smiled awkwardly, looking everywhere but at this five-foot tall propositioner with mesmerising eyes. 'I'm in a relationship. Sort of.'

'Sort of?'

'On and off.'

'Well, then?'

George had agreed to coffee. That was all.

The walk back to her place, up the steep incline of Castle Hill and along the Huntingdon Road, took place in anticipatory silence. But the noise in her head was unbearable. *She's going to expect more from me. I haven't slept with a woman in years. I wasn't looking for this. I don't even fancy her. I love Van den Bergen. But he's an arsehole and treats me like an afterthought.*

'You okay?' Sophie asked, as they stood on the front doorstep to George's shared house.

'It's a bit messy,' George said. 'The communal area, I mean. But my room's a clean space, so you'll have to take your shoes off before you go in. I'm a bit funny about …'

Key in the lock. The flickering light on the wall of the living room said the other housemates were watching TV. George bypassed them and led Sophie up the narrow Victorian stairs to her room.

The door was open. The lock bust. Splintered wood on the architrave.

'Shitting Nora!'

Key still uselessly in hand, George walked in and surveyed the mayhem. The room had been ransacked, top to bottom. Bedclothes on the floor. Contents of drawers strewn all over. Pot plant spattered mess across the carpet. Typing chair upended. Desk drawers flung hither and thither. She ran over to her desk. A space where the laptop had been.

'Fuck!' she shouted, staring at Sophie with desperate eyes. 'My research is gone!'

CHAPTER 10

Amsterdam, Sloterdijkermeer allotments, then, an apartment block in Bijlmer, 4 March

'For Christ's sake! When will it bloody rain and wash this crap away?' Van den Bergen shouted, trying to manoeuvre his car into one of the only spaces at the allotment complex that had been shovelled clear of snow over the past few weeks. Not shovelled well enough though. There had been another downfall overnight, covering the icy rectangle with virgin snow that creaked in complaint when compressed. Now, compacted beneath the tyres of his rear wheel drive E-Class Mercedes, the snow caused him to skid back and forth, back and forth, as if in some kind of retribution for being sullied.

'Fuck this!' he growled, slapping the steering wheel in frustration. He realised the car was at an awkward angle but had had enough and clicked the brake button on. He turned the engine off and stepped outside into -22°C. Perhaps it was lunacy coming here in this weather. But he needed to get away from the station. Here, at the otherwise empty Sloterdijkermeer allotment complex, he could sit in his wooden cabin in a state of suspended animation. Pretend just for an hour – or, as long as he could bear in these ridiculous Arctic temperatures before hypothermia set in

– that everything was alright. That life was normal. That he still had a measure of control over his own destiny.

Carrying the portable heater in one gloved hand, his Thermos flask and an Albert Heijn supermarket bag containing a fat file in the other, he trudged through the malign winter wonderland. More than two feet deep. It was heavy work. He eyed with suspicion the icicles that hung everywhere from sheds and cabins; he noted the sheer volume of snow that now sat on top of every roof, threatening to slide off at any moment and engulf a hapless victim below.

Snowmen leered at him from other people's patches. Jolly characters, easily identifiable as figures of fun on the day they were created by gardeners' children and grandchildren. Now, covered with yet more snow, they had become ghostly amorphous blobs, with drooping carrots for noses. Their sinister pebble smiles with those crow-like raisin eyes made Van den Bergen feel like he was being watched.

'Stop being a prick,' he told himself.

He kicked aside the snow on the step. Grey-white sky threatened another blizzard of bloated flakes. Better not get stranded here. Better keep an eye on the time.

He unlocked the cabin. Got the heater going. Sat uncomfortably in the padded salopettes that were relics of the time he had taken Tamara and Andrea skiing in Chamonix, just before the divorce. A last ditch attempt at happy families. He cracked open the flask, steam rising in whorls on the freezing air. Sipping at the oily coffee, laced with a little medicinal brandy, he pulled his phone out of his pocket, and re-read those poisonous emails. There were so many of them.

Jesus can see your soul, Paul van den Bergen. You are a weak man. You are the scum of the earth. There's a special space reserved in purgatory for you because you failed.

This was just the latest missive from what appeared to be his bank. When the emails had first started to arrive, he hadn't been sure they weren't part of some phishing scam, encouraging him to phone a bogus hotline and give all his financial details away. Then, as the contents of the emails became increasingly unpleasant, wishing him dead, saying the Devil was coming to claim him, he realised someone had created a false email address in order to spam him with pseudo-religious loathing. But the bogus Verenigde Spaarbank was not the only source of electronic woe.

I know where you live, you fucking paedo-loving pervert. I hope you get raped up the arse and beaten to death by those other useless pigs you work with.

This had allegedly been sent by a government official in the Hague, whom a little digging revealed to be an entirely fictitious person. Email account-holder unknown.

After a month or two of filing the hate mail into a folder, he had shown the first few to Tamara, not daring to let George see them for fear of her protective outrage and apocalyptic desire for revenge.

'You're being trolled, Dad,' Tamara had declared. 'I'd say go to the police, but you *are* the police! Get Marie to track down the sender and get whoever it is arrested. Or ignore it. Don't feed the trolls, right? It's your call.'

Sipping from the plastic cup, scrolling through this virtual bilge, he realised he had made a conscious decision to do nothing, hoped it would all go away over time … assumed he wasn't actually under any kind of real threat. And today, he had come to his allotment to do a little thinking. Perhaps there was something in this hate mail. Perhaps the senders were tied to the case that Kamphuis had ordered him to archive under S for stone-cold dead. Or maybe he *was* just weak and a failure. Either way, the words gnawed continually at his conscience so that he had endured yet another lonely, sleepless night, resolving to come to the cabin at first light and go through the missing persons' case notes yet again.

Repositioning his slightly foggy glasses on the end of his nose, he took out the hefty A4 lever arch file he had taken from the archives. Started to leaf through the list of suspects he had interviewed in the beginning. Were there any fervently religious types among them?

Outside, he heard creak, creak, creak, growing closer. Louder. Someone else was mad enough to come to the allotments in this infernal cold. Van den Bergen realised he was all alone out there. He hadn't spoken to a soul yet that morning; had deliberately turned the ring off his phone to avoid Kamphuis' nagging.

Footsteps trudging up his little path. Creak. Creak.

Raising the bulk of the Thermos over his head, he stood behind the door. Wondering if some bum was trying to break into one of the cabins in search of shelter. A cough, as the intruder stood on the other side of the flimsy wooden door. Trying the handle. Up, down. Up, down. The door opened inwards.

Van den Bergen brought the Thermos down heavily on a man's shoulder.

'Ow!' the unexpected visitor cried.

'You!'

Elvis rubbed the sweet spot where the boss had caught him, wincing at the pain that shot down his right arm.

'Jesus Christ! It's only me.' He eyed the giant flask, wondering fleetingly if there was anything hot left inside and whether Van den Bergen would offer him a drink in this biting cold.

'What the hell are you doing here, Elvis?' the boss asked. He looked pale, as though he had seen a ghost. Mind you, he looked like that most of the time these days. They were lucky if they could get him to leave the air-conditioned warmth and artificial light of his office.

'Kamphuis made me come and get you,' he said, pulling his woollen hat off, realising that it was sub-zero in the cabin too, and promptly pulling it back on again. 'I've been calling you for the last hour. When you didn't pick up and didn't answer the landline at your apartment, I figured you were here.' He gestured at the mildewed chair that sported a bag of compost on the opposite side of the beat-up table. 'Can I sit?'

Eyes darting side to side, Van den Bergen towered above him, still holding the tartan-patterned flask, as though he might hit him again should he put a foot wrong.

'No. What does the fat bastard want? Am I not entitled to some space? Am I some wet-behind-the-ears constable that I should be at his beck and call all the sodding time?'

'He insists you come back with me to Bijlmer to do door-to-doors. Marie's doing Internet research on that London Jack Frost case George emailed you the details of.'

'Insists, does he?'

Van den Bergen was staring at a curling poster on the wall of Debbie Harry from the early 1980s. There was an embarrassing moment where he noticed Elvis watching him ogle the faded, semi-naked star.

Elvis blushed and cleared his throat. 'Kamphuis said you need the fresh air, boss. And I need the backup.'

'Get in your car and bugger off back to the station. I don't need a babysitter and neither do you. We're men, Elvis. Men!'

'I can't boss. Came in a taxi.'

Van den Bergen switched off the fan heater and made that telltale growling noise that always said he was utterly pissed off. It was going to be a long morning.

There was silence in the car as they skidding along the icy patches, going too fast at times.

Elvis wondered if the boss was going to kill him before he made his thirtieth birthday. Not long, now. Mum was going to go into the home for the weekend, so he could have respite and go out for a drink with the lads.

He stared at the side of Van den Bergen's face. Saw the split veins that had appeared around his nose. The open pores. Dark circles underneath his eyes said he rarely slept. Funny, how he had to guess at what went on in the boss's private life. Neither of them knew that much about each other after all these years. He knew the Chief Inspector had been having an affair with George McKenzie for quite some time. Knew he popped those painkillers like sweets and disappeared off to sulk or wank or both in his super-shed at Sloterdijkermeer. But that was all. And did the boss have an inkling that his mother was on her last legs with Parkinson's? That he was the main carer? Probably not. Van den Bergen had never asked.

The flats in Bijlmer were soul-destroying. As Elvis and the boss moved their way through the block, proceeding along landing after landing, climbing from floor to floor, front doors were opened reluctantly by the residents. Hitting them time and again with a fug of exotic cooking smells, unsanitary living conditions, piss, pet-stink, unwashed bodies, carbolic soap. All of life was here. But Elvis had just long enough to glimpse the common denominator of poverty beyond the threshold, before those doors were slammed resolutely in their faces.

'No. I didn't see a thing. Nope. I was at work/my parents'/the mosque/in town.'

Ghanaians. Somalis. Moroccans. Sometimes pretending not to speak Dutch. Hell, maybe they couldn't. Every ethnicity Amsterdam sheltered lived here fearfully, silently, treading lightly. You could see the fear in their eyes and smell the desperation coming off their bodies. *Please don't ask to see my paperwork*, their pleading glances said. When the El-Al jumbo had crashed in one of the old multi-storey blocks in 1991, the death toll had been officially set at forty, but had been estimated to be over two hundred in reality, since most of the dead had been illegal immigrants.

'Are you sure you don't recognise the photo of this man?' Van den Bergen said, stooping to speak to an old Asian guy who couldn't have been taller than five foot five. A shake of the head said no.

After an hour with no joy, and the boss getting more and more surly, they followed a woman dressed head to toe in black Arabic robes, wearing an oversized anorak over the top. She kept looking back at them furtively.

'Look at this! Someone knows how to spot a cop when she sees one,' Elvis said.

The boss nodded. 'My instincts say, stay on her.'

The woman picked up her pace. Shuffling along the communal landing at speed, she looked over her shoulder. Wide-eyed. Shoved her key in the lock of a door some twenty metres away. Ten. Five. Desperately trying to wriggle her key free. Still clocking their approach with a nervous expression that screamed guilty conscience. Key free, she disappeared into the apartment's hallway. Tried to close the door. Except the door wouldn't shut.

The woman glanced down and frowned at Van den Bergen's enormous foot in the way.

'Police, madam,' the Chief Inspector said, showing his ID.

Tears in her eyes. Screaming in Arabic maybe, to people beyond the hallway out of sight. Hands flailing, she ran inside. Van den Bergen took out his service weapon and pushed his way in.

Ten or more men scattered at the sight of them – some white, some black – into the bedrooms and kitchen. The air rang with the sounds of panic in several different languages. In the middle of the living room were two kids on mattresses, playing some board game or other. They looked up at the policemen. One had a familiar face.

'It's the boy from the playground,' Elvis said. 'Imran.'

CHAPTER 11

Amsterdam, apartment in Bijlmer, then, police headquarters, later

'We're not interested in whether you're legal or not,' Van den Bergen said. Shouting at volume as though his audience were communally deaf. Might as well be, judging by the silence. Holding his hands up in the hope of demonstrating to the cowering gaggle of eight men, one woman and two children that he meant them no harm. It was hard enough to inspire any kind of trust in the residents of Bijlmer. Now that the two uniforms had shown up as backup for what was potentially a combustible situation, he could see the naked scepticism on their faces.

He turned to Elvis. 'Tell them, for God's sake! Tell them we don't give a shit about their status.'

Elvis shrugged. 'I don't know Arabic, boss!' He sighed heavily. 'Does anybody here speak Dutch? English? French? Come on! Vous ... Oh, fuck it. I can't speak French either. Nobody?' He pointed at the two white men. 'What nationality are you?'

Kneeling with their hands in the air, as though they were about to pray to the Netherlands Police for absolution, or, at least, asylum, the two men spoke in what sounded like Russian. Polish, maybe.

Feeling the agitated lava of his stomach acid spurt into his gullet, Van den Bergen stalked towards the boy from the playground. 'You!' he said. 'You understand what I'm saying, don't you? Imran, right?' The boy peered sullenly down at the board game. English Monopoly. Pieces strewn over the dirty mattress. Metal car, iron, top hat. Half-eaten remnants of lunch on a plastic plate. A piece of pitta bread on Trafalgar Square. He remained silent, looking intently at the younger boy who was building a house out of Community Chest cards.

Van den Bergen knelt and tried to gain the boy's attention. 'It's okay, Imran. I just want to ask you some questions about the man that died. The man in playground.'

The woman lurched forwards. Prodded Imran in the back. Said something in her native tongue, though the tone was castigatory, Van den Bergen could tell.

'Is this your mother?' Van den Bergen asked.

Imran shook his head at the same time that the woman nodded.

'Mother. Yes. Yes,' she said, breaking into an unfamiliar and excitable string of consonants and vowels. Clasping the boy to her chest. Kissing the top of his head.

'Chief Inspector!' one of the uniforms shouted from another room. 'You'd better come and see this!'

Backing towards the bedroom, quickly assessing whether Elvis was at risk or not from the jittery, diasporic occupants of the apartment, he poked his head in on the scene in one of the bedrooms. A dark-skinned man lay on a squalid, single camp bed, clutching at his stomach. His nether regions were wrapped in soiled bandages, a foetid stink on the air of infection. Beside his cot, balanced on top of a stool, was a cardboard vegetable tray from a supermarket. Filled with blood-caked plastic bags containing white powder.

'Call for an ambulance,' Van den Bergen told the uniform. Eyeing the bloody ooze that had contaminated the sheet beneath the man's body. Sweat rolling from his brow, the whites of his eyes on show as he trembled and winced. 'I think we've got ourselves a flat full of drug mules. Looks like some cargo has burst inside this poor bastard's stomach.'

Back in the living room, Van den Bergen glanced at the soiled mattresses that the boys sat on. He cast an appraising eye over the visibly jumpy men in the room, shared a knowing glance with Elvis, then turned to the second uniform.

'Contact social services, as well. Tell them I've got two at-risk kids. And get the van. This lot are coming down the station for questioning.'

'Death by snow,' Marie said to her flickering screen, momentarily catching sight of her face, reflected on its shining surface. Despair etched in parallel lines onto her forehead, their depth and permanence accelerated by the world of Internet filth that Marie inhabited, as her police specialism dictated. *Blot it out.* She refocussed on the Google list.

'Snow-related deaths. Ice as a weapon. Right. Come on, Google. Come on, Europol database. You're my best girls. Don't disappoint me.'

Marie was happy to be alone. The silence was comforting. There was no expectation for her to make polite conversation with Elvis and the boss, although she rarely did these days, in any case. She could just concentrate on the information that came whizzing down the fibre-optic cables to her machine. A world of pain. A world of hate. But, a firewall of gigabytes and machinery that put a couple degrees of separation between her and the places where the world was truly broken.

As the results appeared on the various search engines, she slurped from her lukewarm coffee. Pulled the collar of her top wide, sniffing and wondering if it had another day in it. Probably not. She knew what the other detectives said about her, although she had never heard Van den Bergen or Elvis complain about the smell. That George could be cutting, though. But then, she had a problem with OCD and was okay otherwise. It was the admin-bitches Marie couldn't stand. Other women were always the worst.

'Harpies,' she said, staring at the wall whilst visualising the cows upstairs. Kamphuis' harem. She looked fleetingly at the photo of the six-month-old boy on her desk. Swallowed hard. The world at this end of those fibre optic cables was broken too.

Her focus returned to the Google list that went on for page after page after page. Jack Frost was not the only damaged soul using snow and ice to kill. Mother Nature had previous. She was the Queen of the psychopaths. Avalanches. Ice falling from a great height that could take out an entire car. Frozen corpses scattered along the base of K2's North Face; marble-white near-perfection in perpetuity, only broken in the parts that had trifled with the mountain on the way to the bottom.

Marie skimmed over Marianne de Koninck's forensic report again. Conical wound. Water permeating the surrounding cells. No trace of a blade.

'Got to be an icicle. What else could it be?' she muttered.

Her practised, analytical gaze scanned the contents of story after story. Page after page. Deftly click-clicking her mouse, until she happened upon what she had half hoped the search would throw up. She allowed herself a broad grin.

'Ha! Hello, Jack Frost. Looks like you have very itchy feet.'

Her private celebration was interrupted by Van den Bergen bursting in. Grim-faced.

'I need you to be my wingman. I've got to question a minor. Now, please!'

In the quiet of the meeting room – the only relatively relaxed space they could source at short notice where a child might be questioned – Marie sat next to Van den Bergen. She studied the little boys, who, in return, seemed to be getting the measure of her. Two sets of clear brown eyes fixed on her red hair. Two furrowed brows. Cynical expressions that, by rights, belonged to

64

far older children. The smaller boy couldn't have been more than six.

'Imran,' Marie began, turning to the older boy. A flicker of a smile playing on her lips. She scratched an angry patch of dry skin on her chin. 'You told the Chief Inspector, here, that the woman in the apartment isn't your mummy.'

The boy shook his head. 'No. She's not my mother.'

'Where is your mother, then?'

No answer. She turned to the younger boy, who started to suck his thumb, stroking his nose with his index finger.

'What does she do, that woman? What do those men in the apartment do? Do you know them?'

Imran shrugged. 'She looks after us. The man says she's our aunt, but she's not our aunt. She's mean.'

Van den Bergen leaned forwards. Kept his voice deliberately quiet. 'Mean in what way?'

'She beats us, sometimes.'

'Why?'

'When we don't do our job. I hate her. She stinks.'

Running her fingers along the edge of the table, Marie breathed in sharply, as though she had considered something and then decided against saying it. 'What's your job, Imran? I bet a clever boy like you can do lots of things?'

'If I tell you, she'll beat me.'

'The woman?'

Nodding. The smaller of the two boys said something in his native tongue to Imran. Startled eyes. A look of fear. Wiped his thumb on his trousers and started to hug himself. Imran spat harsh, unfamiliar words at the side of his head in response.

'What about the dead man?' Van den Bergen asked. 'What's his name?'

The boy's reluctance to respond made the air in the meeting room feel heavy, loaded with stifled possibility. In a sudden eruption of emotion, the smaller child started to sob. Van den Bergen's fatherly instincts screamed at him to hug the little boy. His profes-sionalism held him in his seat. Rigid. Unflinching on the outside. Anguish manifesting itself as chest pain on the inside.

'Let's turn them over to social services, boss,' Marie said. 'Get them a safe bed for the night and hot meal. We'll try again tomorrow.'

Angered by the haunting phenomenon of the crying boy, Van den Bergen marched into the interview room that held the woman, her interpreter and Elvis. At his behest, Elvis switched on the recording equipment.

Carefully, deliberately, Van den Bergen shoved a photo of the dead Bijlmer man under the woman's nose. Tapping on the table next to the photo, he said, 'You know who he is, don't you?' He scowled at her impassive face. 'I've got a man in A&E, found in that apartment … looks like he's going to die from septicaemia. A drug mule. I've worked enough drugs cases in my time to know that much. Carrying bags in his stomach and shitting them out once he's been safely trafficked from some far-flung shithole to Amsterdam. Bringing poison and death into *my* town. Are you a drug mule, too? Are you a dealer? Did the dead man use those boys as dealers? Scouts? What? Tell me!'

'No comment,' the interpreter told him. 'She has no comment. She wants to speak to someone at her embassy.'

He turned to the diminutive woman who was acting as linguistic go-between and steeled himself to remember she was just the messenger, that he should not shoot her. 'There are two little boys who are going to spend the night in an emergency foster placement. Frightened out of their wits, saying she'll beat them if they speak. Tell the hatchet-faced cow that if she doesn't give me the info I require now I'll have her on the next flight to whatever warzone she's crawled out of.' He was shouting. He knew he was shouting. He didn't care. Let this bitch come at him with whatever she could muster. Let her try to level an accusation of intimidation or sexism or racism at him.

'Syria.'

'Right. Well, Syria can fucking have her back before the weekend, unless she talks.'

'She wants a Dutch passport.'

'Talk!'

There was a heated exchange in the woman's native tongue. She treated Van den Bergen and Elvis to looks of utter disdain, as though she were a Red Cross nurse, rather than a woman somehow embroiled in drug-dealing and human trafficking.

Finally, the interpreter turned to Van den Bergen, alarmed and disconcerted, judging by her look of disgust. 'The dead man is called Tomas Vlinders. He paid her to take the boys to rich men's houses. They were delivering drugs for parties. Parties held by powerful men.'

Van den Bergen sat back down. Pushed his knees beneath the low table. Leaned forward in a measured manner. 'What powerful men?'

CHAPTER 12

A village south of Amsterdam, 25 May, the previous year

'Phone, door keys, bag,' Gabriella Deenen said, staring blankly at her possessions on the passenger seat. 'Car keys. Where's the—?'

The police officer leaned in through the driver's open window. His hat and the bulk of his navy and yellow Politie jacket filling the space. 'Are you sure you want to drive yourself?' He sounded incredulous. His furrowed brow said he didn't believe her. 'You can come in the squad car and get someone to pick your vehicle up later.'

Gabi started the engine. The key had been in the ignition all the time! Which made sense, since she was sitting in the damned car and had to have had the key to unlock it in the first place. *Pay attention, for god's sake. Breathe in. Breathe out.*

'I'm fine. I'll meet you at the house.'

She was surprised by how strong her voice sounded. She didn't feel fine. She felt like she was going to be sick. *Pull yourself together, you weak woman,* she counselled herself. *You'll get home. This will all be a big mistake.* With a click of a switch, the window closed, shutting the irritating, well-meaning and concern of the policeman outside.

Pulling out of the parking space, she almost crashed into the police car. Almost. Not quite. She was fine. This was okay. It was going to be a mistake. Except she had that horrible feeling in the pit of her stomach. Not butterflies. More like flapping, desperate moths, blind to the direction in which the light lay.

Breathe in. Breathe out.

When they had turned up, in the middle of her fundraising presentation, at first she had been annoyed. Knock, knock on the door of the meeting room, right as she was delivering a heart-rending speech about the hope that the charity's medical research brought to families affected by traumatic brain injury. The donor – a director in a multi-national mining company with a shocking health and safety record – had been rapt with attention; cheque-book open, hoping to buy the company a better public image. But just as things were going well and she had enjoyed that rush she used to get back in London, when she had pulled off a particularly good PR campaign, propelling Schoen Engineering Systems to the top of the aerospace heap, *they* had barged their way in. Flashing ID.

Yes. She had had a bad feeling. The moment she had seen them in the doorway. Eyes only for her.

'Can you come with us, please, Mrs Deenen?'

The policewoman's face had been arranged into an expression of kindliness and sympathy. She wondered if the Dutch Police HR department had arranged training for that kind of thing. Body language was so important.

Now, her hands shook, though she was gripping the steering wheel as tightly as possible. Skin stretched tight over white bony knuckles.. As she waited at the traffic lights, fragmented thoughts punctured her apparent composure. Josh and Lucy missing. A slight chip on her bronze nail varnish. Trip to the nail bar was in order. But Josh and Lucy were missing. Missing.

The traffic lights turned to red. Slamming hard on the brakes, the police car almost ran into the back of her. Suddenly, her foot was disobeying her brain. Trembling. Jerking. Kangaroo petrol, she lurched away on green.

'What do they mean, missing?' she asked the road sign as she pulled into their street.

There were two police cars outside their hydrangea-fronted house. The lawn needed a trim, she noted. Her Dutch home in this Amsterdam satellite town – quiet but for the Schiphol to Rotterdam line that ran at the back of the long garden – was hardly in the same league as the Victorian house they had had in London. But at least it was detached. She didn't feel ashamed to have the police officers in and offer them a cold drink. Perhaps Piet would already have made them one. The kids were almost certainly playing in the back garden in this weather.

The kids.

The kids weren't playing in the garden. The police were here. Josh and Lucy were missing.

Almost ploughing into the back of a small white van that overhung the paved driveway by a small margin, Gabi parked up abruptly, only an inch or so between the bumper and the brick wall. Light-headed, she patted her hair. Phone. Bag. Keys. Going through the routine. Imposing some normality on the abnormal. Staring at everything but seeing nothing. Fingers fumbling with the fob. Locking the car. Turning her ankle as she walked in through the open front door. Unaware of the pain. Past the constable on the step, talking into his hissing walkie-talkie. He reached out to try to stop her but she strutted on into the kitchen.

Look for Lucy and Josh. They'll be there. Sitting at the table, drawing. Bet Piet hasn't washed their hands all morning. If they're not there, they're in the garden. Yes, they'll be outside.

At her back, the police officers who had come to the office were saying something to her, though she wasn't listening. She heard her name. 'Mrs Deenen.' But the rest was rhubarb, rhubarb, rhubarb.

'Rhubarb,' she said under her breath, remembering stage

instructions for extras in the school play when she had been a child, though she had always taken the leading role. 'Rhubarb.' Josh's favourite kind of crumble pudding, though Lucy often gagged on the stringy consistency.

Steeling herself to connect with here and now, Gabi took in her surroundings. So many police officers were encroaching on her space. There was a man in plain clothes, talking to Piet, taking notes at the island in the middle of the kitchen. He had a glass of water by his right hand. Good. Piet had offered them all refreshments.

Beyond, she saw the empty lawn. The enormity of the situation started to dawn on her.

Piet was crying, staring at her, with tears coursing down his cheeks. Red-eyed. Red-nosed. Snot on his upper lip and the white fluffy remnants of kitchen roll stuck in his stubble.

He held his arms out as he stood and stumbled towards her. 'I'm so sorry, darling.'

Gabi put her bag carefully on the work surface. Pushed Piet back towards his stool, walked to the sink and washed her hands carefully, running the water until it was boiling hot. Rubbing and rubbing the astringent lemony hand-wash between her fingers. She dried her hands methodically on a clean towel. The garden appeared empty of children. Nobody on the slide. No Josh, jumping up and down on the sun-lounger, trying to launch himself onto his sister or clutching his ears as the train roared past.

The policeman who wore his own clothes was speaking to her – a detective. Yes. He must be a detective. She stared at him blankly. Little Gabi, blinded by the glare. Silenced by the attention. All eyes on her. Struggling to remember her opening lines. Rhubarb. Rhubarb. 'You're in shock, Mrs Deenen. Shall I make you a cup of coffee?' a policewoman said. Who was she? Oh, that's right. One of the constables who had shown up at the office.

'Where are Lucy and Josh, Pieter?' Gabi asked her husband.

No longer was she a child. Big Gabi needed to take control of this shambles. Big Gabi would sort it. 'What have you done with our children, you fucking useless bastard?'

She marched up to Piet and thumped him squarely on the side of the head, with such force, that he fell off his stool onto the kitchen floor. 'All you had to do was babysit them for half a day, while I went in to give that presentation.' Big Gabi was screaming. 'And you couldn't even do that. You miserable, useless fucking wimp.'

'Mrs Deenen! Please to try stay calm.' The detective grabbed her by the forearms. He was tall. Authoritative.

This badge-toting turd wasn't the boss of her. She shook him off.

She ran into the garden, screaming at the top of her lungs. 'Josh! Lucy! Mummy's here. You can come out now!'

'Can you think of anyone who might have taken them, Mrs Deenen? A relative? A friend? Neighbour?' the detective asked. He had followed her outside. Now, he was standing between her and the climbing frame.

Interfering pain in the arse, she thought. She could find her own children. They were obviously just playing hide and seek.

'Move! I want to check under there,' she said, pointing to the void beneath the platform.

'We've had a team combing the garden and all along the train track at the back for the last hour. There's no way in. There's no way out. The train track is clear for a mile in each direction, though they've stopped the Schiphol to Rotterdam service until we've searched the entire line. No trace of them.'

When she tried to push him aside, he stood his ground.

'Mrs Deenen. Your children aren't hiding, I'm afraid. They're gone. They can't have wandered off. They're not in the house or the garden. They've been taken. Abducted.'

Gabi looked at the Sesamstraat tricycle and an abandoned Iggle Piggle doll Lucy had brought from the UK. She sank to her knees, arms crossed tightly over her bosom. Big Gabi, wrapping Little Gabi in a protective embrace. Keening. Cursing god that her babies were gone. That her life had been thrown into chaos.

'This can't be happening. This can't.'

The detective put a large hand on her shoulder. 'I'm so sorry.'

CHAPTER 13

The City of London, 5 March, present, mid-morning

'My Lord,' the chauffer said, holding the door of the Rolls Royce wide. He touched the brim of his cap.

Gordon Bloom shook his head. He looked longingly at the plush cream and truffle interior of his car; he knew that the heated leather seats would offer some measure of comfort in these infernal sub-zero temperatures. Last night on the TV, the weatherman had been bleating on about Arctic Sea ice melts causing high-pressure weather systems over the Barents Sea and northern Russia, icy wind blasting mainland Europe and the UK as a result. Nobody had seen off-the-charts temperatures like this in England since the big freeze of 2012. Global warming or some bullshit. Whatever the cause was, he was sick of it. Sick of having to wear uncomfortable thermal underwear. Tired of having to be driven everywhere. Bored with being under constant scrutiny since Rufus' death.

'Thanks, Kenny, but I'll walk,' he said, stamping his feet. The snow at least a foot deep, even in EC1 where his meeting had taken place. Strange, to sit at the head of a boardroom table, discussing a major acquisition and then having to change back into skiwear in the men's. A man like him shouldn't be inconvenienced by this nonsense. Though he may not quite have all the money in China, his assets bettered many a country's GDP. He was an übermensch, after all. A Titan from a long line of Titans. Shame then, that those like him blessed with demigod status couldn't control that insane bitch, mother nature. 'It's not far. You can pick me up afterwards. Go and treat yourself to a hot coffee and a cake or something.' He unfurled a twenty from his wallet. 'You need a break. I need some air. This weather is making fools of us all.'

Kenny touched the brim of his cap again, and pocketed the twenty. 'Mental, isn't it, my Lord?' he said, his breath steaming on the air as he blew uselessly into gloved hands. The broad, older man wore a smart coat in thin fabric – far too flimsy for this weather. His wind-burned face and bulky build gave him the appearance of a builder nearing retirement, at odds with the dapper uniform of someone who drove a Rolls Royce for a billionaire.

Bloom remembered his father's driver. Jenkins, wasn't it? He had been cut from similar cloth. Poor old bastard. He made a mental note to furnish Kenny with a better coat. And a gun. Definitely time he had a gun.

'It never snows in central London,' Bloom said, pulling the fox fur flaps of his Russian hat down over his ears, obscuring his peripheral view of this blinding winter wonderland. The chrome pipes and corkscrews of the Lloyds building towered above him like a bartender's tool kit, thrown into an ice bucket. 'People skating on the Thames! How is that even bloody possible?' The icy air made his filled tooth sensitive. He winced.

'It's a long way to Southwark Cathedral, sir,' Kenny said, closing the car door with a thunk. 'You sure? Police said you shouldn't go anywhere unescorted.'

Bloom nodded. Squeezed his eyes shut. Showed he appreciated Kenny's concern for his employer. But inside his gloves, he balled his fists at the thought that the police should dictate to a man like him what to do and where to go in *his* city. 'I need a bit of space. Especially today. You know?'

Kenny cocked his head to one side. Narrowed his eyes. A gap-toothed half smile whispered uncertainty.

'Don't worry. I'm a big boy.' He patted the driver's arm.

'Of course, sir. As you wish.' His formal, stilted turns of phrase always sounded stiff and superficial, with that horrible east end accent. Bloody performing monkey.

Sighing deeply, Bloom turned towards Leadenhall Market. Trudging through the snow, he headed through the brief, dry respite that the gaudy red and gold Victorian arcade offered. Glum in the post-Christmas slump, where all the Yuletide tat was now 75% off, hanging unwanted on rack after rack.

He looked up through the vaulted glass ceiling, blurred around the edges by his halo of grey fur, and saw that the sky was perfectly white. Then, peering through the opening at the far end which led in the direction of Bishopsgate, he could see fat flakes start to come down again. Unrelenting. Forcing the grey-faced denizens of the City of London to hasten home early before public transport ground to a halt. Ice on the roads. Wrong kind of snow on the train lines. Broken-down, blizzard-blinded this and that.

He would definitely be better off crossing London on foot. Catching sight of himself, reflected in a men's suiting shop window, he decided that he looked like an Inuit. Unrecognisable with the hat on and the glasses. On the periphery of the reflection, he barely registered a shuffling figure several paces behind him.

But never mind that. He was thinking about Rufus.

The memorial service was a nice idea, in light of the fact that the police were still refusing to release the body. Everyone would be there, of course. Rufus' widow, sobbing, no doubt. He had always wanted to fuck her. Maybe now, he would have his chance. Hadn't *Harpers* named him as Europe's most eligible bachelor? Yes, he would enjoy sliding his hand between her gym-honed thighs. Riding her throughout the night, innocently comforting her throughout the mourning.

Rufus' beleaguered children would be there too, wondering what the hell they had done to have their father taken away from them. Squalling, snot-nosed pug-faced little fuckers of ten, six and three. Jesus. The fallout the murder had caused was unimaginable, the most unfathomable injustice being his own loss of a trusted super-lackey and friend of old.

The press would be gathered outside, no doubt, snapping the staff of Bloom Group plc, as they entered the hallowed cathedral to bid farewell to their Chief Executive, dabbing at their eyes to show their commitment to the company, whether they had ever met Rufus or not. Nobody had liked him, that's for sure.

Gordon Bloom allowed himself a wry chuckle as he neared London Bridge. He looked into a café window at all the city office workers, trying to thaw themselves out by wrapping their gloved hands around cups of steaming coffee. He caught sight again of the shuffling figure, some way behind, entering the reflected scene as he exited, huddled up in clothes that seemed too big for him. Perhaps a homeless man, making his way towards a shelter. Nothing to worry about, though Bloom did pick up his pace. Tripped on a kerbstone as he crossed the slush-logged street onto the Bridge itself. He had difficulty with his depth perception these days. The surgeon had said the ocular nerves were too badly damaged. At least the glass eye was the finest money could buy. Couldn't be helped. If the worst thing that ever befell him was visual impairment, he was doing reasonably well. Better than Rufus, at any rate.

As he crossed London Bridge with snow whirling around him, settling on his hat, drip-dripping freezing water onto his tingling nose where it melted, he imagined himself trapped inside a snow-globe. No escape from this claustrophobic scene. Just falling snow and the same chain of events replaying in his mind.

He and Rufus had had lunch. They had parted company. Now,

Rufus was dead. Drowning by snow. Holes in his neck like the Devil's stigmata.

Who was this Jack Frost that the press referred to? Why had he wanted Rufus Lazami dead? Was he, Gordon Bloom next on the hit list?

Glancing behind, he was pleased to see the homeless man was no longer on his tail.

'Stop being so easily spooked, you bloody idiot,' he counselled himself, clutching the handrail as he made his way down the gritted stone stairs to Southwark Cathedral, where he would say goodbye in public.

Cameras flashing, as anticipated. Paparazzi pests, swarming like unseasonal flies on a frozen carcass.

'Lord Bloom! Aren't you worried that Jack Frost will come after you?'

He was careful to maintain an air of sobriety. 'I am here to bid adieu to a dear friend and longstanding business partner. Thank you. Good day.'

Their voices rang in his ears, as he stood in the threshold of Southwark Cathedral's great stone hall.

'Are you taking measures to protect yourself, Lord Bloom?' they shouted.

Inside, an organ ground away at a hymn he didn't recognize. The place was packed with mourners wearing snowboots and colourful ski-jackets that were at odds with the sombre occasion. All eyes were on him. He nodded to the young man with the plucked eyebrows who stood in the aisle, ushering family to the left and business colleagues to the right. Recognised him as one of his rising stars.

At his back, the journalistic hordes continued to bay for a response.

'Is it true that the killing was ordered by someone in the criminal underworld? Did Rufus Lazami have many enemies?'

Their questions bounced off him thick and fast; those

cadaverous flies throwing themselves against a sealed window. He would not answer. He would not give them the satisfaction. Let the press and Scotland Yard keep digging. They wouldn't find a fucking thing.

CHAPTER 14

London, Westminster, later

'What are you going to do?' Sophie asked, her Doc Martens scuffing up snow onto the hem of her floor-length batik-print skirt. She grabbed George's hand, as they walked along Millbank.

The Thames was on their left, a white ribbon twisting through a cityscape that looked like it had been dipped in liquid nitrogen. On their right, Millbank Tower loomed: a 1960s brutalist monolith with windows. Somewhere, on one of those dizzying levels that stood sentinel over Albert Embankment, the Open Society Foundation was situated.

George shook Sophie's hand loose, swiftly switching her rucksack to her right shoulder to prevent her from trying to hold her hand again. She sighed heavily. Wondered whether to say anything about this unlooked-for physical contact. Perhaps some things were better left unsaid. 'I don't know. Sally's on my case. The Home Office is burning my ear about deadlines. If I don't find that fucking laptop and my USB stick, I might as well apply for a job stacking shelves at Tesco. Maybe my Aunty Shaz can get me back my old cleaning job at the titty bar. It's at least a years' worth of work. Gone. Just like that.'

'What did the pigs say?' Sophie asked. Her earrings, necklaces and the buckles on her flowery satchel jangled as she walked.

'Don't call them the pigs,' George said. 'My partner's a Chief Inspector in the Dutch police.'

'Your partner? You were slagging him off the other night. Blows hot and cold, you said.'

'That was then. A lot's happened since.' George noticed the expectant expression on her newfound friend's face. She remembered the awkward moment when Sophie had propositioned her in the pub, and regretted even having asked her back for a coffee with no strings. Today, every gesture of camaraderie seemed like a cloying advance. Every knowing glance on the tube had felt overly suggestive. 'Right now, I wish I had six foot five of policeman to stand guard over my place. It's freaky having someone go through your stuff. It happened to me when I was living in Amsterdam.' She shuddered, thankful for the long johns she wore beneath her jeans, though it was the memory of the Firestarter, touching her things in the little bedsit above the Cracked Pot Coffee Shop that caused the hairs on her skin to stand on end.

The brightness of Sophie's green eyes seemed suddenly dimmed, or was it just the shadows cast by the covered approach to Millbank Tower's lobby? George quietly chastised herself for being arrogant.

'You're welcome to stay on my sofa again tonight, if you want,' Sophie said, holding the door open for George. 'I might not be able to offer you pig protection, but at least I'm on your doorstep if you need me.'

Sophie's sofa had been less than comfortable. A battered old thing, covered in cigarette burns and cat hair. Next to it, a large coffee table, festooned with carelessly abandoned coffee cups, wine glasses, ashtrays, Rizla packets, a hairbrush, several hefty academic books and the latest by Donna Tartt. But the anticipation that George would join Sophie in bed in the middle of the night had occasioned something far worse than simple discomfort. It had brought on an unwelcome bout of insomnia.

'Darkest hour is just before dawn,' George muttered beneath her breath, remembering how the night had felt like it would never end.

'What?' Sophie asked.

'Nothing.'

Together in the cavernous reception area, they signed in. All brown, white and black marble harked back to a time when London was swinging and fabulous. Now, rendered fashionable again by a passion for all things mid-century, George reflected. If she could only afford her own place, she might go for that retro-look too. In fact, she'd settle for bloody Ikea if it came to it. As long as it was hers.

High above the city, George and Sophie sat in comfortable armchairs. Biscuits artfully arranged on a plate. Herbal tea in hand-painted mugs. They were facing a dumpy middle-aged project worker called Graham Tokár. He oozed well-meaning and an energy that almost audibly crackled, directed, quite plainly, towards Sophie. Had Sophie at some juncture also offered him a fuck in a pub over a burger, George wondered?

'So, I've told George, here, about the charity funding initiatives that lessen the poverty and social exclusion of the Roma,' Sophie said.

'That's right,' Graham said, angling his body towards George but not tearing his gaze from Sophie's eyes. 'Musical institutes. Education grants. Lobbying European parliament for change. We work with the poorest people in some of the most financially stagnant and racist environments in Europe.' He finally looked at George. The spark had vanished. 'And many of the staff, Europe-wide, are Roma too. Like me. I've got a Scottish mother, but a Hungarian Roma dad.'

George looked down at her notes. She followed the line of her pad to Graham Tokár's shoes. He had a piece of chewing gum stuck to the heel of his left foot. This much, she could see, as he crossed his legs. In his right ear, he wore a small, silver sleeper.

He was clearly an articulate and interesting man, but she hated his earring. His ears were wrong.

'You know you've got an infection in your piercing,' she said, pointing to the inflamed flesh of his earlobe.

He touched his ear self-consciously. George made a mental note not to shake his hand when they left.

'Have I?' he asked, face flushing red right up to his hairline where his greying hair had started to thin. 'Oh, well, did Sophie tell you about—?'

'Look,' said George, blinking hard. Checking her phone. No messages from the police about her stolen laptop. *Shit*. 'I'm a criminologist. I'm doing research into trafficking. Not the Roma. Sophie asked me to come here today, and it's nice of you.' She rammed a biscuit hastily into her mouth. 'And these biscuits are great.' Speaking with her mouth full. 'But to be honest, I can't see the point—'

George could feel her colleague's eyes boring into the side of her head. She felt instinctively that both Sophie and this charity project worker thought her an outrageous arsehole. Was she being rude? Probably.

'I spend a lot of time in prison,' she said by way of an apology. 'I'm specifically interested in hearing how the Roma are embroiled in human trafficking. As victims. As perpetrators. Anecdotes. Groups you can put me in touch with. Stats. That sort of thing.'

Graham Tokár was looking at her with his mouth hanging slightly open. He glanced at Sophie, a look loaded with judgemental import.

'What about criminal empires in countries where the Roma live?' George asked.

'Shqipëtar,' he said.

'What?'

'It's an Albanian legend.'

At her side, Sophie started to nod. She closed her eyes, as

though Graham was about to give a virtuoso performance. 'It refers to the Son of the Eagle,' she said.

Graham rubbed his earlobe. 'Albanian legend has it that there was an eagle soaring in the sky with a fat, venomous snake in its mouth, right?' He sniffed his fingers. 'Below it, the eagle's defence-less eaglet lay in the nest, watched by a young man.'

'What young man?' George asked.

'It's not important. Just this young man. Anyway, when the eagle dropped the snake, presuming it to be dead, the snake fell into the nest, right? Apparently it was still alive. So, it was about to attack the eaglet, but the youth shot it with an arrow. Then, the youth takes the eaglet but is confronted by its parent …'

'The eagle,' Sophie said. Grinning.

'Right. The eagle who thought the youth was deliberately kidnapping its offspring. So anyway, the eagle realises the boy had saved the eaglet and …'

George checked her phone again. 'I'm listening. Go on.'

Bunched eyebrows said Graham Tokár was getting annoyed with her. 'So, the eaglet flies over the boy for the rest of his life, acting as his guardian, and he becomes the best hunter. A real hero. The son of the eagle.'

'What's that got to do with—?'

'Rumour has it that the big-wig who runs trafficking out of Albania – and lots of Roma kids get sucked into that – goes by the nickname Shqipëtar.'

'I've read about him,' Sophie said. 'Apparently only people high up in the trafficking network know who he is, but his tentacles stretch into Western Europe.'

George frowned. She wrote three lines of notes, then ate another biscuit in silence. 'Eagle,' she said. It rang a bell, but she wasn't sure why. She rifled through her memory of all the names on her homespun trafficking database but nothing resonated with her. Thought about the pile of handwritten notes from her women's prison sessions. They, at least, were still at Aunty Sharon's.

There was something in among those notes. Something that almost clicked but didn't quite. Eagle. She needed to get out of this air-conditioned box and get her hands on that paperwork while her hunch was still fresh.

She stood abruptly. Stuck out her hand. 'Bye, then. Thanks for the biccies.'

Outside, Sophie ran after her. 'You are such a dick!' she said. 'I thought you were cool, but you're really not. You're a fucking … a fucking …' Her attractive face screwed up in undisguised irritation.

'Psychopath?' George offered, walking as briskly as the poorly gritted pavement would allow. She headed towards the Palace of Westminster, the pale stone towers of which seemed to reach up into the white sky; trying to poke a hole in snow-heavy clouds so that they might pull more clement weather forth.

Sophie grabbed her arm.

George shook her loose. 'Please don't touch me. I don't like being touched unless I invite it.'

Halting by Victoria Tower Gardens, which was playing host to a pack of American school kids engaged in a snowball fight, Sophie swung her satchel across her body. 'I don't think I want to work with you. Sally seemed to be describing another bloody person. You're strange!' Sophie looked her up and down. Those green eyes were now judgemental and hard.

By the time George had thought of the right thing to say to her, Sophie had crossed the road and was already some two hundred yards away, making for St. James's Park tube, in all likelihood. 'Fucking hippies!' George said, thinking wistfully of her former landlord, Jan. He had been one for grabbing her in suffocating hugs. But he had never condemned her. She was torn. She wanted to like Sophie. Found her charismatic. But … perhaps she *was* becoming strange.

Bound for Waterloo Station, she crossed Westminster Bridge, barely glancing up at Big Ben as it chimed 4 p.m.

Darkness had already fallen. Her breath steamed on the air, catching the light cast from the street lamps. Workers, heading home early in the bitter chill, passed her by. Her heart was heavy. Her feet were leaden. County Hall seemed a long way away, on the other side of the river. The train station, even further.

'Eagle,' she said, dodging a red Routemaster that spattered grey slush over the pavement. Aunty Sharon said the new buses weren't a patch on the old. 'Son of the Eagle.'

As she traversed the slippery backstreets behind county hall, making her way down to York Road, she saw the homeless making their beds for the night in doorways. Begging for spare change. Selling the *Big Issue*. Many were drinking super-strong lager and cosying up to their dogs. The lucky ones had cocooned themselves inside cardboard boxes. Poor bastards.

The smell of urine was strong, even in this cold. She shied away from them. When one of the forlorn figures lurched at her from who the hell knew where, she balked.

'I'm skint, mate!' she cried, clutching her bag close.

But the face was familiar.

'You!' George said, scrutinising the woman's pinched features, barely concealed by the hood of an old, soiled parka.

The woman's blue eyes were sharp, focused on her goal. 'If you want the laptop back, I need a thousand in cash.'

George grabbed her arm, pulling her close so that she could smell the woman's stale breath. No alcohol on it. She smelled thirsty and of sore throat. 'You been stalking me? Have you been to my fucking place in Cambridge. Was it you?'

'No,' the woman said. 'But I know where your laptop is. You can have that and the stick back. Intact. For a thousand in cash. I'll come to your aunts. Call the police, and I'll make sure it's destroyed.'

'But ... I haven't got—'

The woman dug her fingernails into George's hand, so that she was forced to let go of her. Nostrils flaring, she had the desperate, haunted look of someone who was standing right at the edge of life and sanity.

'A thousand by the end of the week, or you can wave goodbye to your research.'

CHAPTER 15

Amsterdam, police headquarters, 5 March

'What do you think?' Van den Bergen asked the forensic pathologist. He gesticulated with his unshaven chin towards a pile of paper, the top sheet of which stated this was the property of the Landeskriminalamt Berlin – specifically, the Kriminaltechnisches Institut.

'Berlin forensics reports on two men found dead a couple of weeks ago,' he explained. 'Marie came across the cases during an Internet trawl. From what my German colleague tells me, there are too many similarities for them not to be connected to our Bijlmer guy and this Jack Frost murder in London that George flagged up. The German press is calling the murderer 'Krampus' – a kind of Alpine folklore horned monster who punishes badly behaved children around Christmas time. What are the odds, eh?'

'Let me see.' Marianne de Koninck hooked her hair behind her ear. She slid a pair of frameless reading glasses on and started to examine the reports that had been sent over from Berlin. 'You'll have to bear with me. My German's not all that.'

'If you think there's something in them, we'll get them translated into Dutch,' he said.

The chunkiness of her cable-knit black jumper made her hands look more delicate and feminine than usual: elegant fingers, removing the contents from an A4 manila envelope. Images of the dead men, laid on the table side by side, one by one, until there was a long row of photographic evidence that said someone had snuffed out these two lives with unfettered rage. One man fat. One man thin. A deathly balaclava of coagulated blood encased the ruined head of the larger of the two, a mess of spoiled flesh where his penis had been.

'The thin man's got the same puncture marks as our Bijlmer victim,' Van den Bergen said, studying the pathologist's face in profile. Pointed chin. Sharp nose. No-nonsense features on a no-nonsense woman. 'And so does the murdered entrepreneur in London.'

'Hm.' Marianne steepled her fingers together and pursed her lips. Her gaze shifted back and forth in a contemplative relay race from the start of the row of photographs to the finish.

She was ageing well, Van den Bergen mused. Bright-eyed. Clear-skinned. Obviously slept at night. Clearly untroubled by the fact that she was responsible for introducing him to the Butcher, who had almost sliced and diced him into the next life.

'You okay?' she asked, peering over the top of her glasses. 'You seem a little tense.'

'Fine,' he said, turning away from her. Fingering the ever-deepening grooves either side of his own mouth, which bore testament to the fact that he was now not ageing so well. He crossed his legs uncomfortably beneath the low desktop, the uncharacteristic beginnings of a paunch in the way; it has begun to appear when he had stopped gardening quite so regularly.

Presently, Marianne cleared her throat. She nodded slowly, as if processing the facts weighed heavily on her sinuous runner's neck. 'I see what you mean. The murders certainly share similarities. Same waterlogged conical wounds in the thin man. Presumably inflicted by an icicle used as a shiv. Snow in the air passages of both victims, though they differ in that the fat man

has been bludgeoned to death and his penis has been severed ...
and not by a sharp blade, by all accounts.'

Van den Bergen breathed in sharply and grimaced. Felt a
sympathetic twinge in his groin and thought briefly about getting
his testicles looked over and his prostate checked during his next
check-up at the doctor's.

'Anyway.' Marianne stacked the reports in a neat pile. 'Let's get
a translation of these pronto, just to make sure I've got the right
end of the stick. Maybe I need to see the bodies, if they haven't
been claimed.'

'They haven't,' Van den Bergen said. 'My guy in Berlin says
neither the police nor their forensics service has had a break-
through in ID'ing them yet.'

'Well, I think a little jaunt to Berlin is on the cards for us,'
Marianne said, unexpectedly reaching forwards and rubbing Van
den Bergen's forearm. Smiling.

He snatched his arm away and touched the skin there, gingerly,
as though he had been burned. Flustered. Felt unwanted heat
creeping into his cheeks. Hadn't he and Marianne been down
this road two years before, when she had broken up with that
dick, Jasper? Before George. Before the Butcher. Hadn't they
mutually decided there was no chemistry there, though neither
had needed to say a single word? Sharing an embrace in her
kitchen that had, on paper, supposed to be electrifying but which
had been devoid of any spark whatsoever.

He pushed his glasses up his nose. 'If we're looking for a killer
who's operating in at least three countries and we've only got two
of the victims ID'd, we'll need to look at the modus operandi and
try to come up with some kind of a profile. Could be a serial
killer, though I think I've had enough of those to last me a lifetime.' How desperately he wanted to fix her with an accusatory
stare. The resentment effervesced inside him. But it wasn't her
fault. *Stop being a bastard, Van den Bergen. She didn't have a
crystal ball, for god's sake. She's got past the whole unpleasant*

episode, and so should you. She's grinning at you! 'Could be a hit man, if there's drugs involved. Christ only knows what we're dealing with. I'm going to get George involved.'

He had hoped the mention of George's name would dim Marianne's hopeful smile. It hadn't.

'She'll need to come to Berlin too, of course,' he said.

Then, the smile faded from Marianne's face.

'What do you mean, how do I fancy a trip to Berlin?' George shouted down the phone. Sitting on the toilet at Aunty Sharon's, hoping to snatch five minutes of privacy in a packed house. Patrice and Tinesha were downstairs, fighting over the TV remote control whilst their respective girl- and boyfriends sat primly at the kitchen table, making conversation with Aunty Sharon as she prepared a chocolate-orange soufflé. The recently appeared and self-installed Letitia was lying on the couch, awaiting the working class woman's last rights of barbecue Pringles, a double rum 'n' Ting and Jeremy Kyle. 'Fucking hell, Paul. Haven't you worked it out yet? I'm ignoring you! You're in the dog house, man!'

The line went silent. 'Dog house?'

She tried to explain the turn of phrase that had been lost in translation. She spoke quickly in Dutch, laying it on the line that he couldn't toy with her feelings like this, two years in.

'You know it's nothing to do with how I feel about you,' he said. 'I just think you deserve better. I'm old, for god's sake! I'm broken, George. I can't offer you anything. Not on a personal level. It's not fair on you if we …' He sighed heavily, filling the phoneline with melancholy.

Scratching at a patch of mildewed grout that she had missed during her big clean with the end of Patrice's blue toothbrush, she visualised Van den Bergen lying in the intensive care unit of the Amsterdam hospital. She saw herself weeping over what she had presumed was his dying body, machines no longer beeping. Disconnected. Then being told by the consultant who had eavesdropped on her mournful prayers to an indifferent god that his oxygen had been switched off because he had no longer needed it. He had finally come out of the coma that morning and was just sleeping. The peritonitis had been defeated. The Butcher's best efforts at killing him had failed.

'Listen, you miserable, self-indulgent man,' she said, barely able to conceal the irritation in her voice, 'I'm sick of this.' She wiped her cousin's toothbrush on her dressing gown, poised to return it to the beaker, then noticed the beaker had a layer of toothpaste spatter in the bottom and started to wash it out with one hand. She clutched the phone in the other hand as though it were her lover's cheek. 'I love you. You love me. We're right for each other. We always have been. I nearly lost you once, and I'm not losing you again. So, stop dicking me around. You can't switch me on and off like a tap. It's not like I'm not asking you for marriage and babies.'

'Good, because you're not getting them.'

She wanted to flush her phone down the toilet with exasperation at that moment. 'Fuck you, Paul! You know I'm not interested in all that!'

'Maybe might not be right now, but once your clock starts ticking—'

'Don't you dare!' She flung the beaker and five toothbrushes into the sink in anger. She noticed that the bristles of her own toothbrush had touched those of her mother's and immediately washed it under scalding water from the hot tap. 'Don't you patronise me. Telling me what to do with my ovaries! And much as you'd like to be consigned to the trash heap, you bloody masochist, there's nothing wrong with your spunk, old man. If I wanted a child – which I don't – you're perfectly capable of giving me one. All you need is a change of scenery, a more patient therapist and a hot fortnight between my thighs.'

On the other end of the line, she could hear her lover growling with dissatisfaction. Stubborn old bastard missed her, she was sure. She tried to keep the smile out of her voice. 'Don't play games with me. They're a waste of my time. We're on. Right? That's it. George and Paul. I don't own you. You don't own me. But we fuck like Olympic champions and we fit. I can't have you acting like we're some failed formula you'd like to expunge from a bloody whiteboard. Now, what the hell do you want?'

He explained the probable link between the four murders in three countries. Her interest was piqued, but her mind was still on the missing research and her stalking rough-sleeper.

'Look,' she said, staring blankly at opaque glass in the bathroom window, a swirling pattern that didn't quite disguise the falling snowflakes outside or the ten-inch icy stalactites that hung from the eaves of her aunt's house. 'I've got a heap of shit going on here.' She considered telling him about the break-in and the blackmail, but thought better of it. And telling him about her new research partner's advances would not serve any purpose either. 'A looming deadline for my prison project, massive computer issues that need sorting urgently, and my idiot mother turning up here, insisting she's dying.'

'Don't you want to see me?' Van den Bergen sounded wounded. Hot and cold, like an unpredictable jet stream ushering in ice one minute, melt the next. 'The department will pay. Obviously.'

'You don't have to pay for my time, Paul. I'm not a bloody prostitute.' *He's offering you money, you daft bitch! What is the thing you're desperately in need of?* She thought about the burden of paying rent on her room in Cambridge and having to give Aunty Sharon money for her keep. Her stipend from the university was peanuts. Hell, the funding she received from the Peterhulme Trust for her prison research barely made a dent in her travel costs! And now, didn't she need a cool thousand?

'I know. I didn't mean it like that,' Van den Bergen said. Contrite on the other end.

Though she wanted desperately to see him – she imagined lying in a warm bed in his arms, listening to the rich rumble of his voice – he had been so intolerable of late that she was tempted to rebuff all of his recent conciliatory approaches. But she was pragmatic, if nothing else.

'I need two grand. Upfront. Paid into my bank a.s.a.p. I've got commitments.'

'I can't authorise that. You'll have to invoice accounts.'

The red mist descended then. 'Find another fucking criminologist to torture. And get yourself a new lover, while you're at it.'

CHAPTER 16

South East London and Amsterdam, 6 March

'Hello, love. All right? Bet you're knackered after all that travelling,' Aunty Sharon said, as George hung her Puffa jacket up in the cramped hallway. The place smelled of something meaty. Stew, maybe. Her stomach growled. The only thing that had passed her lips since breakfast was a bag of Quavers.

'Last interview with the ladies at Her Majesty's leisure,' George said. 'Same tragic shit. Different day. I'll be glad to sign off on this bit of work.' She tugged her boots off. 'Still, got to make my name somehow.'

'Bring us a cuppa, will you?' Letitia shouted from the living room. 'I'm dying of thirst here.'

In the dim light of the hallway, Aunty Sharon rolled her eyes. 'Coming!'

George sucked her teeth. 'When are you going to tell her to clear off back to Ashford?' she whispered. 'Don't be keeping her here on my account!'

'I ain't. She won't fucking go.' Aunty Sharon peered mournfully down at her broken nails, which were less than pristine, having to clear up after five people in a tiny house that was supposed to hold maybe three, at most. 'What am I supposed to do? She might

95

be the sort to put her own sister on the street in this shitty weather, but I'm a soft touch, innit? And she knows it. Always has.'

Looking worn down in old jeans that were going at the knees and a fluffy red jumper that made her look even heavier, Aunty Sharon made a move in the direction of the kitchen. George held her back.

'There's nothing wrong with her, you know. She doesn't need to be here. This is just because of Leroy.'

'It ain't just Leroy dumping her, though, is it?' Aunty Sharon bit her bottom lip. She fingered the locket that contained little Dwayne's photo. She still hadn't taken it off. 'She knows you've been in touch with your dad on the email.'

Reaching forwards to pull the living room door shut, George plunged the two of them into near-darkness. 'You what? How the hell did she find out about that?'

Even in the murk, she could see that her aunt's eyes were fixed worryingly, steadfastly, revealingly on her fur-lined market slippers.

'You told her!' George gasped. 'I said that to you in confidence, Aunty Shaz. Aw, man!' A loud tut. A shake of the head. 'All this pulmonary hypertension rubbish and, 'I'm dying' act. It's attention-seeking! You played right into her hands.'

'What could I do?' Sharon asked, squeezing her niece's hand. 'I was so cut up about, you know … the anniversary of little D. Then, I'm watching telly with her.' She gesticulated with her thumb towards the living room. 'There's something on *Lorraine* about people who lose kids to meningitis. Spotting the signs and that, before it's too late. One of the mums had a lost a disabled kid.' She clasped George's hand. Sweaty fingers said she was reliving her grief anew. 'It was like they'd done a programme about me. It broke my heart, George. Then we got talking about the bond between a parent and a child.'

'Like she'd fucking know!' George scoffed.

'How it never breaks, even when you ain't seen them in years.

It slipped out. About your dad. Sorry, love. I ain't been myself lately.'

'Forget it,' George said, resentful that Letitia the Dragon was still encroaching on their limited space. 'She's a using cow. I'm gonna sort this. We'll get her off our backs.'

Over a dinner of lamb stew, Letitia winced at every opportunity.

'Get us a cushion, love,' she told Tinesha. 'I'm in agony here.' She rubbed her heaving bosom with a perfectly manicured hand. Red talons today. Hot-pink satin pyjamas beneath her dressing gown said she, at least, wasn't feeling the cold. 'It's my pulmonaries. When I married that fucking Leroy, I never thought it was possible to actually break a person's heart. Do you know what I'm saying?'

She followed Tinesha with bloodhound eyes as she returned with the pillows from the sofa.

'Don't be running after her, Tin,' George said, snatching the pillows from her cousin and ramming them behind her mother's back. 'Leroy didn't break your fucking heart! He made a lucky escape and not a moment too soon.'

But Letitia wasn't listening. She was shovelling stew into her mouth at almost breakneck velocity, pulling G's, a fighter pilot with a fork, executing nifty potato-based manoeuvres. She stared at the portable TV that flickered in silence on the kitchen counter.

'Leave it, George,' Aunty Sharon said, standing by the sink, eating her own dinner from a bowl. Eyeing her son, her daughter, her niece, her sister, who had left no room for her at her own table, George realised.

'Sit down, Aunty Shaz.'

Standing by the flickering television, George watched the seconds hand marking time on the kitchen clock. Tick, tock. Seven o'clock. End of the week, her homeless stalker had said. Their impending confrontation was drawing close. Tonight, by George's reckoning. And she needed cash upfront. That sinking feeling that she would fail to get her laptop back dragged on her like heavy antimatter. Her felt her career disintegrating in a cloud of radioactive decay, over before it had even begun. And why had this raggedy bitch targeted her as a walking ATM, after all she had done for her? Breaking into her room in Cambridge to steal her livelihood, perhaps because she thought George was a soft touch? Were there not eight million people in London alone that she could have stolen from?

George could guess why. But that wasn't the issue. Money was.

Dropping her empty plate into the sink with a clatter, she regarded Letitia the Dragon, who was smoking at the table, flicking her ash onto token-gesture leftovers, clearly unperturbed by her sister's admonishing looks. George thought about the handbag that never left her mother's side, even when she went to the bathroom. There was only one reason to guard a handbag that jealously.

'I heard Leroy left you because you had a big win on bingo,' George said.

Her mother looked up, breathing smoke all over Patrice's head. 'I don't know what the fuck half-arsed idea you got into your head, girl. I'm skint. I told Shaz. I ain't got a single penny. He sold the fucking house from under me, that stone-cold wanker.'

'You had a gambling problem, he told me,' George said. 'You cleaned him out. Then you hit the jackpot at Mecca Bingo and wouldn't share it.'

'I got sickle cell anaemic and pulmonaries.' She thumped her chest, barely able to make a fist with those fat fingers and those nails. 'That Leroy couldn't cope with my illness. He didn't care enough, cos he's a selfish bastard. Like all men.' She turned to Patrice, who was blithely licking the fingers of one hand and thumbing a text into his phone with the other. She sucked her teeth.

'My son ain't *all men*!' Aunty Sharon said. 'Don't you be judging my Patrice.' She slapped the phone from Patrice's hand. 'Manners at the table, bwoy!'

'Ow!' Patrice grimaced at the womenfolk around him, fingering the smattering of fluff above his top lip. George watched his Adam's apple ping up and down inside his stringy neck. All arms and legs at that age. He stood, abruptly, scraping his chair on the highly polished lino. 'I don't need this crap. I'd sooner do homework than sit and listen to her.' Flicked a thumb in Letitia's direction.

Aunty Sharon jumped out of her seat. Standing on her tiptoes, she clipped the back of her son's head with a swollen hand. 'Hey! Show some respect for your elder, you little rarseclart.'

A knock on the back door. Insistent, meaning business. Glancing at the clock, George knew who it was calling time on this family drama, credits rolling on her deliberations.

'Who the hell is this? I ain't expecting no one,' Aunty Sharon said, yanking open the kitchen drawer and pulling out a wooden rolling pin.

George unlocked the door and ushered the shivering figure inside, relieved to see she was clutching a supermarket bag containing a rectangular object.

'You've got some front coming here again,' George said, pushing the women into the living room. 'You're testing my patience.'

The woman removed her hood. Matted hair clung to her scalp. 'I'm sorry. I had no option.' Her eyes darted nervously this way and that. She bit her lip, and seemed genuinely remorseful, though that changed nothing.

In the doorway, Aunty Sharon hovered, rolling pin at the ready.

'Give us a minute, will you?' George said.

Alone now, she tried to snatch the bag from the woman's filthy hands. Brittle, frost-bitten twigs, protruding from dirt-caked fingerless gloves.

'Not so fast,' the woman said, clutching the booty close. 'Where's the money?'

Poking, accusatory finger. 'If you ever do this again, I'm going to blow the whistle on you,' George said, her voice shaking with a mixture of fear and venom.

'Money.'

Prickling around her lips. She stared longingly at the plastic bag that contained everything she had worked for for so long. If she screwed this up she was finished. She was unsure how to make this problem go away.

It was a gamble.

She visualised Letitia's handbag. Bingo winnings. What if she was wrong and Letitia really was potless? No time for procrastination though.

Marching into the kitchen, she spied the handbag by her mother's feet. She snatched it up and ran into the living room. Letitia was out of the blocks like an overweight sprinter.

'Give me my fucking bag back, you thief.'

George swung the open bag high in the air out of reach. Lipstick, compact, mirror, Tampax, keys all clattering out onto the floor. Then her finger tested the zippy pocket. Notes fluttered down to the ground. Munificence from Mecca.

'Bingo!' said George.

'Do you want to show me what the men did, Imran? Use the dolls.' the child protection officer said. A kindly woman with a soft voice in non-threatening surroundings. The room was brightly lit, though it was late in the evening. Comfortable, colourful furniture. Toys. These things had to be sensitively handled.

Van den Bergen watched from the other side of the one-way mirror, dreading the outcome of the ghoulish session. Two nights in temporary accommodation under the supervision of experienced staff had flagged up emotional and physical problems with the two boys that seemingly extended far beyond what was normally seen in a drug-dealer's underage foot soldiers. Now the older Imran used tragic puppetry to tell a shocking tale.

'Fuck,' he said to Elvis, thumbing his eyebrows, wishing George was there. 'Why do we do this job again?'

'Never gets any easier, does it, boss?' Elvis ran a shaking hand through his hair. Quiff all but crushed by the hat. 'Poor little bastard. What do you think his story is?'

Looking down at his phone, Van den Bergen saw that he had an email pending from George. He wanted desperately to speak to her, but she would have to wait until later. Though she, of all people, would understand the plight of these children. 'I would think they've been trafficked over here from some far-flung shithole, and now they're being rented out to every perv in Bijlmer and beyond.' With long fingers, he felt the length of his scarring. He stopped at the abdomen when he realised Elvis was frowning at him. 'It hurts in the cold. Alright?' He tutted loudly. 'I'm glad Hasselblad turned the woman down for asylum. She's these boys' chaperone. No doubt in my mind. The way she claimed them as her sons. Full of shit. She said she was going to give us names of powerful men. Did she?'

'No, boss.'

'Did she fuck. George says traffickers often use women. Better people skills. Less likely to attract unwanted attention if they're ferrying kids or girls to and from customers' houses.' He checked his watch. It was late. His stomach growled, but food could wait too.

Relenting, he punched out a text to George.

New development. Bijlmer man ran a
paedophile ring. Trafficked boys of 8 & 6.
NOW will you come? P.

Five minutes later, he received a reply.

Booking my flight, you pain in the arse.
Make sure you pay me.

101

CHAPTER 17

Amsterdam, police headquarters, 30 May, the previous year

The flashbulbs were blinding. Each one leeched away a little of his dignity, stripping him of any semblance of poise, exposing the raw, seething anger and grief beneath.

'Mr Deenen! Piet! Who do you think took your children?'

'Gabi! Gabi! Do you blame your husband for your children going missing?'

Piet squinted at the paparazzi pitch-forked lightening, striking him through and through with its pointed glare. Husband to blame. Lackadaisical dad loses toddlers. As if it wasn't bad enough that the disappearance of the two things he loved most in all the world – his gifts from god – had left Josh- and Lucy-shaped holes in his heart.

On his left, the detective in charge of the case cleared his throat. He tapped the microphone. Television cameras rolled, silence engulfing the room as the press watched and waited. The Deenens were on show to the world, exposing their delicate, flawed underbelly. Gabi sat to Piet's right, pale-faced but immaculately put together. Unmoving. She was staring intently at the policeman as he spoke.

'The Netherlands police has launched a nationwide manhunt

for Josh and Lucy. We will stop at nothing to find the Deenen children,' he said. Grim-faced gravitas. He held the room in thrall. Turning to the cameras he said, 'If you think you have seen the Deenen children or know anything of their disappearance, please call the witness hotline.'

Heartbreaking photos of the children appeared on a screen behind him. There was a portrait of Josh that had been taken at nursery. Tiny pearl teeth framing a beguiling smile. Big blue eyes and short golden curls. His angelic appearance belied the challenging behaviour that drove them all to distraction on a regular basis and kept him and Gabi up at night, arguing, planning on how they might deal with his condition. But boy, was he beautiful. Then, Lucy. Tiny Lucy. Two-year-old perfection with cherubic cheeks and long dark lashes. The same blonde curls as her brother, though wispy because of her infancy. Her father's dark eyes. Daddy's girl, through and through. The thought that his perfect babies were gone, that he would never again stroke their brows and tuck them in at night or feel their dribble-kisses soften the hard stubble of his cheek …

Hubbub in the room. Questions shouted from this media jury.

Now, his treacherous heart was thudding, thudding, thudding though it was broken, broken, broken. The tinkle of a pen struck against a glass. Ting, ting. *Can I have your attention, please?* Time for the father to say a few awkward words, though he had never guessed his moment in the spotlight, pronouncing on the fate of his children using cue cards, with all eyes trained on him, would see him clad in a mourning suit.

'I, er …' Piet spoke into the microphone. He felt tears threaten. How desperately he wanted to maintain his poise, had planned to be a rock for his wife.

He put his arm around Gabi, hoping the warmth of her body would somehow melt free the words that were frozen in his craw, but felt her stiffen. He turned back to the microphone and the assemblage of journalists, remembering what he had been told by the media person: talk to the camera … appeal directly to the abductor.

'Please give us back our children,' he began. 'Please—'

Wracking sobs shook his body, stemming the flow of coherent words from his mouth. Overwhelmed by a sense of loss and emptiness, crippled by the guilt that he had not kept a watchful eye on his babies, he wished, at that moment, that he could just wake up from this nightmare and find it had all been the ungodly workings of an overburdened brain.

Gabi's sharp elbow jabbed his ribs. 'Pull yourself together, for god's sake,' she whispered in his ear. 'You're not helping anyone.'

But all he could see in his mind's eye were his children playing on that fucking climbing frame. Laughing, squealing with delight, down the slide with their chubby legs in the air, Josh's big boy nappy making his shorts look overstuffed. Didn't matter so much when he was in the garden with his baby sister, but the nappy made him stand out amongst the other four-year-olds at nursery who maybe now only wore a nappy at night. It hardly mattered, for his were happy, carefree children, bearing his Deenen genes into a bright future.

Gone.

Dreams of a perfect family unit wiped out inside a five-minute window.

He pictured them, now, ghostly white and silent. Lying with startling dead eyes in a wood somewhere. Defiled by whatever monster had taken them. Stockings around their necks, perhaps. Or else held prisoner in some dank basement, subjected to …

'I can't. I can't.' He pushed his own microphone away, and shook his head apologetically at the policeman.

The sorrow was more painful than any torture he could ever imagine being subjected to. The dread weighed him down, four times the Earth's normal gravity. How could he bear such agony and yet still breathe? He glimpsed the country's press through the blur of his tears.

Then he heard Gabi's voice at his side. Loud and clear. Controlled. Grown-up. 'I'm speaking to the person that has taken our children,' she said. Commanding the full attention of those fickle, spying lenses. 'Josh and Lucy are their names. They're lovely children. Friendly and sweet-natured. Maybe you're afraid right now. As afraid as Josh and Lucy. Maybe you didn't mean to take them. I know you don't mean them any harm. So, please do the right thing and hand them back. And if any member of the public has spotted Josh and Lucy or has any information they may think will help the police, please, please call the hotline so we can get our babies home.'

A glance told him she was still pale, opaque, hard. A mother made from marble. He admired her. He knew that she must be suffering just like him, except Gabi always hid her distress.

Flashbulbs. Poor Piet Deenen: the proverbial Dutch rabbit in the headlights. An outpouring of collective grief had already hit the newspaper headlines. The Netherlands up in arms that two of its perfect blond children had been taken. The old guard, complaining about permissive society. This country used to be safe, said outraged of Utrecht. Now, look at it! Our children can't even be left to play safely in the gardens of the suburbs, said terrified of Tilburg.

But things weren't quite so black and white, once Piet and Gabi returned home and were alone in the kitchen.

'Jesus. That was one of the worst experiences of my life,' he said, putting the kettle on. He perched on the stool by the kitchen's central island, head in hands. 'I've never felt so powerless.'

Gabi was staring down at her smartphone. Scrolling, scrolling. Glass of whisky already in her other hand. 'Worse than losing our children?' Clipped consonants, not taking her eyes off the small screen. 'Don't be fucking ridiculous! We had to do that press conference. It might get us the kids back. That was the whole bloody point.' Finally she looked up, pinning him with unforgiving eyes. 'The more publicity we get, the more likely someone will spot them and call it in.'

Nodding contritely, he ran his fingers along the cold, smooth Corian of the worktop. He looked around at the luxurious proportions of the room. Just a damn room, after all. Bricks and mortar. Perhaps he could do a deal with God. 'I'd give all of this up to have them back. Every last thing we own.' He bit his lip. An architect's folly, moving to this house, demanding this space.

As if Gabi had sniffed out the strong odour of guilt, she tapped her wedding ring on the counter. 'If we'd stayed in London, none of this would have happened.' Her lips thinned to a straight line.

'Are you blaming me?' Piet asked. 'You're not seriously blaming me?'

Thumping the worktop, the fury behind Gabi's eyes had an energy all of its own, smashing together the particles of her being in some kind of violent reaction. He found himself shrinking away from her.

'I wanted to stay,' she said. 'I had a good job.'

'You were made redundant!'

'Do you think I couldn't have found another?' Her words resonating around the room. The air rancid with bitterness. 'Do you think I wanted to work in some shitty charity? Doing marketing in some suburban hellhole in Holland?'

Piet stood abruptly, wiping the hot tears that streamed in rivulets down the sides of his face. 'That's not on, Gabi. This is … Jesus. We made the decision to come home—'

'Your home. Not *my* home!'

'You said yes, for Christ's sake. A better quality of life, right? That was the whole reason we came back. And my mother. Who the hell did you have left in London?'

Gabi took a loaf of bread out of the bread bin and started to carve in to the loaf too fast, too aggressively. She cut her thumb and a fat bead of red immediately oozed.

'Is that my fault too?' Piet asked, clicking the kettle back on.

'Fuck you!'

He was contemplating a sharp retort when the phone rang. It was the detective on the line. Hopeful smiles on the both of them, as though they had never shared a whisky-sour word.

'Well?' Gabi asked. Blinking hard. Eyebrows buoyed upwards on a warm jet stream of optimism.

Inside, Piet's heart turned hopeful somersaults. 'Someone's spotted the kids! Some gypsies in a campervan, parked up at a service station near Maastricht.'

CHAPTER 18

Berlin, Zoological Gardens, 9 March, *present*

'Well, isn't this nice?' Marianne de Koninck said, as the three of them sat penned in together in the back seat of the unmarked Volkswagen Passat. The car was driven by a lumpen-faced uniformed female officer of the Berliner Polizei. They were under the stewardship of one of Berlin's finest detectives, according to the rumours on Van den Bergen's Europe-wide grapevine. They bounced along the perfectly paved and gritted Berlin road from their terracotta contemporary Lego-block of a hotel just off Potsdamer Platz towards Tiergartenstrasse and the white expanse of the Tiergarten beyond.

George poked her ear, still blocked from the flight, and looked askance at the pathologist. 'Are you taking the piss?' she said.

Sandwiched in the middle, Van den Bergen looked beyond uncomfortable. Legs bent in extraordinary fashion, he had gallantly placed himself between a vengeful George and a superficially friendly Marianne. George just wanted to reach beyond her lover and deck the flint-faced bitch who had introduced her man to his almost-murderer.

'Can we not do this in front of our host, for Christ's sake?' Van den Bergen said, staring at her with those hooded grey eyes.

Full of castigation, frustrated passion and a myriad other conflicting emotions, no doubt. Daft old bastard.

She wanted to kiss him, there and then. Grabbed his hand surreptitiously and held it tight, sandwiched between their thighs where nobody else would spot the connection.

'I'm not here to start a thing with you, Georgina,' the pathologist said, gazing ahead. She spoke in a calm voice, as though she had the higher moral ground. 'I know why you're being hostile. I understand you're being prickly out of some kind of loyalty to Paul. But guilt is only yours if you choose to accept it, and I don't choose to accept it, I'm afraid.'

Marianne looked like a sartorial accident from a Winter-Olympics village, in her pristine snow gear and walking boots, George assessed. Months and months since she had last seen her and even now, it felt like an unhappy reunion taking place too soon.

'I don't choose to accept it, I'm afraid,' George repeated in a childish, mimicking voice. Realised she was being churlish. Didn't care. 'Shove it up your arse!' George said in English. Sucked her teeth slow enough to make her disdain incontrovertible.

Tapping on the passenger side window, their host spoke, unaware of the friction that was taking place behind him in deadly rapid-fire Dutch. 'See that building on the right?'

His halting English was heavily accented. Mainly German but with a hint of something else. Looking at his black hair and dark skin, George assessed he was probably Turkish. What was his name again? Fatigued as she was from travelling, she had laughed out loud when he had given her his business card. She pulled it from her jacket pocket and checked it. Hakan Güngör. Sounded like a Transylvanian despot, or some shit. Looked like a matinee idol in detective's cheap plain clothing.

'That is the Berlin Philharmonic Orchestra,' Hakan said. 'My ex-wife plays cello, there.' No hint of acrimony in his voice. 'I also played violin in the youth orchestra a long time ago.' Matter of fact. Efficient Berliner. Obviously.

'Oh. Nice,' George said drily.

Van den Bergen glared at her. He hadn't even looked at the contemporary sprawl that looked like municipal swimming baths to George, whose taste had moulded itself over time around the jagged medieval spires of Cambridge.

At the zoological gardens, they passed through the giant, green iron gates, where majestic stone lions presided over the snowy scene. Kings of the jungle, wearing sparkling white robes, spattered with hardly any birdshit at all from two robins that hopped bravely over their snowy hind legs and heads. The freezing crystalline air was sullied by the diesel stink of the bus station opposite; buses were pulling in and out, empty of travellers. Unsurprising in these weather conditions. Only the sluggish, passing traffic and dedicated staff in the art nouveau kiosks bore testament to this being one of Berlin's main attractions. George hated zoos.

'The bodies were found at the polar bear enclosure,' Hakan said, beckoning them further in along the gritted pathways; open spaces that must have been landscaped garden areas, unrecognisable as anything but indistinct blobs beneath two feet of snow.

They trudged past the rhinos on their left. Then, the glass-domed ceiling of the hippo house appeared, Pig house in the distance on the right. George remembered a disastrous trip to London Zoo with both parents when she was very small. Letitia the Dragon had sharpened her claws to tear chunks from the frail flesh of George's father. He had looked pasty and browbeaten, even in the blistering heat of an unseasonably hot British summer. His half-Spanish blood quietly coming to the boil. The fire in Letitia's Jamaican belly had erupted in balls of angry patois; George had been piglet in the middle. She shuddered.

'Cold?' Van den Bergen asked, rubbing her upper arm gently.

'Someone walked over my grave,' she said in English.

At the enclosure, one polar bear was visible outside, having a ball. Skidding around in its Arctic-like surrounds. Fake rocks covered with genuine snow and ice. The semi-circular pond seemed to be frozen solid. Ah, there was a second polar bear, George noted. Damned hard to see against all that white. It looked up and fixed them with hungry eyes as soon as they approached. A sly, blood-stained smile on its lips.

'At least someone is enjoying this weather,' Hakan said, grinning abruptly.

Nice straight teeth. Black lashes like brushes, fringing almond-shaped dark eyes. George could imagine him playing the violin with great sensitivity. Unbidden, a memory of Ad popped into her head. Adrianus Karelse – her olive-skinned pretty boy, physically reminiscent of Hakan. But oh, how that sweet first love had turned so sour. She shook the thought away.

'I presume the bodies were found this side of the enclosure,' Van den Bergen said, peering over the boundary wall at the steep drop into the pond below.

Hakan nodded. 'One man was draped over the wall. Another on the ground where we're standing.'

George looked around, drinking in the vibe and trying to imagine the scene.

'What time of day were the men killed?' Marianne asked, rubbing her red nose with the back of her ski-glove.

'Night time. We think around 2 a.m. for the time of death.'

'How did they get into the zoo?' George asked.

'That's the big mystery,' Hakan said. 'There was no break-in. One of the men must have had a key to the gate.'

'Were either of the victims employees or related to employees?' Van den Bergen asked, pulling his woollen hat over his earlobes.

Hakan shook his head. 'We interviewed everyone who works here and prepared artist's sketches of the men. Nobody has been able to identify them. Nobody's been missing from work.'

'Sketches?' George asked.

'Their faces had been badly beaten,' Hakan said, breath steaming into the air. He stared at the largest of the polar bears

111

as he reared silently on his hind legs, as if to get a better look at this potential meal, care of the Berliner Polizei. 'That's partly why we haven't been able to identify them. Their teeth were knocked out and splintered so badly from some kind of blunt trauma that our forensics guys are only now trying to do a dental reconstruction.'

They had nothing.

As Marianne examined the two men's bodies at the morgue, George sat in the zoo's café with Van den Bergen and Hakan. Frostbitten fingers clutching at hot chocolate. She was hastily devouring a cheese and ham sandwich when she suddenly felt self-conscious that she was eating ham.

'Sorry. Am I offending you?' she asked the detective.

'Eat whatever you like,' Hakan said. A kind smile with eyes closed. 'I'm not fussy about other people's eating habits. Anyway, my wife was a lapsed Lutheran. Honestly, it's fine.'

Van den Bergen looked momentarily at his own salami baguette and rammed what was left into his mouth, whole, and shrugged.

'The thing that occurs to me, seeing the crime scene,' George said, chewing thoughtfully, 'is that there was definitely some kind of a planned showdown here. Signs of a struggle. Two men, brutally killed. I'm thinking this couldn't possibly have been a two-on-one fight. The murderer must have had some help in overpowering two men.'

'We did think it was about drugs,' Hakan said, draining his espresso cup. 'But of course, with no evidence to support that; it's just an educated guess. We have no record of the dead men's fingerprints being in the police's database of convicted or cautioned felons.'

Van den Bergen cleared his throat and pushed his chair out so that he could cross his legs comfortably. He pulled his glasses on their chain out from his coat, pushed them onto the end of this nose and scrutinized the cake menu. 'It's a peculiar place to commit a murder,' he said. 'Somebody broke in with their own key, maybe. That tells me they were either an employee, which you say is not feasible, or they came here regularly out of hours.' He tapped on the menu with a long finger. 'Chocolate cake for me. George? What would you like?'

'Nothing.' George leaned forwards towards Hakan, an idea forming in her mind. 'Could the dead men have been involved in some kind of illegal trade of rare animals?' she asked. 'I've heard about criminals stealing tigers from zoos and selling them to buyers in the Far East to be butchered and used in virility treatments.'

Hakan nodded. 'Could be. There has been the odd exposé article over the years about the fate of some exotic species in the zoo. There is no saying that the dead men or their murderers weren't involved in some kind of animal rights activism as well. I hadn't thought of that.'

'Have you got the artist's sketches to hand?' George asked.

'Why?'

'I'd like to see what they looked like.'

The Berlin detective produced from his coat pocket two folded-up photocopies of the artist's sketches. One fat man. One thin. Ordinary-looking men. It was hard to tell from sketches.

'Let's see what Marianne finds out at the morgue, if anything,' Van den Bergen said.

CHAPTER 19

Berlin, a hotel in Potsdamer Platz, later

'There's no doubting the similarities between those two men and our paedo pusher in Bijlmer,' Marianne said, sipping her mojito in the hotel bar.

An entente cordiale of an Anglo-Dutch G3, seated on brown plush velvet barstools in a quality boutique hotel that Kamphuis had certainly not signed off on. Outside, the snow had started to fall again in earnest. Inside, the mood lighting and cranked up heating had tried hard to recreate a summer's evening but had merely left George with a headache and dried-out eyes. She sipped beer from a glass, half-wondering if Hakan had ever tasted alcohol.

'Same modus operandi? An icicle?' she asked.

Marianne nodded. 'Yes, but there were additional injuries that weren't evident in the London and Bijlmer murders. Severe facial lacerations.' She raised an eyebrow coolly. 'And I think the fat man's penis was severed with the same blunt blade.'

'Murder weapon ... hazard a guess?' Van den Bergen asked, peeling the label on his beer bottle, making a mess of sticky paper peel on the marble counter. George put her hand on his, compelling him to stop.

'I'd put my money on a snow shovel,' Marianne continued.

'They must have scores in the zoo alone. You can buy them on every street corner since the big freeze. And on such a large campus and in such extreme weather conditions, it's hardly surprising nobody's come across a murder weapon. Easily covered in a blizzard within an hour or two. Or maybe the murderer just took it with him.'

George gnawed at the inside of her cheek. 'These two murders don't sound quite as carefully thought through as our guy. The facial wounds and severed penis smack of heat-of-the-moment frenzied injuries.' She regarded her glass carefully, and suddenly realised there was the shadow of a lip mark on the rim. She pushed it away in disgust. Where on earth was the barman? 'The London and Bijlmer murders come across as cleverly planned hits to me. No murder weapon to find. No witnesses. Apparently quick and deadly, given the built-up, busy areas where those men were killed. But this zoo business …' She tailed off. Craning her neck to see where the damned barman was. Dirty glass in a nice hotel like this; it would never pass muster with her Aunty Sharon.

'It takes some planning to get into a zoo at night,' Van den Bergen said.

George examined her fingernails. 'I guess so. Okay, maybe that sounds premeditated. But what might have been a clean, controlled hit like the others seems to have turned nasty. You've got two men in a deserted location with all the gates locked – not a crowded thoroughfare. And they're chopped into dog meat. I just don't understand it. It all feels … off.'

Silence fell upon the three, as though the snow that fell steadily outside had enshrouded not just Potsdamer Platz in a sound-swallowing blanket but also this beige and anodyne hotel communal area. The contemplative silence was broken only when Hakan came striding over to them, all smiles. He really was handsome, George decided. But not Van den Bergen, of course.

'Good evening, my friends,' Hakan said, his English stiff like a limb that had not been exercised often enough. He nodded at the barman who had miraculously reappeared and who wordlessly poured the detective a Diet Coke.

A lone female drinker, whom George had earmarked as a prostitute, rose abruptly from her seat at the far end of the bar and left.

'I thought that I would drop in, now that my shift is over, to see what you are discovering.'

George was aware of Van den Bergen studying her body language intently, then diverting his attention to Hakan, as though deciding if this younger, obviously handsome man was a sexual threat. She was careful to conceal any telltale signs of superficial attraction to Herr Güngör. After weeks of estrangement from her emotionally unpredictable lover, the last thing she needed to come between them on the night of their reunion was unfounded jealousy.

'Were there any other interesting cases reported on the night of the zoo murders?' George asked. 'Robberies. Fights. Drug-related trouble. Anything to do with children?'

The black bow of Hakan's right eyebrow lifted. He tapped a slender violinist's finger against his glass. 'Actually, yes. I have been transferred to this case because my colleague, who was called to the murders in the first instance, is falling on the ice and breaking his leg. When the men were discovered in the zoo, I was investigating a call from residents in Kreuzberg. Five young children were found wandering the streets in the middle of the night.'

'Oh?' Van den Bergen said. 'What do you mean?'

Hakan stared intently at George until she blushed.

She felt herself coquettishly toying with one of her curls. When he looked up to the ceiling, moving his lips, she realised he had merely been thinking of how to vocalise his German thoughts in English.

'We have found a dirty old house in the district where nobody is officially living. There are mattresses in the basement. The children we found had been held there as prisoners. They were mainly gypsy children we are putting into care while we find their parents and make a note of their stories.'

'Roma?' George asked, curiosity piqued. Her mind raced remembering her conversation with Sophie and Graham Tokár at the Open Society Foundation. The Son of the Eagle.

'Ja.' Hakan nodded. 'Roma. Precisely.'

Staring at the bubbles rising in her glass, George pondered the Jack Frost and Krampus murders. Vulnerable migrants' kids thrown into the mix. What or who was the common denominator?

Later, away from her compatriots, sitting on the perfectly clean-smelling hotel toilet, George thumbed out a text to Marie. It was a gamble as to whether she would respond at all. Who knew what the hell Marie got up to in the evenings?

'Come on, for fuck's sake,' George told her phone display.

After five minutes she checked her watch. Still nothing. Her bottom and the tops of her thighs had gone dead by now, seated uncomfortably as she was. But then, just as she was about to flush and give up all hope of a response to her question, a text pinged back.

```
Checked Vlinders' phone records. There
are four texts to a German number. Owner
answers to the name Gerhard.
```

When she returned to the bar, Marianne was draining her mojito. Hakan was shaking Van den Bergen's hand, as though he was about to leave.

'Gerhard,' she said.

All quizzical eyes on her.

'You go through the interview records from those Roma kids,' she told Hakan. 'See if that name crops up. Maybe check who owns the properties neighbouring the house where the kids had been. And you need to keep an ear out for The Son of the Eagle or Shquipëtar, too.'

Marianne swung her bag on her shoulder. 'While you were on the loo, I had a text through from the forensic pathology guy I met today,' she said. 'The ETA for the finished dental reconstruction is tomorrow.'

'Well, I've got a feeling one set of teeth might belong to a paedo called Gerhard,' George said, feeling a triumphant smile creep into the reluctant corners of her mouth. She grabbed Van den Bergen by the hand, swinging to and fro like a child, eliciting the glimmer of a grin in the grim-faced bastard. 'London, Bijlmer and Berlin Zoo might seem to be disparate dots on a map ... but something tells me that all of this – and that includes the kids from the house in Kreuzberg – it's all somehow connected.'

It felt like a hopeful conclusion to the evening. George looked for a frisson of excitement in her lover's eyes. Wasn't she holding his hand? Wasn't this the first night they had had together since she had stormed out on him and told him to grow a pair? And yet, though Van den Bergen's eyes shone, they sparkled not with romantic anticipation but with that familiar, dogged curiosity she knew so well.

He cleared his throat, fixing Hakan with his laser-like gaze, and shook his own hand loose from George's grip. 'Take us to this derelict house,' he said. 'I want to have a look round.'

Twenty minutes later, the unlikely team of four stood beneath the naked bulb in the basement of the house in Kreuzberg.

George held her nose. 'Aw, it fucking stinks, man. Mould. Dust. Dirt. Stale food. Misery. You name it ...'

Fingerprinting dust from the police around the already grubby architraves bore the hallmarks of the place having been thoroughly searched. It was a once-grand house, reduced to dereliction beyond squat-like neglect. High ceilings in the basement bore testament to the building's age, as did the nooks and crannies and an old fireplace – still working, judging by the fresh-looking ashes in the grate.

'I am not sure what your Chief Inspector is hoping to find,' Hakan said to George, as Van den Bergen stalked into a dingy kitchenette that was lit only by his pocket torch and the moonlight that struggled its way through opaque blocks of two miserly sub-floor windows.

'It's freezing in here,' Marianne said, grimacing. 'I'd rather go back to the hotel and have another mojito before bed, if it's all the same to you guys.' She pulled a hat out of her handbag and rammed it onto her head. 'Berlin forensics will have been all over this place. Their pathologist's good. I like him. Thorough guy. And need I remind you, Paul, that this is not Amsterdam? It's not our turf!'

'Shut it, Marianne,' George said, ramming her hands into her Puffa jacket pockets, narrowing her eyes at the know-it-all inter-loper. 'Nobody asked you to come with.'

'Nothing that I can see in the kitchen,' Van den Bergen said, emerging from the adjacent room. He scanned the walls with his torch, assessing every square foot.

Hakan shook his head. 'Perhaps there is a link to the zoo murders, but I cannot see the value in us being here tonight. Not when the light is so poor.'

Van den Bergen came to a halt before an alcove. Shone his torch on some scribblings there. Perched his glasses on the end of his nose, though they steamed up momentarily with the drop in temperature. He beckoned George to join him.

'Look at this!' he said. There was excitement in his voice. 'Graffiti. Kids' graffiti.'

George approached and stared at the childish drawings. 'Animals,' she said. 'Elephants. Giraffes. Lions.' Though the doodles were out of proportion and unaccomplished, the representations were clear enough. 'Zoo exhibits.'

Van den Bergen nodded. A wry smile, lighting the dark places.

Snapping the images with her phone, just as she was about to turn away, George noticed a cupboard set into the wall. Curiosity tugged at her, dragging her inexorably towards the battered louvre doors. She opened them to reveal a stinking, cobwebby nook, cleared of its contents, now. But there inside, almost every inch of plaster had been covered with one particular kind of cartoon.

'A man crossed with a bird of prey?' Van den Bergen asked, running his finger over the peculiar hybrid of a stick-man with a beak, enormous feathered wings and claws on the ends of his stick arms.

George nodded. Pulse racing. Suddenly no longer cold.

'Shqipëtar,' she said. 'The Son of the Eagle.'

CHAPTER 20

Berlin, Neukölln district, 10 March

'What's this area called again?' George asked Hakan, squinting up at the harsh winter sunlight that ricocheted from one pale rendered apartment block to another. Everything seemed amplified to blinding point with that snow, icicles hanging threateningly from eaves, window ledges, balconies. She instinctively took a step backwards towards the road.

'Schillerkiez,' the Berlin detective answered. 'Although this is just a part of a bigger district called Neukölln.'

Hakan nodded at a woman emerging from a corner shop, bent double with age. A flicker of recognition on her craggy dark, olive-skinned face, headscarf tied beneath her chin. Her floor-length, embroidered skirt dragged in the snow as she tried to wheel her tartan shopping trolley along an almost-impassable pavement.

'It is the biggest area in Berlin for Roma settlers,' he said.

Van den Bergen strode over to the old woman. He picked up the trolley and asked in English where she wanted to go. He was met with a look of disdain and a hoarse mouthful of a language George didn't recognise. Arms flailing dramatically, the elderly woman snatched her trolley away out of his hands, gesturing that he should leave her alone.

George laughed. 'That'll teach you to be so bloody gallant!' she said, as he traversed the snowbound road, tutting.

With a breakfast of cured meats and too much bread weighing her down, causing her to sweat despite today's temperatures of -21°C, George stood and belched quietly in this run-down locale. She looked up at the shabby apartment blocks, abandoned stiff washing covered in snow, strung across balconies, with graffiti on the walls at street level. 'So, this looks okay,' she said. 'No different from any other poor neighbourhood in Europe.' She surveyed the cars parked in orderly rows, covered like misshapen cupcakes by a thick icing. 'I was expecting an encampment. Some mess. Isn't that the stereotype?'

Toying with his thick blue scarf, Hakan nodded. 'There are still some travellers parked near the autobahn. Caravans and RVs holding families of eleven ... sometimes more. We cleared one encampment a couple of years ago that had started up in a park in Kreuzberg, where the house we visited last night was situated. But the families in caravans are all new arrivals from Romania and Balkan states.'

Van den Bergen was watching a man intently pushing a rattling supermarket trolley full of scrap metal down the street, the air ringing with the deafening clash of corrugated iron against an old radiator. He made sluggish progress in the deep, deep snow. Above them a baby started to squall in one of the apartments. Raised voices, spilling out onto a balcony. Further down, somebody flung steaming liquid onto the street from on high. In a snow-covered park at the end of the street, just within sight, they could hear the delighted screams of children. Their white snowballs pinged through the air, hitting the windows of parked cars, where the heavy, glittering topping had started to slide to the ground. 'These don't look like persecuted fugitives,' he said. 'Not what I imagined, anyway.'

Hakan beckoned them towards a run-down café called Sofia's, which advertised curious delicacies in childish writing daubed on the window in white paint. Inside, it smelled of animal fat and strong coffee.

'What language is that?' George asked, pointing to the window.

'No idea,' he said. 'Bulgarian, maybe? Bosnian, Albanian, something from South Eastern Europe. Many of the Roma here came from Balkan states that were ravaged by war. We are having twenty thousand or so living in Berlin now. And the city is trying to integrate these families with other Berliner citizens and migrant groups. They may be self-employed – cleaners and so forth. Learn language. I sometimes do outreach work with the Roma advocacy group, Amaro Drom. Crime prevention with teenagers and that kind of thing. These people face many challenges still.'

A surly-looking man behind the café counter poured them the strongest coffee George had ever drunk. She sipped gingerly from her tiny cup, reminded of the utter poison her old landlord Jan used to brew at the Cracked Pot Coffee shop in Amsterdam. Crude oil and burnt molasses. She eyed the owner's dirty fingernails suspiciously. 'Jesus. This is so sweet.' She stuck out her tongue. Clocking the café owner's look of disapproval, she smiled coyly. Feeling guilty she raised her cup, as if in toast.

'*Haben Sie etwas ungewöhnliches während die letzten zwei oder drei Wochen gesehen?*' Hakan asked the owner. He then explained to George and Van den Bergen that he was asking if the man had spotted anything untoward in the neighbourhood in the last fortnight or so.

'*Nein,*' the man responded in the negative.

Hakan approached the counter and proffered a twenty Euro note – far in excess of what three coffees might have costed. No reaction. The man thumbed the stubble on his double chin, wearing an expectant expression, staring at Hakan's still-open wallet. Another twenty was laid on the counter. Hakan's hands in the air said that was as good as it got.

For several minutes, the two men conversed together. The café owner's eyes darted to the glazed door, as he apparently conveyed news of something that was, indeed, out of the ordinary.

Sitting back down triumphantly at the table, Hakan pursed his lips and drained his coffee. 'There is talk around here of the missing children being returned,' he said. 'I am already knowing this from my contacts in the community. He has heard of the Son of the Eagle, but only that it is an Albanian legend. Maybe it is a drug-dealer, he has said.' He frowned and cocked his head to one side, thoughtfully. 'Not all the Roma are poor. Some have been very successful in business. Especially those using clubs and discotheques as legitimate fronts for criminal activity.'

George nodded, remembering the seedy-looking venues they had passed on Karl Marx Strasse on the way, advertising Bulgarian gypsy chalga singers in the window.

'The only other thing that is unusual in this area,' Hakan continued, 'is the local locksmith has not been open for a while. The café owner has had his premises burgled and when he went to get new locks put on ...'

'The shutters were down,' Van den Bergen finished.

'Let me guess,' George said. 'This locksmith guy hasn't opened up since the morning the murdered men were found in the zoo.'

Pulling his mobile phone from the pocket of his parka, Hakan started to dial a number. 'It is easy for me to find this information. I will call you before you are checking out of your hotel.'

Freshly damp from a hot shower that had been intended to thaw her out, George twisted a clean towel around herself. Flapping around in the flimsy complimentary slippers, she flung her empty suitcase onto the bed and sighed. With a heavy heart and a feeling that she should have remained behind in Cambridge to work on her prison project now that she had her laptop back, George started to pack. Her mind whirled with the dizzying detail and mystery of this hastily arranged Berlin trip. She was still reeling from the bedtime rejection she had received from Van den Bergen, once Marianne had finally sloped off to bed and all was quiet in the hotel bar.

'Are you coming upstairs, then, old man?' she had asked him, stroking his hand. 'For a nightcap!' she'd said pointedly, winking, treating him to that mischievous grin he always said got the butterflies in his stomach a-flutter. 'I've missed you.' She raised an eyebrow, holding her fingers aloft. 'See these? I've nearly worn them to stumps, thinking of me and you. So, what do you say?'

But Van den Bergen had merely shaken his hand loose to drain his beer. He'd set the bottle back down on the bar carefully. 'No,' he'd said. No clarification. 'Night.'

He had neither softened the blow by kissing her, qualifying this flat rejection of romance with some excuse that he was tired, nor had he trotted out his usual line of late: that he could offer her nothing; that he was broken and washed up; that it was unfair to snatch away her prospect of a family like a cheap magician whipping a tablecloth from under a place-setting.

'Is that it?' she had shouted after him. 'You ask me to come all the way out here. *You*. Asked *me*! Not the other way round.'

'I'll see you at breakfast, George,' he had called over his shoulder.

A strictly professional arrangement. After two years. The cheek of it!

Now, as she packed her case, angrily flinging her bra and used ski-socks on top of the fluffy hotel towel she had liberated from the maid-service trolley for Aunty Sharon, she chewed on the inside of her cheek. 'Fucking liberty,' she said. 'Who the hell does he think he is? Blowing hot and cold. Pushing my frigging buttons, the stupid Dutch tosspot.'

Pre-packed biscuits from the tea and coffee making facilities went into the case. All the hotel toiletries from the bathroom were souvenirs for Tinesha. Patrice would have to make do with a hug. There was nothing worth stealing for him apart from a shoe-cleaning sponge and some shitty hotel stationery.

When there was a knock on the door, George jumped. She tightened the towel around her naked body, and looked through the spyhole.

'Hakan,' she said, opening the door.

The Berlin detective stood outside, looking away when he saw her state of undress.

'Don't mind me!' she said. 'Come in! I don't bite, man. Promise.'

As George stood by the king-sized bed, with Hakan perched awkwardly on the end, she failed to suppress unbidden images popping into her head: femmes fatales in Hollywood movies dropping their towels to the hotel room floor to reveal their nakedness to a potential lover. *What if my towel falls off?* she thought. *I can feel it's loose. It's going to fall. He'll see my droopy big tits and my belly. I need to eat less crisps and take up exercise. Got to start cycling again.*

'I have good news,' Hakan said, running his hand through his hair, smiling uncertainly. 'I have the name of the locksmith.'

'Oh, yeah. What is it?'

'Hans Meyer. It turns out that the zoo had contracted him to fix new locks to the Lion Gate after a break-in some time ago. He was one of their regular suppliers.'

'Okay,' George said. 'Well, that's a start.'

'This is not all,' Hakan said. 'The dental reconstruction is finished on both men. There is a match in the thin victim with this locksmith, Hans Meyer. And you were right. The larger man is called Gerhard. Gerhard Hauptmann. He was a slum landlord, running houses in the Kreuzberg and Neukölln districts. He was owning a property next door to the house where the Roma children were found. We are now starting to unravel the Krampus case, thanks to you.'

'Brilliant!' George said, flinging her arms around the detective, unaware that somebody had walked into her room through the self-closing fire-door she had presumed had clicked shut behind her guest.

Van den Bergen. Towering above them both. Hooded eyes appraising a situation where a semi-naked George had her arms around a younger, attractive man, who was sitting on the end of her bed.

'Paul! It's not what it looks like,' George cried, as he turned to leave.

CHAPTER 21

Amsterdam, police headquarters, 11 March

'Why haven't you caught me a bloody murderer yet?' Kamphuis asked, slamming a meaty fist onto Van den Bergen's desk. Sweat glistened on his top lip, his shirt visibly stained beneath the arms in wet, discoloured rings, like chromatography gone mad. 'I mean, what exactly are you trying to pull here?' He looked to the side and squeezed his eyes shut, as though he were hoping for insight and strength from the universe or some other-wordly authority. 'You go on an unsanctioned trip to Berlin with *her* and Marianne.' He jerked his thumb in the direction of George, not even bothering to glance her way.

Van den Bergen could feel his stomach propel hot lava into the back of his mouth. He imagined himself a komodo dragon spitting venom on his prey.

'Don't speak to Dr McKenzie like that, Olaf,' he said, pushing his typing chair backwards so that he could throw one long leg over the other. He took off his glasses in a bid to show Kamphuis that he wasn't remotely intimidated by his bullshit.

His view of George was partially obscured by the Commissioner's rotund belly. But he glimpsed enough to know that she was holding the middle finger of her right hand aloft. Van den Bergen widened his eyes, keen to communicate that matters would not be improved if Kamphuis realised the freelance criminologist was flipping him the bird.

'Look,' he said. 'We helped my guy in Berlin to ID his two Krampus victims.'

'ID'ing the murder victims of the German police is not within my remit, Paul!' Kamphuis yelled. 'And neither is paying for a dirty overnighter at a boutique hotel so my Chief Inspector can indulge himself in a threesome with the fucking head of pathology and his girlfriend!' He finally turned to George, looking her up and down pointedly. 'On my payroll for some spurious profiling nonsense that I've yet to see the benefit of.'

George was out of her seat, of course, pointing, clicking her fingers to emphasis her words, spoken just as rapidly in Dutch as they ever were in English. Her beautiful, easily outraged head moved from side to side as though it was a remote-controlled device on a track of sorts.

'Are you behaving in an inappropriate and disrespectful manner towards me in the workplace, Commissioner? Because I don't need to put up with this shit from you. I'm freelance, see? Paul pays me to do a bloody good job, which I do, because in the world of criminology I'm no basic bitch. Right? And until you got *me* on the scene, nobody really knew jack shit about Roma involvement or child trafficking in this poxy murder case. Right?' Hand on hip now, she took two steps towards Kamphuis, who straightened up and almost backed into Van den Bergen's typing chair. She pointed at him. 'And while we're at it, you can stop verbally abusing your Chief Inspector, because he's doing a damned terrific job and I think they call what you're doing bullying in the workplace. Are you a bully in the workplace, Commissioner Kamphuis?'

Kamphuis puffed his cheeks out, clearly gasping for a response that would match George's in eloquence and fervour.

At that moment, Van den Bergen had never felt prouder of

his little Detective Lacey. He maintained a dour expression, however; he didn't want her to notice the ardour behind his eyes. It wouldn't do to let her know that rejecting her at that hotel had been an extraordinary feat of masochistic self-discipline for him – that he had restrained himself royally in resisting the urge to punch Hakan when he had found them in an embrace. She had insisted it had been a chance encounter, rather than a planned tryst, but he barely knew up from down anymore.

'Thank you for your input, Georgina,' Van den Bergen said, putting his hands behind his head, watching with wry amusement as Kamphuis' complexion grew dangerously red. 'And thank you for your derogatory remarks and your enquiry about my case, Commissioner. I'll keep you posted.' He inclined his head towards the door of his office, making it clear in which direction he wanted Kamphuis to walk. Thankfully he was saved from a bout of prolonged one-upmanship with his superior by Marie knocking and entering.

Kamphuis' eye started to twitch. He rubbed the sweat from his top lip with a slightly trembling hand. Marie was standing too close to him, pinning him to the spot with accusatory, narrowed eyes and something bordering on a sneer: a mouse, challenging an elephant to a stand-off and winning hands down.

With the Commissioner gone and the door firmly closed behind him, George bellowed with laughter.

'Man alive!' she said in English, slapping her knee, before switching to Dutch. 'He's totally petrified of you. What have you got on him, Marie?'

Marie hooked her hair behind her ear and blushed, fidgeting with one of her pearl earrings. Her blue eyes showed a little sparkle, which Van den Bergen had not seen evidence of for a long, long time.

'I threatened to whack him with sexual harassment. It's a while ago, now.' A sly smile and a wink in George's direction.

Van den Bergen spied camaraderie between the two that had

not been there at the start. But abruptly, Marie's smile and the friendly rapport evaporated. All business, now.

'While you were both in Berlin, I've been checking out the bank details of our Bijlmer man, Tomas Vlinders,' she said, brandishing an A4 notepad.

'Go on,' Van den Bergen said, pulling a third chair up for her to sit on, making an effort not to wrinkle his nose when he caught a whiff of her body odour.

Marie stared down at the words she had written in a neat hand. Line after line after line. Figures and sub-totals and notes in the margin. 'Okay, so there's just welfare benefits going into his current account. He was claiming disability because of his addiction. Me and Elvis went to scope out Vlinders' registered home address. Typical junkie's dump.' Rolled her eyes. 'Works from using, everywhere. Dirty syringes. Burnt teaspoons. Tin foil. Loads of paraphernalia on his kitchen table from cutting and bagging coke. I'm surprised Amsterdam's junkies having been dying in droves. He's been watering down pure Colombian with scouring powder, from what I can see!'

'No wonder junkies' baths are always bloody filthy,' George said. 'They're too busy snorting their cleaning products to use them on scum rings!'

A flicker of a smile played on Marie's lips. Perhaps she was uncertain as to whether George had cracked a genuine joke or not.

'Marianne de Koninck phoned through and arranged for Strietman to take a forensics team there yesterday,' Marie said. 'Results won't be back for a few days yet.'

'Any evidence of child abuse? Kids' toys?' George asked.

Shaking her head. 'Nothing obvious.'

Van den Bergen steepled his fingers together and frowned. 'Any computer equipment?'

'Yep. Quite a bit of it, actually. A PC and a laptop. Lots of CD-ROMs and USB sticks. A digital camera. I'm going to start going through it all, now I've finished looking at his bank stuff and phone records. But it's his credit card transactions that I wanted to tell you about.' She flicked the page with her index finger, raised an eyebrow and looked at Van den Bergen. 'Vlinders had travelled to Berlin. He bought train tickets for one adult and two children.'

It was as though a shadow had been cast over Marie. Her eyes were dirty sapphires once more, put back into the ground by sorrow and loss. Van den Bergen opted to say nothing.

'And Gerhard Hauptmann's number was on his phone, right?' George asked.

'Yes,' Marie said, scrutinising her grubby fingernails.

The train-track furrows across her forehead were more pronounced than usual, Van den Bergen observed. And not just down to the cold weather and a redhead's delicate skin.

'I had a call from Hakan Güngör's tech person, Franz,' she said. 'Now they know where to look, they're going to be seizing all Hauptmann's computer equipment and any phones they find in the houses he owns. The other guy too.'

'Hans Meyer. The locksmith.'

'Yep. Between me and Franz, we should be able to unravel at least a motive for our killer. As if the killer needed one, apart from the fact that all three guys seem to be raving paedos.'

The shadow lifted somewhat, along with the corners of her mouth. Van den Bergen detected the spark of intrigue in his junior detective.

'And here's the interesting thing ...'

George leaned forwards in her seat. Van den Bergen sat upright. All ears on the always oh-so-humble Marie.

'... The two children that accompanied Vlinders to Berlin never came back with him. According to the ticket bookings, it was a one way trip.'

'Trafficked!' George gasped. 'He'll have passed the kids off as his own and then dumped them onto Hauptmann for a finder's fee, maybe. I bet they ended up in that basement with the Roma kids.'

'It doesn't take a genius to work out that the children have been abused by a paedophile ring,' Van den Bergen said, feeling suddenly queasy. 'The Kreuzberg house was in too busy an area for men to be coming and going without raising suspicion. So, possibly they were taken to the zoo at night. Let in by Meyer. I'm guessing Meyer liked to watch the visiting children during the day, when he was working on the zoo's locks. School kids. That sort of thing. Perhaps it gave him the idea to use it as a venue.'

'Or, perhaps he pursued the zoo account – doing the zoo's lock repairs – *because* there were children around and he wanted to gain easy access to a place where you can just get lost at night,' George said. 'Paedophiles work in professions where they can get easy access to children.'

Van den Bergen nodded. 'Anyway, my guess, given the modus operandi of our killer, is that we're looking for some kind of organised crime hitman taking out traffickers who weren't dealing with a clean deck.' He turned to George. 'We need to find out more about this British victim. What was his name again?'

'Rufus Lazami,' George said. 'Millionaire captain of industry. Respectable, by all accounts, if you believe what you read in the papers. But maybe he's got skeletons in his closet too. Didn't you tell me that the kids from Bijlmer were pushing drugs and being pimped to rich and famous men?'

'Exactly. You need to go straight back to London and do some snooping.'

George narrowed her eyes at Van den Bergen.

He gulped, knowing he'd said the wrong thing.

She was out of her seat. A greyhound chasing the rabbit, as though ripping its throat out would be the finest sporting pursuit life had to offer.

'You fucking *what*?'

CHAPTER 22

Amsterdam, Marie's apartment, later

'Dinner time, Hugo!' Marie said, emptying the tin of cat food into the bowl.

Soiled kitty litter pebble-dashed the kitchen tiles where Hugo had kicked out the tray's contents. It embedded itself uncomfortably in the soles of her bare feet. But after a hard day chasing the bad guys, even if Marie had been bothered about that sort of thing, she would be too tired to stand there with a remedial dustpan and brush at the ready. To hell with it.

'Hugo! Come to Mummy!'

The tortoise-shell, emasculated tomcat padded up to her, mewing. He arched his lithe back and rubbed himself against his mistress's legs.

Marie stroked the cat, scratching behind his ears as he started to chomp away at the fishy-smelling lumps she had spooned out for him. 'You're my gorgeous man, aren't you, little puss?' The cat ignored her now, of course. Like most of the men she had met in her thirty-one years, his interest was only ever fleeting. Once his needs were met, that was the end of that.

Sighing, she flung the dirty spoon into the sink and the unwashed tin into the recycling bag. She wiped her hands on a tea towel, which she would definitely throw in the laundry by the weekend. Definitely. No point putting the washing machine on for one tea towel, though. Especially not before she had washed the dishes from the last few days. Peering cursorily into the sink, she wrinkled her nose and shrugged.

None of that mattered, because Marie had a Skype conversation lined up with a certain Berlin police cyber specialist.

'Franz Dinkels,' she said, wrapping her tongue around the German name. It had a happy ring to it. She liked it. Wondered what Franz Dinkels would look like. Perhaps as friendly and approachable as his name and the affable, almost jokey tone of his emails suggested.

Clicking the kettle on, Marie made her way along the dark hall to the bathroom, passing the wooden crucifix she had bought in Spain whilst on holiday with her mother some years ago, and the Jan Breughel the Elder reproduction of the Blessed Virgin Mary. She made the sign of the cross and then glared at the BVM.

In the mirror of her admittedly underused bathroom, she spied a medium-sized spot on her chin. That would be easily sorted with some concealer. Her hair was probably reasonable. She pulled her ponytail free, bushed the shoulder-length hair out and assessed that it was not entirely reasonable as hair cleanliness went. To shower or not to shower? Looking at the mildewed shower curtain and contemplating taking her three layers of clothing off when the apartment was so darned cold, she decided there was no real logic in showering. She sniffed her armpits. They seemed okay and, besides, Franz could hardly smell her through his computer monitor.

'Mascara!' she told the mirror. Rummaged in a make-up bag that was stuffed full of out-of-date cosmetics her mother had bought her. Five-year-old Chanel eyeshadow, pretty much untouched. Yves Saint Laurent lippy. In blood red, for god's sake! The old lady liked expensive beauty care and insisted her daughter was fashioned from the same mould. Marie chuckled at the thought, accidentally stabbing her eyeball with the mascara wand. It was as though her mother was punishing her remotely for her slovenly grooming ways with a bloodshot right eye.

'Fuck!'

BVM wouldn't appreciate the swearing, but she and the BVM weren't exactly on normal speaking terms since Nicolaas. And she had not quite made her peace with the Father, the Son or the Holy Spirit.

A film of glassy wet sorrow appeared unbidden on her already aggravated eyes. Stung like stink. She blew her nose, even redder now. 'Pull yourself together, idiot!' She switched off the flickering light above the vanity mirror, refocused on the prospect of Skyping, and checked her notes.

'Hi Franz. Is that you?' She adjusted her camera. 'Can you hear me?' She tapped the speaker on and off but still couldn't hear him, though his lips were moving.

A hairy arm in close-up said Franz was faffing with his camera. It looked as though he was in his living room, maybe. Shelf after shelf was laden with books behind him; crime novels, judging by the bold print on the spines. Grinning. Blushing. Looking at himself. Looking at her. Nobody ever seemed to know where to look on Skype.

Marie cringed anew at the sight of her own head and shoulders, cast in an unflattering light beneath the living room ceiling lamp. Mascara made her look like a prostitute. She turned the footage of herself off. No need for that.

'Hiya, Franz. Nice to put a face to the email address. Ha ha.' Was that stupid or acceptably friendly? She could feel a rash crawling up her neck and that terrible flush of red seeping through the powder that covered her cheeks, making her look as though she'd been slapped hard.

Franz nodded. 'Ja. I am pleased to see you also.' His English was not as fluent as hers. But she liked his face. It was a kind face. Double chin and eyes slightly squinty. He wasn't too perfect.

Good. Mousy hair, thinning on top, but that was fine. That bastard Diederik had had magnificent caramel-coloured hair and he had brought her world crashing down around her. Hair counted for nothing. No evidence of children or a woman's influence on those bookshelves. Good.

Except, now she had run out of conversation. 'Do you like cats?' she asked.

'Ja. I have a ginger cat.' He made kissing noises, leaned out of shot and presently filled the screen with the fattest cat she had ever seen. The cat struggled free. 'Lancelot,' he explained, taking a deep breath from an asthma inhaler. 'I am loving him but also allergic to him.'

Laughter between them. Good.

Except, she had definitely run out of conversation. And apparently, so had he. He was grinning at his camera like a slightly demented schoolboy. Opening and closing his mouth like a goldfish gasping at the top of a dirty tank.

'So!' He had broken the awkward silence. Thank God. 'We are finding that Hauptmann has an apartment near Zoologische Garten, and that he is running a child pornography website from there.'

Marie felt herself relax a little. Onto business. That was a territory in which she felt comfortable.

'I suspected you might. What's the web address?'

Franz told her. She inserted the URL into her browser and a standard porn site popped up.

'Is it encoded?' she asked.

'Several clicks through, there is a login page for extra content. A site within the site.' He talked her through the various firewalls which users had to penetrate to gain access to the illegal content. Eventually, the illicit material came up. She hadn't told Van den Bergen, but of late, since Nicolaas, she was finding it harder and harder to look at this bilge. Realising, now that those were people's children: missing, miles from home, their abuse photographed, filmed, shared and billed for. Before Nicolaas, it had seemed almost an abstract concept but now …

'Are you okay?' Franz asked. 'You are crying?'

Marie hastily wiped her eyes with the end of her jumper sleeve. 'No. I'm having a reaction to my mascara,' she said. Chiding herself for allowing the vulnerability to show through in front of a camera, of all things. Idiot.

She cleared her throat.

'I've been unravelling Tomas Vlinders' phone records this end. Seven calls between him and Hauptmann in a seventy-two hour period. Several emails exchanged – cagey about the nature of the product that was changing hands for money but talking about a finder's fee for Vlinders and a purchase price, payable by Hauptmann *and* 20% on the top as a kind of royalty to someone our people found out is 'The Son of the Eagle'. Whoever this Eagle is, he seems to be a, if not *the*, lynch pin in a transnational child trafficking network. Judging by the locations Vlinders had been calling from, he was taking those two kids with him to Hauptmann's house in Kreuzberg.'

Franz was nodding now. Smiling.

'Excellent,' he said. 'We have not been finding Hauptmann's phone, unfortunately. But with a little more work, I should be able to crack the encrypted credit card information from the porno website and have a list of names of those accessing images. So, we have established that all three men are involved in the same chain of supply and demand.'

Marie wondered if she dare ask Franz if he would like to come and visit the Amsterdam head office at any point if he was ever in the area. She rehearsed the words in her head. They came out perfectly in her head. Poised to say them, however, she could not find enough spittle to speak.

'Are you sure you are okay?' Franz asked.

Bordering on breathless, Marie nodded. A toxic mix of emotions. Anticipation, hope, sorrow, dread.

'I've got to go,' she said and turned her camera off hastily.

But Franz's voice continued though his image had been replaced by a blank screen.

'Will we speak again tomorrow? I am finding this very useful and also enjoyable.'

Marie severed the Skype connection. She allowed herself a glimmer of a smile, but immediately hated herself for it because she didn't deserve happiness. Not if she said the rosary every day. Not if she went to church every single Sunday. Not even if she read the Bible in her every spare moment.

Marie deserved to suffer.

CHAPTER 23

A village South of Amsterdam, 8 June, the previous year

Leafing through *de Volkskrant* and *de Telegraaf*, Gabi could see nothing of their plight until ten or more pages in. Grim photos of the two of them, snapped by the paparazzi that had set up camp on the curtilage outside for the first week, much to the neighbours' chagrin; a throng of fifty, maybe, plus TV vans, which had dwindled to about ten now. She scowled at the photo of herself in a tabloid newspaper, *Algemeen Dagsblad*, leaving the house with her hair in a mess. They had been going to Amsterdam to endure yet another seemingly pointless conflab with the police.

'For God's sake!' she snapped, slamming the papers down onto the counter, one after the other. Glaring at Piet who was slumped over a coffee, as usual. Bloodshot eyes and a hangdog expression, like that would fix things. 'Two weeks and nothing! Nothing!' He still didn't look up at her, even when she started to shout. 'The Roma sighting turned out to be a dead end. Two thousand calls to the missing persons' helpline and not one lead has panned out. Not one! The public's losing interest.' She reached out and grabbed his arm. 'We've got to do something, Pieter!'

But he merely looked up at her, tears standing in his eyes. 'I'm going back to bed. I never should have got up. I can't …'

He shuffled off, scratching the arse of his pyjamas. Typical.

'That's right!' she bellowed after him. 'You go and curl up like a bug under a stone. Don't bother talking this through.'

'I haven't got the energy to talk,' came his voice from the stairwell. 'I'll see you at lunchtime.'

'Wanker!' Gabi said under her breath. 'I married a weak-willed man-child. Jesus. What the hell was I thinking?'

Rinsing her breakfast pots and loading the dishwasher, she contemplated her next move. Ever-decreasing publicity for the case meant the public wasn't on the lookout for Josh or Lucy any more. The charity didn't want her to go back into the office, although she would have loved to have done so, if only to enjoy some semblance of normality for an hour or two. Her buffoon of a boss had bandied about the word 'inappropriate' like he was in a position to decide what was and wasn't an acceptable way to deal with such intolerable stress and loss. Dick. She couldn't deal with her feelings. And they weren't important anyway. What was important was having a plan. Seizing some control from this. Imposing order on chaos. Grief must not compute. Only positive action.

'Gabi! Gabi! Come to the door!' One of the photographers camped on her driveway had caught sight of her through the kitchen window. Goddamn it. And she was still in her nightie. How embarrassing.

But her thoughts were diverted by the sound of the mail plopping onto the doormat. Be positive. Stay focussed.

'Aw, I don't believe this!'

Hard to do when the post included three death threats, a bank statement that showed they were overdrawn by several thousand and five large overdue bills.

'Piet! I told you to pay the car and you still haven't paid it, you arsehole!' she shouted up the stairs.

No response. She gnawed at the inside of her cheek. This was down to him, of course. If he'd held it together, he'd still be working. Billing for plans. Getting on with the day-to-day like a man. A provider. Leaving the evenings free to fall to bits. Selfish, self-indulgent prat of a kidult.

She closed her eyes as she walked past Lucy's room. Tasteful John Lewis zoo animals theme, imported from London. Mismatched *Frozen* bedding, which Lucy insisted on, even though she was too young to do anything but burble and hum along to the theme tune of 'Let it Go'.

Don't look inside. She'll be back soon.

She kept her eyes tightly shut as she walked past Josh's little den with its *Noddy*-themed decor. *Noddy*'s on his way. *Noddy* will sort things out. Bright yellow walls. *Noddy* with his Toy Town full of friends. A sunny disposition, unlike Josh. But often getting into trouble. Like Josh.

Walk, goddamn it! Don't look. Those beds aren't empty. That dust is not gathering on the toys. Walk.

Glimpsed Piet in bed as she passed their bedroom. Body quaking beneath the duvet. Crying again.

Under the shower in the family bathroom, the hot water was invigorating. Washing away the memory of the death threats.

@Gabi_Deenen Die, heartless bitch. #FindTheDeenens

@Gabi_Deenen Jesus took your children because you didn't love them. #JesusLoves

@Gabi_Deenen @telegraaf So much money. So little time to look after your kids properly. #BadMothers

Haters got to hate. It came from having a nice life where others didn't. Beautiful children, where others weren't. A luminous career, where others couldn't. Wash that envy down the drain.

Luminous career.

It was then that the way forward unfurled itself like a fine rug.

What was she equipped to do, better than anybody else? How could she seize control of this fiasco?

Under the steaming water, she clapped her hands together. 'Mummy's got a plan!' she told Josh and Lucy in her mind's eye. 'Mummy's going to sort it all out.'

A phone call was all it took. London was poised and ready. Strings pulled.

Throwing her best clothes into the case – the quality stuff she had worn before this lo-fi, homespun crap she was forced to endure in the Dutch backwater – she imagined herself around the boardroom table of Pickwick Welcome PR. West End offices. Intelligent, quick-thinking people who knew how the world worked. Yes! This was where she could usefully take centre stage in this tragedy that their lives had morphed into.

'What are you doing?' Piet asked, standing in the doorway.

How long had he been there? Had she been speaking to herself?

'I'm flying to London,' she said, unable to keep the odd mixture of relief and vitriol out of her voice. 'I'll be back in three days. I'm going to sort this.'

Piet scratched his head. Scratching, scratching, like a monkey in the zoo. Flea-bitten. Semi-sentient. Useless, if he was unable to provide food and a roof.

'We've got to go to Amsterdam this afternoon,' he said. 'The police are expecting us. We're going to get an update. They've got more questions.'

'I'm going,' she said, slipping into her killer heels. 'I'll text.'

She carried the case downstairs as he shuffled along behind her, hand down his trousers, playing pocket billiards, hair plastered to his head because he hadn't showered in days. A week's worth of stubble, now more of a beard, masked his face.

Bracing herself for the flashbulbs and questions from the remaining journos, hand on the door handle, she turned back to him.

'And do me a favour,' she said. 'Pull yourself together while I'm away. Or else …'

'Or else.' Piet repeated his wife's words. Or else what, precisely? What could she possibly threaten to do that would be any worse than what he was already going through? If she ran a knife through his heart, she'd be doing him a favour.

The cameras belonging to the remaining paparazzi whined and clicked as they snapped at the heels of Gabi Deenen. Currently The Netherlands' most famous mother. Gabi holds it together. Gabi, the super-stylish Brit, mourns the abduction of her little ones. And there, standing by her side, is her loser of a husband. Pathetic Pieter. The man who lost his children.

'Look at the camera, Piet!' one photographer shouted – a man with a giant beer-gut and a hairstyle that was way too young for him, trying to make a living out of someone else's misery.

'Where's Gabi going, Piet?' shouted another, advancing down the path. Click, click, click.

But Piet flung the door wide, momentarily, not caring that they could all see him for the unwashed, unkempt mess that he had become.

'Get off my property!' he shouted, emerging to meet the trespasser. A slight man in his thirties, maybe. If need be, he'd punch the bastard. Yes he would. 'What gives you the right to intrude on our lives like this? Camped out at the end of my drive every goddamn morning, like we're some kind of side-show curiosity?'

Click, click, click. Still snapping away at the ranting and raving shambles of a man.

'Well, the lot of you can go to hell. Do you hear me? Go home. Leave me alone, you parasitic bastards.'

Tears streaming down his face. Bare feet, slapping up and down on the rough flagstones, as though he might somehow yet anchor himself to this cursed life simply by gripping the ground with his toes. He approached the photographer with a balled fist as an offering of non-hospitality. The anguish and emptiness left by the disappearance of his children had amassed to become a canker, infecting him, eating him from the inside out, leaving only a shell of a man. Perhaps he could take this intrusive fucker with him.

'I'll call the police!' he shouted.

The photographer backed away, still snapping.

'Are you having a breakdown, Piet?' someone asked to his right.

Piet swung around to see where the voice had come from. A woman's voice. Gabi's voice? No! Of course not. Through the blur of tears, beyond the bobbing heads of these piranhas with zoom lenses, he could see Gabi's car, already a black speck at the end of the long, long road.

'Come back,' he said under his breath.

Suddenly, he felt foolish and exposed. If he were Gabi, he would never have said those things to the paparazzi. If he were Gabi, he wouldn't be standing in the middle of his front garden in his pyjamas. If he were Gabi, he'd be holding it together for the kids. For their little family.

Pain lanced through his head, suddenly. A thunderclap of agony. He'd been getting them the last day or two. Blinding pain. Like being shot in the head. Clutching his temples. Sinking. Sinking. Not here, Piet. Don't lose it in front of strangers.

He ran inside and up the stairs. Opened a barrel of the tablets his doctor had prescribed. Poured fifty or so into his hand. Might give him peace. Might plug the chasm inside him that his children had filled.

'I can't do this anymore,' he said. 'I can't live without them. I can't live with myself,' he told his reflection in the mirror.

Three or four at a time, he started to take the tablets, swallowing them down with a glass of water. Looking forward to oblivion, now, he could feel his world getting fuzzy at the edges.

More tablets. More water, until he sank to his knees. An unbearable feeling of wanting to vomit and feeling he might pass out. And then, when the darkness came, it was sweet relief.

CHAPTER 24

South East London, 15 March

Wrapping himself in the fleece blanket he had stolen from the mountaineering shop on Oxford Street, he wriggled down onto the thin, single mattress in the back of the Transit van. Parked unobtrusively in a side street of South East Docklands. Surrey Quays and Canada Water stations nearby, where the respectable tax-payers filed in and out during the week on their quotidian travels to some heated workplace, perhaps suspecting but studiously not thinking about what went on just in their peripheral vision. The saying goes, you are never more than a couple of feet away from a rat in the city. And he was now that rat.

How did he feel?

He felt nothing. Just glad he had broken into this van, seemingly forgotten by its owner during this spell of extreme weather – a builder's vehicle, judging by the mud encrusted workman's boots and bucket in the back. Who could build in two feet of snow and rising? The van was unobtrusive. Dry. Most importantly, he was finally away from the other rough sleepers.

Try to get some sleep, he counselled himself. At least it was quiet, here, close to the icy vastness of Greenland Dock and the Thames on a frozen Sunday night. Outside, the snow was falling yet again, but still only covering the dirt of London with a superficial pristine layer. Underneath, the filth was still present, merely awaiting a thaw to reveal everyone's dirty secrets. And the thaw was long overdue.

Slowly his body began to relax. The stolen paracetamol and ibuprofen were keeping the shakes and sweats at bay. For now, at least. The newspaper strapped next to his skin with parcel string kept him as warm as possible, though the piss in the lemonade bottle had turned to ice next to him. *Pissicle*, he thought as fractured dreams started to push the salient thought aside. A soldier must defend his island of beauty. *All's fair in love and war.* Fleeting memories of the enemy that had been felled. The entrepreneur. The locksmith. The fat man. One more, that the police knew nothing of. Icicles burning the pads of his fingers and palm through the rotten woollen glove. So cold that the makeshift shivs had stuck to him. Difficult to cast off down the drain, along with the guilt. *All's fair in love and war.* Childrens' tiny hands trying to press their way upwards through the bars of the storm-drain covers. *Don't worry. I'll pull you free.*

The banging on the side of the van woke him. Heartbeat pounding, he wondered momentarily where he was. Sat up suddenly in almost pitch-black. There was nothing with which to defend himself, so he held one of the heavy work boots aloft. Opened the door a crack, -20°C whipping inside.

'It's me.'

The familiar voice and silhouette told him this man was not a threat. Not police moving him on. Not the van's owner. Not another homeless person, vying for somewhere to get their head down for a few hours. Torchlight shone inside, making him squint. He held his hand over his eyes.

'Turn the damned torch off!'

Then he saw the visitor clearly in the phosphorescence of dancing snowflakes that had taken the shaft of glum yellow streetlight and refracted it into a shower of gold leaf. The fake ID man. *The man who can*, as those in the know called him. Tall, young, mixed race with shapely eyebrows that gave him an over-groomed, feminine appearance. He was wearing a Canada Goose Parka. Real fox fur-trimmed hood. The kind of down-filled technical outdoor wear you could wear at the North Pole and successfully fend off the jaws of the biting cold.

'Nice coat. Can I have it?'

'Fuck off.' One of those shapely eyebrows raised. 'Let me get in, man. Can't have no-one eyeballing me while we're doing business, yeah?'

Sliding the van door aside, he let the visitor clamber in. He squatted carefully. The torch sat on the floor of the van, lighting everything from a strange angle. Sinister.

'I wanted to steal one of those coats from the outdoors shop the other day. They've got more security than a bank.'

'You can't afford one of these, bruv,' the man who can said, running his gloved fingers along the snow-sodden fur. 'Not if you want what I've got in my pocket. Now where's the money at?'

'Show me the weapon first.' His voice was hoarse. He wished this ghetto-glam Arctic arsehole had brought him a hot coffee.

'Money. Don't fuck me around. You know I'm packing my own.'

Counting the notes out, now. One hundred. Two hundred. Three hundred. Lost count. Tutting from the man who can. Eventually he approached a thousand. A tenner short.

'Sorry. I was starving and freezing. I needed to eat. Ten pounds won't make a difference, will it?' He looked into the young man's dark eyes. Hoped that the sensitivity he saw there wasn't a mirage.

It was. The cuff on the side of his head stung.

'Cheeky scavenging bastard with your skanky rash face!' Sucked his teeth. 'You wasting my time, you short-changing arsehole! If I say it's a thou, it's a thou. You axed me for a gun and new ID. I brought you a gun and new ID, right? Because business is business and I don't wanna know what the fuck you want all this shit for. I just provide the product. And you pay for it, innit? That's a transaction, man.'

'Please!' He was desperate. All he could do was appeal to the better nature of this cocky, corrupt bastard. 'I'm just trying to—'

Holding his hands up, the man who can shrunk back into the shadows at the rear of the van. 'Woah, mate! I don't want to know what you trying to. That ain't my problem.'

'Come on! I paid in full in the past. I'm ten lousy pounds short. You know I'll be back. I'll make it up next time. I'll pay you double what I owe.' Coughing. Wheezing so that the breath was almost squeezed out of him.

The visitor emerged from the dark again. Contemplative look on his face. 'Next time, you'll pay me two hundred in lieu of the tenner you owe. No negotiation. You're fucking me around and it ain't like there's some other mug you can go to for this kind of thing, right?'

What choice did he have? He had a job to do. His role had been agreed. He received his orders. He knew he was in no position to bargain. The cough came on again, even more violently this time. A hacking cough that just wouldn't shift. A sitting tenant, abusing his hospitality; slowly usurping its host.

'Jesus. You need to see a fucking doctor with that. You sound like an old tramp.'

The visitor was grimacing, screwing up that pretty-boy face. He held his sleeve up to protect his own nose and mouth from contamination.

'I am an old tramp, remember?'

'Nah. You ain't no tramp. Tramps don't buy guns and fake passports for a grand. You some MI5 shit? Nah. You ain't that neither, cos you would get that from them. I reckon you're a renegade, innit? Getting your money from somewhere, but deep undercover.'

Suddenly, he felt his bloodlust rising. Maybe this little shit knew too much. Maybe he could just kill him and take his coat, leave him in the shitty van. Eyeing the bulging pockets on that parka, he realised his gun was in one, but what was in the others? Money. Drugs. Enough to live on for a few weeks. But then, where would his project be without this chump and his ready access to counterfeit ID?

'Can you get me broad-spectrum antibiotics?'

'A monkey.'

'What is a monkey?'

'Five hundred quid. Includes the two hundred you owe me for being short tonight.'

Breathing heavily through flared nostrils, coughing as the van's dusty interior and the astronomical fee caught the back of his throat, he felt something hot and semi-solid plop into his mouth. Spat it into an already wet tissue. 'Fine. Give me the gun and the ID and just go.'

'Where will I find you next time?'

'I'll need a couple of days to get the money.'

'You might be dead in a couple of days, man.' The man who can handed over the gun.

It was surprisingly heavy and painfully cold to touch. But he knew how to use it. Not dissimilar to the weapons he had handled during National Service. He pocketed it, along with a box of bullets. Flicked through the fake passport. Looked convincing. Even had a decent photo of him. He looked nothing like his old self, obviously. But then, that man had been replaced by a machine. Now, he was Jack Frost. The Krampus. The bringer of cold endings. His orders were nearly all fulfilled. The finale was surely near.

'Just get me the meds. I'll let your boy know where you can find me.'

'Where you going to with that passport? Warmer climes?'

'Roma.'

CHAPTER 25

Amsterdam, police headquarters,
16 March

Footsteps clicked from the sink to the hand-dryer. The hot air began to blow. A man was sniffing. Belching. Blowing his nose. Footsteps away from the hand-dryer. The main door of the toilet slammed shut. Van den Bergen was finally alone.

'Son of the Eagle,' he said, spreading the sheaf of notes over the tiled floor of the disabled cubicle. 'Come on, you bastard. Have you been mentioned in here somewhere?'

He sat back down onto the pan, regarding the paperwork. Rubbed his scarred stomach and popped an anti-spasmodic tablet onto his tongue. Menacing noises emanating from his abdomen. He grimaced, though more from the frustration of feeling that he had many of the jigsaw pieces laid out before him, but that they still steadfastly would not fit together.

'Fifty-odd interviews with gypsies and not a single mention of eagles or hawks or even so much as a bloody pigeon.'

A disproportionately lavish media campaign for the missing persons had had Jaap Hasselblad in an apoplexy of vengeful enthusiasm.

'When we find these fuckers and bring their kidnappers to book, the whole of Europe will celebrate *my* police force,' he had eulogised, frog-eyes bulging, shaking those infernal brass buttons like he had some kind of shamanic powers. Prat.

Faces of the missing had been all over the tabloids: the television, on every radio station, with posters in every school, workplace, shop window and every transport hub, throwing up the general public's favourite hate figures as potential kidnappers. Somali, Italian, Russian gangsters. Immigrants, obviously. One week in, with a flurry of phone calls to the missing persons hotline, the gypsies had suddenly trumped every other ethnic group and the Netherlands' least-wanted.

'I want dawn raids!' Hasselblad had shouted, showering Van den Bergen and Kamphuis with evangelical prejudice and spit.

Twenty targets in five different illegal Roma encampments spread around Amsterdam suburbs and satellite towns. The late summer sun had risen just enough to light up the scrap metal, makeshift toilets, refuse and the embers of camp fires that caused the local tax-paying residents to complain so bitterly about these uninvited new neighbours.

Young men, brought in in their underpants. Processed, interviewed, released.

'It's a waste of time,' Van den Bergen had reported back to Kamphuis. 'Investigative cul-de-sacs, the lot of them. A tonne of admin. No kidnappings. No ransom plans. No forced migration or slave labour.'

Kamphuis, for perhaps the first time in all the years Van den Bergen had known him, had put his hands behind his head, revealing those dark-stained armpits, had nodded sagely and had committed the ultimate act of betrayal. 'I think our Chief of Police is wide of the mark with those gypsies.'

'You? Disagree with Hasselblad? Sorry! I seem to have lost my hearing.' He remembered having poked at his ear for dramatic effect. Provoking his nemesis into some sort of prickly smart-arsed reaction that would set the world back on its usual axis.

Kamphuis had started to stroke the naked lady statue on his desk, eye twitching. There was no hint of sarcasm in his voice.

'I fancy the family. In fact, I'd put money on it. Nine times out of ten, the murderer is the next of kin.'

'But this is missing persons. We haven't got bodies, Olaf. All we can go on is facts and right now, we've got sweet F.A., as the English say.'

'As that girlfriend of yours might say.' Kamphuis had rearranged his mouth into a leer. He'd leaned forward and touched the nipple of the naked lady statue. 'Actually, I've been thinking of her.'

'Oh, you've crossed a line—'

'No, I mean in a professional capacity. I think you should get her in. Get her to look at the case and profile the family.'

At that point, George had been drafted onto the payroll, though she had hardly needed any encouragement at all to fly over to see him.

Sitting on that dismal toilet in the disabled cubicle, Van den Bergen remembered the sound of her voice at night as she lay in his arms in bed. Night after night at summer's end, remaining at his apartment as the falling rain and dropping temperatures had issued in autumn. The feel of her embrace. The smell of her skin. The wisdom of her counsel. She had helped him to heal. She had chased the spectre of the Butcher away. And though he had been reluctant to begin a fully-fledged relationship with his much younger lover, he had. Even he, miserable old bastard that he was, had readily admitted to himself that stifling his feelings for George had almost led him to his grave prematurely. And, at a point where he was too close to the case, George's insight had been valuable.

'I don't think the family has any part in this,' she had said, having trawled through hours of TV footage, files full of information and having met those who had been left behind. Shaking her head as she sat cross-legged in just her pants on his bed, surrounded by paper. Pulling on one of those corkscrew curls until it was straight. 'They're reacting in the way you'd expect them to react. I think Kamphuis is like the Internet trolls. He's using the relatives as convenient hate figures to make him feel better about his own helplessness and perceived uselessness. He's a prize cock.'

'That's what I thought,' Van den Bergen had said, tracing the outline of her belly with his index finger. Round and round in ever diminishing circles to her belly button, where she had no unsightly scarring. Unlike him. His wounds had still been a livid purple all those months ago. Stitched together like a mailbag. But George's skin was smooth. Just a few stretch marks from weight gain and weight loss. Otherwise young and unsullied. Except one day she would almost certainly want to grow a child inside that shapely belly and he felt too old to give her such a gift.

The memory of George, sitting semi-naked on his bed, enthused about the case and their romance, suddenly twisted and distorted to become a recollection of her standing in the doorway to his office at the station glaring at him, telling him she was leaving and that he was a bastard. When that unwelcome memory popped unbidden into his head, he started to gather the paperwork up off the disabled toilet cubicle floor.

'I never make promises I can't keep,' he said under his breath. He slotted the case notes back into the lever arch, feeling that the ache in his chest was so much more than indigestion.

They had argued over the long-term potential of a forty-six-year-old from Amsterdam conducting a childless long-distance relationship with a twenty-six-year old from London.

'You're a prick, Paul,' she had said. Anger setting her soft face into hard lines. Animated hand gestures like a vengeful ninja, aiming to decapitate him, perhaps. 'Find your own missing persons. I've given you all the pointers I can. I'm going home to *not* have babies and *not* be a domestic drudge and *not* give up my dreams to wash your underpants on my own. Don't phone me. Don't write me. Shove it up your hairy arse.' Tears had stood in her rueful brown eyes. And then weeks passed before they had spoken properly again – only then, because of the Jack Frost murders and their child trafficking implications.

'Why do I always screw everything up?' he asked himself.

Emerging from the cubicle, carrying the heavy file, he was horrified to see Elvis standing right in front of him.

'How long have you been there?' he asked, grimacing at his protégé. 'Have you got nothing better to do than stalk me in the toilets?'

Elvis smiled fleetingly and then looked at his feet. 'I wasn't listening, boss, if that's what you mean,' he said.

Clearly he had been listening, and now everyone would know that Chief Inspector Van den Bergen talked to himself on the toilet. Great.

'You've got a visitor in reception, boss,' Elvis said. 'Your daughter.'

The corners of Van den Bergen's mouth twitched upwards. 'Good. And I wasn't talking to myself. I was ... er ... recording a memo on my phone.'

Out of the corner of his eye, he could see Elvis grinning. Little shitehawk.

In the foyer, Tamara was sandwiched between what appeared to be a homeless man and a harried looking woman who toyed with rosary beads. His daughter spotted him and stood awkwardly, straight-backed, bending at the knees. Burdened by the extra weight.

Van den Bergen strode briskly over to help her, struck by how much bigger she had grown in only three weeks.

'Good to see you, Dad!' she said, kissing him on the cheek. Taking his hand and putting it on her hard, swollen stomach. 'Or should I say, Granddad?'

CHAPTER 26

The City of London, 16 March

'I'm here to speak to Rufus Lazami's PA,' George told the incredibly well-groomed receptionist. A pin-stitched navy skirt suit; hair in a chignon; flawless make-up and sparkling blue eyes that said this woman had not drunk a bottle of merlot last night in a club in Brixton and stayed up until the small hours, watching the room spin. Bloom Group plc clearly demanded perfection even in its admin staff. Or perhaps for this giant international conglomerate, it was all about image, even down to those who signed you in and out.

'Bloom Group, good morning,' the receptionist said into her headset, smiling inanely at George.

George leaned over the gleaming beige counter and felt the smooth granite, devoid of all dust and fingerprints, also immaculately presented. 'I said, I'm here to speak—'

The blonde girl touched her headset. 'Putting you through.' Tapping on a computerised phone system with long, blood-red nails. Then she refocused on George. Sized her up blatantly. Perhaps Puffa jackets didn't cut the mustard here, even when it was Arctic conditions outside. The smile was still fixed in place, though.

'Can I help you?' she asked. Pearly white teeth like a child's.

'Rufus Lazami's PA.'

'Have you got an appointment?'

'Yes.' She glanced at her discreetly elegant Raymond Weil watch, a gift from Van den Bergen when they had been on better terms. 'Now.'

'Sign in, please.'

George entered her details onto the visitor's badge. Dr McKenzie, Research Fellow, Cambridge University. Sounded respectable enough. The receptionist beamed and raised an eyebrow when she read it. Clearly the title had convinced her that George was not some anti-capitalism protestor. Judgemental cow.

After George had spent a good ten minutes observing the beige corporate sophisticates coming and going in this bland, glittering foyer, a thick-set woman, wearing a skirt that was too short for such lumpy red knees, approached the reception desk. She beckoned George over, gesticulating that she should follow through the security rigmarole of turnstiles and men bearing metal detectors.

'Glenda Cameron,' the woman said in a Scottish accent. She stuck out her hand and grasped George in a tight, clammy handshake. The inoffensive taupe twin-set and pearls she wore and her naff helmet of backcombed short hair belied the almost military aura she had about her. A no-nonsense ball-breaker from the Gorbals of Glasgow, by the sounds.

Sitting in the almost-empty office of Rufus Lazami, dabbing the coffee spillage in her saucer with a clean serviette, George had fed Glenda a line about conducting research into the heightened risk successful business people ran of becoming victims of violent crime, kidnapping and terrorism. The Scottish Rottweiler seemed to have swallowed it thus far. But now George wondered how she should broach the subject of his connection to paedophiles and drug pushers.

'So, do you think there was anything in particular in Mr

Lazami's business affairs that might have led to the murder?' she asked.

Glenda dabbed at her eyes, making a fair fist of grief. Not a tear in sight.

'He was a good man,' she said. 'A very generous boss.' She touched her pearls. 'Well-liked by everyone.'

Sipping her coffee thoughtfully, George tried to read Glenda's body language. She was blinking too much. Looking at the wall behind her, rather than making genuine eye contact. Something about her downturned mouth and crossed arms.

'Did he have business interests outside of the realm of Bloom Group?'

'I don't know what you mean.' Any warmth in her tone of voice had chilled down to hard frost. 'Look, Rufus Lazami was a revered entrepreneur. Lord Bloom's right-hand man. There was no gossip about him. No tittle-tattle. Nothing shifty. He was a pillar of the community.'

Glenda was still staring beyond George so intently that she was compelled to look round. Framed photos hung on the wall behind his empty desk, as though the ghost of the plundered Rufus Lazami was watching over his loyal PA, even now, peering out from eyes family snaps, mainly – judging by the glamorous trophy wife on Lazami's arm, and the overweight children who looked like her, positioned artfully in front of the couple. But in the middle of the wall was one large photograph in a gold frame. A photo of Lazami, standing with someone clearly of note in a room furnished with ostentatious red curtains and a red patterned rug or carpet. Shaking hands.

Feeling that she was getting nothing from the impenetrable Glenda, George set down her drink and strode over to the gold-framed photo.

Lazami had been a reasonable-looking man with dark hair, greying at the temples. But then she'd seen his photo plastered across the front page of every British newspaper at the time of his murder. Nothing new there. And the man whose hand he was shaking looked like a civil servant of some kind. She saw enough of those regularly in Westminster. A diplomat, perhaps.

'I haven't quite had the heart to take those down yet,' Glenda said, approaching the desk. 'I said I'd box everything up personally for his wife. But it seems so final.'

George moved to turn away, feeling heaviness in the pit of her stomach. Despite her best intentions, this interview had revealed nothing useful whatsoever. Perhaps Lazami's murder had been an anomaly or a copycat. Who knew? But just then she spied a flag in the background of this gaudy, self-congratulatory photo – a red flag with a black double-headed bird on it. Tingling in George's stomach and tightening in her chest told her she'd stumbled across something of note.

'Rufus Lazami was of Italian descent, wasn't he?' she said, turning to Glenda, who was standing just by her shoulder now. She smelled of sickly, floral perfume. 'Is this him at the Italian embassy or something?'

Glenda smiled. 'Oh no. That's the Albanian ambassador he's with. Lazami's an Albanian name – from Mr Lazami's father's side. He was quietly proud of his heritage. Did a lot of charity work.'

Nodding. George steeled herself to ask the question, though she hardly needed to. 'Is that a phoenix on the flag?'

'An eagle.'

George was breathless; she felt light-headed with anticipation. She knew what she was about to ask would get her into trouble and bring security thundering down these corridors of power. But what did she have to lose?

'Was your former boss into drugs, Glenda? Did he like children?'

Trudging down the street in thick snow, George acknowledged that she was lucky not to have been arrested. She couldn't help herself from grinning as she started to thumb out a text to Van den Bergen.

```
Put money on it that …
```

As she crossed the road, making her way towards Bank tube station, she almost walked straight into the slush-splattered bonnet of a black cab.

'Watch where you're going, you dopey cow!' the cabbie called at her through his window. He honked furiously, as if the reprimand hadn't been enough.

George stepped back onto the safety of the pavement, tapping into her phone with one hand, giving the cabbie the finger with the other.

'Fuck you, wanker!' she shouted, not bothering to look up. Texting with fervour.

```
… Albanian, Lazami was the Son of the
Eagle. Just been to …
```

She was so lost in reporting back to her partner that she wasn't paying attention to the world around her: a traffic warden advancing towards her; people barrelling out of a sandwich shop at her side; cars, splattering her boots with slush; icicles falling from above and shattering only feet away from her; the man three paces behind.

But still she texted.

```
… the Bloom Group offices. Very swish. PA
obv didn't rate her boss. Photo on the
wall of …
```

Glancing up, she opted to cut down Lothbury – a back street that would bring her out by Bank tube's entrance with less splash back from mouthy cab-driving arseholes. The hubbub of City of London life stilled, and presently, she was surrounded by silent old buildings on one side, the monolithic high wall at the back of the Bank of England on another. She pictured the red circle slashed through with the blue UNDERGROUND sign up ahead. *Not far, now, girl. Do a left at the Bank of China. Down Princess Street and you'll be there. Keep going!*

Walking through this shit was hard work, but the council had run out of grit. White stone buildings round here were starting to look dirty against the brilliant white blanket that covered everything. Thaw was on its way, apparently. Thank God. Back to the text.

```
... his office at the Albanian ...
```

George sensed that something was wrong but she was so wrapped up in the Lazami revelation to identify precisely what that could be, and she shrugged the niggling feeling off. Walking. Walking. Texting.

When the man grabbed her from behind, she dropped her phone into the deep snow. Kicked. Struggled. There was barely time to register that her attacker wore a dark woollen overcoat. His fingers smelled of cigars; his grip was pincer-like. But George's mouth was covered. She couldn't scream. Nobody around. She braced herself to feel the icicle breaching the soft skin of her neck.

CHAPTER 27

City of London, then, Aunty Sharon's house, South East London, later

George struggled against the grip of her attacker. Thrashing this way and that like a small water buffalo trying to throw off a rolling crocodile. Trapped, she bit her assailant's hand. No time to balk at the bitter taste of second-hand tobacco. He released his grip immediately, yelping.

'I'm gonna kill you!' she screamed. She spun around and punched the man squarely in the face with her leather-gloved hand. She watched with split-second satisfaction as his head flicked backwards, then kneed him squarely in the groin.

The man crumpled, clutching his crotch. George pounced on him, knocking him to his knees.

'You're not Jack Frost!' she shouted, picking her phone out of the snow and cuffing him on the ear with it, before drying it on his coat.

'No, I'm *not* Jack Frost,' the substandard assailant said, rubbing his reddening jaw. He looked up at her, wincing visibly.

She tried to melt him with her scowl. 'Well, who the fuck are you, then, you pervert?'

Wanting to test this bastard's metal, George feigned another swipe at his head. The man held his hands up in front of his face.

'Please don't punch me again!' he cried.

Grabbing him by his collar, George pulled the mewling figure to his feet channelling the strength of a woman far larger than her diminutive stature suggested. She was running on pure adrenalin and anger, blood running hot and fevered pulsating in her ears.

'I said, Who are you? What do you want?' she screamed.

'Dobkin,' he said in a small voice. 'Professor Jim Dobkin from UCL.'

'Dickwad Dobkin?' George asked, rubbing her neck. She stared at the beady-eyed man, with his increasingly swollen jaw.

'Not Dickwad. Jim. I'd like to speak to you about your research.'

'It was horrible.' George wept, pushing Letitia's feet off the sofa as her mother tried to use her as a footstool. 'H-he just came up behind me, a-and—'

Perched on the arm of the sofa, Sharon clasped her sobbing niece into her ample bosom. Consoled the girl in the only way she knew how: plate full of homemade Swiss roll on the coffee table; a nice shot of brandy to warm her up after her ordeal.

'Darling, you gotta be more clued up when you're out. Know what I mean?' she said, kissing the top of George's head, eyeing Letitia as she tried to perch those pig's trotters on her daughter's thighs yet again. 'Your line of work attracts nutters, yeah? You're supposed to have street smarts. I think you're going soft, all that living in Cambridge with the posh white people.'

'B-but this wasn't a nutter. I was sure h-he was going to kill me.' George hiccoughed. 'I thought he was that Jack Frost, but it turned out it was—'

'Danny,' Letitia said, finally sitting up and lighting a cigarette, eyes narrowed, nodding as if she knew the way the world worked better than anyone. 'Danny bloody Spencer finally catching up with you, girl.'

George shook her head. 'No! Are you not listening?'

'Thought you was dying,' Sharon said to Letitia, standing to locate a clean ashtray for her sister. 'You shouldn't be smoking if you're that ill.' She wafted the blue-yellow cloud away, unable to open the window because of the cold outside. Yellowing nicotined condensation poured down the panes.

Letitia the Dragon blew smoke through her nose onto George's hair. Flick, flick with her ash that missed an ashtray the size of her dinner plate. Almost like clicking her fingers, since she knew her younger sister would come running to wipe up.

The air crackled with tension, but Sharon remembered this was George's spotlight moment in the ongoing Williams-May family drama.

'Go on, love. Tell us about the man. We're listening, babe.'

George shook her head. 'It wasn't an ex-convict or anything.' She wiped her eyes and blew her nose loudly on the tissues Sharon offered her. 'It was this academic from UCL. Professor Screw Loose Dobkin. Guy's a twat. He grabbed me from behind.'

Sharon sucked her teeth. 'Cheeky fucking rarseclart. What about that, eh? What did he want?'

'I hope you kicked him in the bollocks,' Letitia said, then inhaled sharply so that the end of her cigarette glowed brightly in the murk of the room.

'Yeah,' George said. Tears stemmed, now. She sniffed and shook her hair out regally. 'I bit his skanky hand too and threw him like a fucking ninja. Right on his arse in the snow. Then, I punched him in the ear with my phone. He had horrible ears, man. Hair coming out of them and everything.' She started to chuckle.

Letitia nodded sagely, full of 'that's my girl' platitudes.

But Sharon was at pains lay claim to some of that fighter's instinct in her niece. Hadn't she been the girl's surrogate mother getting on for six years now? She made sure she laughed louder and harder than that presumptuous fatty boom, her big sis.

'Sounds like you give as good as you got, darling,' she said, plonking herself on the sofa between George and her mother. 'What did he want then?'

'We ended up going for a coffee, would you believe it? Me, half strangled and him all mashed up from my right hook.'

George took a cigarette out of her mother's packet and lit up – rejecting the Swiss roll, Sharon noted. Her heart sunk like a bad sponge mix.

'So, turns out, this Dobkin twat thinks I paid someone to steal his research, right?' George exhaled. She looked pointedly at her aunt and mother. 'Remember how I got my laptop and USB stick taken from my room in Cambridge?'

'Yeah. I fucking remember,' Letitia said. 'You nicked my bingo winnings to pay that blackmailing homeless skank what keeps coming after you for money, like you're some cash machine.'

'I didn't nick them. I borrowed them.' George pursed her lips and glared at her mother, hand in the air in faux horror. 'Cos God forbid you should help your daughter in a tight spot.'

With a degree of satisfaction, Sharon swiped the uneaten Swiss roll and listened to the story unfold. George's voice was hoarse from crying.

'So, turns out, this Dobkin has had his *entire* research nicked a month ago. He's been working on a trafficking project that sounded almost identical to mine.'

'Maybe he's been pinching your ideas,' Letitia suggested.

George shook her head. 'Sometimes duplications like this can happen and it means whoever gets their paper published first renders the other academic's work useless. It's a bloody nightmare. You can lose years just by being pipped to the post.' She sniffed and stubbed her cigarette out. She spotted the fast-disappearing cake and looked apologetically at her aunt. 'I was going to eat that, you know.' She squeezed Sharon's hand. 'You're the best baker in the world.'

Sharon felt heat creep into her cheeks and grinned, just as her sister's mouth curled downwards like a stale sandwich. 'Go on, love. Was it the homeless bird what nicked his stuff, like what happened with you?'

Shaking her head, George chewed her lip. Sighed. 'A bloke, apparently. Dobkin said there was a student eyewitness, clocked this guy running away from the office – one of those old houses around the little park by UCL. A lot of the academics have got rooms there. But get this!' She leaned forwards, a gleam of intrigue in her eye. 'The student described the thief to the police as looking like a roughsleeper.'

'So, was this homeless guy just after money, like the bird?' Sharon asked.

'No. Apparently not. Nobody's been back and tried to extort cash out of Dobkin.' George smiled ruefully and touched her neck. 'Dobkin's got a grip on him, even though I put him down. Terrible breath too. He could have taken out a burglar with his breath alone!'

Letitia pulled an old blanket around her knees defensively. 'What did Dobbins have that you didn't, then? How comes just you got fleeced for money?'

George turned to her mother. That gleam of intrigue looked suddenly like a fire had started somewhere inside the girl. 'Dobkin has been sleuthing on the side for years, acting as a decoy in online chatrooms where paedos hang out – international ones, as well as British – trying to lure them into revealing shit about the big players in these huge underground networks. Over the years, he's built a database with the names of sex offenders, child pornographers and child traffickers that the police wouldn't touch. Maybe because there were some pretty fucking big and powerful names on his list. He wasn't just doing research ...'

Sharon set the half-eaten Swiss roll down in silence, rapt with attention as her niece spoke.

'... he was planning an exposé in *The Times*. Dobkin was going to blow the lid off the whole shitty shebang, just as his research was stolen.'

'By a homeless man,' Sharon said, her curiosity piqued. She fingered her locket. 'And yours by a homeless woman, right? That's gotta be more than just coincidence.'

CHAPTER 28

A village South of Amsterdam, 4 August, the previous year

'Do you think you could get out of bed at some point this week and do some work?' Gabi asked, teeth clenched, as she looked at the recumbent form of her husband beneath the duvet, sleeping like the dead, almost around the clock.

Piet groaned. He shifted slightly, farted, rolled over and looked at her with an alarming directness. The sight of his haggard, stubbled face, that dimpled chin and those weak lips, continually on the point of trembling. Puffy eyes, perpetually red from self-indulgent tears.

'I can't, Gabi,' he said quietly. 'I'm ill.'

'You're not ill, for God's sake.'

'My stomach's still raw. I'm in agony.'

'Self-inflicted! Nobody asked you to overdose, did they? What they did ... what *I* did ... was ask you to be strong. To hold it together. And did you? Or did you stuff tablets down your gullet as a cry for help?' She approached the bed. She could smell his unwashed body, sickly breath, greasy hair, sweat. 'Our children are missing, and all you can do is seek attention!'

He pulled the duvet tighter to his chin and closed his eyes in answer.

'The bills need paying,' she continued, dragging the duvet down, forcing him to acknowledge she was standing there, though it pained her to look into those bloodshot eyes. 'I've got to go into the bank today and beg them not to foreclose on the car loan.' She flung a pile of opened, white envelopes onto the bed. 'Bills, Pieter. Utilities. All overdue. My shitty charity salary won't pay for this all on its own.'

Piet threw the duvet off suddenly, as if in defiance, revealing his naked body. His face twisted with emotion; he festered with resentment or anger or whatever else he clearly thought he was entitled to feel.

'I don't give a shit about your car,' he said. 'It was your bright idea to set up the Josh and Lucy fund. There must be nearly €200,000 sitting in it by now. People are throwing money at us. Can't you ask the trustees for a handout to keep us going? They're all your bloody cronies anyway.'

He pushed past her, beat a path to the en suite and slammed the door.

'It's for them!' she shouted. 'Someone's got to pay for the PR campaign. Marketing and advertising and all that stuff doesn't come for free, you know.'

His bitter voice emanated from behind the closed door, possibly stripping the paint on the other side. 'PR! PR, this. Advertising, that. You've turned our kids into a portfolio-building opportunity.'

Anger burned inside her with a scorching incandescence. She pushed the door open abruptly.

'Everyone on the continent is looking for our children, thanks to me.' She poked herself hard in the chest. She marched over to the television, flicked through the stations until she found a news programme and forced a satisfied smile when photos of Josh and Lucy popped up onto the screen. She silently acknowledged the crippling ache in her heart at the sight of those children she had grown inside her body and nurtured into toddlerhood. The twin-centres of her world feeling like they were spinning satellites lost on the dark side of the universe; a lifetime away now. 'See?' she said. 'International news. How else do you think we're going to find them?'

Piet, enthroned on the toilet, looking fragile and crumpled, like a ruined king, picked up a toilet roll and flung it at Gabi's head.

'It's been ten weeks!' he yelled. 'We've got nothing. Absolute zero, you self-serving, blinkered bitch.'

Cranking the volume all the way up, Gabi tried to drown out her husband's defeatism. She sat down at the stool in front of her mirrored dressing table, switched on the elegant porcelain lamp and sprayed perfume on herself to dispel the funk of Piet's spending day and night in denial that summer and fresh air ever existed.

'I can't hear you, and frankly, I'm not interested in anything you have to say, Piet Deenen.' She had one ear on the television report, admiring and approving of the gravitas that the rich-voiced presenter added to the latest developments in the case:

'Sightings of the Deenen children have consistently pointed the finger of suspicion at the Roma camps that litter Dutch suburbs, and even the countryside. The Chief of Police, Jaap Hasselblad, has remarked that the Albanian and Romanian Roma setting up camps around Amsterdam, where they beg and target tourists in particular as easy victims of pick-pocketing, are a scourge.'

'You're not even listening to me!' Piet shouted, flushing the toilet. 'I'm trying to talk to you about the disability allowance and ...'

But no, Gabi wasn't listening. She was focussed on the TV screen, feeling where she should slide the pins into the back of her blonde curls to tame them as befitted a trip to see the bank manager, proud of the national fervour she had inspired with her efforts. And there was the montage of photos of Josh and Lucy, together with snippets of happy holiday film that her colleagues in London had so professionally, so slickly, put together. A heart-rending appeal.

Whilst she listened to public opinion, she applied her moisturiser. A retired bus driver from Amstelveen spoke with passion.

'Everyone knows the gypsies snatch our blond children. Didn't they find that little girl in Greece a couple of years ago?'

A woman who worked in Duty Free at Schiphol Airport beamed down the lens of the camera, clearly delighted to give her opinion.

'Kids don't just disappear, though. Do they? I mean, I know where my kids are 24/7. Why didn't that Gabi Deenen? What kind of sub-standard mother is she?'

Gabi felt the blood drain away from her lips. The room felt suddenly too small, the strong scent of her perfume cloying and suffocating. She could see the sneering disapproval in that overly made-up woman's face. She had seen tight lips and accusatory eyes in the supermarket. She swallowed hard and switched the TV off.

Piet was cocooned in bed once more. 'See? This is what more publicity gets you, Gabi. Heat. Hate. And a pile of propagandist bullshit about gypsies. But no kids!'

'They'll find my babies,' she said almost inaudibly. Feeling tears track along the lower rims of her eyes, she hoped they wouldn't fall and ruin her freshly applied mascara.

She stood slowly, her movements measured, seeing her Twitter feed scroll down in her mind's eye: an outpouring of national grief; an unfurling of love and support like a blooming hothouse flower – artificially cultivated and nourished by the rich, frequent supply of heartbreak, hysteria and mawkish photographic evidence that two perfect, blond tots ever existed. But carried on this rising tide of love were poisonous spores of mistrust and harsh judgement. Feeding the trolls.

Gabi blinked those thoughts away.

'I'm going to the bank. Then I'm going into the office.'

In town, she carried her sense of loss around like a hidden, malignant tumour. People were staring, but they didn't see how grief ingested her. They kept their distance, though she could still hear the indistinctive chummer, chummer of small town rumour on the wind.

Ignore them, she told herself.

She approached the counter inside the bank with an optimistic smile and braced herself for the warmth and fiscal understanding that would undoubtedly envelop her.

'Sadly, Mrs Deenen, your children have nothing to do with the bank's policy on defaulting,' the dispassionate, lard-faced manager said.

His name tag told her he was Dr Joost Bregman. Pockmarks in his cheeks – the scars of teenaged acne – put Gabi in mind of Leerdammer cheese. What sort of charmless underachiever studied for years and years at university to become the manager of a village high street branch of a poxy bank?

'For Christ's sake! Have you no heart?' Under her breath, she said, 'My husband's having mental health issues. He's self-employed. If he can't work ...'

'Can you sell the car? Didn't you secure the loan to pay for a—' He looked down at a sheaf of notes, printed out from some database that probably told him which breakfast cereal she preferred. 'Volkswagen Touareg. Nice car. Do you need such a nice car?'

At that point Gabi wished the malignancy inside her would stop her heart and end this pain and humiliation.

But wait. That was how Piet thought, too ready to throw in the towel. The kids needed her to be strong.

'I'll get your money,' she said. *Just say the words in a convincing way. Smile. Bat your eyelashes. You have friends who will help you.* 'Next week.'

'Please see that you do, Mrs Deenen. My hands are tied, you see.'

As she emerged from the bank onto the pristine cobbles of the village high street, she caught sight of the electrical shop opposite. Huge flatscreen TVs sat in the window, next to vacuum cleaners and washing machines, cake mixers, irons and a cornucopia of appliances to help every Dutch housewife in this Amsterdam backwater lead a life not far removed from that enjoyed by women in the 1950s. Wholesome. Easy. Less labour-intensive. The sign in the window in gold lettering said this was a family-owned business since 1956. Everything with a plug under one roof.

But it was not the seasonal 30% reduction or 0% APR that drew her gaze to the flickering screen of the Panasonic HDTV. It was the sight of the detective heading-up the investigation. In impressively high definition, he was standing in a field in the middle of the good, green, flat land.

Two older women had also stopped in front of the window beside Gabi. Respectable parishioners, idling the morning away with coffee and cake from de Vries bakery and patrolling the high street on the lookout for gossip, as though it might be left unattended, like a suspicious package or abandoned bag. And here that gossip was, in the form of Gabi Deenen. *The English woman – you know?! That one with the neglected kids.*

They were pointing at the soundless footage and talking animatedly. Noticing Gabi drawing ever closer at their side they nudged each other.

'What do you think? It's her! She's hanging around the village with her make-up on. Why isn't she out looking for her children?'

Ignoring the judgemental subtext that hung heavy in the air, Gabi stood, almost with her nose pressed against the glass. Looking at the news footage of that Chief Inspector. Wearing overshoes and giving orders, it seemed, to officers in frog-suits and some who wore waders up to their waists. They were standing in the watery artery that bisected the too green field, like water boatmen, skimming the surface to see what lay beneath.

'What's going on?' Gabi asked the women.

One looked at her askance. The other had something akin to bitterness etched into her hatchet-face.

'Haven't you heard?' Hatchet-face asked, eyeing her up and down like a photocopier light, capturing every detail to reproduce faithfully for easy redistribution amongst other information seekers. 'They're dredging the canal that runs through the polder near that disgraceful gypo encampment.'

Gabi gasped. She scrutinised the TV screen to see if she recognised that field – that wide, grey stripe of water with the slowly turning wind turbine in the background.

'You should know this, shouldn't you?' the woman said, reaching into her shopping bag. 'They're your bloody children the cops think are dead at the bottom of that canal.' An unpleasant glint in her septuagenarian eye. 'But then, why would you? You lost those babies in the first place, you evil English whore.'

The woman withdrew from her shopping bag a large brown egg. Gabi had no time even to fathom what she might be doing with the smooth egg in her wrinkled hand before it hit the side of her face, oozing down onto her work suit. A snotty, yellow mess covering her broken heart.

CHAPTER 29

Amsterdam, Oud West district, 12 August, the previous year

'Is the dress for a special little girl?' the shop assistant asked, beaming at him.

Clearly she hadn't recognised his face. She wrapped the little pink party dress in pristine white tissue paper. The dress was so small, it folded over only once and would still fit inside the crisp card bag.

'Yes. It's for my daughter,' Piet said, touching the tiny raspberry velvet bodice before it was hidden from view in the upmarket packaging. €60 but worth it for Lucy. Smart new summer sandals for Josh too, now that his feet were growing. Dinosaurs on the straps, no less. 'And the sandals for my boy. He'll love them. He outgrows his shoes every five minutes!'

The assistant rang the sale through using Piet's credit card. Still full of smiles for this clearly doting dad, out on a shopping spree for his little darlings. Strange, only in that he seemed to be wearing pyjamas and slippers beneath his denim jacket. But otherwise he'd made it past the gatekeeper on the door in this exclusive boutique. Walk in like you belonged there. That was the key.

When her smile faltered, he knew things were about to go wrong.

'I'm sorry, sir,' she said, her finely plucked eyebrows gathering together in apparent consternation. 'There seems to be a problem with your card.' She handed his card back. Bright smiles once more. 'Have you got another method of payment?'

He tapped his pockets, as though he were making a genuine effort to pluck a card from some forgotten hidey-hole in his jacket. He started to back away from the cash desk.

'Sir, shall I put it behind the counter for you?'

He turned quickly and walked away.

Two women with pushchairs recognized him on the way out. They were pointing, nudging, nodding, tittle-tattling that he was the one from the television. The man from the newspapers. The one who had lost his kids. Shit Dad. Irresponsible husband. Loser.

'Move!' he shouted to another shop assistant who was now standing between him and the door. He could feel the walls drawing in on him, like curtains closing on a theatre scene. Threatening to swallow him. But he was still in the spotlight. Too bright. Too bright. Faces turned to scrutinize him in that bastion of appearances-mattering, with its neatly folded, colour-coordinated jumpers and novelty ranges of children's wear. 'Get out of my damned way!' He pushed an elderly woman aside and stepped out into the fresh air.

Breathe. Breathe deeply. He leaned forwards and clutched his knees. In and out through his nostrils. Heartbeat slowing. Back on Pieter Cornelisz Hoofstraat, where Tiffany & Co. tipped the wink to Tommy Hilfiger and Dior that everything was fine, here. The beautifully renovated three- and four-storey houses that were now home to Louis Vuitton and pals were going to shelter him from the ugliness in the world. Here he was, just a regular man, pushing the boat out for his exemplary family amongst the tanned and toned patricians of Amsterdam.

'You can't sit here, sir,' a doorman said. He emerged from his perfumed and air-conditioned haven with its buzzer-entry door, looking like an upmarket bouncer, and grabbed him by the lapels of his jacket. 'Not on the step. Move it elsewhere, pal.'

'I felt funny,' Piet said. Looking round, bewildered. 'I'm fine now.' He pushed the brute away.

His phone started to ring, but there, at last, he had spotted Lucy and Josh. Shopping with some woman he didn't recognise. Lucy in a Bugaboo pushchair. Josh at the side, walking like a big boy.

'Ah, at last!' he cried. 'There you are, you little monkeys!'

The woman was walking away from him now. Her back turned to him. The children had not seen him. He started to run, ignoring the phone. That could wait. When Gabi found out he'd found the kids at long last, she'd be overjoyed!

'Lucy! Josh!' He was shouting now. People were looking at him askance, as he pelted down the street after his children. Twenty paces away. Ten. Josh's hair had started to grow. But it was definitely him, with those sturdy little legs. Except he was narrow in the hips. No nappy peeping out the top of his camouflage-patterned shorts.

'Josh!' he reached out to touch his boy on the shoulder.

The boy yelped and looked around. Angry little face. Not Josh's. The woman had swung around too, revealing the small girl in the Bugaboo. So like Lucy. But not Lucy.

'Do I know you?' she asked. Hard eyes and a grimace on her immaculately made-up face said she was unimpressed by this interloper touching her son. Handbag at the ready, like a weapon.

'Sorry.' Piet felt the sorrow pushing upwards in his throat, constricting everything, an anguished ache in the glands beneath his ears that quickly crippled his entire body. 'I thought you were somebody else.'

And the phone was still ringing. Gabi's photo was on the screen, insistent that he should pick-up. The tears made it difficult to speak. The ice in his stomach made it impossible to stand. He sat down in the middle of that grand street, with its temples to consumerism, where the tables were never overturned.

'Piet! Where the hell are you? I've been waiting for twenty minutes. I'm starting the interview without you.' No pause for breath. Gabi was on a roll. She didn't need him anyway. He knew where he was going.

An hour later, he had driven to the canal that the police had dredged only days earlier to no avail. He stood and peered at his fractured reflection in the dank, still water. Maybe his babies were in there, entangled in some weeds growing on the bed. Maybe they weren't. But he needed to sleep. He needed respite. And that overgrown bed of forgetful silt with its blanket of sluggish, dark water seemed as good a place to lie quietly as any other.

'Let's just start without him,' Gabi said, turning to the journalist with a half-smile.

She felt suddenly alone and exposed inside this pub – dismal, silent, all but empty, apart from a surly-looking landlord who was wiping glasses clean with a filthy rag. It was hardly surprising they were the only customers inside, given the glorious sunshine. The cobbled pavement directly outside was still festooned with tourists who looked like bunting, dressed in colourful Hawaiian shirts and sun dresses. Soaking up Amsterdam's cosmopolitan vibe, they sank beer after beer until the flimsy stainless-steel tables groaned under the weight of different-shaped beer glasses. Cherry beer. Trappist ale. Duvel was your date with the devil. Hoegaarden with a lemony twist. Not a care in the bloody world, those nauseatingly chipper Americans and photo-frenzied, deferential Japanese.

'Are you okay?' the journalist asked. He touched her upper arm briefly. A caring gesture. 'You look nervous. Honestly, you don't have to be nervous. We're just chatting.'

'I'm fine,' Gabi said, blinking away the thought of Piet on the other end of the phone before he had cut her off. Who knew where he was or what he was doing? He was a liability. She had lost two children and gained a third.

The journalist clicked on his voice recorder and smiled blankly as he set it on the table between them. His twinkling, inquisitive blue eyes were impervious to the suffering of others, she could tell. Just chatting. Gabi knew journalists better. They never just chatted. He was after his story and that was that. But she needed all the publicity she could get.

'How does it feel to know all the leads from your big campaign have come to nothing?' he asked.

Somewhere inside her, her pride – patched up so regularly of late like an old cycle inner tube, beset by unforgiving road surfaces – was punctured. She felt herself deflate until she had to lay her hands on the sticky table or else risk collapse.

Sit up straight. Show him no weakness, you idiot.

'It's devastating, obviously,' she said, willing her voice to remain even and strong. 'The Chief of Police was convinced the gypsies were involved, but—'

'What do you say to the accusations on social media that you've deliberately steered the investigation towards the Roma to deflect attention from you and your husband?' He was a smiling assassin, teeth bared, ready to go in for the kill. They all were now.

Gabi paused. She visualised the tweets that plagued her the moment she opened her eyes in the morning to the moment she closed them at night. Sometimes even pushing memories of Lucy and Josh out of her mind. Hate-soaked vitriol and misogyny, trending on Twitter. Never for Piet. Always for her.

@Gabi_Deenen You killed your fucking kids. You deserve to die, heartless bitch. #KillingDeenens #infanticide

Why pick on the Roma? Because they're easy scapegoats! @Volkskrant #racism #FindTheDeenens

Gabi Deenen cares more about money & fame than finding her children. @ADnl @telegraaf #BadMothers #FindTheDeenens

'I can't control how the public perceives us,' she said. She looked down at her fingernails, and strove to hide the chipped polish by shoving her hands beneath her thighs. 'I'm only concerned with finding my children.'

The journalist drained the dregs from his espresso. 'But it's true, isn't it? That you are the driving force behind the PR campaign, and that includes the telephone hotline for witnesses to report sightings. Which the police are using as a basis for their investigation. That's a conflict of interest, right? You could potentially influence—'

'No! I couldn't bloody influence anything!' she shouted. She leaned in to this young interrogator, poking him on the shoulder. 'I had a big career in PR. I know how to drum up public support. If people forget about us, they forget to look for Lucy and Josh, you damned—'

'Have you run out of money, Gabi?' The journalist sat back in his threadbare seat, put his right foot onto his left knee and his hands behind his head. He glanced down at the recorder.

This wasn't supposed to be that kind of interview. Staring down at her half-drunk coffee, Gabi felt confusion roll in like bad weather.

Consider your answer. Don't snap back. That's what he wants you to do. It's cat and mouse.

'Why are you attacking me?' she asked.

'I'm not,' he said. 'It's just we've had a few close family friends speak to us in confidence.' He opened his palms outwards, as if showing her quite how transparent and honest he was. Fucking snake. 'And they've told us about your financial difficulties. You know? Your personal cash-flow problems.'

'What has that got to do with you?' she asked, folding her arms. Feeling her neat bun too tight against her scalp. 'That hasn't the slightest bearing on this—'

'Is it true you were trying to get Josh diagnosed as having Asperger's in the hope of getting disability payouts?'

181

'I beg your pardon.' Blinking hard, as if she could somehow scratch him from her vision with her eyelashes alone. *Should I leave? Will it make me look worse? Could I threaten him?* 'This is slander!'

'No. It's not slander,' the journalist said, producing an official-looking report, printed on headed paper. 'I have a copy of the paediatrician's report concerning Josh, his condition and how you and Piet as parents were coping with it.'

Gabi made to snatch the paperwork out of the man's hand. 'Where the hell did you get that?!'

'I don't have to reveal my sources.'

'Oh, you bloody well do if the information's confidential.' She narrowed her eyes, scrutinising his cock-sure behaviour as he slid the papers back into his man bag with steady hands, nothing given away by his rictus grin beyond smugness. Never one for reading the subtleties of people's body language correctly, she tried to decide what his was telling her. Piet would know. He had always been the more intuitive of the two. 'I don't believe you. You're bluffing!'

Keep it together, Gabi. You're a professional. But her heart was beating too fast like an overwound clock. Sweat poured down her back, her palms ice cold and clammy. She was unused to listening to its prompts. *Get out of here. Get away from this creep. You're digging a hole.*

'I'm going,' she said, standing abruptly so that the battered table between them rocked, spilling what was left of her drink. She reached out and clicked off the recorder. 'You print any of that in your tabloid rag, I'll sue you so fast it'll knock that super-cilious grin off your coked-up face.'

Outside, her bottom lip trembled. Her hands shook. The canal-side drinkers were an attentive audience, more than just a flicker of recognition on the Dutch faces. Nudging. Tipping each other the wink. There's that woman. There's the terrible mother. Gabi Deenen. Nation's Number One Bitch. Though mercifully, at least those dressed in the bright colours of tourists paid her no heed.

Just walk. Walk quickly. Find that bloody idiot you're married to and go home, for god's sake.

Smoothing down her skirt, she made her way on legs made from jelly towards the smart street where Piet had been shopping. 'For a surprise,' he'd said. And now, he was missing too.

She took out her phone, poised to dial her husband. She jumped when it rang in her hand unexpectedly, showing the name of the Chief Inspector in charge of the case.

'Yes?' she said, willing the swell of tears to break without causing a splash.

'I need you to come down to the station, Gabi.' His rich, deep voice sounded tinged with something else, though the nature of it was just beyond her grasp.

'Do I have to? Only, I seem to have mislaid Piet and I must find him. You should never let men go shopping on their own.' She giggled, putting on a show of confidence, ignoring the gnawing sensation in her gut.

'I'm afraid you do,' the policeman said. 'Social services would like to have a word with you both.'

There was that sensation in her chest again. An over-wound clock, except now, she felt as though the seconds hand was jammed, flicking back and forth, back and forth over the same number. She wanted to run. Run away from this unending nightmare. Run to her children.

'Nothing serious, I hope,' she said. Giggling again.

'Just come straight down to the station, Gabi. Now, please.'

CHAPTER 30

Amsterdam, police headquarters, later

'Why are you bringing this up, for god's sake? It was an accident!' Gabi appraised the row of judgemental eyes before her: one set of steely-grey, partially obscured behind the smudged lenses of reading glasses that hung from a chain; one set, dark and inquisitive, impossible to interpret; one set of blue with watery irises. Sympathetic-looking, maybe; another pair of brightest blue – the pair staring at her, right now – felt like a borehole being sunk into her to see what comprised the hidden strata of her soul.

The woman who owned the hard blue stare poked at her paperwork with a biro, a ring on almost every finger and cheap, polyester clothing. She needed to eat less, do more and shop elsewhere, Gabi assessed. Name badge said Wilhemina van den Broek was something big in child protection. There was that gut-wrenching, icy feeling in the pit of her stomach again. Wilhemina van den Broek was bad news.

'You took your son to A&E on the 24th April this year,' she said. Her thin lips clicked together as though they were magnetised, forming an unyielding straight line.

'Did I?' Gabi asked. The memory of cradling a screaming Josh in her arms, of trying to contain his flailing body in the A&E waiting room jabbed at her.

'With a fractured arm.' Wilhemina had all the details, it seemed. 'Oh, yes. Poor Joshy. He was beside himself.'

Eyes down, scanning the notes, the social worker read out dated entries in a voice that had just too sharp an edge to it to be a monotone. The police and the criminologist on the other side of the table merely looked on in silence.

'It seems you've visited A&E with your son rather a lot. Head injuries. Bad bruising. Sometimes injuries to your daughter, Lucy too. And I've had notes emailed over from London's King's College Hospital ...' Wilhemina produced another sheaf of A4 '... that show this pattern in the UK, too.'

Gabi folded her arms, and crossed her legs, wishing Piet were there as moral support, even if he would just sit there like a mute while she did all the talking. 'You know my son has Asperger's, don't you?' she said.

'That doesn't explain these injuries.'

'Oh, but it does.' Gabi sat up straight, willing herself to hold this judgemental monster's gaze. 'Do you know how difficult it is to raise a child on the Autistic spectrum, Ms Van den Broek?'

'Did you break his arm, Gabi?'

'How dare you!' She looked over at the Chief Inspector, who was sitting with his hands on his stomach, head cocked to one side in non-committal contemplation. Was he an ally or a foe? 'Are you going to let this happen?' she asked him, looking at the two younger women. The red head and the black girl. 'You know I can't have anything to do with such bullshit! I told you about my Josh and his problems. His anger. His fearlessness. The fighting. And you're letting this polyester-wrapped blimp insinuate that I've abused my own children?'

'Well, have you?' the social worker asked, eyebrow raised as if she were awaiting full and heartfelt disclosure that the Deenens were child-beaters.

Gabi felt her brain trying to disengage from her mouth. She was aware of anger trying to sear through the veneer of cool professionalism that had taken years to harden to a point where it was both opaque and unyielding. 'My son pulled the television on himself from the top of the TV cabinet because he was frustrated that I had called time on his jigsaw puzzle at 7 p.m. He's strong. He's determined. He has absolutely no understanding of physical danger or consequences, which is probably why he was lured away by a stranger. You. Unfeeling. Patronising. Cow.' Drumming her nails on the table for emphasis.

'I'm not—'

'All I want to do is find my children and bring them home safe. You speak to Josh's paediatrician. You get references from my doctor. My employers. Any professional you like. You see then if I strike you as a bloody abuser of children.'

Wilhemina van den Broek blanched. 'It's my job to—'

'It's your job to what? Conduct a witch-hunt? Who put you up to this?'

Gabi looked at the social worker, who in turn looked pointedly at the three others in the room. All suddenly examined their knees or doodled in pads, clearly not wanting any part in this farce.

The social worker bitch spoke, jowls wobbling, scratching at a nervous rash at the base of her bull neck. 'Commissioner Kamphuis felt certain that child protection services should—'

'The Commissioner?'

'Okay. Enough,' the Chief Inspector said, removing his glasses. 'I think Mrs Deenen has answered all your questions for now, Wil.' He rose from his seat, towering above them all like a judge presiding over court proceedings. He ushered Gabi into the hallway and beckoned that the young criminologist should follow them. 'Come with me,' he said.

Wondering. Wondering. Wandering through those sterile police headquarters. Gabi was Alice, trapped on the wrong side of the looking glass. A bad trip. Falling, falling down the rabbit hole where her children may or may not lie broken at the bottom.

'I can't find Piet,' she told the criminologist. 'My husband. He's not answering his phone. I'm getting worried. He's not—'

'Come on. Let's get you a coffee and we'll talk,' the girl said, Gabi noting how she carefully stepped into the middle of each individual carpet tile without breaching any joints. 'Take no notice of Wilhemina, by the way. She's one of the Commissioner's kiss-arses. I can see what's happening here.'

Inside the austere office, empty of decoration but for an orchid plant, Gabi took a seat opposite the Chief Inspector, the crimi-nologist at her side. She felt somewhat calmer in here, but only marginally so. The spectre of the journalist she had met in the pub lurked still. A scavenger circling the car-crash carrion of her life. Some dirt wouldn't wash out.

'You think I did it, don't you?' She searched the Chief Inspector's angular face for the truth. Found only flinty enigma there, but perhaps a flicker of warmth in those grey eyes. 'I've had some journalist accusing me of foul play because I can't make my car repayments. Everyone's trying to use Josh's problems as a stick to beat me with. What happened to the gypsies?' Turning to the criminologist in the hope that she would offer some measure of hope where all hope had been lost.

The girl toyed with one of her curls and bit her lip. 'You and your missing children have ended up political pawns, I'm afraid,' she said. 'The Chief of Police is desperate for the glory of finding Lucy and Josh, so he's responded with a knee-jerk reaction to the sitings and theories that the phone-ins have thrown up. Every Tom, Dick and Harry has an opinion. Perverts. Paedos. Gypsies. Paul, here, has been haring down blind alleys for weeks and there's still no trace of your kids.'

'I've made it all ten times worse, haven't I?' Gabi felt tears brimming in her eyes, then overflowing onto her pale-pink silk blouse, like a rain-soaked rose petal.

The criminologist shook her head. Nodded. She shook her head again, then shrugged. 'Without it, you wouldn't have had every pair of eyes on the continent on the lookout for Lucy and Josh. But now …'

'Everyone thinks I did it. No bodies, so maybe I took my own kids, killed them and made them disappear. Am I right?' She sobbed into a child's novelty tissue that she found at the bottom of her handbag. *Sesamstraat*-themed. A pack she'd bought for Lucy when she had had that stinking summer cold in May. Tiny nose, permanently runny. That was before the world had ended. She held the tissue to her chest. 'What have I done to deserve this? God hates me, doesn't he? Everything I love gets taken away. My parents. My reputation. My babies, for Christ's sake.'

The Chief Inspector shifted his position behind his desk and stopped doodling absently in his pad. He sniffed. '*I* don't think you did it. George, here, doesn't think you did it. Only my superior, Commissioner Kamphuis, wants to look into that possibility. And I couldn't speculate as to whether he's a dick or not, because that would be disloyal and unprofessional of me. But me and George … we believe we're dealing with an international criminal network. There's a possible connection to people traffickers in Italy and Germany. England too.'

The criminologist reached out as if to touch Gabi's hand but seemingly thought better of it and went back to arranging paperclips in a perfectly straight line. 'I've read your files cover to cover and I've been to your house,' she said. 'I've visited every suspected crime scene with the investigating team. You're an easy scapegoat for the media. I saw that clip on last night's news, where you took a swing at the paparazzo. You need to dial it down before it becomes a media feeding frenzy. You're a PR woman. You should know the sort of woman the public would fall in love with. Demure. Likeable. Thankful. They don't understand ball-breakers.'

Closing her eyes, Gabi remembered the small man from the gutter press who had buzzed around her at the supermarket like an irritating wasp, snapping away with his camera, his fresh-faced lackey, holding a recorder for her to speak into.

Do you get dolled up for the cameras because you don't care? Is that why you're back at work? Are you glad the kids have gone? Does it free you up to be a career woman instead of a good mother?

She clenched her fist. 'He was lucky I didn't knock him out. I wanted to.'

For the first time in weeks, and certainly for the first time in public, Gabi allowed herself to cry. There was no stopping the tidal wave of grief that drowned out every other salient thought. The words limped out after at least five minutes of unintelligible attempts at speech.

'I-I can't take it anymore. I-I can't … I just …' She scratched resentfully at her wet eyes. It was too late for dignity and poise. She was glad. She turned to the criminologist. 'Are you sure it's traffickers?'

The girl's dark eyes widened, backlit by white-hot enthusiasm. 'I've seen this kind of thing before. Eight months ago, two children were abducted by a player in a paedophile ring in Lewisham. Very similar circumstances. I mean, really similar. Kids went missing from their back garden while they were kicking some leaves about.'

'It might just be coincidence,' Gabi said, wrestling with the intolerable notion of her babies being prey to paedophiles and the familiar sinking feeling of heading down yet another blind alley. 'How can you be sure?'

The girl squeezed her arm with a ferocity bordering on pain. 'This is my field of expertise, Gabi.'

CHAPTER 31

London, Westminster, 17 March, present

She was sitting in the Strutton Ground pub with a middle-aged man, far away enough from the Millbank offices to avoid the scrutiny of his colleagues. Maybe that was telling. Through the large window, he could see that her fingers were interlaced through his. A broad smile that showed teeth and gums. She flicked her hair over her shoulder with her free hand. Definite flirtation. When he wasn't checking furtively over his shoulder, her companion was grinning and blushing too. Toying with his wedding ring, now. This was clandestine. They were both vulnerable. Good.

'Time to go home, lovebirds,' the ragged man muttered, as he shifted his painful position behind the industrial-sized wheelie bin that was standing diagonally opposite. Waiting for bin day. Waiting to rid this cobbled street of its Westminster secrets.

The mystery man inside the pub laughed at something, then ran a hand over his thinning hair.

No mystery here, though. He'd done his research. Judging by the photos that had come up on Google image, this was Graham Tokár from the Open Society Foundation. Also a possible target, until he had weighed up the fact that the man was half-Hungarian and might not speak the language of the gypsies which would need to be the case if he was to be interrogated. Plus, there was the fact that he was physically big. Even though the homeless assassin was now packing a gun, given the amount of travelling they would have to do together, taking a man hostage was logistically risky.

'You'll do me just fine,' he told himself, as he observed Sophie Bartek.

Drip, drip, drip, onto his shoulders as the icicles above him started to unmake themselves, dissolving finally in the falling sleet that had replaced the snow in the last few hours. Already, the two or three feet drifts had thinned to just over one foot of slush. But cold, still biting its way through his newspaper layers and sodden, filthy clothes. Feet, numb, blistered, frostbitten. At least he could still walk in the boots the Salvation Army had given him before they had started to ask too many nosey questions.

He shook. Would his aim be true if he needed to use that gun? It had better be. He was a soldier nearing the frontline. It was his duty to stand his ground even in the face of death.

When the couple emerged, putting up umbrellas, he held his breath, praying that they would part company. Bartek would, in theory, be heading up to King's Cross Station to catch the train to Cambridge. Tokár's online presence showed he was registered to an address in Southwark. If the wedding ring was anything to go by, the girl should not be following him home to bunk up in a cosy threesome with his wife.

The two stumbled into Old Pye Street, the canopies of their umbrellas twirling and clashing in a mating ritual of sorts. Forbidden courtship, where only the residents of the Peabody Trust flats might peer down on them. Kissing flirtatiously, then, passionately. Giggling, as though they had the world at their feet and no hounds at their heels.

'Come on, for fuck's sake,' he muttered, hanging back in St

Matthew Street, only three or four metres away. Watching. Tired of waiting. Feeling the weapon in his pocket.

'I'm cold,' she said. 'This was wonderful.' Held his free hand, pushed away, then pulled herself closer still. Two plumes of hot breath, steaming on the sleet-filled air.

'Stay,' he said, hooking her hair behind her ear. 'She's away on business.' Those words within earshot quickly became something more suggestive that only the intended recipient could hear.

Giggling.

'I can't. Not tonight. I've got to go. Look. We'll do this again.' She checked her watch under the streetlight. 'I'll miss my train.'

The two parted company on Victoria Street amid the perennial throng of snowboot-clad tourists and workers heading home after the pub. Embracing stiffly in public, as though they were only friends with no benefits whatsoever, Tokár disappeared off in the direction of Westminster. Bartek was poised to cross the busy street, no doubt aiming for St. James's tube station.

Now was his chance.

'Don't cross if you want to live,' he said, pressing the barrel of the gun into her kidney.

Sophie Bartek looked around at him. Dazzling green eyes stricken by fear.

'Take my bag,' she said. 'I've got cash. I've got cards. You want to get warm and fed, right? Take it!'

'Don't make assumptions,' he said. 'And don't make a fucking sound. We're going on a little trip.'

The walk up to Charing Cross was one of the most nerve-wracking duties he had had to perform. She just wouldn't stop talking.

'I can help you get shelter for the night,' she said. 'There's no need to resort to violence, dude.'

Kept eyeballing him, though he had pressed the gun harder into her side and told her to look dead ahead.

'You need to see a doctor. You've got some septic shit going on with your face. Seriously. And your fingers, man. You've got bad frostbite. Why don't we go to the walk-in centre? They might be still open. I won't tell them.'

Why did she have to be so bloody nice?

'Shut your mouth, for god's sake,' he said. 'Let's just get on the train. I'll explain what I want you to do there.'

All the way to Sittingbourne, she persisted in shooting him nervous glances. Caring glances. Fixing him with those spell-binding green eyes that gave a glimpse, through their glacial translucence, of the kind soul that dwelled inside this woman. She would be hard to kill.

'Keep looking ahead. You do as I say and you'll be fine,' he said.

'Where are you from?' she asked, peering at the white water-marks on the uppers of his oversized boots.

'It's where you're from that matters. You're Slovakian, aren't you?'

'My Dad is, yes,' she said, her voice tremulous. 'How do you know?'

'You're from Romani stock?'

'Yes.'

'Good. So you can speak the language of Slovakian Roma?'

The caravans were lined up at the entrance to an industrial estate. White elephants, huddled together in the snow. Even in minus twenty and falling, the encampment reeked of fire and human shit. Deeper snow out here. Fat flakes drifting down to the ground instead of sleet, as though rural Kent had not heard that a thaw was on. He shook violently. Felt cold sweat pouring down his back. Time for more paracetamol, though today's supply was all used up already. Death beckoned, offering sweet release, but he still had work to do. He willed himself to hold the gun firm.

'What are we doing here?' Bartek asked.

Accordion music was coming from a large, brightly lit caravan.

Cigarette smoke rendered the windows almost opaque. Men's voices in happy high spirits. He automatically steered Bartek away from that place.

'I need to speak to an elder,' he said. 'A woman, preferably.'

Bartek surveyed the range of vehicles. 'Go for the quiet ones,' she said. 'The women will be asleep in there with the children.' She turned to him. An accusatory look etched onto her pinched face. 'You're not some kind of racist moron, are you? You're not going to kill them?'

'No. I want information. I can't think of another way of getting it. But you'll help me, if you want to live.'

She swallowed hard and rubbed her mouth. She almost tripped on her long, fringed skirt as they approached a large RV where only one window near the driver's cab was lit. She knocked and said something quickly in a foreign tongue that he didn't recognise.

The door opened to reveal an elderly Roma woman, swaddled in a headscarf, wearing several cardigans one on top of the other like skins of an onion. When she caught sight of the gun, she balked and started prattling panicked words that meant nothing to him. Too loud!

'Tell her to shut the hell up. Get inside the caravan.'

The interior of the RV was pristine. Euro-trash-bling shining surfaces. Mirrored this and that, reflecting mood lighting that came from LED lights concealed behind gold trim. Plush carpet. Pristine pink padded sofas covered in showroom plastic. He felt like he had fallen into a life-sized Barbie's world. The smell of heavy floral air-freshener masked odours of sweat and food. At the far end, little lumpy bundles slept beneath ethnic blankets.

'This your family?' he asked, waving the gun in the direction of a gallery of photos. Mainly boys. Some almost adult. Some small children.

Bartek translated. The old woman nodded, chattering away

194

with a loose, toothless mouth. He began to get nervous that they were plotting against him.

'Can it! I want you to tell me if you've seen these children.' He pulled the crumpled photo from his pocket. Didn't feel anything now.

'They were taken. I'm trying to find them.' He poked the pistol in Bartek's shoulder. 'Tell her. Tell her, I've been given information that they might be here or might have passed through here. That these gypsies might know about the Son of the Eagle.'

Bartek's eyes widened. 'Son of the Eagle.'

'You've heard of him?'

She nodded. She turned to the old woman. 'Shquipëtar.'

A sharp intake of breath. The old woman's collapsed, gnarled face contorted into a snapshot of fear.

'Shquipëtar,' she repeated.

There ensued an exchange between her and Bartek that made him momentarily hopeful that some new piece of information would be revealed.

'What is she saying?' he asked.

'Shh! Let her speak,' Bartek said.

After some time, the woman fell silent. She stood and glanced out of the window. Then spoke again.

Bartek turned to him. 'She says we have to go if we want to live. Gun or no gun, if her sons find you here, you're toast.'

He clutched his coat close, shuddering violently, holding onto the gun as though it was the only anchor he had left in this world. 'Tell me what she said. Then, we'll go. Please. Don't make this your last night on earth.' He swallowed two paracetamol with the spit he had left, his teeth chattering.

Tying her hair into a bun, watched furtively by the old Roma woman, Bartek explained, 'The Seful de Platz – that's the guy who runs this encampment's money-making activities—'

'Like a pimp? Or a godfather?'

'Yes. Exactly. It literally means chief of the square. So, the Seful de Platz has been in cahoots with some British child traffickers that run a child trafficking gig all over Western Europe. This woman knows of a couple of Roma girls – no more than ten or eleven years old – who have been trafficked through this guy. He told them he had work for them as cleaners in hospitals. Turns out they just went missing and ended up on the streets in Berlin. Nobody trusts this fucker, but he rules their encampment like a little Hitler. Any dissention, and they're out of work. No begging. No windscreen washing. No cleaning. No mugging. These guys rely on a supportive network and working on a sanctioned 'patch'. If they disagree with him, they're cut off from the community and any chance of a livelihood.'

The old woman nodded, though she couldn't possibly have known whether Bartek was relating her tale faithfully or not. It sounded believable enough.

'What about the children in the photo and the Son of the Eagle?'

'She hasn't seen these specific children, but the missing Roma kids have apparently been drafted into a paedophile ring that runs out of a hotel in Margate. This is all conjecture, by the way. It's visited by the rich and famous, she says. Politicians, celebrities. That sort of thing. The filthy rich and untouchable.' She shuddered. 'Fucking horrid, but then, the Roma are used to being used and abused like this. That's what comes from being classed as Untermenschen. Do you understand that term? Untermensch?'

He nodded. 'Sub-human. Spare me the social conscience. What's the name of this hotel?'

She repeated the words in the Roma tongue. The old woman's face hardened.

'She doesn't know,' Bartek said, stiffening suddenly.

Voices on the freezing wind. One Roma. One instantly recognisable as South East London.

The old woman spoke rapidly. 'The Seful de Platz is coming. Quickly. We've got to get out of here.'

'Tell her, thank you. Tell her, I'm sorry.'

'There's no fucking time, man. Let's go.'

'How do you know you're safe from me but not from whoever's outside?'

'Instinct, dickhead. Move it!'

They slid out of the caravan, the old woman shutting the door softly behind them. He felt a twinge of guilt that he had subjected her to it, but more he felt irritation that he'd failed to get the name of the Margate hotel.

As they crept together into the deep shadows, he caught sight of the two approaching men making their way towards the rowdy caravan where the accordion music still issued forth, accompanied now by raucous laughter. One short Roma man, middle-aged, dressed in an expensive-looking anorak but still shabby-looking next to the younger man at his side. Tall, built like an athlete, overly groomed features of a mixed-race pop idol visible even with his hood up. Fox-fur-trimmed. The finest parka money could buy.

It was the man with the plan.

No more than ten feet away. Perhaps instinctively, the man with the plan turned towards the shadows where he crouched with a shivering Bartek. And for a split second, the ragged assassin could have sworn that they had locked eyes.

CHAPTER 32

St. John's College, Cambridge, then, Cambridge train station, 18 March

'No, I'm afraid I haven't seen her,' Alf, the porter said, scratching his bald pate.

He turned around and checked the pigeonholes behind him – a beehive of dark wooden boxes, mainly stuffed with post, though some were empty. Uselessly he ran his finger around the pigeonhole labelled Dr Sophie Bartek. 'Pretty sure she's had quite a lot of post this week.' He raised an eyebrow and adjusted his glasses on the end of his nose, as though that might change the view. 'She must have been in recently.'

Amid the hubbub of students filing in and out on George's side of the counter, Alf turned to his identically dressed colleague, policing the act of some tweed-clad man, who smelled strongly of pipe tobacco and mothballs, signing into the visitor's book.

'Dave,' Alf said. 'Dr McKenzie here is looking for Dr Bartek. You seen her this morning?'

Dave momentarily abandoned his visitor and took his place next to Alf. Now both men were staring at the empty pigeon-hole.

'She's collected her post,' Dave said, also scratching his scalp, as though the two men were connected on some basic level. Taking his time with those words, as the elongated vowels of the East Anglian accent demand. 'Must have been in yesterday, at least. I didn't see her though.' He turned back to the visitor's book.

'Have you tried Dr Bartek's room, my dear?' Alf asked.

George nodded. 'I've tried the Archaeology & Anthropology faculty, too. She was meant to give a lecture this morning and she hasn't shown.' She ran the nail of her index finger up and down the zipper teeth on her Puffa jacket. 'I need to talk to her.'

Alf's frown gave way to a cheerful expression. The way he rocked back on his heels said he took disappearing Fellows in his stride. 'I'm sure she'll show up. Perhaps she's had some family emergency crop up. I'll try her number if you like.' He took a ledger from a shelf at the back and started to leaf through its alphabetised entries.

'No, that's fine, Alf,' George said. 'I've tried her phone a few times and it went straight to voicemail. She'll be knocking around.' Underneath the down-filled wadding of her coat, George's blood cooled fast. Moisture on her fingertips told her something was wrong. But she had to meet Van den Bergen from the station. The ticking clock on the wall said she could spare the mystery of a missing Sophie not a minute longer. Now, she must focus on her troubled lover, fresh from his breakfast meeting at Scotland Yard.

'If she comes in, tell her I'm looking for her, will you? Cheers, Alf.'

'Yes, ma'am!' The head porter smiled warmly, saluting and clicking his heels together as though George was some captain in the army of academia. Same rigmarole every time. His expectant grin said he was waiting for her retort in this set piece.

'At ease, sir!' She offered him a show of teeth, though all she wanted was to get out of that place and spark her e-cigarette into life.

Negotiating Trinity Street was heavy going in the slush. Skidding over the flagstones that had finally begun to peek through the white covering. The morning had brought with it the first true rain since January, yet the weather could still not make up its mind. Icy precipitation of one form or another, biting through skin that yearned for the tropical climes of her ancestors. Rain. Sleet. Snow. Hail. Last night, Cambridge had borne witness to all four, plus the howl of the omnipresent, chill Siberian wind. It had been a sleepless night for George following her return from London; she wondered about Dobkin, Aunty Sharon's theory and listened to the elements as they had whipped against the draughty window of her room in that hellhole of a shared house.

She dragged hard on her e-cigarette, pure white smoke discharging itself from the tip and from her nostrils. *Got to get in a cab,* she mused. *Got to be there for Paul. But I'll give it one last go for Sophie. Maybe she just pulled someone hot and couldn't be bothered to get out of bed. Maybe she got caned and can't face getting up. Would it be weird to go to her place? Haven't got time, though. Not today. Check her hangouts first ...*

George walked round the whole of Heffers, drinking in the smell of brand new books. Feeling the thick carpet, springy beneath her snow-boots. No Sophie. Peered into every café window. Still no Sophie, though she spied Sally Wright, sipping an espresso and chatting in patient, measured spurts with Professor Stephen Hawking, immediately identifiable from the back in his specially adapted wheelchair with its glowing computer screen. George marched smartly past, keen not to be spotted and subjected to a lecture of one sort or another by her well-meaning mentor. She trudged through the market place where stall-holders were setting up for the day, expecting yet more brisk trade from tourists and students who demanded mulled wine, steaming cups of chai, hotdogs and hand-made tat produced in Taiwan and Thailand but ostensibly from Germany. An opportunistic

Weihnacht's Markt, though the traders were mostly locals, cashing in on the cold, or Romanians on the make. Christmas was long, long gone, leaving only Jack Frost (aka The Krampus) as a hangover.

'Fuck it. I've got to shelve this.' George checked her watch. It was time.

Her pulse rate was thunderous as she stepped onto the platform. She watched the train pulling in, its cab looming larger and larger. The carriage doors beeped as they unlocked, ready to release the human cargo of mainly tourists grunting over their unwieldy suitcases on wheels, as they took in the famous ivory towers on their whistle-stop tour of this strange, quaint continent. They filed off in clusters at first. Then, one or two. No sign of Van den Bergen. George started to walk the length of the train, breath coming short. Where was the pain in the arse?

'Hello, Detective Lacey,' a rich voice said behind her.

Grinning, she spun around. There he was. Six foot five of misanthropic policeman, looking different in this British air than he had in Amsterdam. Less grey. More handsome. Would he embrace her, or continue this 'let's just be friends' crap? She didn't wait for a prompt and grabbed him in a bear hug.

'There you are, you grumpy old fart.'

She drank in the smell of his sport deodorant, still evident beneath the layers of winter clothing. She revelled in his gathering her to him, though her face only reached as high as his sternum. She reached up and caressed the stubble that covered his jaw. Iron filings, prickly like sandpaper, whereas his freshly clippered white hair was bristle-soft. Clasping his face between her hands, she pulled him down for a kiss. She turned her head to the side, open-mouthed, intending to meet his tongue with hers.

He offered her his cheek, which she licked unintentionally. Sharp, against her tongue.

'You're kidding,' she said, taking a step backwards, as the apparent connection was broken.

Those steel-grey hooded eyes refused to meet hers. 'Come on, Detective Lacey. We've got serious work to do. Lives are at stake.'

CHAPTER 33

Doubletree Hilton hotel in Cambridge, later

In the taxi to the hotel; in the hotel lobby as he checked in; in his room, as he unpacked his meagre belongings, where the double bed screamed her failure to seduce a man she had thought loved her, and now, in the dining room, George's head was filled with, *Prick, prick, prick, prick! Emotional cripple! Why the hell am I here? Why should I give a shit about this mind-fucking, milky-white anus-hole?*

But she knew precisely why she gave a shit.

'Give me your bloody notepad, then,' she said, ignoring the disapproving looks of the waiting staff as she covered the floor around their table with paper from Van den Bergen's lever arch file. 'Let's see what Scotland Yard coughed up.'

'Eat your lunch first,' he said, taking a predatory bite out of his steak baguette. 'You look like you've lost some weight.' As he chewed, he took his steel-framed glasses out of their case and hung them on their chain around his neck. He fixed them on the end of his nose, squinting out at the serene, Christmas-card-perfection of the still-frozen river Cam – the start of the Grantchester section. Brave winter birds hopping on its bright surface, providing the only movement in an otherwise stationary scene. He looked around at their dark restaurant surrounds, with its browns and burgundies and teak wood. 'It's weird in here. Like staring out the window of a Bangkok boutique hotel. Except, I'm expecting to see the yellow waters of the Chaophraya river but here we are in Cambridge!'

'I wouldn't know,' George said, stuffing a chip into her mouth, talking as she chewed. 'I haven't been to Bangkok.'

She could feel Van den Bergen's eyes on her. She saw his hand reach out towards her … felt his uninvited caress on her neck.

'Bruising?' he said. 'Have you been mugged?'

She pushed her chair out just far enough to ensure she was beyond his reach. 'What do you care? Maybe I was attacked. Maybe it's medals from an elaborate sex game with the other Fellows after last night's formal hall. Maybe I've developed a penchant for auto-asphyxiation or dogging in Peterborough.' George registered the warning prickle as tears gathered behind her eyes, felt the aching lump in her throat. She willed herself to banish this show of weakness. 'Spare me the fake concern, Paul. We've got work to do.'

'Scotland Yard have got nothing on Rufus Lazami,' Van den Bergen said, plopping an effervescent tablet into his glass of water.

'But I know he was the Son of the Eagle,' George said, curious as to what he was poisoning himself with now but steeling herself not to ask.

'You don't know for sure.'

'I'm pretty bloody certain,' George said, standing to arrange the pertinent notes in a long, perfectly straight line that reached to the large picture window. 'And I've got interview subjects for my *Women in Prison* study who are in their twenties and thirties, talking about a "hawk" who was trafficking underage girls domestically well over ten years ago.'

Van den Bergen pushed his chair away from the table and crossed his long legs. He folded his hands over his slight paunch, fingering the ridge of his scar tissue through a gap in his shirt.

'Tomas Vlinders supplied kids – illegal immigrants and presumably Dutch passport-holding ones too, who he's maybe abducted personally – to a paedo ring in Berlin.' He thumbed his stubble and pursed his lips, the hollows beneath his cheekbones more pronounced than they had been of late. 'It's possible he took the Deenen children who went missing last year, you know.'

George clicked her tongue against the roof of her mouth. She sucked her teeth thoughtfully, savouring the noise it made.

'You never did let that one drop, did you?'

He shook his head. 'The only people looking for traffickers in that case were me and you. Kamphuis insisted the parents had murdered them. Hasselblad had a hard-on for gypsies.'

'Turns out the Roma might be involved in this case after all …' George said, thinking of Sophie and her enthusiastic friend, Graham Tokár, with his plastic shoes '…cos now we've got four traffickers dead, one of whom – Lazami – seems to have been of Albanian Roma descent. He was almost certainly getting a 20% cut of the action, if Marie's research holds water. As if he needed the money! And one who had Roma kids locked up in the basement of a squat in Kreuzberg.'

'I think the Deenen case and these murders are connected,' Van den Bergen said, putting his large hands behind his head. 'We're fairly certain our Jack Frost and Krampus are one and the same man. Thing is, I can't put my finger on who the hell he might be, but he's out to get a tight circle of kiddy-fiddling scumbags.'

Their musings were interrupted when a young waiter dressed in black approached. He leaned into Van den Bergen conspiratorially.

'Can you ask your friend to tidy away the paper, sir?' he asked. 'It's a trip hazard. The other guests … in a restaurant of this calibre. I'm sure you understand.'

George sat open-mouthed, selecting her outraged words and putting them into the correct order before she fired them point blank at this scabby-faced little wanker. Except she didn't have time. Van den Bergen looked at the boy's knees, where the black fabric of his trousers had worn to shiny grey. He peered over his glasses at George. His long fingers reached into the pocket of his chunky cardigan hanging on the back of his chair, and he withdrew his police ID. Flashed it in the waiter's face.

'There's nobody else in the bloody restaurant, sonny, and we are conducting police business. Please don't interrupt me or my colleague again. Do *you* understand?'

George's cheeks flamed merrily in response to Van den Bergen's chilvalrous outburst. But the warm glow was quickly extinguished by the reality of an unpredictable lover. *He loves me. He loves me not.* She entertained an unbidden memory of childhood, pulling petals off the daisies in the park with Letitia and her father. Optimism bloomed, then, as it always had in childhood. *Maybe he does love me.*

'Who's next on his hit-list, then?' George asked. 'We know he looks like a rough-sleeper.'

The Chief Inspector inclined his head towards her. Dark eyebrows heavy over those large, grey eyes. 'Do we?'

George nodded. Pointed to her neck. 'See these war wounds, old man? I did get mugged – well, not mugged, but attacked by another academic, the other day.' She held her hand up. Didn't want to be interrupted. 'Dobkin from University College London. Total twat, but was doing some serious undercover exposé shit on major players in a child trafficking ring. He also had his research stolen a month ago.'

'Also?'

She shushed Van den Bergen and bit her lip. 'I'll get to that. Thing is though, the guy who was spotted running away from Dobkin's office after the break-in was described by witnesses as homeless. Now, you're telling me Scotland Yard has a big, fat zero on Lazami, and Vlinders. Hauptmann and Meyer weren't on a sex-offenders' register or anything. So, it stands to reason, the only way anyone could have known all four victims' names was if they'd either been a player in this trafficking ring themselves, or had somehow got their hands on Dobkin's research. And the woman, who blackmailed me for money in return for *my* stolen laptop and USB stick—'

'When did this happen?'

'About two weeks ago.'

'Why didn't you tell me?'

George stood. She fell silent with her hand on her hip. She snatched a rogue chip that had been left in Van den Bergen's little wire basket, pointed at him with it and spoke deliberately slowly, speeding up and getting louder as she gained momentum and lost control. 'Like you give a shit. Like I'm anything to you beyond a fucking colleague these days. Two years of a relationship. Tamara gets knocked up and suddenly Granddaddy-to-be can't bear to stick it to someone old enough to be his daughter no more? Nice, Paul. Real classy.'

He held his hands aloft. 'There's no need for this, Georgina.'

'Don't fucking Georgina me! And what would you do if I did this?' She marched up to him, grabbed his face and kissed him passionately on the mouth, expecting him to respond, despite his best intentions. She felt like he had thrown a snowball squarely in her face when he didn't.

'Stop being silly, for god's sake.' He wiped his mouth with his sleeve. His words were few but burned like acid.

'Silly?' George could feel the red mist descend.

'I've made my position clear,' he said. 'You're making a fool of yourself.'

He was looking at those ridiculous size thirteens of his. Perhaps he didn't mean any of what he was saying, but those words seared deeper and deeper to the soft places where she hurt. George took a deep breath, not caring that a waitress and the waiter from earlier were eavesdropping from behind a screen. She calmly took his glass of effervescing whateverthefuckitwas and threw it over his chest.

He looked at her with wide-eyed surprise and something bordering on contempt.

Between gritted teeth, she spoke from the blazing river of strength that ran inside her: Letitia the Dragon's daughter, hot jets of indignation buoying her. 'Don't you fucking *ever* mistake my sexual confidence and emotional honesty for silliness and foolishness, Paul van den Bergen. This is not 1950. I am not some little kid. This is all about *you* acting like some mid-life-crisis prick entering his second fucking childhood. Or maybe you just didn't finish your first.'

Dabbing himself with the dry napkin, she could see his Adam's apple pinging up and down like a barometer, assessing the temperature in that room. Boiling for her part. Icy for his.

'You're unfair. Let's get back to the debrief.'

'Am I unfair?' She sat back down. 'You won't allow yourself a shred of happiness, so you're pissing all over mine. Is *that* fair? You use cruel and cutting words to push me away after we've meant so much to each other. Silly. Foolish. Do you think I don't have fucking feelings? Am I some robot or something? Should I be punished for falling for you? *Seriously?* What planet are you from, cos it sure as hell ain't mine?' She examined the bafflement in his expression as if it were a menu. Trying to read into his silence. 'Oh. What? Did you think I'd let it slide? Like I wouldn't come back at you and have my say?' She started to shake her head with ghetto-fabulous drama, normally reserved only for arguments with her mother. 'Cos if you thought we could just rumble on with you insulting me and without me telling you how it is, Paul van den Bergen, then turns out you didn't know me at all, my friend.'

Her Dutch lover looked suddenly at a loss. Opening and closing his mouth, he looked like a guppy, gasping and on show in the tank that was the restaurant of the Double Tree Hilton in Cambridge.

'I'm going to my room,' he said, quietly.

'No, you ain't,' she said, trying to cause him injury with her pointed glare. She gestured at the paperwork on the floor. 'Because we're grown-ups and professionals and we've got a killer to catch and fucking job to do. Right? So straighten you face, bwoy, and think before you fucking disrespect me again. And for the record ...' She arranged the cruet set in a straight line across the table, separating them '... I won't be making no "foolish" advances on your wrinkly arse again, old man. You decide you were wrong and that you want me, you'll have to come fucking chasing.' A lot of waggling of her index finger, loaded with meaning. 'And make sure your tail's hanging between those skinny legs of yours, cos I expect you to be one contrite motherfucker after the merry dance you've been leading me on these past few months.'

'You're intolerable,' Van den Bergen said.

'Oh yeah?' She cupped her ear. 'I don't hear no asthmatic wheezing and I don't see no hives on your skin, so I suggest you suck it up because turns out you can tolerate me just fine.' She stared him down.

'So, you were blackmailed by a woman,' he said, sighing.

No apology forthcoming, she noted. *Fuck him*. He'd come round without water.

'A homeless woman. And I can tell you exactly who she is because she's been tapping me up for cash for weeks.'

'Go on.' Van den Bergen leaned forwards, his disgruntlement replaced by hunger for the truth.

'Gabi Deenen.'

'But Gabi and Piet Deenen are dead. Their coats and shoes were found at the end of the pier in Scheveningen. They had suicide notes stuffed into their pockets. They were driven to it by Internet trolls.'

'But did they ever find the bodies?' George asked, smiling wryly. Something clicked into place in her subconscious, though she couldn't yet put her finger on it.

'How long have you known Gabi was still alive?' A look of pure thunder on Van den Bergen's face said he was incensed.

'The Deenens were off my radar, Paul. I've been busy with my own life. I do have one, you know! And anyway, I had my reasons for keeping quiet.' George pursed her lips and folded her napkin into a precise triangle. Then, the blood froze in her veins as something struck her. Wide-eyed. Tongue-tied.

Van den Bergen leaned forwards, and grabbed her hand. 'You know who Jack Frost is, don't you?'

Breath coming short. The truth surfacing in her deep pool of understanding. Fast enough to give her the bends. 'Jesus! I do. Why the fuck didn't I see it sooner? Dobkin. Dobkin gave me the piece of the jigsaw.'

'Piet Deenen,' Van den Bergen said.

Nodding. Rubbing her numb face. 'It could only be.' She looked up at her lover. 'Shit, Paul. What have I done?'

CHAPTER 34

South East London, later

'Alright, Dan the Man,' the skinny young brother said. 'I ain't seen you round these parts for a bit.'

Danny eyed this shivering little skeez suspiciously. 'I know you?'

The boy's eyes were tarnished medals of dented pride and fear, but he started stepping up to him, striking a bit of a badass pose, like he was some fucking player, making himself look bigger in his shit Lonsdale Puffa. Twenty quid on clearance down Sports Direct on the Old Kent Road, no doubt. 'Yeah. I'm your old next-door neighbour from when you lived round the way, innit?' He tried to fist-bump him, though Danny kept his hands in his pockets. 'You the man with a plan, right? I was wondering if I could get—'

'Step off, little man,' Danny said, only paying part-attention to this wannabe pretender. 'I'm busy, yeah?' He reached inside his Canada Goose, smirking as the boy flinched, expecting him to bring out some metal maybe. He pulled out a roll of cash that could choke the big black cat in Catford, and peeled off a couple of twenties.

'You ain't seen me. Understand?'

'Nice one, bruv.' The boy pocketed the money in his zip pocket,

211

rubbing his chapped lips together, sleet landing as sparkling droplets on his nappy hair.

'What's your name?' Danny asked, never taking his eye from
the little kitchen window of the house.

'Sean.'

Glanced down at Sean's slush-sodden trainers. He peeled off
another few notes and pushed them into the boy's hand.

'Listen, Sean. I need you to do me a big favour, right?'

'Anything, man.'

'Get some proper seasonal footwear and a decent coat and
fuck off.'

Left alone now he waited a further ten minutes, watching the
door of the house where he knew she lived half of the time,
wondering when or even if he should make his move. He had
seen her often enough from a distance. She was still a gift of a
girl, but wrapped in the Kevlar of the pigs and the justice system.
Untouchable, but still a loose end he had vowed to tie off.

His phone pinged, alerting him to a text. He checked the screen
of his brand-new iPhone. The Duke had summoned him, wanting
an update. He turned away reluctantly, disappointed that she
hadn't appeared at the front door. Nobody had. Though he knew
the house wasn't empty because he had eyes and ears all over the
estate. Nothing passed Dan the Man by. Never had. Never would.

'What do you mean it's Danny fucking Spencer?' Letitia said,
trying to push Sharon out of the way. 'I ain't seen that little twat
since me and Ella lived on the estate. I had to change my name
by deed poll cos of him. Left me out of pocket. Bastard.'

But Sharon wouldn't give an inch. She turned around to face
her sister, uncharacteristically clenching her hand into a fist,
though she'd grown up with the threat of hell and damnation if
she didn't dig deep enough for forgiveness and understanding.

'This is my house, Letitia. Back the fuck off! You're supposed
to be friggin' ill. Sit yourself back on the sofa or you can get your
malingering arse on the next train back to Ashford.'

'I'm gonna tell that Danny to do one.' Letitia's eyes narrowed, plotting revenge. 'I am. I'm gonna go out there and give him what for.' She was poised to thump on the window of Patrice's small bedroom. 'He ain't nothing but a snot-nose lickle bomboclart. I ain't scared of his sort.'

Sharon backed away into the shadows of the room, pulling her sister with her. 'You're such a silly cow, Letitia. Everyone knows he's big league these days.' She started to shake, though the heating was still cranked up to downtown Kingston, Jamaica. Adrenalin. 'I bet he's got a gun in that anorak. I ain't trifling with no gun. Don't you be bringing grief to my doorstep ...' She poked herself in the chest '... just because you fancy yourself as some hard case.'

Her elder sister surged back to the windowsill like an unturnable tide, rapped on the glass and shouted, 'I'm going to take the belt to you, Danny Spencer!'

Fearful tears brimmed in Sharon's eyes. 'You stupid, selfish cow! Wat mek yu dweet fa?' She thought of Patrice, at school, and Tinesha, at work. They would be back soon, and she wouldn't be able to protect them. She raised her hand to slap Letitia – ever the more wilful of the two daughters, kicking against their mother's strict upbringing.

But Letitia was fast. She grabbed Sharon's hand in mid-air and guffawed with laughter.

'He's gone, you dopey cow. I'm winding you up, innit?' Continuing mirth as she shuffled downstairs, back to her sickbed on the couch, still wheezing with amusement as she lit her eleventh cigarette of the morning.

Hanging back on the stairs, Sharon prayed for her pounding heart to slow. 'Keep cool. Keep it together for the kids,' she counselled herself. She took out her phone from her skirt pocket and dialled George.

On the other end of the line, her niece sounded irritated and sharp at first. Her voice softened as Sharon spoke, giving way to audible trepidation.

'You sure it was Danny Spencer?' George asked.

'Yes. Definite. I never forget a face. Even if I didn't know him from yous, he was all over the papers for about a year. And now he's here. And he knows you're here.' She scratched with a worn-down thumbnail at the bubbled pattern in her white-washed Anaglypta wallpaper, shaking.

'Did he spot you?'

'Nah.' She sat on her hand to stop the jitters.

'Good. Do us a favour, Aunty Shaz. Get Patrice to ask his mates if they know where Danny's at.'

'No fucking ways, darling. I ain't getting my boy caught up in any gangsta bullshit.'

'He can be discreet and get his mates to do the dirty work. But I need to keep a watchful eye on the bear's den if he's going to come after me, thinking I'm easy meat. Please! It's not just my safety that's at stake.'

CHAPTER 35

London, the West End, later

Strutting his way down to Savile Row, Danny thought about what it was to be rich: to know where the next meal was coming from; to buy himself threads that were correct; to have the world at his feet. He bashed some rich Arab woman in full burka out of the way as she pissed around outside a boutique, digging for some shit or other in her Chanel handbag. He got a kick from it. He was king of the road, off to meet the king of the city. He had come a long way. He wasn't about to let that fucking cow take that away from him.

'Gimme a coffee, yeah?' he said to the suited salesman when he'd entered the store, flinging himself onto a leather sofa. 'This well nice in here, innit?' He looked around at the lofty, bespoke tailor's: an upper crust white-man's temple to style, complete with galleried second floor and vaulted glazed ceiling, like it was some Victorian museum, but with nice tailoring instead of stuffed tigers and that. All white panelling. Dummies wearing thousand quid suits. This is where the real money came, just to restock their wardrobes away from prying eyes.

But the salesman was still waiting, staring at Danny's clothes and the tramlines in his close crop, as though he was from another fucking planet.

'You got a Coke? I'll have that, man.'

Still eyeballing him.

'You know who I'm meeting here, don't you?'

'Yes.'

'Yes, sir.' Danny leaned forwards in his seat, toothpick hanging out the corner of his mouth, legs astride, hands on knees, making himself look bigger with his coat unzipped and hanging open.

'Yes, sir.' The salesman touched his naff college-boy hair and disappeared, almost bowing. Fucking idiot.

In his head, Danny ran through what he was going to tell the Duke.

'Step this way, sir,' some old geez in a waistcoat said.

He beckoned him into a private room, which turned out to be some kind of fitting room on acid; the Duke was stood in the middle on a podium thing, wearing fuck-ugly tartan boxers and old man socks, getting measured with bits of white cloth pinned to his right side. Looked a proper numptee.

'Young Daniel!' he said, swivelling right round so he could see him with his good eye.

Smelled of money. First thing you noticed, when you walked into a room where this geezer was at, even if he was in his undies. And the way the tailor treated him – kneeling at his feet, with pins in his mouth; standing back, laying the praise on thick with a trowel – like the Duke had done something clever, just by standing there. Like it was his pleasure and honour to prance round after a bona fide toff, shovelling up any steaming shit that came out of his sunshiny white arse. Nice.

Danny approached to greet the big cheese. Fist-bumps, of course. No fucking way was he lowering himself to do that formal upper class handshake shit. He was a businessman, but there was no need to sacrifice a brother's stylish way of being to get right with the Duke.

'What do you think of my coat?' the Duke said.

'Sharp, man.' Danny eyed the patchwork of white shitty fabric and pins. 'Think you could do with a bit more coat in your coat, though. If you get my meaning.'

Laughter.

'Bespoke,' the Duke said. 'You must treat yourself one day. They do a wonderful service here.' He patted his belly. 'Hides the vagaries of middle age rather well. Not that you have that problem.'

Danny laughed and ran a manicured hand over his head. He fingered the trim on his hood. 'Nah, man. You wanna get yourself a quality parka. This got genuine fox and down fill for the Arctic, innit? While you be shivering your tits off, I be nice and toasty.'

More laughter all around, like he had said something incredible. The tailor actually clapped like a fucking seal.

'Sir is very witty.'

'Yes, sir is,' Danny agreed, smiling, at ease with his destiny. The man who can. Serious, suddenly. 'We gonna chat business, then?'

The Duke looked down at the tailor. 'Will you give us a moment, Charles? There's a good chap. Perhaps a couple of flat whites would go down a treat. Better still, a drop of brandy for my associate here and me.'

With the tailor gone, the Duke settled himself on the fitting room sofa. Danny, sitting lower on the podium, didn't like the fact he was suddenly a few inches closer to the ground. But what was it his mum said? Life's a shit sandwich. The more bread you got, the less shit you eat. He was working his way to all bread and no shit. The Duke could make that happen.

'You got a space at the top now Lazami's gone, innit?' No point holding back.

Fucking loon started tapping his glass eye with the tailor's pencil, giving a funny tight-lipped smile like he was apologetic or something. He gave off a patronising vibe, which Danny didn't like.

'Rufus possessed many qualities in addition to his Wild West spirit. He was my right-hand man in my legitimate enterprises, as well as my … er … more left-of-field interests. A man you can trust on the board of a plc as well as at the helm of an international trafficking venture is not one easily replaced, I'm afraid.'

He crossed his bony white legs and leaned back on the sofa as if he owned the whole of the West End, which maybe he did. Hard to tell with that old money. But either way, he didn't seem to give a dog's arsehole that his saggy old bollocks were hanging out of his shorts. Big bollocks, at that.

Danny chose his words carefully; he didn't want to put his vexation on show.

'So, you saying I'm no good in a fancy suit round a board table. I get that, yeah? I never been that sort of guy. But that ain't taking into account my talent for the other stuff. The left-of-field shit. I got that covered, man.' He sat up straight. He imagined he was on *Dragon's Den*, pitching for the ultimate business backer. He wanted the Duke to see he was a dependable ally, a man with a plan. 'Running the trafficking. I can do that. I speak Dutch. I speak German. Not brilliant, admittedly, but I lived in Holland for years, yeah? I'm over there, dealing with our pharmaceutical contacts all the time.'

He felt the weight of the piece in his coat pocket. He was sweating now, wishing he could put a bullet in the Duke's scarred head. Hadn't he been top of his own little pile? Hadn't he had the Mohican working for him, taking over the operation Jez had been looking after? Running girls. Dealing ecstasy bought from the Rotterdam Silencer. Heroine from Helmand. Buying weight straight from Colombia. Lining up some tasty deals with a cartel in Mexico. Then, this upper crust wanker swans in and says it's his turf. Suddenly South East London's finest is playing second fiddle to some already billionaire bastard who's in it just for kicks.

Come on, man. Pull yourself together. Bitching ain't gonna pay your mum's bills. Prove your loyalty.

'Listen. You want proof I'm ready to fill Lazami's boots on the

218

non-legit side? Here's proof. I reckon I know who this Jack Frost is ... the bastard who took out Lazami, Vlinders and two pervs in Berlin.'

The Duke leaned forward, a glint in his good eye, the faint scarring around his glass eye crinkling up. 'You do, do you?'

'Pretty sure,' he said. 'He's a homeless.'

'How do you know?'

'Putting two and two together. I been flogging him some ID and other gear. I could hear he was foreign, but his English is good. Barely any accent. So, it took me a while to place it. But then, I realised. Seen him out at the gypsy camp, snooping around. He's on your tail, man. And he's packing.'

A raised eyebrow said the unrufflable billionaire's feathers had been ruffled. 'I can't say for sure what else Rufus was involved with, but I'm fairly certain his getting himself murdered had nothing to do with me. I'm untouchable.' He touched the place on his front tooth where the diamond had been.

Danny's chuckle was hollow, the way he wanted it to sound. He had to make himself indispensable to this arsehole. And to do that, he had to put the fear of god into him.

'Only two people could have known Lazami, Vlinders and the two Germans were all linked. One is a professor type from University College London. Dobkin, his name is.'

'Who's he to me, and how the hell do you know about him?'

'I got my sources, yeah? Brother of a mate just ... er ... got out of Wandsworth a few weeks back. Trevor. He'd been involved in your ventures, right? With Lazami. Getting little girls from Sheffield and bringing them to that hotel you got in Margate. Got picked up for possession, but he's already on the sex offenders register. So, he's interviewed by this Dobkin, who was doing a study into paedo rings. Dobkin lets slip that he was putting a database of names together. Was gonna blow the whistle on *all* the players in the papers. High-level names. Mentioned Son of the Eagle, apparently.'

'Do you know where Dobkin can be found?' the Duke asked.

Danny nodded.

'Make him disappear. If you think you're ready to step up, I need to see your aptitude. Understand?'

In his head, Danny ran through the list of names he could call on to buy the services of a fixer. Killing wasn't his thing. He was a lover, not a fighter. But he had no problems with paying someone to do his dirty work for him. He made a pact with himself not to mention George; he would deal with her.

'Fine. But I know it's this guy I been flogging ID and shit to, because I done some digging, and Dobkin had his computer nicked by someone matching the homeless geezer's description. Too many coincidences, man. Foreigner, needing passports, buying a gun. Maybe someone's taken a hit out on your key people, and you're next. I can protect you by keeping my eye on this Jack Frost. Or I can get him taken care of. Your call.'

Examining his fingernails in silence, the Duke's expression changed like shitty, unpredictable weather. Danny found it hard to read him, especially now his face was tighter since the uplift – a different man from a couple of years ago when they'd first clashed antlers. Some sort of chameleon crap going on. Maybe mid-life-crisis. Maybe hiding from someone who could ID him. Who knew? Guy was a fucking nutcase.

The Duke stood and took a pillbox out of his jacket pocket, pinched white powder between his fingers and snorted hard. He turned back to Danny and smiled.

'I'm invulnerable. I'm the Duke. What have I got to be afraid of? I'm ferried around in a Rolls Royce. I live in a house that has the security measures of a fortress. The minute I start watching my back is the minute I lose my grip on the reins.' He snorted another pinch of coke, put the pillbox away, then sat back down as the tailor returned with a tray of drinks.

'Ah! Perfect, Marcus. Thank you so much.' He sipped his flat white and downed the brandy in one, then fixed Danny with his one good eye. 'Keep tabs on our rough-sleeping friend. Deal with other matter, and you might find yourself promoted.'

PART 2

CHAPTER 36

A village South of Amsterdam, 16 January, earlier that year

'Just pack the fucking rucksacks, you idiot!' Gabi screamed. 'We've got to be ready. We've got to go.' She looked anxiously at her watch. How long would it be? Minutes? Hours? Another few days? 'Kamphuis is going to have us arrested. I know it.'

'I can't, Gab,' Piet said. 'Let them arrest me. I've got nothing to hide. I've got nothing left to lose.'

TV on in the background. Rolling news channel. A weather report, describing the start of a downwards draft of Arctic chill set to last weeks. Heavy snow falling fast, with the double-digit drop in temperature to accompany it. Climate change to blame. The absurdly chirpy meteorologist was followed by a short feature on a turn in the tide of public feeling towards the Deenens.

Piet turned the sound up and stood blankly in front of the strobing box. Soundbite after soundbite: Gabi did it; he did it; both kids buried in a shallow grave somewhere by parents who were unfeeling monsters, utterly self-obsessed and more bothered about money than their 'mentally ill' child.

'Turn that shit off!' Gabi shouted. She zapped the slander into silent submission, as though the remote control were a Taser. She pulled her jeans on, picked up Piet's fleece and flung it at him. 'You need warm clothes. It's insane out there. You'll freeze to death.'

'Good! I've been trying to die for months.'

Enough! She had had enough. Strode over to her husband and grabbed him by the collar of his T-shirt. Put her face right next to his. No space between them. Smelled desperation oozing from his every pore. 'Do you want to find our children? Well? Do you?' Shouting at the top of her voice.

Tears rolled lazily onto his cheeks, dropping onto his slippered feet when he inclined his head forwards. Fat, sorrowful droplets from dark eyes, reminding her of Lucy when she cried. She lessened her grip on his collar, and wiped his tears away with the sleeve of her hoodie. She encouraged him to sit on the edge of the bed.

'What did George tell us in yesterday's catch-up meeting?' She was working hard to soften the tone of her voice. She needed Piet with her. This was one undertaking she couldn't do on her own. 'The convicted paedophile who took those little children – just like ours – from their back garden. Trevor Underwood. He's escaped from prison. Trevor Underwood is walking the streets of London. We've got his name, Piet!' She started to count off the facts they were privy to on her fingers. 'We know he's been sighted in South East London. George even let slip his mother lives in Lewisham.'

She knelt down before her broken husband, quaking as he sobbed. She held his forearms gently, though she wanted to slap him hard. 'I can find him, Piet. Research is part of what I do. It's a lead. The police are less than useless. Kamphuis is poised to fry us alive. We've only made it as far as January because Christmas got in the bloody way! Hasselblad's insisting his detectives look in every direction but the right one. The only allies we've maybe got are George McKenzie and Paul van den Bergen. They've been following good lines of enquiry with this trafficking thing, but they've had no backing from their superiors! In the meantime, everyone's baying for our blood.'

Piet rose and pushed her away.He picked up the rucksack, starting to line the bottom with underwear. He sniffed hard and met Gabi's gaze.

'It's our last chance, isn't it? Our last pop at finding Josh and Lucy.' He hiccoughed the words out, his voice hoarse from crying, and Gabi was pleased to hear them at last.

She nodded.

'We've got some money,' she said. 'I've not touched the accounts because they'll only know we've gone on the run if I do. But I had a bit of cash knocking around. When Mum died, I found wads of fifties and twenties all over the bloody house. You know what old people are like.' She chuckled mirthlessly. 'I didn't want to declare it.'

Piet looked at her. Frowning. 'You never told me this.'

Gabi put her hand on her hip and cocked her head to the side. 'Why would I? You're financially incompetent. It was rainy-day money. And it's not just raining. It's frigging snowing a blizzard!'

Abruptly, he flung the rucksack back down. 'You're the one who insists we live beyond our means.' He held his hands up. 'I'm not even getting into this bullshit again.' He blinked hard and exhaled slowly 'What's the plan, then?'

'London bound,' Gabi said. 'It's big enough to disappear in. I've paid a man who sails in and out of South Docklands in a disused lifeboat. He's got a mooring in Surrey Quays. We'll be rough sleepers. Nobody notices them. No one wants to.'

'How are you proposing to find this Trevor Underwood if we've no technology?'

'Internet cafés. Libraries. People do it all the time. Leave that to me. We sail tonight, but we've got to stop off at Scheveningen pier first.'

'Why?'

'To buy us time. To stop them looking for us.'

As winter-dark evening turned into deep night, Gabi led Piet along the deserted pier, already buried in places beneath snow-drifts of four feet. The wind whipped her face cruelly; a thousand lashes reminding her that she must be punished for her poor mothering. She must be punished for failing to curry the public's favour. Now, at least, she had a chance at redeeming herself.

'Got the note?' she asked.

'In my coat pocket,' Piet said.

Together they put their coats and spare shoes gingerly on the ground at the very end of the pier. They held each other for the first time in months, though Gabi knew the warmth of another human being could not thaw her heart. She was numb to the core ... had been for years. Looking into the inky black sea, she wished, just for a moment, she could jump into it and wash all conscious thought and the agony away. But she was not like Piet, and those self-indulgent reflections were soon replaced by resolve.

'Use the snow shovel as we walk back to smudge out your footprints. They'll soon be covered in this downfall, but we can't be too careful.'

CHAPTER 37

London, South Docklands, 17 January

Awoken by a thump, Gabi looked up at the oppressive mass above them. A low ceiling, pitch-black but for a shaft of weak light coming in from the far end of the cavity. No windows, this deep in the boat's keel. With Piet beside her, they were covered by coats and blankets that stank of diesel. An inch of icy water formed a puddle at their feet where the vessel wasn't quite water-tight.

'Jesus,' Piet said, sitting up and hitting his head. 'We could've drowned in the night.'

'But you didn't,' came the unfamiliar voice of a Dutchman. More light then as he opened some sort of hatch, daylight streaming in.

Gabi blinked hard. The ceiling above them had been papered with nicotine-stained naval maps and hand-written shipping reports that looked like they'd been torn from a ledger. Lifejackets and rope were piled high around them. Seeing a child-sized lifejacket, she remembered all she had left behind. She felt relief ... pain ...intense grief. She wondered how bad her hair must look.

'We're in London?' she asked.

'You bet,' the hoary old captain of the leaking vessel said, shoving a rolled up cigarette in his mouth. He cupped his hand around the end against the wind, so he could get a light. His craggy, red face looked like it had been marinated for years in the brine of the North Sea. 'We were lucky with the weather. It was dead calm most of the way. But I've never seen snow like it. Good for doing things without attracting the interest of Thames River Police.' He tapped the side of his bulbous purple whisky-drinker's nose, and looked expectantly at Gabi. 'I can swap you a nice breakfast of wafels and hot coffee in exchange for the other fifty per cent of what we agreed.' He winked.

Scrambling to her knees, Gabi pulled out a bank teller's plastic bag containing a roll of money. She made her way up onto the deck and peered around at her new surroundings, shivering violently even in her chunkiest sweater and a heavy ski jacket, but elated. Glacially fresh air sliced into her lungs. To the north, some two hundred metres away, the River Thames flowed slug-gishly past. Beyond it, the corporate monoliths of Canary Wharf glowed merrily in the whiteout. Red lights winking on the top of each – a giant's Advent candle. Christmas had come late and her present was freedom from the trolls and the long arm of Olaf Kamphuis. But it came at a price. Josh and Lucy were still missing. They had a battle to fight and prisoners of war to retrieve.

She handed the money to the captain. 'Count it, if you like. It's all there. When I make a promise to do something, I keep it.'

Boosting the Transit van was easy, surrounded by the appar-ently deserted, uniform townhouses of the Canada Water development. Snow swallowed the sound of two opportunist thieves. Nobody would look askance at two middle-aged white people, even if they were carrying the tools of a car thief's trade.

'How the hell do you know how to do this?' Piet asked, quaking with fear as much as near-hyperthermia. Fat flakes settled in his hair, on his shoulders.

'Google,' she said.

With the engine running, it was not long before her feet began to thaw a little. The drive to Lewisham took only twenty minutes, even on poorly gritted roads.

'I don't like this,' Piet said, peering grey-faced out of the foggy passenger window. 'What if we get pulled over?'

'Stop looking like you're going to throw up, and then we won't be pulled over,' Gabi said, trying to see the way ahead through the greasy windscreen, not helped by windscreen wipers flashing two and fro, scraping against the glass with a whup, whup that set her teeth on edge. It stank of stale cigarettes and sweat in the cab. The diesel in the tank was worryingly low. With the snow settling in earnest on John Silkin Lane, she could only risk fifteen miles per hour. The tyres needed replacing. Typical. She dreaded the hill starts as she manoeuvred the clumsy beast across the Deptford border and into the hilly urban terrain of Lewisham.

'Can't we go and find somewhere to stay the night first?' Piet asked, blowing on his reddened hands.

'No! I told you. We've got no fixed abode now. It's doorways and underpasses for us. The minute we register in hotels, we're spending cash we could use better on finding the kids. Plus, most importantly, we'll have to give some sort of ID, and we left our legitimate passports and driver's licenses behind. Nobody commits suicide and takes ID with them.'

'Doorways? Are you fucking mad? In this weather?'

'We've got to suck it up, Piet. Anyway, if we make our move now, we'll get where we need to go before the owner even realises his van is missing. Vans are easy pickings in bad weather. Builders can't build in snow. My dad spent thirty years as a ground-worker and we were always skint in January and February.'

They skidded their way into Lewisham, surrounded on either side by elegant Victorian gentleman's residences that were now split into seedy flats. Dated floral curtains hung crookedly from their poles, like disgruntled erotic dancers; bare bulbs behind filthy windows; dead plants on the sills; wheelie bins out front, covered in thick snow. The odd BMW or Audi on a drive and plantation shutters at the big bay windows said the march of the affluent middle-class hipsters was upon the area, pricing the rough-shod, beleaguered locals out.

'We'll park up and go to the local library. Lewisham High Street.'

Putting their rucksacks on their backs, the trudge through the snow towards the pint-sized centre was hard. But it felt something like home to Gabi, after a year of lily-white faces *op het platteland* – in the Dutch countryside. A small-town existence, rubbing shoulders until static buzzed unpleasantly with bland, Aryan-looking people who talked about the price of cheese more than politics.

Lewisham Library loomed in the snow. An angular mid-century building. More famous as the scene of a stabbing than as a place of literary inspiration or learning, it looked like a smaller version of the police HQ in Amsterdam. Déjà vu.

'What if the van gets a ticket?' Piet asked.

'Jesus. It's stolen! Relax, will you? We're soldiers of fortune.'

Inside, with their clothes still fresh, they attracted no attention whatsoever.

Gabi slid onto a computer as a library-user disappeared off to the toilet in the middle of a browsing session.

Her fingers flew back and forth over the keyboard. Confident. Hopeful. Pragmatic.

Underwood. Gladys. Mrs. Registered to an address in SE4.

She turned to her husband. 'We're on.'

CHAPTER 38

South East London, later, then 21 January

'How the hell are we supposed to know what he looks like?' Piet had asked, adjusting his rucksack on his back, wishing they could get to a café and grab a snack. He'd looked down at his wife, a feverish look about her.

From inside her ski jacket, she had produced a print-out from an online newspaper article. The photograph had showed a dead-eyed white man in his late twenties, with a shaven head and a tattoo of thorns scrolling around his bull neck. Reported in London's *Evening Standard*; February, one year ago: *Candy Man finally under lock and key after Met police crack down on paedophile ring.*

'He's been inside for the best part of a year,' Gabi had said, 'I guess he might have changed his appearance – especially if he's on the run. But that tattoo's got to be a dead giveaway, if it's visible. And those eyes.'

Her beautiful features had hardened to something akin to a mask of pure hatred. Piet had flinched. He understood why the media had latched onto the possibility of Gabi being a kid-killer. She had no idea she came across like a stark photo, taken with a hi-res camera – no filter or special lens to soften what was there, so that it appeared endearing or sympathetic.

'This is a waste of time,' he had said, staring up at the unbe-coming low-rise block of flats, facing onto beautiful Victorian villas; reminding the flats' residents that they had drawn the short straw in life. 'What do you propose we do, now? Hang around until somebody who looks like a pervert miraculously emerges and says hello.'

'What else do you suggest?'

Four days later, stiff from spending nights locked inside the freezing stolen van, praying the silence of a snowy backstreet would keep them safe from prying eyes and traffic wardens, they stood together outside the same block of flats, still hoping their optimism would bear fruit.

The pain of a snowball in his ear took Piet by surprise. He yelped, then sought out its originator, heart pounding as though this were a fight or flight situation. But he sighed with relief, as he connected the dots: school children filing past them, throwing snowballs at each other. He watched them fronting minus twelve out in flimsy uniform trousers and cheap supermarket shoes that had taken a battering on the football pitch. Girls wore skirts, rolled up too many times at the waist, so that they swung a good six inches above the knee. Some of the children were young, accompanied by Mum or Grandma, holding hands, wearing bright wellies and multi-coloured gloves. Hats with earflaps designed to look like woodland creatures. Excited chatter sounded as they made footprints in the virgin snow by the kerb. But the older ones – year six, at a guess – walked unchaperoned. Pre-teens full of SE4 swagger: precocious sexu-ality in the coquettish girls; alpha male posturing from the still-squeaky boys.

Realisation dawned like the first February sunrise after a five-month-long Arctic night.

'Where would a perv hang out if he wanted to get to children?' he asked, feeling the sudden rush of adrenalin, a feeling of anticipation he wasn't used to. The thrill of the chase. 'Let's follow them.'

The wave of school children flowed over the main road and filtered down a side street in twos and threes. Cars double-parked and school-crossing signs said they were nearing the epicentre of this youthquake.

Gabi stopped outside a neat Victorian terrace. Cream-grey bricks and white lintels. She looked up at the single-glazed windows. So picturesque in the snow.

'What's the matter?' Piet asked, noticing the downward turn of her mouth.

'Nothing.'

But he knew. Apart from the red door, where theirs had been black, the terrace was almost identical to the home they had lived in for almost five years, only two or three miles from that place, as the crow flew. A reminder of better times. She was right. They never should have moved.

'What the hell are we doing here, Piet?' she said, turning to him. Red-rimmed eyes said her resolve had all but left her. 'If the police haven't caught this bastard, what chance do we have? A million to one. London's massive. There's a school on every corner. He could be anywhere.' She exhaled heavily. 'Let's go. Let's get a hot drink and something to eat. I've fucked up.'

Piet reached out to comfort his wife; he squeezed her shoulder, though she shrugged his comfort off. She started a brisk onwards march away from the school up towards New Cross, negotiating these back streets as though she knew precisely where she was going. A human tracking device, bound for some unspoken target.

'Slow down, Gab!' Piet said, panting. Having to use his inhaler, as Gabi started to take longer strides, impossible to keep up with her long distance runner's idea of pace-setting.

It was too much. He swept the snow off the low front garden wall of a house and sat down, forcing Gabi to retrace her steps. Yet another school looming behind high Victorian walls at the end of this street. Though Gabi was right. What use was it? The bell had rung now, in any case. All the children tucked safely inside while they still wandered aimlessly; parental diaspora in a not-quite-familiar land.

She sat beside him in silence, breath steaming on the crisp air. The snow started to fall heavily. Settling on the two of them – a frozen representation of grief sculpted by a callous God.

Sitting there, watching cars crawl along the slippery snow-bound asphalt, Piet noticed presently that one or two children were still skidding their way down the street towards that high wall. Slightly older children, wearing blazers and carrying fat book bags slung over their shoulders. And there was a chubby black girl – probably eleven or twelve, though she looked no older than nine – struggling with her bag. She fell over, landing on her side in the snow, looking like she was about to cry.

Piet stood, preparing to cross the road and help her. But Gabi's fingers, crab's stubborn pincers digging into his arm, held him back.

'Hang on,' she said. 'What's this?'

CHAPTER 39

South East London, later

A man advanced swiftly towards the girl from who knew where? Perhaps he had been waiting, just beyond their field of vision. Perhaps he had followed the girl. He was a non-descript character of medium height and medium build, dressed in unremarkable clothing. Jeans. Quilted navy jacket. Trainers. Wearing a beanie hat that was pulled low over his ears. But the collar of his jacket was open just enough to reveal distinctive ink, as though he had been barcoded to be scanned and identified at this very moment.

'Fuck,' Gabi said, pulling the car-thief's slide hammer and screwdriver from her rucksack with shaking urgent hands. 'Grab him!'

Adrenalin powered Piet across the road, sent him bowling into their quarry just as he had grabbed the little girl, putting his gloved hand over her mouth. Gabi rounded on the predator, holding a screwdriver to his neck, the slide hammer to his stomach.

'Bugger off!' she said calmly to the little girl. 'Go to school. You never saw us.'

The weeping child scrambled to her feet, nodding wordlessly, and scurried away, leaving them with the Candy Man.

Piet had no doubt they had the right man when he looked

into those soulless eyes and then caught a proper glimpse of that tattoo.

'The universe provides,' Piet said in Dutch, feeling hate mushroom inside him as he imagined this man defiling Lucy and Josh.

'Get your fucking hands off me,' Trevor Underwood shouted. 'I was just helping her, you crazy bastards.'

When he started to struggle, Piet felt certain he would not be able to hold him for long. He felt his breath coming short as the adrenalin worked his lungs too hard in the cold. But he yanked the man's arm up his back, gaining mastery over him.

'You do as I say, or I'll cut your throat.' Gabi said, pressing the screwdriver into his neck so that she drew a bead of bad blood.

Underwood nodded.

'Start walking.'

The awkward salsa in the snow, executed clumsily as a threesome, brought them several streets down, where they came upon a semi-derelict pub. A once-beautiful Victorian hostelry on the corner. It was surrounded by poorly erected metal fencing, warning kids to keep out. Telling them that this was a construction site and that hard hats must be worn at all times. A portaloo, standing like a bright-green frozen sentry alongside a giant, yellow skip in the road – its half-empty bulk delineated by flashing traffic cones. Scaffolding criss-crossed the facade, with a giant white tube that shot down from the topmost level into the low mound of snow-covered rubble.

'Get in there,' Gabi ordered Underwood. Gestured with her chin towards a gap in the fencing that was just about navigable.

They trudged inside, crunching broken glass underfoot and stepping carefully over red steel beams, clearly destined for the roof. Piet looked up. A large expanse of white sky above them. Snowflakes drifting down past the naked spires of buddleia that grew like bristles of a witch's broom through gaping apertures in the partially collapsed roof; down through the giant hole in the first floor, where damp had maybe caused the floorboards to rot and give way. Nature was taking the place back. To an architect's trained eye, the building didn't look structurally sound, but he had no time to ponder his safety.

'Sit down. Try anything funny and I'll kill you,' Gabi said.

Piet forced their captive onto a stack of timber. He climbed a ladder to the first floor, spying what he sought through that giant hole. A builder's bucket with a length of sturdy rope tied to the handle. He untied the rope, shinned back down and bound Underwood's hands behind his back.

Still holding the screwdriver at his neck, Gabi was the first to begin the interrogation. 'Where are my children?' she asked.

'How the fuck should I know?' Underwood said, sneering at Piet, who stood before him, wondering if he looked threatening enough.

'Lucy and Josh Deenen,' Piet said. 'What do you know about them?'

'Never heard of them.'

Unexpectedly, Gabi flipped the screwdriver and used the handle to treat Underwood to a sharp blow to the temple. 'Lying bastard. Two blond children. A boy of four. A girl of two. Living south of Amsterdam. They were abducted from our back garden. You've been convicted for an almost-identical offence. Spill the beans or you're dead meat.'

Underwood tried to look round at her. He clutched his hand to his head, as blood tracked between his fingers to form bright red circles on the filthy ground. 'You ain't got it in you, you stupid tart.'

He suddenly kicked out in front of him, catching Piet squarely in the kneecap. Piet's vision clouded with pain. No time for salient thought. Within seconds Candy Man had somehow wriggled his hands free of the rope and grabbed a piece of four by two from the timber stack. He brought it crashing down on Gabi's shoulder and hand, knocking the screwdriver from her determined grip.

The wood whistled through the air again as Underwood hammered it home on the top of Piet's head.

'Gabi! Get help,' he moaned, slumping to the floor, feeling nauseous and dizzy, struggling to say anything more.

Lucidity coming and going, he watched his wife fighting valiantly for her life with a tattooed paedophile. Was he dreaming? Were they both back at home, the children tucked up in bed? Perhaps he had just fallen asleep on the sofa and slipped into a strange dream world.

'Piet!' Gabi's shrill voice brought him to his senses.

He crawled forwards through the rubble and detritus. Underwood had Gabi by the neck and was squeezing with his hands. Gabi's face grew redder and redder, eyes bulbous, staring.

Come on, Piet. You can do this. Step up. Grow a pair of balls.

He rose to his feet, pain from his knees so acute that he almost vomited. He grabbed Underwood from behind and punched him repeatedly in the kidneys, wrestling with him for longer than he thought possible.

Suddenly, there was the sound of a bottle smashing. Gabi, brandishing the deadly shards of an old wine bottle, cuffed Underwood in the neck with it. Blood spurting onto the pile of virgin timber. Then, in one final gesture of defiance, she plunged the broken bottle deep into his chest.

The fight went out of him immediately. He clutched uselessly at the neck of the bottle as Gabi backed away, wide-eyed at what she had done. But Underwood's breath was already coming short. A gurgle in his throat. Blood bubbling up at the corners of his mouth. He sank against the timber, leaning back onto its bulk. Panting. Grimacing. His face turning purple-black with effort, as the air failed to reach his punctured lungs through the slashed windpipe.

'Jesus. What have I done?' Gabi asked.

The noises emanating from this Candy Man were anything but a sweet offering. Gasping. Groaning. His skin fading to grey-blue, now. Deep red flowering around the wounds. All the colours of the rainbow; no treasure at the end. This defiler was not bound for paradise. But it was still a grim sight. Death looked like hard work.

Piet put his arm around Gabi. Still dizzy. He tried to pull her head to his chest, at least to shield her eyes from the spectacle of a dying man. But she stood like a pillar of salt. Lot's wife staring down at Sodom.

'What do we do?' she asked.

Her voice was small. For the first time since they had met, she seemed utterly helpless. Some primal emotion swelled inside Piet's chest, warming him, emboldening him. He covered her ears, trying to muffle the incessant noise coming from Underwood taking his last laboured breaths.

'It's alright, my love. It's going to be alright. Keep breathing. We'll find a way.' Stroked her hair. 'I'm here. I'm here.'

The anguished look on Underwood's face lessened. His breathing was shallow now. Only the prickling sound of blood bubbling inside him. Then, it stopped. He stopped. He was gone.

Gabi howled. Head in hands, she flung herself onto a stack of roofing felt, wracking sobs shaking her body. She clutched at her heart as though she had been stabbed there, not Underwood. But Piet guessed she was crying for more than a dead child sex offender.

'We've got nothing,' she said, after her tears slowed.

Tearing his gaze from the dead man, Piet braced himself to take the reins. He rummaged in Underwood's jeans pocket and found a phone. He took the cash out of his wallet but left the rest. An old carpet lying in the adjacent lounge would do. He dragged it through to where Gabi sat.

'Come on. Help me.'

'I can't,' she said. 'I just can't.'

'You can. You will.' More than at any other time in his life, he needed to be strong and persuasive, bend his normally inflexible wife to his will. 'We've got to hide the body and get out of here.'

She nodded.

Together they lifted the leaden weight of Underwood onto the filthy carpet and rolled his body up like an enchilada stuffed with their murderers' guilt, his evil and the undiluted tragedy of the young lives he had ruined. They checked first that the street was deserted – nobody peeking through their windows – then carried the carpet to the skip and slid it onto the mound of old bar fittings, broken roofing and discarded bricks.

Piet looked up into the snow-heavy sky, descending flakes seeming grey against the white of the heavens.

'They'll find him,' Gabi whispered. 'They'll find him and trace him to us.'

Taking her by the hand, he led her away from that street at a brisk pace. 'In this weather, they won't find him for weeks, if at all. With a bit of luck, he'll end up in landfill, with nobody any the wiser.'

'He'll start to stink.' Her eyes darted this way and that, seeking witnesses from behind their net curtains.

Piet kept his voice calm. 'He won't even stink if it stays cold like they say it will.'

Later, sitting in a café on the A2 in New Cross, warming his hands on a mug of hot chocolate, Piet looked down at the phone. 'Now all we need to do is hack into this. How the hell are we going to do that?'

Gabi looked at him through watery, bloodshot eyes. 'I know who might help us.'

CHAPTER 40

South East London, Aunty Sharon's house, 22 January

The crack of stone against glass. Several heartbeats passed, but there it was again. George opened her eyes, clutching her duvet to her neck. Praying the knack-knack insistence would stop. The clock on her bedside table said 4 a.m. Still dark outside, but the dark before dawn. Not a time for vandalism. Those little arseholes were in their beds now.

Maybe she had been dreaming.

Knack. Stone bouncing from the window onto the path below. Knack.

'What the fuck?'

George sprang out of her camp bed, gathering her duvet to her in the icy chill of Tinesha's bedroom. She pushed the curtain aside and rubbed the condensation from the window. It was freezing to the touch. She peered below, dumbfounded as to who she could see looking up at her.

'What the hell are you two doing here?' she asked, a few minutes later, stirring her instant coffee, twice clockwise and once anti-clockwise. 'Van den Bergen emailed me to say you'd committed suicide.'

Gabi and Piet Deenen were seated at Aunty Sharon's kitchen table. They gripped the cups of tea she had made them with grubby hands, and ate toast savagely, as though it were their last meal. Blackened fingernails made her cringe. It was the first time she had seen Gabi looking anything but immaculately presented.

'As you can see,' Gabi said, wiping crumbs from her wind-burned cheeks, 'we're not dead. We're looking for Lucy and Josh.'

She began to cry. Shaking hands relinquished the mug as though it were radioactive. Trainee tears gave way to fully qual-ified wracking sobs within seconds. She clutched at her chest, showing signs of emotional frailty George had not thought Gabi capable of.

'Did we have an option?' Piet asked.

He put his arm tenderly around his wife. No tears in his eyes, which were clearer than the last time George had seen him. His voice was strong. His posture said confident. A sudden role reversal, she observed, where the meek had inherited the Earth and the strong had been brought to their knees.

Gabi put her head on her husband's shoulder. She wiped her tears on his coat, then turned to George. 'You're the only person we could come to.' There was a pleading look in her bloodshot eyes. 'You won't turn us in, will you?'

'Won't turn you in for what?' Aunty Sharon asked, padding into the kitchen while tying her pink fluffy dressing gown tight around her middle, clippety-clop in the fur-trimmed mules she wore on her small feet. She picked up the kettle and took the lid off pointedly, as though it were a metaphor for her discovery of this clandestine dawn summit. 'Who the fuck are these white people sitting in my kitchen, Georgina?'

As George related the tale of the past eight months, her aunt's sceptical expression softened, giving way to sympathetic tears. Half an hour in, Sharon clasped Gabi's hands, stumbling through heartfelt words.

'I know what it is to lose a child,' Sharon said. She released herself from Gabi's grip, moving to a heavy old sideboard and opening a slim drawer, secreted inside the centre cupboard. She pulled out a shining silver locket and showed the visitors the photo inside. 'See him? That's my Dwayne. He was only seven when he died. I fell pregnant with him when I was still a girl myself, really. Stupid cow, I was. Still. The Lord giveth, right? Ended up my own Mum raised him as much as I did. I tried to do right by little Dwayne, though. It weren't easy, I can tell you.' Her brow furrowed deeply. She fell silent, gazing at the photo. She took a ragged breath and continued, placing a hand on top of the locket on her large bosom. 'He had Duchenne Muscular Dystrophy – not the sort of thing your boy had. But I feel for you, cos I know what it's like, trying to bring up a kid what's different. Then he got meningitis. There weren't nothing they could do. Just one of them things. The Lord taketh away, innit?'

George put her arm around Aunty Sharon, and felt a pang of loss for a cousin she only vaguely remembered. A smiling boy who had been slow to walk and who, at times, resorted to a wheelchair. Born around the same time as she had been. She wondered what kind of man he would have turned into, had he lived.

'How do you cope with the grief?' Piet asked. 'Does it ever get any easier?'

Sharon shrugged. 'I only bring the subject of him up once a year on the anniversary of his death. I made a vow that I'd keep my sorrow to myself, especially since I got Tinesha and Patrice. I fell pregnant with our Tin a year after little Dwayne passed. I couldn't let Tin and her babyfather see how I was hurting. It wouldn't have been right. So, I decided I'd put a brave face on.' She looked down at her work-worn hands as though some wisdom were inscribed in the brown lines etched into her pink palms. 'But there ain't a day I don't think about him and what might have been.' She dabbed at her eyes with a piece of kitchen roll.

Pushing more toast into the toaster, George turned to face the

Deenens. 'I just don't know about this.' She sighed, wrapping her old mohair cardigan tight around her and wriggling her freezing toes in her bedsocks. 'By rights, I should turn you in,' she said.

'Turn us in for what?' Piet said.

He had a point. 'You've still defrauded a nation by pretending you're dead,' she said, feeling like the right thing to do was lurking at the edge of her conscience, like a reluctant wallflower at a school dance. 'And if Hasselblad was about to order your arrest …'

'The Commissioner is a dick,' Gabi said, squeezing the bridge of her nose. 'The Chief of Police is a clown. You and Van den Bergen were the only hope we had. I know your hands were tied, though. Look …' she reached out to George, but George remained by the toaster. Didn't want to make contact with those unscrubbed digits '… we're here to find our children, not commit a crime.'

Aunty Sharon wedged her chair backwards and manoeuvred herself so that she was facing George. Her judgemental eyes narrowed, still tired-looking from her night shift, working the bar at Skin-Licks. She tapped on her locket, now hanging round her neck. 'You grass these poor fuckers up, girl, maybe you ain't got my blood.' She sucked her teeth long and low. 'Maybe you got too much of Letitia in you. And you know, she's so cut-throat, she ain't got any real blood left in those clogged-up veins of hers. She's a fucking reptile, your mother.'

'Please, George,' Piet said. 'Help us find Josh and Lucy.'

Torn between the law and her innate empathy, George was swayed finally by the strength of her aunt's conviction that the Deenens were victims who deserved a chance. She sighed, and ruffled her hair. 'OK. If my Aunty thinks I should cut you the slack, then I will. It must be dreadful for you. I really genuinely feel for you guys. But why have you come here? How the hell did you even find me?'

'Doesn't matter how we found you,' Piet said. 'The fact is …' He seemed to be mulling something over, chewing his bottom lip, looking at his wife as some sort of unseen exchange of information took place. 'We've got a lead. I don't want to discuss it right now, because I don't want to incriminate you in any way. What you don't know won't jeopardise your career, will it?'

'I don't like the sound of this,' George said, biting into her toast, handing her aunt a plate of her own.

'It's nothing to worry about. Nothing criminal, like I said. Gabi's very good at Internet research, so we're just having a feel around.' He produced a slim smartphone from his coat pocket. 'It's just we wondered if you knew someone who could unlock this.'

George pulled her sleeve over her hand and took the phone from him. She wiped it clean on her pyjama leg and pursed her lips. 'Whose is this?'

'Nobody's.'

'Doesn't look like nobody's. Nobody doesn't generally fork out on an iPhone.'

Piet rubbed at several-day-old stubble with his index finger, eyes darting furtively to the cooker and back. 'I picked someone's pocket. That's all. Someone of interest in a pub last night. He won't miss it. Not his type. It's probably stolen anyway. Best you don't ask.'

Four digits. No idea of whose phone it was. At 5 a.m., George's mind was sluggish. She keyed in the obvious ones that she remembered from her days as one of Danny's girls.

'Nada.'

'Give us it here,' Aunty Sharon said, reaching out for the white lozenge. She left the kitchen. The sounds of footsteps on the stairs. Patrice, in the room above. Complaining that he'd been woken in the middle of the night. Sharon's voice was shrill in response. Footsteps back down. A smug look on her face as she handed the phone to Piet. 'There ain't no pin on it now. Some things only kids can do. Like believing in Santa and that.'

Circumnavigating the cramped kitchen, George peered over

Piet's shoulder, munching toast that had already turned cold and damp, watched him scrolling through the contacts list. Then, checking the gallery, where photo after photo of children, snapped from a distance, were stored. His thumb slowed as there appeared a series of blurry shots of two small blond children. One boy. One girl. It was hard to tell if they were Josh and Lucy, but George intuited from the knowing look that the couple shared – loaded with anguish and optimism, both – that they felt they had glimpsed their abducted son and daughter.

She swallowed hard, unexpectedly touched by their optimism after all this time.

'That it?' she asked.

'Can you lend us some money?' Piet asked. 'We've only been here for a few days and we're already out of cash.'

Shaking her head, she held out empty hands. 'I'm on the bones of my arse myself. I haven't been paid yet.'

But Aunty Sharon marched over to the tins cupboard, reached in and pulled out a clean, empty Heinz container with the lid missing, in amongst the legitimate beans.

'There's a couple of hundred, here. Electric bill money. But go on. I'm getting good tips at work at the moment.'

'I'll give it you back, Aunty Shaz,' George said. 'It's my fault they're here.'

Her aunt shook her head and pressed the roll of cash into Gabi's hand. 'Go on. Have it. Find your kids, for the love of God. But don't bloody come back here no more. If you get caught and you go down, I can't have you taking my niece down with you. Right?'

By 5.23 a.m., the only sign that Piet and Gabi Deenen had ever outlived their alleged suicide attempt were two dirty tea mugs sitting in the sink.

PART 3

CHAPTER 41

London, Liverpool Street Station, 19 March

'I wish you'd come back with me so I can protect you,' Van den Bergen said, holding George's hands on Liverpool Street Station concourse as though they had never argued, his nose touching her nose, he, stooping, and she, forced to stand on tiptoes. A tingling lover's kiss in the rush-hour chill air as commuters scurried hither and thither, marching smartly towards another day of corporate containment and profitability.

'I don't need protecting, Paul,' George said, pulling his head towards her so that her face pressed against his, feeling the warmth of his freshly shaven skin caressing his forehead. 'If Piet Deenen wanted to kill me, he'd have done it by now. And searching for him in a city of nearly ten million makes trying to find a needle in a haystack look like a piece of piss. This isn't Amsterdam.'

Van den Bergen sighed resignedly, holding her so close that she could smell the residue of hotel shower gel on his body through the fabric of his coat.

'I should tell my colleagues at the Met,' he said. 'There aren't ten million homeless men in London. I'm sure they'd pick him up. Every day we leave it, there's a risk he'll kill again.'

She shook her head. 'Things have gone quiet. Gabi's bound to come and find me next time she runs out of cash. She knows I'm a soft touch. And if she knows where Piet is, I'll convince her to give up his whereabouts. *If* she knows. But I'll put feelers out myself in the meantime. Contact homeless shelters. There's a few places I can look. And when I find them, I'll string them some bullshit so we can get them back to Amsterdam. Under your jurisdiction.'

'I don't like it.' He gazed blankly at the busy blur of other travellers, darting to their various destinations. 'It's my duty to go after Jack Frost. This is my case. I catch criminals.'

George felt a knot of anxiety in her stomach; her instincts screamed that doing things by the book was no way to skin this particular alley cat. 'Paul, if you launch an international manhunt, we'll never see either of them again. You know I'm right. The Deenens have already proven they're pretty astute at staying off-grid. And who knows what they've found out? Dobkin was onto something. Piet and Gabi are onto something. Their kids are still missing, but there's something much bigger lurking just over the horizon than two abducted toddlers. A real fucking kill, if you can bide your time and use the Deenens to hunt it down. You want medals in the war on crime, General? You'll get the Victoria Cross if you bring a huge trans-national trafficking network to justice! And more importantly …' she poked him affectionately in his shoulder '… as far as your sanity goes, Kamphuis will be toast!'

'Jesus.' Van den Bergen emitted a low growl. He grimaced, then rolled his eyes and treated her to a half smile. 'Okay. Why the hell are you so good at destroying my resolve, Detective Lacey? First, in the bedroom, now—'

'Ha! I knew you'd put out in the end, old man,' she said, winking. 'I'm irresistible. Admit it.' She put his hand on her bottom.

Van den Bergen coloured up. He smiled knowingly and sighed, looking up at the departures board. 'You're persistent and a corrupting influence, Georgina McKenzie,' he said. 'I have to go. I'm going to miss my flight.'

In amongst the din of thoughts vying for precedence in her head, all George could think of was her lover's naked body entwined with hers: a triumph where he had promised failure.

After they had finally been shooed out of the brasserie of the hotel by the maître d', they had repaired to Van den Bergen's room with the various sheaves of case notes. They'd discussed Gabi Deenen's three impromptu visits to Aunty Sharon's house, where Gabi had told them she and Piet had fallen out – that his mental health had worsened. She had thrown George off the scent by saying her husband had absconded on a coach to the South of France, or even Spain, maybe, where the freak Arctic weather manifested itself as cold showers of rain and the odd gusting wind, instead of minus twenty with two or three feet of snow.

'She tapped me up for cash,' George had told him, remembering Gabi's thin frame and filthy clothes. 'I helped her out. She cut a sorry bloody figure, I can tell you. No woman should have to live on the streets. Especially not in this weather. We let her get showered and Aunty Shaz slung her clothes in the wash.'

At that point, she had been sitting on the end of Van den Bergen's bed. He had been perched at the head, propped on cushions, sketching her, using hotel stationery.

'I still can't believe you kept it from me,' he'd said, and stopped sketching, studying the line of her face with his pencil held in front of him to get the angle right. 'All this time. You didn't trust me.'

George had tutted. 'It was a bond between women. For Aunty Shaz, it was about the pain of losing a child – whether through illness or abduction. Two bereaved mothers. Gabi was looking for her kids and didn't feel she could ever go back to her old life until they were found. I swore I'd keep quiet. Promises like that, you just can't renege on, man. It's not cool.' George had straightened the wrinkled bedspread as she'd considered the spectre of an ailing Leitita and the unexpected communications she had suddenly started receiving from her father, who had found her on the St. John's College website. 'I may not have my own kids, but I've got enough emotional intelligence to understand the strength of even the shittiest parent-child bond.'

Paul had put his sketching materials to one side, folded his hands in his lap and appraised her with those shrewd grey eyes. 'Then you should understand why Tamara's pregnancy has made me think twice about us,' he'd said. 'You're my daughter's age.'

She had crawled the length of the bed to meet him, sinuous movements designed to weaken his resolve. She knew he would be seeking out her cleavage, visible in the V-necked top she was wearing.

'But I'm not your daughter, old man,' she had said, pulling his shirt free from his trousers with her teeth. Toying with the naval hair that grew thick on his abdomen, looking for the line where the Butcher had unzipped him. Kissing along the scar tissue until she reached his chest. Butterfly kisses along his collarbones. Caressing him with her breasts. She'd felt his body relax and his desire registering hard and insistent against her inner thigh.

He had grabbed her by the waist and rolled her over, peeling her clothes off as though she were the last shrink-wrapped snack in a chiller cabinet and he were a starving man.

'You said I'd have to come running with my tail between my legs,' he'd said, caressing the sides of her breasts, tracing a line around her erect nipples, deliberately not touching them.

'I'm not very good a bearing a grudge,' she'd replied, voice hoarse as he'd teased the resolve out of her. She'd stroked herself with his erection so he could feel the hot pool of her own desire. 'Anyway. Tail seems present and correct, old man.'

'You drive me insane,' he had murmered, pinning her arms above her, describing a figure of eight as he caressed the curves of her body, finally licking her nipples with a firm tongue.

'It's my job.' She had pulled him inside her without further preamble, and for the first time in more than two months, they had made love. It had been urgent and intense, all of Van den Bergen's reticence evaporating in the burning passion of their union.

The following morning, beneath the departures board in Liverpool Street station, she registered the satisfied warmth between her legs and a heart that felt full. 'I love you, you know,' she said. 'Now, are you going to stop shutting me out?'

'I'm so sorry I've been an arsehole.'

The creases at the sides of his eyes said he was happy. For now. He stroked George's cheek with his forefinger and sighed contentedly. The unforgiving angles of his face seemed to have softened into something more hopeful and youthful.

'You're so fit,' she said, smiling. 'I forgive you, arsehole.'

As he pushed one of her wayward curls to the side, a memory pressed its way to the fore: Sophie calling Paul a pig; Sophie, pissed in a pub, waxing lyrical about stolen Roma children; Sophie, now also missing in action.

'What is it?' Van den Bergen asked, pulling up the handle on his small suitcase, the lines in his brow deepening.

George shook her head, as though she might shake her hazy thoughts into sharper focus. 'Nothing.' She kissed her ageing lover on his sizeable hand and started to back away. 'Go back to Amsterdam. I'll call you tonight,' she said. 'I'll be over within a week or two. I promise. Granddad!' She winked, waved and then was gone.

Sophie. Piet targeted Dobkin, who had information on the Son of the Eagle. Now, Sophie's absent without leave. Christ on a bike. How could I have been so fucking blind?

As George marched smartly towards the Underground station, she called Graham Tokár, asking if he'd seen his Roma-championing ally. He hadn't. *Shit.*

But there was an email from her father, saying he was in town for ten days only and did she want to meet for coffee? *Shelve it for now. He's waited twenty years. He can wait a bit longer.* A text from Letitia, saying her consultant's appointment had come through for her pulmonaries and that, and would George come with her to it? *She can fucking take a ticket and wait her turn too.* Finally, a text from Patrice.

    Danny Spencer is living Greenwich.

The world stopped turning. Her lips prickled, blood draining away at the whiff of a ghost. There was her old flame's address, displayed in black and white on the small screen. George Googled it. A penthouse in a block of recently constructed executive apartments right by Crowley's Wharf in Greenwich – the jewel in South East London's crown. Blistering views of the river. Isle of Dogs on the opposite shore with the upturned fruitbowl dome of the O2 Arena visible in the distance as the river bent round to the right.

'Nice one, Dan the Man,' she said, feeling jealousy, like sickly poison creeping along her veins, leeching the well-being from her body that a night with Paul had given her. 'Crime really does pay, you bone-headed, egomaniac, plucked-eyebrow twat.' Fleeting memories of being ensconced in Danny's drunken mother's unmade bed with him and Tonya. Two's company. Three's more limbs than an Argos divan could technically cope with. Teenage kicks in a filthy, standard issue Borough of Southwark box.

George thought, then, about the cramped conditions at Aunty Sharon's and her revolting room in the college house. On a material level, Danny's life had improved significantly. Hers had not.

'Cunt.'

How would she feel when she saw him? Would she even see him? As she disembarked the Docklands Light Railway at Cutty Sark, the harsh wind blowing off the Thames almost knocked her off her feet. With a thunderous heartbeat and thoughts of Van den Bergen and Sophie long gone, she made her way past the National Maritime Museum and down to the river. There was hardly any snow left here, apart from huge grit-strewn mounds that looked like dirty icebergs. They had been shovelled by council workers from the site surrounding the Cutty Sark. And there, to George's left, was the fully refurbished tea clipper, looking resplendent in the harsh winter light. Masts, towering above her, with the vessel's taut rigging and fluttering international bunting lending itself more to a summer's day than deep mid-winter and one criminologist's hunt for a two-bit crimelord.

Catching her breath, she walked gingerly along the river, slippery in parts where the melting snow had hardened to ice. On her left, the Thames flowed into town, bearing all the secrets of the sea, large tracts of ice still floating on its surface. Snow clung stubbornly to the lesser towers of Canary Wharf's skyline in the distance. The old Royal Naval College loomed in front of her, to her right, with its neo-classical columns and Georgian windows. Christopher Wren would be turning in his grave, George mused, had he known a Danny was living within spitting distance of this World Heritage Site that was still crawling with tourists even on the shittiest of mornings.

Having weaved her way through the historic complex, she finally came out the other side. Danny's lair in her sights.

'I can't believe I'm doing this,' she said, peering up at the penthouse. Using her smartphone to zoom in on the large living room window. As if she'd even see him from this angle! It was ridiculous. 'This is bullshit.'

George hung around by the block of apartments for another half an hour, feeling silly. Obviously there was no Danny to be seen … what the hell had she been thinking? And what would she even do if she saw him?

At midday, with a rumbling stomach, she walked back into

Greenwich Village. She decided she'd reward her failed sleuthing attempts with an opportunistic trip to Noodle Time on Nelson Road. A nice bowl of ramen would defrost her fingers and toes.

Picking up her pace, she walked past Nauticalia, selling all manner of maritime-related nick-nacks, the orange and white frontage of Noodle Time visible further down on the other side of the street. Giant photographs of various dishes hung in the window. *Noodles. Chicken. Hot, salty broth. Van den Bergen's sizeable manhood finally having put in an appearance, thank fuck.* These were her only thoughts as she prepared to cross the road. So when a tall, athletic figure emerged from Greggs bakery in her peripheral vision, she almost didn't register him.

But he was crossing over now, apparently coming her way. Closer and closer.

George stepped back into a doorway, put her hood up and watched this tall, swaggering figure making short shrift of something greasy in an almost-translucent paper bag.

She swallowed hard, seeing her ex-lover at close quarters for the first time in six years. Boy band good looks. Shaven headed. Plucked eyebrows. Still the same. He'd hardly aged.

Danny Spencer. No more than four metres away. Danny. The man who can. The man with a plan. The man she had betrayed, and who had put word out on the street that one day he would come for her and that that day would be her last.

CHAPTER 42

London, South Bank, at the same time

The tick, tick of time running out syncopated perfectly with the steady, loping beat of Piet's heart. So unlike the paralysing panic when despair first came knocking; when he had opened the door to an event horizon beyond which all hope and light would inexorably disappear. But his heartbeat was unhurried now, after all that had happened. Only dead calm and focus remained.

Focus.

From his vantage point some way behind his quarry, he checked the cracked face of his watch yet again. Precision timing was needed to pull this off.

Over the Millennium Bridge they walked, battered by almost-horizontal sleet, the churning waters of the Thames swollen beneath them, carrying the first of the glass-roofed tourist cruisers upstream, like foolhardy salmon. The brutalist tower of the Tate Modern art gallery loomed before him, a judgemental index finger on an unforgiving fist of a building pointing skywards to God. Always watching. Never caring. To his left and right workers trudged past this ragged, unremarkable man, knowing only that it was an ordinary day full of work and woe and domestic disappointment, unaware that the dark, foreboding Tate tower stood sentry over two men – a man with nothing, about to kill; a man with everything, about to die.

The gun felt heavy in the pocket of Piet's sodden overcoat, freezing in his hand as the chill wind bit through the fabric. Silently, he prayed that his aim would be true and that just for those moments where he put a bullet in the head of Gordon Bloom his shaking body would be still. That he had not died from exposure was a miracle, but he had no doubt that without proper treatment he would be dead inside a week from infection in any case. At least, if it was his fate to depart this hateful world early, he would take this black-hearted bastard with him to hell.

Gabi's research had been detailed. Gordon Bloom was to meet one of his criminal underlings on the South Bank path that runs beneath the Millennium Bridge at 9.30 a.m. He had attended a typical City breakfast meeting at the Worshipful Company of Something or Other, near St. Paul's at 8 a.m., which meant, given his habits, the proximity of the two venues and parking restrictions, he would probably walk, rather than take his car. Once the underling left, he would be vulnerable.

Bypassing Bloom, who stood by the barrier at the river's edge, as though he were merely taking in the view of St. Paul's dome on the far side, Piet continued several paces in the direction of the gallery entrance. He sought the cover that the bridge's ramp afforded him. In the shadows, he would not be seen by security cameras buzzing overhead in that very public place. Recording every move, every word, every expression. At a glance, he was just another rough-sleeper. Caught on camera, however, at the side of a revered entrepreneur and peer of the realm, his would be an instantly recognisable face. Mindful of this, he pulled on the hood of a fleece he had liberated from somebody's long-forgotten, snow-bound washing line, thawed out and dried over a fire some other rough-sleepers had started in an oil barrel.

9.30 a.m. arrived, bringing with it promptly a jogger in full winter gear – thermal leggings, hat, wind-cheetah. Nothing out of the ordinary, even in the sleet. The paths that ran along the Thames on either side were always studded with lycra-clad fitness fanatics, pounding through their commute to work in return for tight abs and admirable cholesterol levels. At first, Piet was not even certain that this jogger was Bloom's associate. But when the man stopped by the rail and started to stretch his hamstrings out – when his lips started to move, even though he and Bloom were standing a metre apart, not looking at each other – Piet knew that Bloom's criminal rendezvous was taking place.

The exchange took only ten minutes. An almost-imperceptible nod from Bloom designating a satisfactory conclusion.

The jogger moved off towards Southwark Bridge, loping quickly out of sight. Bloom was alone.

Game on.

Bloom checked his watch, made a short call, then started to walk towards him.

Emerged from his hiding place, Piet gripped the gun in his pocket. Bloom was getting closer and closer; Piet would finally get a good look at the Bloom plc demi-legend. The buzz cut hair. The prosthetic eye. With a subtly different shaped nose now, his face was hard to recognise from the three-year-old photos that had sat on Dobkin's laptop. But it was him, alright. The King of the Shitheap. The lynchpin in the devil's own conglomerate. The Duke.

Piet felt momentarily as though ticking time had frozen; as though the sleet hung motionless in the air; as though this was the turning point of a life which had once been full and grounded but which was now empty and anchorless. Now, he was hurtling through the hostile vacuum of space – a lone astronaut in a flimsy capsule fashioned from grief and anger. Heads, you make it home alive. Tails, you burn up on re-entry. Just keep flipping the coin.

'Don't make a sound or I'll shoot,' he said, pressing the barrel into Bloom's cashmere-clad back, just over the kidney sweet spot. He frisked him with one deft hand and withdrew a pistol from his breast pocket, wedging it into his own waistband. 'Keep walking.'

Jagged breathing in. Jagged breathing out. A cold sweat breaking out in already-drenched clothing.

Bloom stiffened but continued to look straight ahead with his good eye.

'Walk!' Piet steeled himself to keep the adrenalin out of his voice, lest his captive took it for fear. Prayed he didn't look as ill as he felt. *Focus.*

'You want money—' Bloom said.

'Shut your mouth!' He pressed the gun harder into the man's bulk. Was anybody looking? No. Too wrapped up in their own lives. 'Come with me if you want to live.'

Bloom turned around abruptly and looked at Piet through his sole, operational eye with a directness that made him flinch. 'I know who you are,' Bloom whispered, a smile playing on his lips. The filler on his front incisor that covered the hole where a diamond stud had once sat was just visible.

'Then you'll know why I've come for you,' Piet said.

'I'm not afraid of you, you tin-pot scribbler of shitty suburban hovels. I'll see your body concreted into the foundations of the next city skyscraper to go up before you'll get me.'

Piet considered Bloom's words. His cool demeanour. His apparent lack of fear. It was as if he'd been expecting the ambush and had already planned for it. He looked around furtively, wondering if Bloom's muscle was about to appear. His heartbeat quickened, his composure all but gone. But nobody did come forward. And a light, white dusting of powder around Bloom's left, dripping nostril told Piet exactly from where Bloom's confidence flowed forth.

'Move!' he said, pushing the gun further into Bloom's back. 'Round the back of the gallery.'

Together they marched diagonally across the busy concourse in front of the Tate. Heading away from the South Bank down

Holland Street, where they shuffled along an icy pavement past glittering modern office blocks to their right. Nobody looked at them askance. Londoners with their heads and umbrellas bent against the flurry of sleet were the most inattentive citizens in the world. Thankfully.

Bloom neither attempted to speak nor escape. On they stumbled. Nearly there, now. To the white Transit van in the parking bay, with its engine running. A small figure, dressed in black, just visible in the driver's seat.

Piet slid back the door to the loading area with his free hand. 'Get in!' he said, praying his teeth wouldn't start clacking.

'Where are you taking me?' Bloom asked.

'I ask the fucking questions. Get in and kneel down, you piece of shit!' He slid the door shut. A makeshift light he had rigged came on. He grabbed Bloom's manicured hands roughly and strapped them together at his back with electrical cable ties. Then he banged on the steel wall that separated the loading area from the cab. The van pulled away.

As his temperature soared silently going over the plan in his head became more difficult. He shivered, and every joint, muscle and fibre of his body ached. He strapped the billionaire's mouth with duct tape and remembered what Gabi had told him: 'We get him in. We sit him down. We get every shred of information out of him that we can. We do *not* kill him until we've done that! Don't forget it!'

This was the first time they had actually been together in the same space for weeks. It had felt strange. Where physically and emotionally she was a wreck, intellectually Gabi was still the nerve-centre of their operation: the brain telling him – the body – how best to execute this mission. Researching his next target and emailing over the details, like a brief from MI5. He had taken his orders from her dutifully and stepped up to become the alpha male she hadn't chosen but had always secretly hankered after.

Sitting on the floor next to him at 2 a.m. in the doorway of a closed minimart, encasing his feverish hand inside her skinny cold fingers, Piet had remembered, however, that they were looking for their children. Not playing some ridiculous spy game. And that she was not just a tangle of electronic impulses and words pinged from one library computer to his email account, picked up on another. She was his wife, made from flesh and blood; the woman he still loved.

'I won't forget,' he had said. 'We have to find Lucy and Josh. That's all that's left.'

Sitting in the back of that van, staring at the man who orchestrated an elaborate puppet show for gargantuan profit, jerking the strings of traffickers, paedophiles, pornographers, drug dealers, junkies and abducted children as he made them dance a gruesome jig across lost continents, he wasn't entirely sure if he wanted to remember.

The van came to a halt. The acoustics outside had changed, more muffled now, as though they had pulled into a cavern. The driver got out of the cab, making the vehicle lurch slightly.

Bloom cocked his head in the murk, observing his kidnapper coolly with one functioning eye, making Piet feel as though this might be a flat calm harbinger for the deadliest of storms.

'We're here,' Piet said. 'Up you get.'

Grabbing Bloom under the arms, Piet hoisted him to his feet. Dead weight. The door slid to the side, revealing the diminutive figure and stern, drawn face of Gabi. A dank railway arch beyond. Strip-lighting flickering on and off overhead. The drip-dripping of moisture coming from who knew where? Giant wooden doors, rotten at the bottom and missing chunks, like decaying teeth. The place reeked intensely of damp that stung in the nostrils, but it was perfect for their purposes. Better still, Piet had discovered on the local Borough town-planning website that the entire row had been condemned, ensuring nobody would disturb them today.

'Sit on the chair in the middle,' he said, pointing to a low wooden seat he had liberated from a derelict school.

Bloom complied. Good eye darting everywhere.

Gabi stuffed the van's keys into the pocket of her hoodie. Stepped forward and ripped the duct tape from his mouth.

'Thanks for dropping by, Lord Bloom,' she said. Her hoarse voice sounded hollow in that place. 'Or should I call you the Duke?'

'Gabi Deenen,' Bloom said, scrutinising her slowly. He leaned back in his small seat, as though it was a minor throne, legs splayed wide. 'Long time, no see. You're quite the celebrity these days. Could do with getting your roots done, though.' He tutted. 'Very shoddy for a PR woman like you. You used to be quite shaggable.'

'Where are my children, you evil bastard?' she asked.

Piet held the gun with both hands, aimed at Bloom's head. 'Answer my wife! Where are Lucy and Josh?' he shouted.

No response from Bloom, however. He merely chuckled malevolently, following the line of the filthy vaulted ceiling with that staring orb, appraising every inch of the murky space until his gaze came to rest on a large object in the corner. His brow furrowed as he struggled to make sense of what he was seeing.

When his face contorted into an alarmed grimace, Piet knew he'd worked it out.

Sitting in a chair in that dark corner, wearing a potato sack over her head, was the body of a woman, wearing a batik print skirt and Doc Marten boots.

CHAPTER 43

London, later

'But the hospital sent this appointment through. It's the only date they got. You promised me. You said you was gonna come with me.' Letitia's voice was thick with guilt-trip melodrama and indignation on the end of the phone.

'I'm cutting you off, Letitia,' George whispered, eyes on Danny, some two hundred yards further up the road. Walking from Russell Square towards Euston. She had tailed him successfully all the way from Greenwich. Now where the hell was he going? 'I'm busy.'

'He's telling me about my pulmonaries, you heartless cow! Don't you want to know if your mum's dying?'

'Get Leroy to go.'

'Ha fucking ha. Is that meant to be some kind of dig at me? Cos if it is and you think—'

Pressing the button to end the call felt good. Cathartic. Then, almost immediately, despite her best intentions, George felt a prize shit. But this was no time to get entangled in her fucked up relationship with Letitia. She was busy with Danny, who was hanging a left into Gordon Square, strutting in step with some shady-looking arsehole she had seen him meet in the Hare & Tortoise noodle bar in the ugly concrete temple to middle-class consumerist woe, the Brunswick Centre. His companion had a tough, brutish face, not softened by the severity of his cornrows. He was wearing ghettofabulous designer gear: flash baggy jeans with various zips, appliqué and patches; a Puffa jacket, two sizes too big, judging by the shoulders – looked as though it was made from leather. It must have cost him a couple of grand, at least. He hadn't taken it off in the noodle bar. Probably thought someone might nick it from the back of his chair. Wanker.

The two men strode on ahead. Purposeful. Suddenly more puffed up. Shoulders wide. Starting to look to their left and right, as though something was on the brink of going down.

Now, George found herself only metres behind two dangerous psychopaths, who had started to dawdle. The large dome of UCL's main building was not visible beyond the neighbouring rooftops, obscured as it was by the bare-branched tangle of frosty trees in the little private park that serviced the surrounding houses. But she knew it was there. With a sharp prickle of dread that lanced along her spine, she realised where Danny had led them. The surrounding Georgian townhouses were all occupied by lecturers at the college. Had Danny come for Dobkin? Was Danny somehow embroiled in this mess of paedophile rings, trafficked Roma children and Jack Frost?

Shit. Shit. Shit.

The guy with the cornrows reached inside his coat and kept his hand there. He leaned up against the park's iron railings further down. Danny, chewing on a toothpick, looking furtively up at the second floor of one of the houses. Checking his watch he nudging his compatriot and nodded, two fingers in the air. What the fuck did that mean? Two minutes? Started to peer into the rear window of a red estate car.

No time to connect the dots.

I've got to warn Dobkin. What's his number?

Retreating to the cover offered by a BMW, parked in one of

the bays that ran alongside the park, George looked for Dobkin's name in her phone. She was certain they had exchanged numbers after he had ambushed her and then eccentrically taken her for coffee. But it wasn't there. Checking her email inbox, she looked for the last angry missive he had sent before their meeting. Buried beneath an avalanche of other correspondence.

Too slow. Too late.

A loud crack. Shattering glass. A car alarm ringing shrilly across the square. Danny, standing beside the red car, deftly concealing a crowbar inside his parka. The two men edged several metres away from the noise. Eyes on the house. Hoods up.

The door opened. And there he was, right on cue. Shambolic and puzzled-looking in the doorway. Dobkin. White-man-book-junkie's pallor. Same balding dark hair and overgrown goatee. Same heavy-framed glasses. Now, wearing a cardigan and cords. Running over to the red car, fob in hand.

But there, waiting in the wings, was Danny's associate, pulling something from his coat. Car alarm still honked. Diverse alarums.

George stood uncertainly in the midst of this theatre of certain tragedy. Split-second pondering: fight or flight. *Fight*. Poised to run to Dobkin's aid.

But the gun had emerged: a black, semi-automatic bringer of death at the end of cornrows' large hand.

A thunderclap, ricocheting around her.

One bullet finding its home in the middle of Dobkin's forehead. Even from her vantage point at the end of the street, George's sight was keen enough to register the black spot in the pallid skin. The end of a brilliant mind.

Dobkin crumpled to the ground like the last falling leaf of winter.

'Jesus!' George said, eyes wide, phone in hand, watching the madness unfold.

Dobkin lay sprawled in the street, beyond her help now. Students and academics started to stream out of the surrounding buildings to witness first-hand the fate that had befallen one of their number. Bewildered screaming from the girls. Confusion abounded. The scratching of heads. A profusion of mobile phones – their owners uselessly dialling for an ambulance or pointlessly filming the dead body of poor Professor Dobkin. Police sirens starting up in the distance, getting closer, moment by moment.

But George had no time to ponder her academic rival's fate. Danny and cornrows were walking briskly towards her. Only metres away on her side of the road, for god's sake! Making herself as small as possible behind the bumper of the parked car, praying she would not be discovered, she eavesdropped on the men's now-audible conversation.

'Just keep walking, bruv,' an unfamiliar voice said. Cornrows. An indelicate Peckham patois, not unlike Danny's. Sounded older. 'Which way you wanna go back?'

'Cops are coming.' Danny's voice. Two metres away and gaining ground. Sounded breathless. 'Backstreets are quiet.'

'Nah, man. Got to get into the crowds. Hiding in plain sight.'

'Whatevs. You wiped your prints of the gun? Ditch it, yeah?'

A thunk, as something heavy hit the frosty ground at the base of the trees in the park.

An amused chuckle. 'You telling me how to do my job, man?' Cornrows sucked his teeth. Moving further away now. 'You the one paying me for my expertise, innit?'

'Respect. Listen. I got to be someplace else, bruv. Laters.'

George took the arrival of several police cars as her cue to move. Last thing she needed was to get roped in as a witness.

With a thunderous, disbelieving heart, she emerged from her hiding place. She spotted Danny on the other side of the street, on his own once again. No sign of Cornrows.

Go home or keep on his tail?

A snap decision, fuelled by anger at the theft of an innocent criminologist's life. George determined that she would follow her ex-lover, as he made his way briskly to some other terrible rendezvous, wondering how long it would be before she joined Dobkin in his one-way journey to the other side …

CHAPTER 44

A railway arch in South East London, at the same time, and flashbacks to early February

'Tell me about your sordid little enterprise,' Gabi said, pushing the razor blades further into the flesh between Bloom's fingertips and his nails.

A muffled cry was the closest she got to eliciting a scream.

'Made of stern stuff, are you?' She moved back round to the front to examine his face. He was biting his lip so hard that the skin was turning purple. Eyes screwed up tight – the prosthetic orb not quite concealed by the lid – a solitary tear trickled its way along his jawline. But the sweat beaded freely on his brow and his nostrils flared as he breathed in, out, in, out heavily. Good. He was in agony. Blood had started to flow in earnest from the wounds, pooling on the floor behind him, beneath where Piet had tied his hands together.

'Come on, you entitled piece of shit,' she said, savouring this switch in the balance of power. No longer a sycophant, servicing the ego of her fee-paying client.

She took a stiletto flick knife out of her jeans pocket. A handy weapon for a woman living on the streets. The thin blade sprang to attention in her slender hand. She stuck it deftly up Bloom's right nostril. 'Tell me, or you'll never snort a line of coke again, the Duke.' Her clipped annunciation of his underworld moniker was laced with mocking cynicism.

Bloom's eyes shot open, his good eye, staring at her, as though she were deranged. He shifted his focus to Piet, standing behind her. Grey-faced and waxy-looking, holding the gun, which looked too heavy for him.

'You two are fucked up,' he said.

But Gabi inserted the knife several millimetres more into his nasal passage, knowing she was about to draw blood. 'Spill the beans, old bean.'

'Okay, crazy tits! Take the knife and the razors out before I bleed to death.'

'No.'

'Then you might as well kill me.'

'That can be arranged,' Piet said, clicking off the safety on the gun. He gesticulated at the recumbent shape of Sophie in the corner. 'You can join her in hell, if you want.'

'Alright! I'll talk. But only if you take those goddamned razors out of my nails.'

Gabi withdrew the various blades. She bound his hands with a filthy rag, then returned the stiletto to his jaw, pressing into pink fleshy jowl.

'Speak!' she said.

'I run a trafficking ring,' he said. 'But you already know that, because …' he grimaced at Piet '… you killed my fucking business partner.'

'Did I? Did I really?' Piet's voice, behind Gabi, so unlike the downtrodden ghost of a man who had departed those lowland shores in the belly of an old lifeboat. Even though he shook with illness, his was a confident voice now.

But Bloom was not displaying the requisite amount of fear and respect owed to Jack Frost.

'Yes,' he said to Piet. 'You murdered Rufus Lazami. Three

children, now without their father. I hope you're proud of yourself. I've had one of my people watching you. Did you really think you were off the radar?' He started to laugh. Menacing and derisory. 'Amateur! You can run, but you can't hide, Mr Deenen. I know it was you who took out one of my players in Amsterdam. And two associates in Berlin.'

'You know less than you think,' Gabi said, scrutinising Bloom's pudgy, cosmetically altered face, biting back the urge to tell him exactly how the drama had unfolded in the Zoological Gardens on that snowy night.

*

In addition to discovering on Trevor Underwood's phone a text exchange with Gerhard Hauptmann and photos of children they had been certain were Lucy and Josh, she and Piet had found the details of a man called Tomas Vlinders. It had taken days of painstaking and logistically difficult Internet research in libraries and Internet cafés to track Vlinders down to a run-down block in the Bijlmer district of Amsterdam, and Hauptmann, the owner of several tenanted houses in Kreuzberg and Neukölln, to a smart, second-floor abode in a historic block near the Zoological Gardens in Berlin.

The decision to travel back to mainland Europe had caused a great deal of consternation between them.

'We've only just got to London, for God's sake!' Piet had said, warming his hands by an open fire that the other rough sleepers had set beneath a Camden railway arch. 'We haven't got passports!'

'Piet, we've got to follow every available lead,' she had said, feeling the ever-deepening snow that had gathered in drifts – even here – creeping through the soles of her inadequate boots. 'Because one of them might lead us straight to the kids.' She had lowered her voice, looking over her shoulder at the drunks knocking back stinking bottles of cooking brandy and tins of strong lager. 'Underwood was worth going after, wasn't he? Haven't we got a new trail to follow?'

Nodding, Piet had said, 'Yes. But I thought you couldn't face it. I thought you were in bits. Having second thoughts about it all.'

His words had stung. Gabi had always been one to thrive under pressure; the orphan who coped with adversity. The little hard-nut daughter of a South East London builder, making her way in the middle-class world of marketing and PR. Holding her own with the likes of Gordon Bloom. In her marriage to Piet, she was undoubtedly the stronger of the two. Or had been. Until killing Underwood.

'I'm fine,' she had said, batting away the memory of the paedophile as he had drowned in his own blood. 'I'm over it. Now, are we going to track down these animals and get our son and daughter back?'

'How the hell can we travel without passports?'

'This is London. You can find anything here.'

The recommendation to make contact with a man called Danny had come from a homeless man called Irish Tony. Living in a Kilburn squat, Tony had offered them shelter for several nights in exchange for a bottle of single malt and a hand job from Gabi. They had negotiated amicably, settling on two bottles of whisky, no hand job. Danny was your man, apparently. Purveyor of fine counterfeit identification and other contraband articles of great practical value – for a fee. She had left Piet to seek this man out, while she had made another fundraising approach to George and her endlessly empathetic aunt.

Travelling to Zeebrugge in the cab of a Polish truck driver had been painless enough. Nobody had been looking for dearly departed Gabi and Piet Deenen, let alone interested in questioning the well-faked identities of a rather dishevelled René Vandewinkel and his wife, Bouvien. Even the authorities were too preoccupied with the freakish weather. Stories of the Deenen children had been replaced by rolling news shows depicting gridlock, whiteout and record-breaking icicles hanging from every rooftop.

But once on Belgian soil, rather than go immediately in search of Vlinders in Amsterdam and risk discovery by the Dutch authorities, they had opted to continue with the Pole through to Berlin.

Sleeping in a strange land, with three feet of snow for a bed and unforgiving Arctic temperatures as their blanket, had become the toughest of survival challenges. Days had passed, as Gabi pieced together information about Hauptmann, sneaking in and out of hotel computer rooms, where lazy residents had failed to log out of their guest accounts, consuming what was left of their daily Internet allocation.

Huddled together, trying and failing to sleep in an old Volvo estate car they had broken into, they contemplated what she had discovered: the porn sites, registered in Hauptmann's name, that had given way, several pages in, to a new log-in; a firewall she simply didn't know how to bypass, though she could guess the content on the other side. 'If only I could have cracked the password,' she had said, pausing to cough violently in the car's freezing interior. The smell of plastic and diesel had caught at the back of her throat, making it harder to suppress the tickle. 'Maybe I'd have seen Josh and Lucy.'

'Is that what you'd want?' Piet had asked, holding her close. 'To see our babies in stomach churning photos?'

She had bitten her lip, shaking her head fervently. 'I'd rather. I'd—' The unpalatable words had stuck. 'I'd rather they were dead.'

It was a thought she had entertained a hundred times or more in the privacy of her own mind. It had been the first time she had ever said it aloud, and had felt immediately guilty, as though she had, indeed committed the infanticide that the Twitter trolls had accused her of.

Piet had merely squeezed her hand. 'We'll get them back,' he'd said. 'They're young. Maybe they won't even remember. Maybe some rich lunatic who desperately wants a family has bought them off these traffickers. Maybe they're ...'

At 4 a.m., the air was too cold and thin to sustain anything akin to promise or hope. Piet had fallen silent. Gabi had slept fitfully for only an hour.

Sustained only by partially eaten falafel that they had salvaged from a bin outside a kebab shop, they had used the cover of darkness the following evening to advance on Hauptmann's apartment. Second floor up, the light had been shining in his living room. Slipping into the communal entrance hall, as a neighbour had left the building. Whispering in the shadows; hatching a plan.

'Is that you, Hans?' The response to Piet's authoritative knock. A muffled voice had come from somewhere inside the apartment.

Unhurried footsteps had gotten closer on the other side of the heavy, ornate door. The light that had been visible through the spy-hole had suddenly snuffed out. Hauptmann had looked out onto the landing. 'Hans? Hans! Are you there?'

Would he open up? Gabi had held her breath, praying he wouldn't slide some large bolt home, pad back to his living room, rendering their visit useless. But curiosity had clearly got the better of him. When the lock clicked and the door had opened a fraction, Piet had thrown all of his weight against it, pushing the rotund Hauptmann onto his back in the hallway. Scrambling to his feet with astonishing speed for a fat man.

They had chased him down along the slippery polished floor of the hall into a bedroom to the left. An acrid stench had hit Gabi on entering the room – unmistakeably tomcat urine. An overfed Persian cat had sat on almost every available surface. Newspaper had covered the floor, dotted with cat turds and pools of thick yellow pee. Dust had hung heavy in the air, along with the foetid tang of old, soiled bedding. But the most distasteful sight of all had been three lots of computer equipment, each hooked up to wide-screen monitors: a pornographic image of a pre-teen girl up on one of the screens, opened in Microsoft Paint;

two more suggestive images of naked boys on the remaining equipment, clearly in the midst of being photoshopped.

'What do you want?' Hauptmann had shouted. A thin, reedy voice for such a large man. 'I've got money.' He'd backed towards his wardrobe, though there was nowhere to go.

'Money won't be necessary,' Piet had said. 'It's you we've come for.'

The crotch of Hauptmann's trousers had stained dark as he'd urinated. 'Please don't hurt me.'

Together they had wrestled him onto the bed, tying him up with electrical cable from his own computer equipment, kneeing him in the small of his back, straddling him so that he was face down, gasping for breath.

'Where are these children?!' Gabi had shouted, twisting Hauptmann's head with a nauseating crack so that he was forced to look at the monitors. She'd wanted to snap his fat neck, but the hunger for answers had been gnawing. 'Where are *our* children? Two Dutch toddlers.'

'Lucy and Joshua,' Piet had said, emerging from Hauptmann's kitchen, carrying a meat cleaver with purpose. His dead eyes had given him an utterly sinister aura.

After twenty minutes of quietly terrorising Hauptmann to no avail, but then finally persuading him to give them access to his computer suite by threatening to dismember his cats, Gabi had uncovered his website and database. It contained thousands of images of children. Feeling a mother's anguish, manifesting itself as almost crippling dyspepsia, she had looked to Piet for guidance.

'What the fuck shall we do with him?' she had asked.

Piet had raised the machete. 'I'll kill him. It'll be messy, but it's something to do on a cold snowy night, I guess.'

'Kill me?' Hauptmann had squealed. 'No! I'm innocent. These are just photographs, nothing more. I'm a photographer, specialising in children's portraits.'

Gabi had brought a computer keyboard smashing down on his head. 'No photographer I know photographs the abuse of abducted children and calls it portraiture, you fucking moron.'

'I don't know where your children are!'

But they had rifled through the drawers of his desk. That had been the point at which Piet had found the keys, labelled up with the address of the house in Kreuzberg.

'Keep an eye on him,' Piet had said, handing the machete to Gabi. 'I'll be back.'

*

'Are our children living with the Roma?' Piet asked, moving closer.

Bloom looked askance. 'Roma? Gypsies, you mean? How the hell should I know?'

'You took them!' Gabi screamed.

Shaking his head vociferously, Bloom scowled. 'No, I fucking did not!' A flash of anger unexpectedly blurred the lines as to who was really in charge here. 'And what have gypsies got to do with your missing brats?'

'Your trafficking ring preys on kids from Roma camps,' Piet said. 'You use corrupt Roma men to provide you with a steady stream of children as young as four or five. And the Roma are mobile as well as desperately poor. Why the fuck wouldn't you move our children around with them, so they can be abused all over Europe, you scum bag?'

He lunged forwards and pistol-whipped Bloom on the temple.

*

Finding the house in Kreuzberg had been the toughest challenge Piet had yet faced during this mission: the basement of a semi-derelict Berlin townhouse where the stuff of nightmarish news reports was reality. Ten children had been locked in together in the dark, sleeping on filthy mattresses spread across the floor. No Joseph Fritzl or Fred West had stood guard, yet this situation had seemed so far worse to Piet: missing children, at the mercy of not one psychopath but an entire network of traffickers and abusers that saw young lives only as commodities to be exploited and monetised. To Piet, that basement had represented the ghoulish reality of a ruined world.

'Have you seen this little girl and little boy?' he had asked, showing a photograph of Lucy and Josh taken at nursery.

Shaking heads had told him that none of them had.

Setting the captives free to wander in the snow in the hope that they might somehow be reunited with their parents had felt like an empty triumph. He had wanted to wait with them until the police arrived – to know that they would be safe – but Piet had had no option but to slink away into the shadows, to return to Gabi and Hauptmann.

Climbing the stairs of the paedophile's apartment block, he had felt a mixture of relief and dread: relief that his babies had not been in that house of heartbreak; dread that they might be prisoners inside another. He had determined to make Hauptmann suffer. Where justice had failed, he would avenge those Roma children.

But his rising bloodlust had been quelled at the sight of the door to Hauptmann's apartment standing ajar.

'Gabi?' He had pushed it open, following a smudged trail of blood that had led to the chintzy living room. His pulse had pounded in his neck. 'Gabi?'

The apartment had been devoid of any signs that his wife and Hauptmann had ever been there, but for the giant message on the wall, daubed in blood. One word.

ZOO.

*

'I've already told you, you piece of shit,' Bloom said, spitting as he spoke in a voice thick with venomous intent. 'I don't know where your kids are. And why the hell would I? I don't keep tabs on every product that's bought and sold under my name.'

Yet again Piet brought the weight of the gun down on his temple, drawing blood this time.

'Product? You see children as fucking products? To be peddled around celebrities and politicians in some Margate hotel, as though they were drinks in a minibar or a room service special.'

Bloom's raised eyebrow showed his surprise.

Piet nodded. 'Oh, yes, I know all about that hotel. And I've got the list of so-called pillars of society that are regular paying guests, *Lord Bloom*.'

For the first time since their interrogation had begun, Piet watched with satisfaction as Bloom swallowed hard, the pupil dilating in his functioning eye betraying fear. 'You're bluffing,' he said.

'Am I? Anything happens to me or my wife, the whole world will know the identities of those perverts. You fail to return Josh and Lucy, my list will be published in every newspaper you can think of. The police will know. You'll be—'

A remorseless face of a man that possessed no remaining shred of humanity spoke then, heartless, empty words coming from his mouth. 'I'm the Duke. The king of the fucking heap, you piece of shit. My business interests are far-reaching. And I'm not afraid of the police. I'm untouchable.'

'Oh yeah?' Gabi said, rounding on Bloom, holding the razor blades aloft in a fan as a warning, narrowing her eyes. 'Who have you got in your pocket? High-ranking top brass in Scotland Yard? Some of your fellow backbenchers? Someone in the cabinet?'

Bloom shrugged. 'That's for me to know and you to find out.' He winked. 'Crazy tits.'

Grabbing his hands, Gabi gleaned a certain sadistic pleasure in ramming the blades back under Bloom's stubby fingernails.

Whimpering, panting, he strained against his bonds but refused to scream.

'Who is protecting you in the police?' she asked, inserting the stiletto knife into Bloom's ear. She cocked her head to one side and frowned. 'I can't hear you!'

'It was you, wasn't it?' Bloom closed his eyes. 'I heard it was a brutal attack. I don't think it was him at all.' He fixed Piet with a disdainful sneer. 'You killed the Germans. Some mother figure you are.'

*

Piet had been gone for some twenty minutes. Gabi had not expected to be defenceless against an unfit man who was unarmed. But a moment of weakness where she had had to use the toilet had been her undoing. Hauptmann's bulk on top of her had been unassailable. Within minutes, a second man had appeared answering to the name Hans: a weedy, sallow-faced man with a comb-over, who fulfilled every physical stereotype of a child molester. She had struggled, at least, and left Piet a desperate clue as to where they were taking her. Possibly her last testament, daubed in her own blood.

It had been unbearably cold in the zoo. Bound and gagged by the periphery wall of the polar bear enclosure, she had felt the end was near, bereft at the loss of her children. Guilty that not only had she failed to protect them, but she had also failed to rescue them. She deserved to die and had been now merely curious as to what form that violent end would take.

She had tried to decipher Hauptmann's conversation with his co-conspirator. Talking, talking in a Germanic monotone. When Hauptmann had leaned her over the top of the thick enclosure wall and grappled inside his trousers to reveal a small, hard cock, she'd realised that a simple death did not await her. Perhaps she deserved the additional pain and humiliation, she'd thought.

She'd braced herself as the thin assailant tore off her jeans, exposing her delicate skin to the sub-zero night, then hope had surged anew at the sight of Piet sprinting up behind him. Carrying a snow shovel in one hand. Wielding an icicle that glistened in the moonlight in the other. Puncturing the man's neck so that blood arced freely onto the snow. Steam coming from the hot liquid, hissing on the frozen ground.

The killing had happened quickly. Frenzied. Snatching the snow shovel from Piet, she had beaten Hauptmann repeatedly over the head with it until he became docile and confused. Severing his penis with the blunt blade. Violence that had been fermenting inside her all these years had suddenly issued forth with every blow; every kick; every fistful of snow that she had forced into his windpipe. Retribution for the suffering of those children. Revenge for the disappearance of her own. With his dying breath, he had uttered but six words.

'Gordon Bloom. Find Dobkin. He knows—'

She had pronounced her final judgement upon him and brought his end with the blade of the shovel, a deadly smile rent across his face. There had been silence at last in the Zoological Gardens.

'What have I done?' she had asked, still clutching the snow shovel. Staring at the two men that were now nothing more than macabre trim on the edges of the polar bear enclosure. 'I'm a murderer, Piet. You're a murderer.' Holding her blood soaked hands aloft like Lady Macbeth. *Out damn spot. Out, I say.* 'How can we live with ourselves after this?'

'Look, neither of us ever wanted any of this to happen,' Piet had said, plucking a mobile phone from Hauptmann's trouser pocket, then searching Meyer's body. Eventually he had stopped, regarded his wife, then held her shaking body to him. 'But I could have lost you back there. Those men were going to rape you.' He had touched her bloodied head. 'They would have killed you. I went to that house in Kreuzberg and set a load of kids free. It

broke my heart to see them huddled together in a squalid basement. Wouldn't anyone kill to stop that?'

Gabi had shook her head. 'Going off grid was a mistake. We've
ruined our lives.'

'Our lives were already ruined.'

'You're turning into someone I don't recognise, Piet. We both
are.' She had searched those killer's eyes to find traces of the
warm, gentle soul that had once been evident in them. She had
seen a hopeful glint, but realised it was merely moonlight
reflecting on their glassy surface.

Piet had led her away from Hauptmann and Meyer's bodies
– already covered with a dusting of snow. 'The police failed us.
So, *we've* become the police. This is our life now, Gabi. We're
going find our kids. We're going to bring these bastards to justice.'

*

'I'll ask you one more time,' Gabi said, pressing the stiletto further
into Bloom's ear. 'If you don't answer me and or I think you're
lying, I'll drive this knife right through to your brain.' She took
a deep breath, remembering Piet's words, spoken with such
conviction in Berlin's Zoological Gardens. *We're going to bring
these bastards to justice.* 'Who in the police is protecting you? It
is someone in Scotland Yard?'

Silence.

'You have a house in the Netherlands, don't you? I remember
you telling me when I was handling the Bloom Group account.'
Memories flickered through her mind like damaged footage from
an old movie. Gabi, working on a PR presentation. Cheesy smiles,
cheesy patter all to keep the big cheese happy. She knew he had
been checking out her arse in her tight skirt and heels. Those
moneyed types always treated women as though they were orna-
ments, positioned strategically in the workplace like exotic
arrangements of plants: pleasing to the eye but superfluous to the

real business of work, which was tended to by men. 'When I told you I was married to a Dutchman. Remember? A mansion in Wassenaar, you said.' She dug further into his ear. Blood starting to trickle out. 'Is it someone on the continent?' Pieces of the puzzle arranged themselves into a coherent pattern ... the upper echelons above Van den Bergen insisting their Chief Inspector hare down blind alleys in the search for Josh and Lucy, always pointing the finger everywhere but in the direction of child traffickers. 'A member of the Dutch police?

Bloom winced, then sighed heavily, contemplating his fate, perhaps. He looked over at Sophie, slumped in her chair with the potato sack still on her head.

'He's just a golfing buddy, but a buddy nobody would ever dare cross,' he said.

'Tell me!' Gabi shouted.

'The Chief of Police. Jaap Hasselblad.'

CHAPTER 45

South East London, at the same time

Tailing Danny was hard work. Fresh from a crime scene, his tendency to look over his shoulder regularly meant that George had to hang a good way back, darting into doorways, whenever he jerked his head in her direction. Her composure disintegrated fast, like decay on an overused cassette recording, leaving her feeling thin and exposed, jittery with hunger. Paranoid. It wasn't helped by her phone going into overdrive.

Letitia, of course.

'Yes, I got your bloody texts. I'll speak to you later, for god's sake,' she had told her mother, praying the wind didn't carry her voice to Danny. Four times, now, with the same bullshit. No. Five. Letitia – insistent, shrill, making George's eardrums quiver, bitching about Aunty Sharon, as if her aunt were anything but hospitable and long-suffering. Hospital appointment this. Pulmonaries and sickle cells that. 'No, I can't come back,' George said. 'I'm in the middle of something. I ain't telling you. That's none of your business. Listen, if you phone back again, I'm putting you straight to voicemail. Right?' Verbal abuse coming at her in a tinny, crackling package. Pain in the arse. Fuck you very much, Mommie Dearest.

When Danny had ducked into London Bridge station, George

had lost sight of him for five minutes. Maybe more. Heart thumping. She couldn't see him. Perhaps her momentary lapse in concentration had left her exposed; he was now the predator and she the prey. But no. There he was, only three or four metres away, emerging from a coffee kiosk. Mercifully not looking in her direction, rising on the escalators to the main concourse. The Shard outside, towering above them – a dizzying dagger of glass and steel – made her think of the icicles used by Jack Frost. Piet Deenen, impaling the delicate necks of men on winter's weaponry. She shuddered.

There was Danny, juggling his coffee and an Oyster Card. A flash of his perfect teeth as he smiled at some girl in a short skirt, wiggling her way to the tube. He was strutting towards the barriers in that blinging parka, the spoils of an urban war, well-won on his back, carrying the muscular bulk of the man he had promised to become as a lithe young brother, when he and George had been together. She felt a strange pang of nostalgia, though she had sought to bring him down for good.

Sucking Danny off in her tiny, dingy council house, when Letitia had been at work. Kissing Danny in a stolen car and imagining just for a second that he cared. Fucking Danny's friend, at his insistence, while he watched, Tonya sprawled naked on his lap. George ushered the memories into a box and locked them safely away.

Concentrate, girl! And don't get too close. At this time of day, if he was taking an overground train, she would be too easy to spot.

South-easterly bound, he alighted after only one stop. New Cross Gate. George sought the cover of a group of rambunctious pensioners making their way home from town, carrying Blue Cross sale bags. She waited until Danny had rounded the corner and then crept forwards, spotting him making his way down a busy street. Chicken shop, newsagents, cash your gold, a barber's shop for the super-fly of SE5. Checking his watch. George had a feeling he was heading to meet somebody. A change in his deportment. Walking with even more swagger. Keeping tabs on time. Anticipatory behaviour she had seen many times in this man she had once known too well.

Advancing towards some railway arches that were boarded up, he took out his phone. Made a call. Turned around towards George. But she had already darted behind a board that had become all but dislodged. A soggy, torn notice on the mildewed ply saying that the entire row was condemned. Trespassers keep out. Fly posters will be prosecuted. Partially covered, of course, by a fly poster.

Downwind of the conversation, George could hear Danny speaking.

'Yeah, man. I'm here, now. Yeah. I got them. You better have the cash and you better not be short, right? Alright. In a bit.'

Her hiding place was flawed. If he were to look in her direction, not only would he see her feet peeping out from beneath the board, but he would undoubtedly see her face through the gap, where the wood had been ripped askew from its fastenings. Worse still, once his rendezvous was over, Danny would have to pass back this way. How the hell could she hide from him then? And what if Letitia or Van den Bergen called? In this quiet alley, she was sure he would hear her phone. Cold sweat started to roll down George's back. A myriad of things that could go wrong.

The distinctive sound of a Zippo lighter springing into action told her that her ex-lover was waiting patiently. She smelled the smoke from his cigarette carried to her by the wind. Caught sight of him thumbing a text to someone. Then, finally, footsteps approaching from the far reaches of this dead end street. George pressed her eye right to the gap to get a clear view of whom he was meeting, gripped by curiosity and dread in equal measure.

A shuffling, ragged figure coming towards him. Getting closer, closer.

'You've got them?' the man asked in English with a barely discernible Dutch accent. 'Amoxicillin?'

'I got what you asked for. You wrote it down yourself, didn't you? My man can fucking read. It's on the packet, see?' Danny proffering what appeared to be a box of tablets. Pointing at the label. Cigarette hanging out the side of his mouth. Eyes screwed up.

And there was Danny's clandestine customer. Barely recognisable, now with overgrown, greasy hair – suddenly silvered as though he had aged ten years in those few weeks. Florid scabs had colonised his haggard face. But still, a trace of the sensitive-looking architect that George had met several times in Amsterdam's police HQ, whose eyes had been continually puffy from the desperate tears of the grieving.

'Piet Deenen,' she whispered to the chill wind.

Money changed hands. Danny moving off, now. Advancing in her direction. George stood to attention, rigid with fear. A solitary sheet of ply standing between the huntress becoming the hunted. Perhaps he wouldn't see her. *Walk on by*, she thought. The Dionne Warwick ringtone of dearly departed Derek's phone suddenly springing to mind.

Just walk past. Just walk past. Thudding words in time with her heartbeat. *Walk on by.*

But the spirits of the musical greats were busy in George's world today. James Brown in her pocket, singing that Papa had a brand new bag. Letitia the infernal dragon. Why hadn't she turned her phone's ringtone to silent? Idiot!

Danny's eyes swivelled toward the sound. He stopped walking, shoving a hand inside his coat, where a bulked pocket implied he was packing, a puzzled look on his overly groomed face.

George held her breath. The godfather of soul, still warbling away in her pocket, immune to the danger he and Letitia had put her in. Please god, please god, please god.

Too late for disingenuous prayer.

'Who's there?' Danny said, marching up to her arch. 'I can see your fucking feet! Come out, you spying bastard.'

A tight, tumorous knot of panic in her stomach sapped the strength from her. How should she play this? Give in to fear or front it out?

'What you going to do, Danny Spencer?' she asked, stepping out from behind the flimsy board. Speaking loud enough, hopefully, for Piet Deenen to hear, still visible, as he trudged further and further away from her. It was a punt, but it was the only card she had to play. 'You going to put a bullet in a criminologist? You really wanna fuck with someone under Her Majesty's special protection? Cos I know you've been staking out my aunt's place, like some shitty little child-trafficking pervert.' Shouting, now. Desperate for her voice to be heard by anyone. A passing stranger would do. Just buying her enough time to bluff her way out of this.

Surprise registered on the man with a plan's face. A raised eyebrow. A half-grin that could denote anything from genuine pleasure to menace, knowing Danny. Turned out, it was menace. Something metallic being pulled from Danny's coat. Of course, it had to be a semi-automatic. Pointing at her head, he clicked the safety off.

'Ella. Just the girl I wanted to see. You must be telepathetic, innit?'

In George's peripheral vision, hope blossomed at the sight of Piet turning around.

'Georgina?' he shouted. 'Georgina McKenzie.'

'Yes! Over here! Piet! I've got news for you. I've been looking for you.'

A gun in Jack Frost's hand, now, though. This changed things. Did Piet view her as an ally or a foe?

'Put your weapon away,' he told Danny. 'I don't give a shit what sort of beef you have with her. I want to hear what she's got to say.'

Danny sucked his teeth, grimacing at Piet, and swung his weapon around to aim at the ragged man's head. A ludicrous standoff, where George was certain Danny would always win. His turf. His formidable reputation. And his upper hand wasn't shaking with ill health.

When the gun went off, George yelped. Ears ringing for the second time that day, she stared in horror at the bloody mess of Danny's knee. The tall, powerful figure of a two-bit back-street gangster lay prone on the cobbled ground, writhing in agony.

'You fucking psycho bastard!' Danny cried, wide-eyed and incredulous as he looked up at Piet.

'Get up,' Piet said, holding the gun with two quivering hands, smoke rising on the icy air from the barrel. 'You're coming with me.'

'I can't walk!' Danny shouted.

'You'll walk if you don't want another bullet somewhere more deadly.'

Piet turned to George. 'Let's go somewhere private.'

Van den Bergen. I have to tell Paul. Could I text him? But what good would that do? He's in Amsterdam. I'm here. Jesus. I never expected this. Fuck. I'm such a dick. I could dial 999, but I don't want the Met crawling all over this. So much more at stake than a dead millionaire. Feeling like she was trapped in some surreal dream, George ran through her options silently. It took her only moments. Her only option was to follow Jack Frost.

With Danny limping ahead of her, dripping blood onto the cobbled street and Piet at her back, holding the gun, George silently considered the arguments she could use for her life being spared, should things turn nasty. Had she not helped the Deenens thus far? Could she not act as a go-between with the law? Surely, all she had to do was remain positive and confident.

I'm going to die. I'm going to end today with a bullet in my head on the floor of a condemned railway arch, and I haven't eaten since the bowl of Rice Krispies at breakfast. Thanks, God, for fucking nothing. What a shit life.

'Get in there!' Piet said, using the gun to point to the ominous black opening in the penultimate arch. Bypassing a white van that was parked, discretely obscuring the fact that a board had been ripped clean off the entrance.

The stench inside made George gag. Intense mildewed damp, rotting vegetation. Something else. She peered down at the cracked concrete of the floor, once painted red, now peeling with naked buddleia stalks bursting through. Noticed small, round figures dart quickly out of view. Telltale black balls dotted everywhere. Rat faeces. Plus, the ammonia stink of their urine. But another scent on the air. Metallic tang. Unmistakeably blood.

'Further in,' Piet said.

In the dingy light rigged from the lofty, vaulted drip-dripping ceiling, she spied the truth of this subterfuge. Gabi, sitting on a chair with a stiletto knife in her hand, painted bright red with blood that was not her own, staring intently at a man, bound to another chair, some two feet away: well-dressed and bleeding from his hands into a puddle on the concrete, filthy ground. A fat rat, sipping at this nutritious pool. The man jerked his head upwards to examine the newcomers with one roving eye. He focused on her ex-lover first, recognition clear in his somehow-familiar face.

'Danny? What the hell has he done to you?' A cut-crystal accent George had heard before.

'I know, man.' Danny clutching at his knee, whimpering, putting George in mind of an overgrown boy who had hurt himself in the playground, playing football on unforgiving tarmac. 'He shot me in the fucking knee! Nutcase bastard. I was only doing him a frigging favour.'

'Get this asshole tied up,' Piet told Gabi. 'And put some duct tape over his mouth. He talks too much.'

Hanging back in the shadows, relieved that she was apparently not being treated as a captive – not yet, in any case – George studied the scene. A figure slumped in the corner, with a bag on its head. No, a woman. Wearing a skirt and Doctor Marten boots. But the man with the bleeding hands and one eye … gripped by an intense feeling of déjà vu she took a step forwards, heart pinging like a bagatelle ball gone mad against the inside of her ribcage.

That one exorcet orb switched from Danny, locking onto her. The line of his nose had changed subtly. His face was scarred and bloodied. But it was his grin that gave him away. Slight discolouration on his incisor where a hole had been filled but had since stained with coffee.

George swallowed hard as the clues lined up to conjure a coherent chain of events. A man she had last seen two years ago in an industrial unit near Laren in the Netherlands. A man who had had a diamond stud embedded in his tooth. Whose eye she had damaged irreparably with a makeshift knuckle-duster fashioned from her keys. The driver of a Bentley. The partner of the Butcher. The Duke.

'You!' she said, backing away.

'You!' he said, shuffling forwards. His mouth arcing downwards, his bull neck straining. A shark of a man, poised to snap her up, as though she was nothing more than chum in the water.

'You know each other?' Gabi asked, forcing Danny to sit on the ground.

'This little whore owes me an eye. It's because of her I had to change my appearance. She's the only one outside my circle of trust who could ID me as anything other than Lord Bloom, Chairman of Bloom Group.'

He spat at George, missing her by a good metre or so, but George cringed at the gesture of ill intent.

'I knew you'd be a loose end. I should have killed you when I had the chance,' he said. 'Cheap black bitch.'

'Fuck you!' George said. She approached Bloom, remembering the feel of his hands squeezing around her neck. She felt the grip of indignation, more current and pressing than his fingers had been on her windpipe. 'You'll have to try pretty fucking hard to kill me, you piece of trafficking shit. Last things living after the fucking apocalypse will be cockroaches and me.' She poked herself in the chest for emphasis, head tracking from side to side as she channelled pure Letitia the Dragon. 'And my name's McKenzie, you one-eyed pig's arsehole. Not black bitch.' She spoke slowly, annunciating every syllable. 'Dr Georgina Avenger-of-the-innocent McKenzie. Bad cook. Good fuck and eater of fine crisps!' She balled her fist and punched him in the mouth so hard and so suddenly that his head flicked sharply to the side, making an unpleasant clicking sound.

'Ow!' she said, shaking her throbbing, sullied knuckles. 'Ew.' She wiped the mess of Bloom's blood and saliva onto the fur trim of Danny's parka, ignoring Danny's muffled protests. 'Ugh. Is that real fur, you moron? Who the fuck wears real fur anymore? You're such a ponce.'

Bloom breathed heavily through his nostrils. His mouth was livid red where his lips had split. His face twisted into an expression of pain, fear and suspicion as he appraised George. 'There's something wrong with you,' he said. 'You're not right in the head.' He scrutinised Gabi and Piet, then the mysterious slumped figure in the corner. 'None of you are.'

'Says the self-confessed king of a criminal empire that trades on abducted children?' Gabi said, standing next to George.

'So, is this the Son of the Eagle's *boss*?' George asked, folding her arms, stroking her chin thoughtfully. She was aware she was in the company of a serial killer and that, though she understood Piet's motives – though the architect and father of two was still inside him, buried beneath the filth of the streets, the heartbreak and the infection – it might not take much for him to turn on her. She would have to tread carefully.

'You know Gordon Bloom?' Piet asked, waving the gun at her, non-committally. 'Is that why you were lurking outside?'

George related the story of how she had, in fact, been trailing Danny in a pre-emptive bid to become the hunter instead of the hunted, and told the tale of Professor Dobkin's untimely demise at the hand of a hired fixer. She turned back to Bloom. 'You think this bastard just runs a big old paedophile ring? That's only half of what he's into!' She turned to Piet. 'If you're on a vigilante killing spree, this is your man.' She jerked her thumb in Bloom's direction. 'This is the pinnacle of the shit heap. Drugs. Sex slaves. Slave labour. Organs. You name it. If this bastard can get his hands on it and sell it at a profit, he will. And now I know his true identity. I've seen him on the telly. He doesn't even need the sodding money. Greedy twat.'

'Kill him!' Gabi said. 'He won't tell us where the kids are. So just end this. Kill this other idiot, too.' She pointed at Danny whose body heaved with silent sobs.

'I can fix it so you get away with this, guys,' George told the destitute couple, playing her trump card. 'I know people in the secret service who have been after these evil bastards for years. I can convince Van den Bergen to let his Jack Frost case turn cold.'

Piet was sizing her up, lips pursed, as though he were trying to work out if she were bluffing. He glanced over at Gabi, who jerked her head once in consent, then he turned back to George and nodded. He gripped Bloom by the shoulder, put the barrel of the gun against him temple, safety clicked off.

'Wait!' Bloom shouted. 'Wait! I can help you find your children.'

'How?' Piet asked.

'Well, it stands to reason, doesn't it? If anyone can find two toddlers who have been snatched by perverts, it's going to be my people.' He looked pointedly at George. '*She's* not going to bloody well track them down after all this time, is she? She's not even police. In fact, what are you, exactly?'

George sucked her teeth at Bloom. 'Your worst nightmare. That's what I am.'

'An empty promise that you'll find Josh and Lucy if I let you go?' Piet said, pressing the gun harder into the side of Bloom's head. 'Not good enough.'

'I've told you about my connection to Hasselblad.'

'Hasselblad?' George said, puzzled.

'I'll give up the bloody lot,' Bloom said, blinking too much. It was hard to tell if it was sincerity or trepidation. 'The corrupt politicians. The celebrities. Every last name in my network. But don't kill me.'

Coughing frenzy. The crackle of infected mucus deep in his lungs. Piet began to sweat, but still he held the gun in place. 'I need a gesture. A mark of your commitment.'

Bloom nodded. Hope in his disingenuous face. 'I'll let you, your wife, even this stupid black cow go.'

'More,' Gabi said.

'Give me back my gun. I'll show you.'

'No.'

'I promise, I won't harm you. Just untie my hands and give it me. Just for a second. Let me show you. You can still put a bullet in me if I try anything funny.'

Piet rummaged inside his coat, then produced the handgun he had taken from Bloom by the Tate. Gabi cut loose the billionaire's bonds. Everyone was poised to end this monster. George knew instinctively what was about to happen but was unable to prevent it, lest she jeopardise her own life and the life of the still-breathing figure slumped in the corner with the potato sack on her head.

Bloom grabbed his handgun and shot Danny between his beautiful brown eyes.

'There,' he said, placing the spent weapon in his own breast pocket, then holding his bloody hands in the air. 'Was that a big enough gesture?'

CHAPTER 46

South East London, Aunty Sharon's house, later

'Pack your shit up,' George said to Letitia, flinging a suitcase on the bed. Aunty Sharon crowded in behind her on the landing. 'We've got to get the hell out of here.'

'What do you mean, we?' Aunty Sharon asked, elbowing her elder sister out of the way.

George took her underwear out of the small chest of drawers that she shared with Tinesha, and flung the items into her battered case. She resisted the urge to fold them in a certain way and make the shapes fit together like a jigsaw. No time for that. 'All of us. Me, you, Tin, Patrice, Letitia. The lot. We're not safe.' She conjured a picture in her mind's eye of Danny and felt a bittersweet pang in her chest. Poor, poor Danny. A twat of a man she had once loved, despite her best intentions. Dead on the floor of a condemned railway arch. No more big plans. No more swagger. No more spreading the love around the ladies. Not yet thirty and a life snuffed out with one bullet.

'Where the fuck we supposed to go, exactly?' Letitia asked, barging beyond the threshold to sit on the end of George's bed, marking her territory, though it wasn't hers to mark. 'I got that consultant's appointment next week.'

'Not now, you haven't.' George wedged her make-up bag into the corner, along with four different pots of hair product. 'You can see someone in Amsterdam. Paul will swing it for you.'

'Fucking Amsterdam?' Two sisters in union, like a conflagration of outraged gospel singers with Tourette's.

George nodded. 'Danny's dead. You heard of the Duke?'

Both shook their heads. Aunty Sharon started to fold George's T-shirts neatly then finally processed her niece's revelation. 'Danny Spencer's dead?'

'We're all in danger. This man – the Duke – it's a long story. But we have to be on a flight this evening. It's all booked. It's all paid for. Just don't ask questions.'

Letitia levered herself off the bed with a grunt and flung two pairs of George's jeans absently into the case, which George removed and folded properly, seam to seam. 'I ain't going to Amsterdam,' she said, arms folded, lips puckered as though she were planning to kiss this spontaneous bullshit from her estranged daughter goodbye. Typical Letitia. I say black. You say white. Mary, Mary, pathologically contrary. Annoying cow. 'I'm dying, or did you forget?'

Wrapping her trainers in a supermarket plastic bag so that they wouldn't touch her clean clothes, George tutted. 'You'll be dead soon enough if you don't get on this flight. Did you miss what I said? Danny. Is. Dead. There's a crime lord coming for us, and he's not after Aunty Sharon's recipe for salt fish and ackee.'

Aunty Sharon scrutinised George's face, then clasped her niece to her bosom and kissed her hair. 'If you say it's a matter of life or death—'

'I do.'

'Well, that's good enough for me.' An anxious tear escaped the corner of her eye, which she wiped away with a trembling hand. 'I thought we was living here on borrowed time. I always knew you were caught up in some bad stuff. It came with the territory and I weren't even bothered, cos I wanted to give you a roof with family.'

George returned the warm embrace from her aunt.

'Yous is making me feel sick,' Letitia said. She stood abruptly, then barged her way back out of the room with hands still folded beneath her armpits. 'Happy family cobblers, like I ain't even in the room. Don't you worry about your old mum, Ella.' She jerked her chin towards Sharon. 'And don't you worry about your ailing sister, neither, you fucking cuckoo-in-the-nest Judas bastard. I can stay and hold the fort, seeing as I'm evidently the only Williams-May with bollocks swinging between my legs.' She patted the crotch of her pyjamas with a manicured hand. Flame red nails today said Letitia the Dragon was on fire.

'Oi!' George shouted after her. 'This is not some fucking council estate game of throwing stones. This isn't some kid from the Pepys Estate threatening to put our windows in.' She ran after her mother, dragging her back from the top of the stairs by the sleeve of her dressing gown. She locked eyes with her and saw the stubborn defiance there, almost as if she were holding a mirror to her own soul. 'We are dealing with serious criminals, Letitia. Hitmen, people traffickers with money to burn. They'll just bypass your loud fucking mouth with a shotgun. Do you want that to happen? Cos they're coming. They're coming now!'

```
Get out of the house a.s.a.p. Even if
your family won't come, you must. Don't
lose the Deenens, whatever you do. X
```

Running a finger affectionately across the words of his text, George swallowed down frightened tears. She wished Van den Bergen were with her, to herd this extraordinary rag-bag of family and Amsterdam's most wanted onto the next flight to Schiphol.

'You phone the taxi?' she asked Tinesha.

'Yeah,' Tinesha nodded, peering nervously through the window of their tiny shared bedroom, still wearing her uniform from work.

'Anything?'

'Nah. All quiet. You sure we've gotta go? Only I had a date for tomorrow night.' Tinesha toyed with her hair, looking crestfallen.

'Yep. Sorry. You can go on your date when this arsehole is behind bars.'

George remembered how Gordon Bloom – his gun back in his hand – had worn the grin of a triumphant cannibal as he had regarded that broken backstreet gangster's lifeless form, savouring the kill of one of his own as though Danny's strength and vitality were now his.

'I'll make some enquiries,' he had told Piet. 'I'll be in touch.'

An exchange of email addresses. The sense of a truce forged between men of the world. But Bloom had focused on George with that one functioning cold, blue eye.

'My deal is with him, not you,' he had said, pointing his gun at her head, miming pulling the trigger with blood-slick fingers. Click. 'You still owe me an eye. Maybe I'll take it from you. Maybe I'll take it from someone you love.'

Now, George's heart was pounding as she zipped up her case in Tinesha's bedroom, shoving her passport into her handbag with fumbling fingers. *There's time. Stop panicking. The taxi will be here in a minute.*

But there wasn't time.

A quick visual check of the street revealed a sleek, black 7 Series BMW gliding slowly down towards the house. Dark-tinted windows, the wintry afternoon sun's reflection on the windscreen revealed nothing of the driver or any passengers inside.

A lump in her throat. The words stuck.

'Go. Out the back. Quickly!'

Tinesha, wide-eyed and uncomprehending.

'*Now!*'

In the cramped kitchen, the windows were steamed with the breath of her mother, examining her nails whilst intermittently sneering at Gabi Deenen; Aunty Sharon, who was bundling a half-eaten fruitcake into a sheet of tin foil; her cousin, Patrice, gaming on his phone as though their lives weren't on the line; Gabi, haphazardly scrubbing Bloom's blood from beneath her fingernails at the kitchen sink, so that she might pass muster at the airport, wearing George's second-best jeans and Tinesha's interview blouse. Piet Deenen looked almost presentable in the coat and suit Patrice had worn to Derek's funeral. He was still shaking and visibly sweating, though he had downed every analgesic Letitia had thrown at him. Only Sophie Bartek was absent, back on the train to Cambridge by now – discovered still alive and well beneath the potato sack that she had consented to wear, agreeing to play dead as a warning to Bloom in return for her freedom. She was clearly delighted that she had mined a rich seam of new research material, thanks to the Roma of Kent and Jack Frost's night-time gallivanting, though forever now holding a grudge against George for roping her into this dangerous world of vigilante killers, missing children and violent criminals. Mixed blessings from the unholy Dr McKenzie.

George had more to worry about than offending Sophie's sensibilities. Death had just pulled up to the kerb outside.

'Out the back!' George yelled.

As she bundled her reluctant mother through the kitchen door, through the front door's safety glass George caught sight of a large figure, dressed in dark clothes. Broad in the shoulders. A white man. Knocking insistently. No taxi firm in South East London ever sent a white man, driving a brand-new 7 Series to do an airport run. Especially not one wearing black gloves.

'I ain't packed my heels,' Letitia said in too loud a voice. 'I gotta go and get my heels.'

Knocking again at the front. The hammering of a meaty fist.

How long before it occurred to the driver to check this back alley, now clogged with brightly coloured suitcases, being dragged along on half-bust wheels by their hapless owners?

'Shut your face, Letitia,' George hissed, pulling the back door shut, as the unwanted visitor started to ram his shoulder rhythmically against the front door. 'Heels are bad for your arteries. Fucking move it!'

Hastily, George redialled the taxi company, told them to wait in the next street. But their getaway MPV, with its beaded driver's seat cover and its shabby, cigarette-burned interior and its almost-bald tyres was *stuck in traffic in Lewisham, love. He'll be there in ten. Sorry, darling. You know them roadworks is a nightmare, innit?*

For seven agonising minutes, they squatted behind an out-of-control leylandii hedge, screening the front garden of a neighbour. Checking they had their passports – faked ID from dearly departed Danny, in the Deenens' case. Double-checking the flights.

Then, just as a beat-up Toyota Previa drew up with its Asian driver full of apology and M25 traffic information, the regal bulk of the 7 Series turned into the road, slowly gliding towards them.

CHAPTER 47

Amsterdam, above The Cracked Pot Coffee Shop, much later, then Sloterdijkermeer allotments, then, even later, Van den Bergen's apartment

It was already dark outside. There was an eerie pink glow in the sky, where the dense, low-hanging clouds seemed to reflect the red lights of neighbours, plying their wares in the windows of the surrounding houses.

'I ain't staying here,' Letitia said, wrinkling her nose at the shabby room with its gabled ceiling.

'Just be thankful we're all still alive,' George said, deliberately keeping quiet about the second coming of the BMW 7 series, just as they had been clambering into the taxi. A miraculous coincidence of biblical proportions, where an identical car had been the wheels of a local dealer, rather than Bloom's black-clad hitman-for-hire. 'It's just for a couple of nights until we sort something better out. Think of it as a holiday.'

'They all on the game, then?' Tinesha asked, peering out of the window at the scene on the other side of the canal.

Patrice giggled beside her. 'Look at her!' He pointed to a statuesque blonde, coquettishly pouting down at a group of young men who were standing by the canal's edge. She beckoned them to her, naming her price using her fingers. The men sized her up, as though she were erotic meat hanging in a butcher's window; deciding if her flesh by the pound represented good value for money.

'Yep,' George said. 'Every time you see closed curtains round here, chances are someone's screwing behind them. Same shit goes on here as any other big city in the world, except the Dutch don't try to dress it up. A turd rolled in glitter might be shiny, but it's still a turd.'

'Patrice!' Aunty Sharon said. 'Cover your ears, bwoy!' She bit her lip uncertainly, eyes roving over the scratched old furniture: the sagging double bed; the chaise longue that had been patched up badly; the thin, office carpet covered in stains. 'You lived here? Serious? *You*?'

George nodded and smiled wistfully. Bed springs squeaking in Inneke's room below. The battered table where she had sat and written essays for her politics course at the university. That glorified bedsit above The Cracked Pot Coffee Shop held both good memories and bad. 'Nobody will come looking for you here. Not after all this time. And Jan's a good guy. He promised me the bedding has all been done on a hot wash. Sit tight. Smoke some weed downstairs. I'll be back in the morning.'

Eyeing Piet Deenen's scabbed, florid face beneath the street light, Van den Bergen touched his own skin, wondering if the bacteria that were clearly eating this man alive were airborne. Could he become contaminated? Gabi started to cough, a rumbling, painful-sounding affliction. As though this were some strange mating ritual between rough sleepers, Piet started to cough too, then spat something almost solid onto the thinning layer of snow that covered one of the Sloterdijkermeer allotments.

'Sweet Jesus,' he said, glaring at the offending body fluid. 'Cover your mouths! And don't dare spit on my bloody plot. You could have tuberculosis.'

'I haven't got tuberculosis,' Piet said, shivering.

'How the hell do you know? You could contaminate my soil.'

'I'm on antibiotics!' Piet looked back at Van den Bergen, took a packet of tablets from his pocket, and waved it around like a white flag.

'Just keep walking, will you? My cabin's next on the left. And I've got a doctor friend of mine coming to look you both over in the morning. You're a mess! I don't know what you were thinking.'

Gabi stopped dead in her tracks on the pathway and scowled at the Chief Inspector. 'We were looking for our children, or had you forgotten?'

Van den Bergen sighed and ushered her onwards. The public thoroughfare through the allotments was not the place for an argument, even if it was currently deserted. And besides, Gabi looked like she was only days away from starving to death. He didn't have the heart to curry confrontation with a woman who had given up everything and lost so much more.

Unlocking his cabin, he checked over his shoulder to reassure himself that their clandestine retreat had gone unnoticed. But it was near midnight – outside the official opening times for the complex. If there was ever a place where two fugitives could slip into hiding unnoticed, it was Sloterdijkermeer by night, when the ground was still covered with snow. He herded the couple inside the freezing box.

On the potting table were bundles.

'I put together some camping gear. It should keep you comfortable enough,' he said, unfurling one of the sleeping bags: Tamara's, from a time when she was still young enough to go camping with her old dad and actually enjoy it. 'There's a fan heater, but it's old. Make sure you switch it off for a bit when it starts to smell.' He fished out a bright orange heater from under the table, plugged it in, ignoring the disconcerting stink of an impending electrical fire that immediately permeated the cabin.

Gabi wrinkled her nose. 'Are you trying to kill us?'

Van den Bergen smirked. 'You could spend the next few weeks in the cells, if you like. I'm sure Kamphuis and Hasselblad will be pleased to know you've come back from the dead. Especially if Hasselblad is, as you say, in cahoots with this Gordon Bloom.'

From inside his backpack, Van den Bergen pulled out his large Thermos flask, which George had bought him. A bulky tinfoil parcel.

'Something hot to drink and some sandwiches to keep you going. You *have* to stay put. Don't go wandering off, will you?'

'What choice do we have?' Piet asked.

'You've murdered four men,' Van den Bergen said, a wrenching sensation in his ageing viscera. He was torn between feeling he should arrest these takers of lives, and the agreement he had reached with George that he should keep them under wraps until they knew more. 'I'm locking you in. Try anything funny and you're behind bars at the mercy of my superiors.'

'What if we need to get out in an emergency?' Piet asked.

'What if there's a fire?' Gabi's shrunken face crumpled with concern.

Glancing at his unreliable fan heater, Van den Bergen merely shrugged. 'Saves you the job of burning in hell, doesn't it?'

Driving through the silent streets of Amsterdam's outskirts, from the allotments to his apartment, Van den Bergen revelled in the thrill of anticipation. George would be waiting for him. Danger had brought his young lover back into town, ahead of schedule. Tonight, his cold, cold bed would be warmed by her body. Didn't the sun stream through the French doors of his patio a little brighter when she was there?

For a moment, with the car's engine purring, the Smashing Pumpkins buzzing on his stereo and the moon shining onto the glittering overnight frost that had settled on the bonnets of parked cars lining the sides of the road, he imagined he had it all. Piet Deenen under lock and key. An intelligent, beautiful woman who

305

loved him. A grandchild, growing healthy and strong inside his daughter's belly. The possibility that he could vanquish his professional enemies once and for all. Then, he realised how ridiculous that sounded. The Deenens would escape and it would be his fault. He and George would inevitably argue because he was the king of self-sabotage. Tamara might lose the child or it would be born looking exactly like Numbnuts, complete with a ridiculous, overgrown beard. Hasselblad and Kamphuis would take him down, if not out entirely.

His hip began to ache. His abdominal scar throbbed. His throat stung as stomach acid barged its way up his gullet. Business as usual.

With the aching legs of the unfit and the heavy heart of the middle-aged, he climbed the stairs. A pinpoint of light emitted through the spyhole in his front door revived his spirits. George would be sitting on the sofa in the living room, legs tucked beneath her, playing with one of her corkscrew curls, a bottle of wine already open. Yes, this was going to be a good night after all.

Key in the lock, he walked inside and smelled cabbage and sickly perfume. Out-of-place aromas. Had George been trying to cook?

Kicking off his shoes, he made his way down the hall to the source of both light and smell. There, on his sofa, lay a woman reminiscent of George, though it was not George. A large, older woman he had glimpsed only briefly two years ago. Sitting at a table in a cheap chain pub, clutching a wine glass, wearing a fun fur that had made her look like a mountain lion with an extreme manicure.

'This is a fucking uncomfy set-up, man,' Letitia said, wiggling her toes at him. 'Thought you was senior. Don't they pay you enough to get proper fucking furniture?' Cheap floral perfume wafted towards him as she arranged herself the length of the sofa.

But the smell of cabbage came from his left, near the windows.

There, seated primly in an armchair ,was Marie, laptop on her knee, files spread all over the floor.

'Hi, boss. I've already accessed the system of one of Bloom's companies,' Marie said, hooking her lank hair behind her ear. Fingers a blur, as she tap-tapped her way deeper into the ether. 'Fashionista Limited. Buys and sells clothing from the Far East to supermarkets across Europe.'

George emerged from Van den Bergen's kitchen, clutching a cafetiere of coffee and four cups, wan with fatigue, or perhaps anxiety. Who knew? No kiss hello. No hug on offer. No smile to warm the place, though by the feel, she, or more likely her ghastly mother, had cranked his heat up to tropical. Top button of George's jeans undone. A telltale empty bag of Croky chips on the coffee table said she had had dinner without him.

'Grab a seat,' she said, though every seat in his living room had been taken. 'You're not going to believe what we've already found!'

CHAPTER 48

Amsterdam, Van den Bergen's apartment, later still

'See these claims for business expenses?' Marie said, turning the laptop towards Van den Bergen. She turned the screen away again before he had even had chance to put his glasses on. 'There's a company car, expensive dinners in high-end restaurants. All Amsterdam. A golf-club membership.'

Perching uncomfortably on the arm of George's chair, Van den Bergen shot surreptitious glances in Letitia's direction. Nobody had yet explained why she was there. Hadn't George said she would install her family at The Cracked Pot for a couple of days until a secure hotel had been sorted out?

'Are you listening, Paul?' George said.

Flick, flicking through the channels with clickety-click nails prodding the buttons of the remote control, Letitia tutted loudly. 'Your telly is shit. Anyone ever tell you that?' She flung the remote onto the coffee table. 'You got anything drink? I could go a rum. Brandy, if you ain't got that.' She clasped her fat neck. 'I'm so thirsty. It's like a desert in here, now I put the heating on. And flying dehydrates you, you know.' She slapped her stomach, which made a hollow noise. 'How about we order a pizza?' She jerked her thumb at George. 'She gave me a shitty handful of crisps, but

I'm still fucking starving.' Examining her nails, the one on her index finger shorter than the rest, she exclaimed, 'Shit. I broke a fucking nail drying my hands on that piece of cardboard you call a towel, hanging in your bathroom. Seriously, man. You call this police protection? Cos you ain't protecting my best interests. Know what I mean?'

'Can it, Letitia,' George said, eyes narrowing as her irritation clearly mounted. 'By rights you should be on the other side of town with Aunty Sharon. This is police work.'

Hands in the air, Letitia's eyebrows disappeared into her hairline. 'I weren't sharing no bed with that fat cow. She farts in her sleep. Always did when we was kids. Stank like a box of rotten eggs. They used to call her Shaz the Spaz at school, cos Dorothea Caines reckoned she had a spastic colon.' She laughed heartily, her ample bosom heaving.

'You're so unpleasant. Did you get lessons when you were a kid?' George asked, diverting her attention from Marie's laptop to glower fiercely at her mother. No response beyond a curled lip. 'And you're well mean to Aunty Sharon. I don't even know why you've been staying at hers anyway. Perched on the sofa like a fucking vulture. Eating her out of house and—'

'Enough!' Van den Bergen stood abruptly, resenting being made to feel an interloper in his own place. He could tell that Letitia was a woman used to dominating proceedings, manipulating people until their choices suited her agenda. But he would not bend to this woman's will. He had met her kind before. He had been married to her kind, hadn't he? 'Letitia. You can stay here for tonight but I'll have a car take you back over to the coffee shop tomorrow morning.'

'Nah. I don't fucking think so, lanky lover boy,' she replied, looking him up and down with a disparaging grin, as though he were a tragi-comic side show in a human circus.

'The spare bedroom is through here,' he said, conceding no ground, using the same firm voice he reserved for angry relatives visiting their incarcerated drunk and disorderly loved ones. 'I'll show you. This way, please.'

Letitia rolled onto her side and grabbed her cigarettes from her handbag, which was lying next to her on the floor. 'Sofa suits me better. I can watch telly and listen to yous, innit? I didn't give up my life to come to Amsterdam to get bored to death, did I?'

Feeling George's eyes on him, Van den Bergen chose his words with care.

'George, Marie and I are discussing a live case, where the people involved pose an immediate threat to your safety. You may *not* listen to us. We are *not* here for your entertainment, Ms Williams-May.' He saw with some satisfaction that this puffed-up armchair-despot was visibly deflating. 'This is *my* apartment. I didn't invite you here. I doubt George brought you along for the ride willingly.'

George shook her head, closing her eyes to emphasize her innocence.

'I can only assume you invited yourself,' he continued. 'So, you will leave first thing tomorrow and await my instructions at The Cracked Pot Coffee Shop. Follow me to the bedroom. *Now*, please. And I forbid smoking in my place. If you want to smoke, you can spend the night on the patio. It's only going to be around minus one tonight.'

With Letitia out of earshot, Van den Bergen perused the Fashionista accounting software Marie had hacked into. Other records listed with Companies House in the UK showed the same name cropping up on the Board of Directors no fewer than six times – six separate businesses that operated as subsidiary concerns in the Bloom Group, showing six lots of business expense claims by the same person over a period of some ten years.

'Mieke Hasselblad,' Marie said, looking to George and Van den Bergen for a reaction with bloodshot, blue eyes.

'Hasselblad's wife,' Van den Bergen said, allowing a wry smile to flick the corners of his mouth upwards. 'Jesus. Bloom was telling the truth. He *is* in bed with the Chief of Police.'

'What are we going to do?' George asked, rubbing his forearm. 'I mean, Bloom's a rich businessman and involved in politics. A toff and a backbencher. He's got legitimate business interests over here, as well as in London. Maybe Hasselblad doesn't have a clue that Bloom runs an organized criminal empire as some kind of macabre hobby.' She chewed her lip. 'I mean, is that likely?'

Van den Bergen shook his head, thumbing the iron filings of his stubble. The clock on the wall in the kitchen said 2.30 a.m. His stomach was growling noisily, but that could wait.

'This is a mess.' He ran his hands through his thick white hair, considering his options, the jeopardy George was in, what to do with Jack and Mrs Frost, ensconced in his allotment cabin, their children still missing … 'George, you speak to as many convicted sex offenders as you can.'

'I'll cross check the Dutch sex offenders list with the names on Dobkin's database,' she said, making notes on her phone. 'See if there's any matches.'

'Good,' he said. Trying to calculate how much time they might have before it got out that they were conducting a separate investigation into the top brass, in addition to harbouring a serial murderer. A week, at best. He'd have to take the wrap entirely if they were caught out, of course. 'I'll give Elvis a list of informants to make contact with. Marie, you keep trawling through Bloom Group's business records and see what comes up. Start digging into Hasselblad's finances. See if his wife's being used to launder money, somehow.' Stinging, exhausted eyes on the two of them. 'But we have to keep this between us. Nobody outside my team can know. Got it?'

'Yeah.'

'Yep.'

'That include me, big boy?' Letitia asked, leaning on the architrave of the living room door, brandishing a takeout pizza menu in one hand and a packet of cigarettes in the other.

CHAPTER 49

Amsterdam, Bijlmerbajes prison complex, then, Marie's apartment, then, Sloterdijkermeer allotments, 20 March

'Son of the Eagle,' George said, pointing to a photo of Rufus Lazami, a promotional shot, taken from the Bloom Group plc website, which depicted him in a sharp, dark suit. His wide smile said he was an approachable and well-liked boss, hiding his true identity beneath a veneer of respectability. 'You know him?'

The man sitting opposite her in the interview room scratched at the tattoo on his neck. 'That the Son of the Eagle?' he said in a strong Rotterdam accent, a sing-song voice marking him as an affable guy, rather than the convicted child abuser that his prison record revealed him to be. 'I know the name, but I never actually met him.'

George noticed the inmate's gaze drop to her chest. She clasped the collar of her shirt closed, wishing she had done up the top button, not that fabric and buttons were a barrier to a determined imagination. 'Eyes up here, please,' she told him, pointing to her face. 'I'm too old to be your type, anyway.'

Her interviewee laughed and adjusted the crotch of his trousers. Fat veins strained against the musculature in his bull neck. Over worked-out in the prison gym. A terrifying prospect for any victim, let alone a child. But at least he was laughing. She wanted to keep him onside; tease any latent information out of this brute.

'I've got a source says you were involved in the Son of the Eagle's network. You were sent down for a variety of offences, weren't you?' She skim-read his record once more. 'Pimping Roma girls of thirteen from a B&B near Rotterdam docks. You had unlawful sex with the girls yourself and coerced them into going with truck drivers for money. Supplying class A drugs too. Starting kids of ten and eleven off as runners for you.'

Holding his hands aloft, the prisoner grinned. 'I paid them well. They got better treatment off me than they did at home. You know how these kids are, don't you?'

George closed her eyes, keeping her own teenaged memories of a disengaged, selfish mother firmly locked in Pandora's Box. 'Then you pressured them into prostitution. Kept them prisoner at the B&B when they tried to leave.'

'I was dedicated to my work. Part of a big, well-oiled machine.'

'Who ran this machine? I mean, the guy at the very top.'

The inmate leaned towards her so that she could see every blocked, black pore in his broken nose. Every split red vein in his otherwise sallow cheeks. 'I know I'm in here for a long time,' he said, as though he were sharing some confidence, as though a prison guard wasn't standing by the door. 'I get that. They got me banged to rights. But I'm not grassing.'

'Your name was linked to the Son of the Eagle. You've just told me you'd heard of him, didn't you? This is not a new police investigation into you. It's a freelance criminologist trying to build a picture of who's who in the...'

The man's face was a blank screen, as though he'd punched the on/off switch and was now hibernating.

'The Duke,' George said. 'Have you heard of the Duke? Runs the whole show from London but also has interests over here and in Germany. Further afield in South Eastern Europe too, if the Son of the Eagle's reach is anything to go by.'

A change in the size of the man's pupils told her he had indeed heard of Gordon Bloom.

'Did you ever hear that a high-ranking policeman is connected to the Duke?'

Eyes narrowing. Darting off to the left. Silence.

'Any top-brass cop ever used your services?'

Examining his bruised knuckles. Fingering a blocked hair follicle on his elbow. Silence.

'Any rumours going round that someone high up in the force is involved in oiling the wheels in this big machine you were part of?'

When her interviewee's furtive gaze honed in on the prison officer by the door, George saw a previously invisible subtext written in a tense, tight hand, hanging freely in the fraught air between them. She nodded. Put her papers together. Thanked the tattooed monster and left.

Franz Dinkels. Images. Click. In the quiet solitude of her living room, Marie revelled in the benefits of working on this tangle of subterfuge and potential libel from home. There was Franz's pleasant round face on her monitor, care of a Google search. Coming up on a crime-writing blog he ran, where he and an American friend called Ned reviewed the latest thrillers from Europe and the US. One photo of Franz in a local newspaper, labelled simply as a researcher in the Berliner Polizei. No mention of him being charming or that he blushed in an endearing way whenever he talked about cases at work that had been cracked thanks to his hard work, trawling through a virtual Sodom and Gomorrah on the Internet. They shared a love of horror films. He, like her, was a semi-lapsed Catholic. One failed long-term relationship. Otherwise, plugging the lonely gaps with work and his hobbies. When, during one of their frequent Skype conversations, she had told him about the short affair with that posing prick Diederik, and how she had gained and lost a son inside twelve months, hadn't Franz's eyes become glassy with empathy? Hadn't she seen him swallow hard when she had turned her favourite photo of Nicolaas towards the camera for him to see? An introduction of sorts. Nicolaas, smiling in his bouncy chair. About a week before that bitch, the BVM had taken him. Wearing a playsuit covered in zoo animals. A picture of health. Too robust to succumb to Sudden Infant Death Syndrome. And yet he had.

Hastily, Marie clicked off the tab containing the images of the irrepressibly cheery Franz Dinkels, reminded that, as a sinner, she didn't deserve happiness, so she might as well give up the ghost of ever finding love with a slightly overweight, empathetic man with a pleasant face who lived in Berlin. She glowered at the Breughel representation of the BVM in the hallway, just visible from where she had perched on her sofa.

'Idiot,' she reprimanded herself, catching her breath as grief washed over her anew.

It had been almost a year, and still the pain was constant and acute. She thought of Gabi and Piet Deenen, not even able to lay their children to rest; letting go of the bad memories and choosing to replay only the good, over and over, like favourite footage taken by an old Hi8 camcorder. Those poor bastards were trapped in a purgatorial sojourn that could last their entire cursed life-times.

Blinking away hot tears, she turned back to the financial records for Bloom's companies. Money going into Mieke Hasselblad's bank account. Everything in her name. But no evidence of a separate bank account in the Chief of Police's name. No sign of any financial transaction occurring between the two men. Not a single thing in the name of Jaap Hasselblad. Clever. Records from an exclusive golf club outside Amsterdam, though, showing Bloom and Hasselblad were both members. Hell, there were even photos on the golf club's website showing the two lifting a trophy together. A picture of middle-aged respectability in colourful argyle sweaters and pale golfing trousers.

Marie scribbled her thoughts onto a brand-new notepad – one that she would keep at home where prying eyes would not discover Van den Bergen's covert investigation.

What is Bloom's connection to Mieke Hasselblad? Did Mieke know Bloom first? If so, how?

The cabin felt cramped with three adults inside it. Van den Bergen stretched his long legs out in the direction of the door. Arms folded, he regarded Piet and Gabi as they hungrily devoured the ham baguettes he had brought for them. He'd also replaced the spent flask of coffee for his old tartan Thermos, full of tinned tomato soup, and brought two large bottles of Evian, which may or may not freeze solid before they could be drunk. Strange to see two fugitives sleeping in his and Tamara's old camping gear.

'My doctor tells me you both need blood tests to see what God-awful infections you've picked up on the street.'

Piet shrugged, and rubbed at the scaly skin on his nose. 'None of that matters.'

'Have you heard from Bloom? Any emails?'

'No. Not a word.'

'The guy's full of shit,' Gabi said. 'I know him well enough. The City of London's a small place. Bloom Group owned Pickwick Welcome, back when I used to do his PR. The guy's a typical politician. He's always been about the spin. He just wanted to get out of that railway arch alive. He won't find our bloody children for us.' She took a hungry bite from her baguette. 'We should have killed him when we had our chance.'

Van den Bergen shook his head, torn between the policeman and the father that warred inside him. 'No. It's bad enough that four men are dead because of you. Killing Bloom would have been a huge mistake. If you'd cut the head off the monster, we'd never get to find how far its tentacles reach.'

Piet drained his cup of tomato soup too enthusiastically. Red smeared on the bottom half of his face made him look like a recalcitrant vampire who had substituted fangs for icicles, bleeding the ungodly dry through punctures in their wretched necks but eschewing their tainted blood in favour of Albert Heijn's tinned best. 'I don't give a shit about the tentacles!' he shouted. 'I just want my children back. Dead or alive!' Tears welled in his eyes. 'I don't care if I spend the rest of my life in prison. I don't care that I was once an architect and a father and a husband and now I'm a murderer. I don't give a flying fuck. I just want this nightmare to end. If I could die, I would. But for some reason, God just won't let me go.'

Gabi looked blankly at Van den Bergen. 'He's right. It's like we're trapped on a shit ride we can't get off. We need closure.'

Van den Bergen stood, stooping slightly to avoid banging his head on the low ceiling of his cabin. Once a place of solitude where he could go to ruminate in peace about the blind alleys that difficult cases and life in general led him down. Now, his special place had been contaminated by somebody else's anguish. He fingered a packet of lavatera seeds on his shelf – seeds he planned to sow later in the spring, as the ground softened. Maybe have George help him thin the seedlings, when the first leaves put in a brave appearance. Hope, even in the dormant seeds and dead soil of winter. Warmer days not too far off. Maybe it would be in police work as it was in life.

'I'm doing everything I can,' he said, looking into the sombre faces of the couple. 'Stay put. Call me immediately if you hear from Bloom.'

CHAPTER 50

Amsterdam, police headquarters, then the Deenen's house in a village South of Amsterdam, 23 March

'What do you mean we've got nothing?' Kamphuis said. Derision dripping from his every syllable. It was hard to tell if he was delighted that Van den Bergen had apparently failed, or disgusted that his subordinate had left him looking like a limp prick with the balls surgically removed.

Distracted. Van den Bergen's thought processes were codeine-blurred, despite his two-year-long abstinence from his old, pleasantly numbing friend. The fogginess this morning was a result of sharing a bed with George for more than a week, knowing that the ghastly Letitia was snoring on the sofa in the living room: a lazy sprawling sentinel, guarding the way to the kitchen, seemingly sleeping with one eye always open. Spikes of false eyelashes barring the way to any hope of freedom. Eavesdropping on every shared thought, every snatched, tender exchange. Storing information like a bank's server in a secure warehouse.

Knowledge, innit? Intelligence, like. You never know when that shit comes in handy. He could hear her voice grating hard inside his head. Insisting this. Prophesying that. *You mark my fucking words. I been to the school of hard knocks. Blah, blah, blah, got any rum, darling?*

'Paul!' Kamphuis slapped his chubby hand on the meeting table. Not in his ceremonial uniform today. Pretending to roll up his sleeves and do, 'proper police work'. The station's central heating was on the blink, rendering the meeting room just a freezing cupboard with chairs, a table and Marie's body odour. Rings of sweat beneath the arms of Kamphuis' red shirt were white ghosts from another day. 'Explain.'

Van den Bergen stopped scrolling through Twitter notifications on his phone. The trolls, still trying to intercept him on his fraught travels down the information super B road, could wait. What the hell had Kamphuis just said?

He shot a glance sideways at Elvis. Elvis grimaced and mimed moral outrage. Ah, yes. The update.

'Jack Frost and the Krampus are one and the same guy,' he said, wondering if the ache in his throat was a symptom of an impending throat infection. Had he caught something from the Deenens? 'A serial killer who targets men involved with child-trafficking.' Swollen glands. Yes. A bloody throat infection. Hoped he wouldn't pass it onto Tamara and put her pregnancy in jeopardy.

Kamphuis leaned forwards. 'You've been working this case for weeks. We've known about the connection for weeks. Is that the best you've got after all this time?' Reminiscent of a stag trying to impale his opposite number on the end of his antlers.

'Is it my fault Jack Frost hasn't killed again?' Van den Bergen he said. 'We've followed every single lead. George and I feel certain—'

'George and I! George and I!' Kamphuis wittering the words in a high-pitched, mocking voice like a gossiping old woman. 'George and I feel certain.'

'Fuck off, Olaf,' Van den Bergen said, scowling at the cock-sure imperiousness of the Commissioner. Hamster-cheeked, buck-passing, Teflon piece of shit. 'You might not want to hear it. Hasselblad doesn't want to hear it. But it's my belief that Jack Frost and the case of the missing Deenen children are connected. It's all about an organized child-trafficking network. I gave you my interim report. I know you read it. But we've come to a dead end. For now.'

Van den Bergen folded his arms, hoping to put a barrier up to further confrontation. On the table, his phone pinged. He couldn't resist checking the text that had just appeared from George.

Another dead end. Sorry. George. Xxx

'What's so interesting? Why are you checking your goddamn phone when you're supposed to be justifying your existence to me?' Kamphuis poked himself in a flabby tit emphatically.

'Georgina has been in prison, interviewing some sex offenders that may have had a connection to one or more of the dead men. When she unearths something new and relevant to the case, you'll be the first to know. She was just texting me with an update.'

Kamphuis thumbed his chin repeatedly, aggressively, close to where he had cut himself shaving that morning. He pointed at Marie. 'What's she been doing for the past bloody year? Still whingeing about cot death?'

Marie said nothing, but her face flushed red like a lobster plunged into a boiling pan, screaming inside her, almost audible.

At that point, Van den Bergen fantasized about picking Kamphuis up by the crotch of his too-tight chinos and throwing him through the window into the canal below. Horrible bastard taking a cheap pot shot at a bereaved woman.

'Marie here has been investigating the finances of Jack Frost's victims, of course,' he said. 'And looking for paedo porn sites connected to the dead men – anywhere pictures of the Deenen children could crop up. Cross-referencing names that recur, in case Jack Frost was known to all four men. Perhaps he worked with them. Perhaps he's a hitman employed by a rival criminal network. These are the theories Marie is looking into.'

Marie was pressing so hard on her pad with her fine-liner that Van den Bergen noticed the nib disappearing entirely into the barrel. A large black blot leaking outwards from the point of contact in an almost perfect circle.

'And him?' Kamphuis scowling at Elvis.

Elvis attempted to fasten the button of his leather jacket. Failed. 'I've been speaking to informants who know what's what and who's doing who in Bijlmer.' He patted his quiff, unencumbered by a hat now that the sub-zero temperatures were starting to climb again. An endangered hair species, reintroduced into the wild.

'And?' Kamphuis barked.

'I've got nothing.' Still fiddling with his button, his slightly shaking hand almost gave the game away. Van den Bergen made a mental note not to entrust Elvis with lying again; he was bloody terrible at it. 'Jack Frost is like a ghost, man. But I'll keep trying.'

Without warning, Kamphuis thumped the table. 'You're a useless bunch of bastards. Do you know that? Useless!' Pointing a nicotine-stained finger at Van den Bergen. Pointing.

Since when had Kamphuis started smoking, Van den Bergen wondered? Was the stress finally getting to him, now that he was clinging on near the very top of the greasy pole? His twitching eye said yes. Olaf Kamphuis was feeling the heat.

'The bodies are piling up and there's not a damn thing the Dutch police can do about it. This is a chance for us to make a real name for ourselves here. And what happens? You fail to solve your last case. You fail to solve this case! Instead, you're bringing some hair-brained theory to the table that our icicle-wielding serial murderer is sitting reading *Where the Wild Things Are* to Josh and Lucy Deenen in some paedo sex dungeon somewhere. Do you know how that sounds?' Hi eye, twitching repeatedly, put

Van den Bergen in mind of a hummingbird beating its wings. 'Far-fucking-fetched! That's how it sounds.'

Kamphuis stood, short arms spread wide along the table's edge, playing a big, angry boss but putting his Chief Inspector in mind of Samwise Gamgee. Fat little Hobbitses wants the precious. Turd.

But something had registered deep inside Van den Bergen's subconscious. A glimmer of a thought, coming fast into focus from the brain's primordial soup. A memory of the book left on Josh's nightstand. Everything in his bedroom intact since the day they were taken. A favourite book, written in English, his father had said. Bought from Waterstones Piccadilly in London when Josh had been Lucy's age.

Where the Wild Things Are. Maurice Sendak.

And yet, Olaf Kamphuis had never been to the Deenen's house. Perhaps it was a coincidence. Yes. That was it. *Where the Wild Things Are* was fairly famous, wasn't it? Although Van den Bergen had no memory of ever having read it to his own daughter when she had been small.

The journey to the Deenens' house was easier, now that the roads were all but clear of snow. Sun broke through the clouds as he pulled up outside the empty house. The front door was secured with an extra padlock, since the couple were presumed dead and the estate was being dealt with by solicitors trying to trace a beneficiary in the absence of their children or a will – the house being contested jointly by Piet's mother and Gabi's uncle.

Making short shrift of the locks, Van den Bergen stepped gingerly inside the musty house. Drank in the sense of abandonment that oozed from every bland wall. Everything left intact. The spectre of family laughter and times well-enjoyed seemed to hang in forgotten corners, along with dusty cobwebs. Hollow, cold and empty. Damp, after a hard winter of minimal heating and no ventilation. Inhospitable. Making a mockery of the Deenens' return to the Netherlands for a better life. A dream crushed during a short window of lapsed attention on an idyllic summer morning.

Swallowing down the unwelcome lump of vicarious grief in his throat, Van den Bergen took the stairs two at a time, focusing on the Maurice Sendak picture book in his mind's eye. On Josh's nightstand. It had been there after the disappearance. It had been there, as he'd glimpsed the boy's room on subsequent visits. This was surely just a misplaced hunch. An overtired Chief Inspector, past his prime, imagining things.

There was Josh's room at the end of the hall. He advanced towards it. Everything else undisturbed since the Deenen's disappearance. Into the little bedroom. Smelling now of dust instead of little boy and washing powder. Looking down at the nightstand, he expected to see *Where the Wild Things Are*. But the wild things weren't there.

The book was missing.

CHAPTER 51

Amsterdam, The Cracked Pot Coffee Shop, then, consulting rooms, then, Kamphuis' home near Vondelpark, later

'Tell them to get in the fucking taxi, will you?!' Letitia shouted through the half-opened rear window, face almost trapped as she tried to lower it further but succeeded in doing the opposite. Engine ticking over; meter running; Letitia in a sparkly batwing top, looking her best for the Dutch doctor, having taken over an hour in Van den Bergen's bathroom, using all the hot water. Impatient now.

'Come on, Aunty Shaz,' George said. She held the door to The Cracked Pot Coffee Shop open, acting as an intermediary between a disgruntled Letitia and a fretful Aunty Sharon.

Jan hovered inside, clutching a jug full of a liquid that looked like treacle and – George knew through experience – smelled like barbecued horseshit, trying to foist it onto Patrice who was sitting in a booth with narcotic intent. His mother, standing over him with hands on hips, turned to George, wearing a thunderous expression.

'I ain't coming until I've told this little rarseclart that if he touches so much as a Rizla, I'll stop his spends.'

'I am sitting here, Mum,' Patrice said, holding his cup up to Jan.

Jan started to wheeze with laughter, as though he'd remembered an old joke. He pointed to the neon mural above the booth of a black girl in hotpants with an Afro. The mural glowed under the UV lights, making the poor execution of her eyes seem worse. One up. One down. At least her tits were on an even keel, George mused.

'This glorious portrait of your big cousin is my lucky talisman,' Jan said. 'She'll keep an eye on you.'

'A boss-eye.' Patrice held his head in his hands, grimacing at the cup of murky coffee on the table in front of him. He looked back up at his mother, wearing a winsome expression. 'I won't touch so much as a blim, Mum. I promise. Leave Tin behind if you don't trust me.'

Jan strode over to the door and planted a wet kiss on George's cheek, immune to the family wrangling going on in his coffee shop.

'Will you come and share a joint with me when you've finished?' he asked. His oversized eyes stared at her, blurry behind the thumb-smudged lenses of his tortoiseshell Trotsky glasses. 'That Five-O hogs you. I barely ever see you when you're over.'

'Five-O.' George smirked at his reference to American crime series, *The Wire*. 'You fucking loon.' She looked down at her biker boots, thinking about the grim afternoon she had ahead of her. 'Maybe.' When had life got in the way of fun? It didn't seem fair.

The specialist peered over the top of his glasses at the motley gathering of people on the other side of his desk.

'Which one of you is Letitia Williams-May?' he asked, skipping over Patrice, Tinesha and George to the older duo of Letitia and Sharon.

'Her,' Sharon said, folding her arms, shuffling up towards George.

'Me, of course,' Letitia said, batting her false lashes at the long-limbed, fair-haired doctor, flicking her caramel-coloured hair extensions out behind her. A budget Gloria Gaynor, all at once afraid *and* petrified, despite the show of bravado. Her breath coming short. A wobble in her voice.

'Then, why are the others here?' An appraising, uncomprehending look at his audience.

'Family,' Sharon said, as if this explained everything. She curled her lip at her older sister. 'You know?'

'We already paid you, innit?' Letitia said, pursing her lips. Now she was strong. And she knew how to get along. 'Just gimme the low-down and stop judging my moral support.'

Sighing, smiling, the doctor clicked on his mouse and turned a screen around to face Letitia. CT scans of a large oval shape. He clicked again and white blobs started to move on the screen. Getting larger. Shrinking. Changing. A macabre animation moving from top to bottom through the cross-section of Letitia's torso.

The specialist pointed to various blobs with his biro. 'There is congestion in your pulmonary arteries. See? The walls are thickening, preventing the easy flow of blood. There's a build-up of pressure.'

Letitia gripped her chest, gasped sarcastically. 'Yeah, I fucking already knew that.'

Nodding, the doctor went on. 'Okay. So, the pulmonary hypertension is because of your sickle cell anaemia, which has shown up in your blood tests, which your GP in Britain suspected. I'm surprised you haven't had this diagnosed decades ago.'

'I don't trust you quacks, innit? No offence, like.'

'Your condition is more common in people of Afro-Caribbean origin, I'm afraid.'

George could see her mother in profile. Gulping. Keeping a brave face. Shitting herself, judging by the sheen of perspiration seeping through the carefully applied layer of foundation on her forehead. '*I* ain't afraid. What you going to do about it? That's what I wanna know.'

327

'You've described several sickle cell crises to me that have occurred inside the last twelve months.'

'Yeah. I always kept a lid on my suffering.' She touched her synthetic hair as if to check her artificial halo was still shining above it. 'But these ones lately was fucking painful. Worst was, nobody bloody believed me.'

Letitia shot a withering glance at her sister to her right. George to her left. Point-blank range. The stench of festering resentment in the room.

The doctor started to talk about putting her on Hydroxycarbamide or some outlandish-sounding medication with oxy in it. George stopped listening to the detail and stared at her mother intently, feeling the thumbscrews of guilt pinion her to her chair. All these long years, she had sought to avoid contact with this loveless woman. Hadn't believed a word that came out of her mouth, blisters on her acerbic tongue from telling so many lies. Crocodile tears seeping from a cold-blooded reptile of a mother. Now, it transpired that Letitia had been lounging on Aunty Sharon's sofa because she had been genuinely too ill to move. In pain. Suffering. Crumbling from the inside out. Fallible and feeling, like any other human being. George felt like a prize shit.

'Am I gonna die, then?' Letitia asked.

'Life expectancy can stretch into your early fifties, nowadays.' The doctor smiled.

A sob from Aunty Sharon. A sharp intake of breath from Tinesha and Patrice. Five pairs of bewildered eyes staring at the man in the white coat.

'What the fuck you talking about? I'm in my late forties *now*,' Letitia said. Her voice sounded thin, as though her vocal chords had been ripped from her throat and only the ghost of speech remained. A shuddering intake of breath. She gripped George's hand with those curling claws.

George stiffened, unsure how to react. She felt she ought to hug Letitia to offer some physical solace but instinctively shrank away from her touch, leaning heavily into Tinesha on the other side.

A snapshot of the here and now.

This frightened dragon, with all her bombast, falling away like the shedding of scales, as her short future was mapped out for her in a spartan Amsterdam consulting room.

A snapshot of the there and then.

The warm-hearted woman who had raised her daughter alone, planting petunias in a window box of their small house, taking little Ella to church on Sundays, with pure white socks digging into the backs of her knees.

And George's father.

George thought of the separate folder in her email inbox, where she had stored his missives. Asking after his former partner – a woman he had once loved enough to stand by, despite her acerbity. Should she tell Letitia? If her mother's days were numbered, should she give her the opportunity to make her peace with her babyfather?

Outside, George held the rear door to Van den Bergen's Mercedes open, as her family – uncharactestunned into silence – piled into the car.

'There's too many of you!' he shouted. Switching to Dutch for George's ears only. 'I said I'd give you and Letitia a lift back. Not half of South East London.' Furrows, deepening in his brow.

George glared at him. Rapid fire retort the others would never understand. 'Just get us all back to The Cracked Pot, for Christ's sake. She's actually really ill.' Her lover looked even more harried and grey-faced than usual, she noted. 'Anyway, you're late.' She checked her watch; she wished she could turn back time, return to a place where Letitia was indestructible and it was safe to hate her.

'I had to go somewhere first,' he said.

She slammed the passenger door shut with a resentful thunk and buckled up. At least she had an ally at her side who wasn't caught in a web of family politics. Letitia weeped dramatically in the back, hiccoughing as though she were choking on what was left of her vitality. Sharon, offering words of solace, volleyed by her elder sister with frosty, 'like you actually give an actual fuck.'

'Let's just get the hell back to Jan's and split these two up before they kill each other,' George said.

Van den Bergen bit his lip. 'Well, before I drop you, there's something I need to … just bear with me. It's not far.'

The six of them were crowded like sardines suffering from ennui and low blood sugar, in the luxurious tin can that was Van den Bergen's car.

He pulled up alongside the kerb, approximately one hundred metres down the street from a large, detached house. It was a standout building on Van Eeghenstraat – an exclusive road full of red-brick period apartments that had been carved out from expansive four-storey houses. So pretty, they could have been fashioned from gingerbread and plucked from a Hansel and Gretel adaptation. Just south of Vondelpark, this was the exclusive address of boutique hotels and home to urban sophisticates. A world away from Van den Bergen's mid-century utilitarian neighbourhood, George assessed. Two cars parked in bays outside the detached house – one, a Range Rover. The other, an Audi.

'Hey! Where the fuck is this?' Letitia asked, leaning through the gap between the front seats. 'I'm dying with sickle anaemic, you know. I'm *supposed* to be resting.' She sucked her teeth. 'And I need a smoke.'

'Doctor told you, you got to stop all that bad habit shit,' Sharon said. 'You're digging yourself an early grave.'

'Nobody fucking asked for your opinion, did it?' Letitia spat, visible in the rear view mirror, smoothing down the front of her glittering top. 'I ain't dead yet.'

'Shush!' Van den Bergen turned round abruptly, holding his

long finger to his mouth. Hooded, grey eyes spoke neither of mirth nor of sympathetic indulgence.

The car's occupants fell silent. Everyone staring solemnly out of the windows, though they knew not what they were looking for.

'What's going on?' George asked.

'Kamphuis' house,' Van den Bergen said, pointing to the elegant home with its impressive stone portico and wide bay windows.

'Why are we here?'

'I think he has the Deenen children.'

'What?' George looked at the back of Van den Bergen's head, as he craned his neck to observe the house. '*Kamphuis*? Olaf Kamphuis has got the Deenen kids? Where in God's name did you get that idea from?'

'Who the fuck is Camp House and why's he getting between me and the bleeding sofa?' Letitia asked, rummaging in her handbag for her cigarettes, tutting and cussing until Sharon slapped her hand away.

In sullen silence, Van den Bergen took out his phone and thumbed a text to Marie and Elvis. George peered over his shoulder.

```
Marie - Start looking into Kamphuis'
finances a.s.a.p. and Elvis — you and me
are on surveillance from end of working
day. Strictly confidential! Meet me in HQ
foyer at 5 p.m. VDB
```

He and George exchanged a knowing glance. He hadn't given her a shred of an explanation, but she knew instinctively he was onto something.

CHAPTER 52

Amsterdam, outside Kamphuis' home, much later

'Did Marie say anything before you left?' Van den Bergen asked, stretching his long legs into the driver's side footwell. He pinched a clumsy mouthful of takeout Indonesian noodles between two disposable chopsticks, dropped them, then started again. 'Had she started on the money?'

'Nope,' Elvis said, chewing his burger. 'She was struggling. We haven't got a warrant, have we? She couldn't even get bank details.'

'Shit. This is going to be harder than we thought.'

An awkward pause. Not quite the man-bonding session Elvis had been looking forward to.

Stuffing his takeout wrappings into a plastic bag and tying the handles tight to avoid his boss' wrath, Elvis gazed idly at Kamphuis' family home – brightly lit on the inside with warm light from chandeliers. The floodlighting on the outside made it look even more stately than it was. 9.30 p.m. now. Frost forming outside, making the cobbles on the street sparkle optimistically. The boss kept having to start his engine and put the windscreen heater on to clear the gathering condensation.

'I think we should call it a night,' Elvis said, wishing there was a nearby toilet.

'Yes. You're probably right. I'm sorry I've ruined your evening. Did you have a date?' Van den Bergen asked.

A vision of his mother, shaking as she heated a meagre tin of soup for dinner. Too stubborn to let the care worker in. Too ill to reach the pizza he had bought for her and placed in the freezer. 'No.'

Van den Bergen gasped as he shifted his position in the driver's seat, hip clicking audibly. He started the engine. 'Come on. We're on a fool's errand. And if he gets wind of the fact that we're keeping an eye on him, we'll be really pissing in the wind.'

The car thrummed. The heated seats, warming Elvis' body, felt like an attempt to reanimate the dead. A subtle change in the position of the car told him the handbrake was off. Ready to go back to his empty flat with the weight of expectation heavy on him to pop over to his mother's. Check she was okay.

'Oh, Jesus,' he said, softly.

But, just as Van den Bergen turned his steering wheel to leave their parking space, Kamphuis appeared above them, standing in the window of his master bedroom.

'Hang on, boss!'

Kamphuis was fastening the cuffs of a fresh shirt. Non-uniform. Running a hand through his hair, gazing at something just to the left of the window, as though he were looking into a mirror.

'He's going out,' Van den Bergen said, raising an eyebrow. 'Bet it's nowhere special, though. That egotistical prick would do his hair just to go for frites and mayonnaise from the local snack bar.'

'Looks like he's prettying himself up, boss. Maybe our luck's in.'

The Chief Inspector made a harrumphing noise at the back of his throat, like he was clearing phlegm. 'At best, it'll be some bar or restaurant where we can't even follow him.'

Five minutes later, Kamphuis appeared at the front of the house, silhouetted against the light of his hallway. The door closed and the light disappeared. Clad in a dark overcoat, he whistled as he walked down the road, hands shoved deep into his pockets. He advanced towards Elvis and Van den Bergen. Elvis' breath caught in the back of his throat. He slid down into his seat, fearful that their position would be discovered.

'He's getting into a car,' Van den Bergen said, peering into his rear-view mirror.

Elvis opened his eyes, and aw yellow lights flashing in the wing mirror as a car alarm was deactivated two or three cars back. Sure enough, Kamphuis was manoeuvring himself awkwardly into an Audi four-wheel-drive.

Their quarry slid off down the road. Van den Bergen allowed one car to pass before following through elegant, icy back streets to the outskirts.

'I think he's making for the motorway,' Elvis said.

'E19. Maybe the airport.' Van den Bergen allowed another car to overtake him, now separated by two cars. 'Did he have a case with him? I don't remember.'

'No. And I checked his online diary before I left HQ. He's in tomorrow.'

Kamphuis' car sped past the giant Schiphol complex, travelling south along the empty road. Rush hour long gone now, everyone tucked up for the night this far out of the city. But then, some way down, indication that he was pulling off. He drove approximately a mile towards a small village, turning into a service station that incorporated a motel.

'Oh, I see,' Van den Bergen said, a wry smile visible in the glow cast by the carpark's floodlights.

'What?'

'Fancy cufflinks? A clandestine meet in the middle of nowhere? What do you think? Our Olaf is playing away from home.'

Elvis' heartbeat picked up its pace as the boss pulled into a space on the far side of the complex, sufficiently out of sight of Kamphuis. The prospect of stalking the Commissioner was perhaps the most daunting challenge he had faced in all his years as a cop. He tugged at his quiff nervously, wishing he'd gone to his mother's after all. That spinach and chicken he had refused to prepare for her and an evening on the receiving end of her verbal abuse that he had turned down sounded quite appetising now.

'Come on!' Van den Bergen slammed the car door shut before Elvis could protest, striding across the almost-empty car park, immediately visible to anyone who happened to be looking their way at the right moment.

Some ten metres ahead, Kamphuis was spraying something into his mouth, then breathing into his hand and sniffing.

Elvis slowed his pace, falling in behind the boss, feeling somehow that their presence there was intrusive. If Kamphuis was meeting a woman, who was he to stand in judgement? He already thought the Commissioner was an amoral piece of shit. How did this risky act of voyeurism ennoble his stance in any way?

As if the boss sensed his reticence, Van den Bergen turned around and beckoned him forwards. He tutted like a castigatory Jedi, glaring down at Elvis, his disappointing Padawan. 'Two children. Missing for months. He's in the frame, somehow.' He prodded himself in the stomach with those long fingers and winced. 'I feel it, here. Am I ever wrong?'

'No. Well...' Elvis thought of how Van den Bergen had misjudged the Butcher, but decided not to say anything more about it. 'No.'

'Are you bothered about being spotted and sacked by that ass-kissing, two-faced, abusive donkey's rectum?'

'Nope.' The boss was right. He was sick of playing the beta male. He was a grown man, for Christ's sake. A catcher of criminals. A righter of wrongs. A possessor of bollocks. He forced himself to remember the time when he had been full of swagger, before his mother's Parkinson's. That Elvis was still there, wrapped inside an extra stone of fat and an ageing leather jacket.

They approached the windows of the motel and caught sight of Kamphuis, walking from the too-brightly-lit foyer into a dismal-looking bar area. A woman rose to greet him. Small, like a doll. Redhead. Kamphuis always went for redheads. Overly groomed with that big bouffant hair that middle-aged women had. A tanned complexion on a frosty winter night said spray tan, and the red was probably fake. Not like Kamphuis' burly wife, who had attended a Christmas party looking like the changing cubicle in which she may or may not have tried her new dress on. Plenty to hug.

'He's got a bit on the side,' Elvis said. 'No surprises there. The guy shags anything that moves. He had a pop at Marie, for God's sake!' He turned to rummage in his jacket pocket for his cigarettes, desperate to have a smoke and get the hell out of there. 'Maybe she's a prostitute!'

But at his side Van den Bergen was silent, eyes narrowed, staring intently at the couple as they air-kissed with the promise of more. Kamphuis' hand on the woman's pert bottom, clad in a figure-hugging bandeau dress. She turned towards the window. Her blank expression said she was clearly unable to see her audience. Lights inside, brighter than outside.

'Aha,' Van den Bergen said.

'What is it?' Elvis asked, a thrill tapping along his spine.

Van den Bergen took out his mobile phone and deftly photographed Kamphuis with the woman.

'You gonna blackmail him, boss?'

'Don't be fucking stupid, Elvis.' He turned to his protégé, wearing a broad grin. Impossible in those light conditions to tell if it was jubilant or malevolent. 'I know her. I know that woman!'

Elvis reappraised the Commissioner's squeeze. No memories triggered. He shrugged.

'This onion has many layers,' Van den Bergen said, snapping again with his phone's camera.

'Who is she, then?'

'Jaap Hasselblad's ex-mistress.'

CHAPTER 53

Amsterdam, Van den Bergen's apartment, 24 March

The bed was empty. The room was dark and silent. Where was he? George looked at the clock and saw it wasn't yet 7 a.m. She wrapped the duvet tightly around her, extreme fatigue making her bones feel leaden and her brain feel like an overwrought computer processor. Sliding her head onto Van den Bergen's pillow, she drank in the scent of his skin; a lingering whiff of sport deodorant, but the essence of him beneath it. Two short, white hairs on the aubergine pillowcase. She wished he was still there to kiss away the heavy feeling before breakfast. She placed one of his tiny hairs on her tongue and swallowed it deliberately, feeling instantly foolish for a romantic gesture that was almost certainly odd by most people's standards. *Fuck most people.* She and Paul weren't most people. She smiled and stretched out.

She remembered all at once that Letitia was in the living room on the sofa. Realised why she felt so dog-tired. There was nothing to smile about. She, her mother, her aunt and her two cousins had crowded into Van den Bergen's apartment, taking advantage of its owner being out on surveillance. Until three in the morning, there had been high drama and hyperventilation surrounding Letitia's health woes. Too many cups of coffee, followed by a bottle of rum, which Sharon had sent Tinesha to the local minimart to buy.

Tears had dripped steadily onto Letitia's bosom, making her skin glisten. Puffy-eyed, she had held court on the sofa. Loving every minute of it. Talking about funeral arrangements, acceptable levels of bling when selecting a coffin and, once the tears had dried, how she was going to apply for disability benefits as soon as she got back to the UK. A broad smile then.

'Can't wait to get back to bingo,' she had said. Turning to George, her smile had faded. The soft face of the emotionally exposed had hardened. 'And you can give me back those fucking winnings what you nicked out of my handbag, you cheeky cow.'

George had been torn. Any kindness the woman had shown her in early childhood had been negated by more than a decade of neglect and toxicity. And yet, here Letitia was. Crying on the sofa. Contemplating the news that she had maybe five years to live.

You're a heartless bastard, George. Hug her for Christ's sake. She's looking to you for solace. Why can't you just grant her that? It's so easy and costs so little. But even a stiff embrace would have felt like daylight robbery to a daughter who had been left to rot at Her Majesty's leisure by Letitia the Dragon.

Pulling on her dressing gown, George padded into the living room. The sofa was now empty.

She spotted the guest duvet in disarray, an indent in the pillow, and reasoned her mother must have gone to the toilet.

In the kitchen, George flicked on the kettle. Cleared out the cafetiere. A hard crust of coffee grouts left by Paul, whom she imagined tiptoeing past his unwelcome, sleeping houseguest before heading out to work. As the coffee brewed, she turned on her laptop, still sitting on the kitchen table after the previous night's family research session into all things sickle cell anaemia and pulmonary hypertension.

There in her inbox was another email from her father.

From: Michael Carlos Izquierdo Moreno (Michael.Moreno@
BritishEngineering.com)
Sent: 23 March 23.58
To: George_McKenzie@hotmail.com
Subject: Meeting up

Hi George,

Thanks for the photo of you with your family. Letitia hasn't changed one bit. She still looks glamorous as ever. Your cousins have grown. They've all got a distinct Williams-May look about them, like your mum and Aunty Sharon. You could pick them out in a crowd any day of the week. Yours, of course, is the standout face. I'd recognize you anywhere. You've grown into such a beautiful woman.

I think it might be quite nice, after all this chat, to meet up. I don't know your movements at the moment, but your web page tells me you move between London, Cambridge and Amsterdam. As it happens, I'm in Amsterdam on business next week. If you're in town, meet me for lunch at Vinkeles, 1 p.m. on 4th April. My treat. Email me if you can't make it. Otherwise, I'll see you there!

Love Dad

George stared at the email. Blinking repeatedly at her father's words. *Meet me for lunch.* The man she hadn't seen since she was a small child wanted to take her to a fine restaurant, as if an afternoon of expensive food and drink could make up for two decades of absence, silence and, by implication, utter disinterest. It felt like a betrayal both to herself and to her memory of the caring Letitia from George's childhood even to consider re-forging contact with this semi-stranger.

George closed her Hotmail tab. She was annoyed. She was excited. Her father could wait.

The kitchen yielded nothing for breakfast apart from a stale crust of bread and a packet of biscuits, which George duly opened. Van den Bergen was no better than her when it came to food provision. But Letitia would be moaning if she found out the cupboard was genuinely bare. 'Where *is* the silly cow?' The apartment was silent.

Pouring herself a black coffee and wedging a ginger biscuit into her mouth, she shuffled back into the living room. Checked the time. Twenty minutes since she had got up.

'Maybe she's gone out for bread,' she told Paul's portrait of Tamara, hanging above his stereo. She rummaged through his execrable CD and vinyl collection, finally finding an old Massive Attack 12". *Unfinished Sympathy.* Unstarted sympathy where her mother was concerned. But where the fuck was she?

George stood in front of the sofa, pulling on one of her corkscrew curls until it was straight. Sucking on the tract of hair, deep in thought, she tried to spot what was wrong about this set-up. Duvet. Pillow. A plate half-pushed under the sofa containing half-eaten toast from 2 a.m. Phone gone. Handbag gone.

'Letitia!' George shouted.

She checked the toilet. Nada. She checked the spare bedroom in which she had refused to sleep. Empty. Her coat was still hanging on the peg by the front door. Not good, given it was snowing outside. Not the sort of fat flakes that settle, but the wet stuff that comes hard and fast. George rang her mother's phone, chagrined to find it kicked straight into voicemail. Letitia trying to sound like a sassy DJ on some sweet soul South East London pirate radio station. Bullshit FM. Carleen Anderson, singing in the background that you better listen to your Mama. *Leave a message, yeah? And you know I'll hit you back later.*

'It's me. Where the fuck are you?' George hung up. Accelerated heartbeat signified her body speaking for her mind. She dialled again, just in case. A third time, because three was a proper number. Still going to voicemail. Shit.

Aunty Sharon might know. George pulled up the number of her aunt. Ringing. Ringing. Answer the bloody phone.

Finally, she was greeted by a slow, lazy voice that sounded thick with sleep and befuddlement: 'Wotcha, darling. What time is it?'

In the background, the sound of snoring reverberated around her old Cracked Pot Coffee Shop room. Almost certainly Tinesha at her side, sharing the double bed. She sounded like a rumbling volcano at the best of times.

'You seen Letitia, Aunty Shaz?'

The smacking of lips. Shifting of position in the squeaking old bed. 'Nah. Why?'

George hung up. A waste of time. She silently prayed her mother would put the spare key in the lock and walk through the front door with a loaf under her arm. But George was still alone with her disquiet.

She called Van den Bergen, aware of a tense, dull ache that had her viscera in an iron grip.

'Van den Bergen. Speak.'

'It's me.'

'Oh, yes. Sorry. We're just trying to get into the bank accounts of—'

'We've got a problem. I think Letitia's gone walk about.'

CHAPTER 54

Amsterdam, police headquarters, then, Carlien Dekker's house, later still

There were two photos on his desk. One of him with George, standing outside the Houses of Parliament in London, taken by a tourist. A summer's day, with azure blue skies above the gothic rooftops. She, a good foot shorter. He, actually smiling for once, though he could remember being in agony at the time – his vertical scar itching in the heat. But there was his arm, protectively draped around her, looking more like her father than her lover.

He grimaced at the thought, attention turning to the photo of Tamara, when she had been four. On a swing in the back garden of his and Andrea's old family home. Kiddy-toothed smile and childish delight in her eyes. Chubby little hands gripping the ropes either side. First, he felt a pang of nostalgia and wistful hope that he could relive that time through his grandchild. Then, a ball of stomach acid propelled itself into Van den Bergen's gullet, incinerating the rosy optimism to ashen grey realism. Tamara, playing in the garden, aged four – just like Josh Deenen. Tiny little blonde girl – just like Lucy Deenen.

He picked up the phone. Dialled Marie's extension. 'Any joy?'

'Morning, boss. No. I've been wracking my brains overnight, trying to think of a way round it that won't get us into a pile of

343

steaming shit. I'm going to have to call in a favour from a … friend.' She hesitated. Van den Bergen knew the silence was loaded. 'We're in seriously dodgy territory here.'

Swallowing hard, Van den Bergen considered 'I know. I'm sorry. You don't have to do it. Any of this. I know I'm putting you in an awkward—'

'I want to,' Marie said. Her voice sounded strangled. Fierce, even.

Tenderly, he ran his finger over the two dimensional souvenir of his daughter's toddlerhood. He thought about the couple, locked in his cabin, subsisting on the sandwiches, soup and flasks of coffee that he brought them. Shitting in a bucket, while he tried to track down their children. An unsustainable situation. Time running out for everyone.

'Me and Elvis are going to drive over to the Kennemer golf club in Zandvoort that Hasselblad and Bloom belong to,' he said. 'See if anything turns up. Somehow, Hasselblad and Kamphuis are both involved in this bullshit. But I'd like you to keep hammering away at the finances and do a bit of digging into Kamphuis' mistress.'

'Ooh. Mistress?' A sharp intake of breath said Marie was not immune to the sensationalist appeal of office gossip. 'You mean he's stopped shagging trainees?'

'If Kamphuis spends time with her, maybe she knows something. I can't keep the Deenens tucked away indefinitely. It's inhumane.'

'Who is this woman, then?'

'Carlien Dekker.'

'Carlien. Rings a bell. Hang on. Wasn't she the auditor who totally pissed accounts off a couple of years ago? She pissed me off too, actually. I've never had such earache over three-year-old expense receipts. Is it that cow? Perky tits and a crepey chest from too much sunbedding?'

'Yep.' Van den Bergen was struck by a memory of Dekker, perched coquettishly on the corner of Hasselblad's desk. Foxy in stilettos. Always heavily made-up. Less interested in spreadsheets than silk sheets. She was the ultimate anti-accountant.

'Leave it with me,' Marie said, hanging up.

'I shouldn't even be here,' George said, moving to fling her bag onto the floor of Marie's office. She considered Marie's habit of dropping shards of crisps all over the carpet and set the bag on her lap instead. 'My bloody mother's gone AWOL.'

'What do you mean?' Marie glanced towards her absently.

A Google search on Marie's computer screen clearly dominated her attention. The image of a hatchet-faced red-headed woman in a corporate power suit – pneumatic tits and a tiny waist – told George this was the accountant Van den Bergen had been telling her about.

'Letitia's buggered off. No coat. No breakfast.' George started to hook paperclips together in a long chain, making a perfect oval shape with them on the desk. 'I spent over an hour in a blind panic. Then I eventually get a text from her just as I'm about to completely lose my shit. She said she had to get out the flat and spend some time on her own.'

'So?' Marie said, clicking on a search result that yielded Carlien Dekker's address. 'Mystery solved, right? I've got a car booked out. Let's go.'

'Go?' George asked, thinking about the benders her mother had disappeared on for days at a time when she had been only twelve, maybe thirteen. Having to get the neighbour to open tins of beans for her because the shitty old tin opener had been too stiff for her small hands.

'Surveillance. You can keep me company. As long as you don't start moaning about standards of cleanliness and the smell of the upholstery.'

Driving down past the airport, hail started to rattle on the bonnet of the Ford Focus. Accompanied by the soporific swish and whine of the windscreen wipers, George found her eyelids becoming heavy, her heart heavier still. She absently – fruitlessly – checked her phone for news, either of her wayward mother or the missing toddlers.

'Do you think we'll ever find these poor bloody kids?' George asked, peering out of the window as the car scudded down the E19. Flat fields quickly turned from grey-green to white, covered with the pea-sized balls of ice that fell from the sky like little pieces of Armageddon.

Marie stared solemnly at the whiteout ahead. 'No.'

'No? Seriously?'

The detective shook her head in silence. George sensed she was agitated. She remembered Marie had lost a baby and probably no longer believed in miracles. George wondered fleetingly how her life would be once she became a step-grandmother of sorts to the child of a woman who was roughly her own age.

The car ploughed on down the straight road, hail turning to sleet. In parts, where the canals had become inundated by meltwater, bursting their banks, the ghostly white of the big sky was reflected in the standing water.

'Hang on a minute,' George said, peering round at the smattering of Dutch barn-style houses. A petrol station, there. A wind turbine, here. A roadside hypermarket. 'Isn't this the way to—'

'The Deenens?' Marie said. A half-smile flirting with the corner of her mouth. 'Yes. Do you believe in coincidences?'

The lights in the dashboard glowed, as the sleet abated. Indicator strobing said they were bearing left.

'The same fucking street? Oh, you are kidding!' Flashbacks in George's mind's eye to the last time she had been here.

The place had been crawling with Marianne de Koninck's forensics team, uniforms, paparazzi, newspaper reporters and TV journalists camped out along the street. Even at night, when she had visited the place with Van den Bergen, red tail lights like demonic eyes had snaked their way to the Deenen's front door.

The world's press, pointing their enormous vehicle-mounted satellite dishes at the heavens, beaming the couple's misery to every bleeding heart on the planet, and perhaps even to the abductor himself.

Today, the place was deserted. A tragedy long forgotten.

'No. I couldn't believe it when I saw Carlien Dekker's address,' Marie said. A grin manifested itself fully on her face now, as if declaring its supremacy over whatever claim sorrow usually staked on her features.

They bypassed the Deenen's house – windows boarded up downstairs, all the homely charm of a haunted house – and pulled up two doors down outside a neat-looking box. Good-sized. Two-storey detached. The sort of executive home one would expect a successful accountant to live in. Chintzy lace curtains hanging at the windows in neat pleats, showing scenes of the countryside. Windmills. Farmhouses. Blue-white clean, George noted. Hiding whatever went on inside from prying neighbours' eyes.

'No one's home, by the looks,' Marie said.

'What does she drive? Do you know?'

'Audi TT,' Marie said, checking her notepad.

George stared at the empty driveway. 'She'll be in work, won't she? Does she live alone?' She imagined Kamphuis showing up here with some shit flowers, a hard-on and a bottle of wine. Carlien Dekker looked like the sort of woman who drank fizzy rosé and pranced about indoors wearing pink slip-on mules with marabou feather trim. George wondered fleetingly if she made Kamphuis talk about VAT returns when they fucked. 'Ugh.' Naked disgust, slipped from her mouth.

Together, they sat in the car with the engine running for thirty minutes, trying to keep warm, though the car was running low on petrol. The warmth of the air-conditioning cranked to twenty-six degrees resulting in the occasional smell of stilton. George looked down at Marie's feet. They looked innocent enough. She looked at her own, horrified by the thought that she might be the source of the stench.

Marie opened her laptop and plugged in a dongle that connected her to a roving Wi-Fi signal, then connected to her email. 'I'm waiting for bank details from a friend,' she said, winking.

'What friend?' George asked, narrowing her eyes at this unprepossessing policewoman.

Marie toyed with her pearl earrings. 'Let's just say not everyone I mix with outside work is entirely law-abiding. And I spend a lot of time online, of course. You can put two and two together, right?'

Laughing, George was almost tempted to pat Marie on the arm, but decided against it. 'Dark horse,' she said in English.

Tapping away beside her, Marie sighed.

'Anything?'

'Nothing. Let's just sit for a bit longer. I'll email the boss. See what he wants us to do.'

Minutes passed during which George rang Letitia's phone another five times, texted a filthy poem to Van den Bergen and sent a noncommittal email to Sally Wright, promising she'd be back in Cambridge 'soon'.

'What we doing, then?' she said, eventually. Chugging on an e-cigarette with the window open only an inch. 'You haven't got a warrant. She's not home. Do you want to break in?' George rummaged in her pocket and produced a bunch of keys. She showed Marie her skeleton key from the time before. 'Because I can get us in if you like. I'm a whizz with alarm codes.' She noticed Marie's questioning look. 'Misspent youth.'

Marie shook her head. 'I'm not risking it. Not without good reason.' She sighed heavily and checked her watch. 'Let's go.'

'Check your emails one more time,' George said. 'You can't go without refreshing the page and checking.'

'Why not?'

'Because it's the rules, right?' A sweat breaking out on her top lip. 'Humour me.'

Tutting, Marie glanced at her inbox. Hit F5. 'Oh. Hang on!' She opened several attachments, figures spilling onto the screen. She scrolling through and through the bank account details of Hasselblad and Kamphuis.

'Well?'

Disappointment in Marie's voice. 'Not a bloody thing out of the ordinary from what I can see. Salary in. Normal bills. Money out. Nothing huge that sets any bells ringing. Debited or credited. Nope. That's it. Let's go.' Marie put her hand on the lid of the laptop, about to send it into hibernation.

Feeling disappointment nibbling away at her, George scrutinised the many attachments, arranged horizontally in a ribbon of icons across the top of the email. 'Woah! Hang on. You've missed something,' she said, pointing to a discreet little arrow that said there was more to come.

Marie blinked hard, clicked on the mousepad, brow furrowed. Her expression brightened. 'It's Dekker's accounts. Credit card statement too. My pal hit the jackpot!' She blushed. 'I owe him a big bottle of schnapps, or whatever his tipple is.'

ABN Amro Bank. Leaning in closer than she was comfortable with, George spied a glut of financial transactions that seemed perfectly ordinary. Until she saw the size of the amounts coming out of this current account to settle Dekker's credit card debt. 'She spends nearly two thousand a month on plastic! Jesus wept. Are people really that rich? Or stupid?'

'What the hell is she buying?' Marie said, opening the credit card statement.

A list of expenses, telling a story of consumption that was more conspicuous than had been intended.

Toys from a toy supermarket on the edge of town.

Children's books from Amazon.

Children's books from a store in Amsterdam.

Children's clothes from a high street children's clothing shop. George swallowed hard as everything clicked into place. 'Oh my days! The kids are here. Come on!'

CHAPTER 55

A village South of Amsterdam, Carlien Dekker's house

George inserted her skeleton key in the lock of the rear patio doors – a lasting souvenir from Danny Boy. The lock relented. Heart pounding and blood rushing in her ears, she pushed the handle down. Opened the door a fraction. Cocked her head, listening for the dreaded beep, beep countdown to bedlam and bells ringing. Nothing.

'We're good,' she said.

Marie glanced over her shoulder. A patch of lawn, studded with melting hailstones and some scrubby evergreen shrubs. A train line running behind the sodden fence sounded deserted for now. 'Jesus, George. We've got no warrant and Dekker is shagging the Commissioner!'

'Oh, shut it, Marie. You want to find these kids, don't you?'

'More than you.' She drew her service weapon.

Inside, George could smell dust and the funk of stale food, though the dated kitchen looked perfectly clean. The sort of hygiene attained by a fortnightly cleaner. The sort of smell that denoted pizza from the supermarket deep-freeze. Dr Oetker in the house. Chicken nuggets or whatever the Dutch fed their kids on. Not George's field of expertise.

'No sign of toys,' Marie whispered, advancing through the kitchen. The barrel of the pistol that she clutched in her hands, leading the way like a deadly beacon.

George followed several steps behind. Eyes on everything. Dreading what they might find in this prissy suburban hole.

The living room, off to the left. Marie, already inside.

'Clear.'

Already advancing to a room at the front of the house. But George wanted to see how Carlien Dekker lived. Lingered in this main reception room at the back. Photos only of Dekker: in eveningwear, glittering with wealthy-looking friends; smiling on what appeared to be a Caribbean beach. Leg, artfully bent to make her look slimmer, though she was already very slender. Rocking a bikini like a girl ten years younger; a professional portrait, hanging on the wall. Hair, coiffed to perfection; elaborate framed certificate from the supreme overlords of accountancy. Feminine, flowery chintz on the sofa. Frou-frou curtains with braided gold tie-backs.

George grimaced at the overpowering scent of narcissism that clung to every surface. No sign of any family life, whatsoever. Carlien Dekker was at the epicentre of her own universe and her strong, magnetic core had attracted Kamphuis. Or had it just been her tits?

'Dining room's empty,' Marie whispered. 'No sign.'

George looked down at the cream carpet, studded with pock-marks that implied stilettos were worn in the house. She was almost tempted to take her shoes off. She drummed her foot on the ground. Solid. No basement.

Marie pointed the gun at the staircase. Gesticulated upwards with the weapon. Started to climb, gingerly. George followed behind.

The master bedroom ran from the front of the house to the back. Window at the side. Window at the front. An entire wall at the rear dedicated to walk-in wardrobes with mirrored doors, uniform in size except for one larger one, no doubt ideal for posing in front of. No fingerprints said Dekker kept her hands clinically clean. The lingering sickly smell of overly feminine perfume and hairspray betrayed a strict grooming routine. Appliqué butterfly bedding that looked as though it hadn't been slept in for more than a day or two. Knick-knacks and beauty products on every available surface. George pulled on her gloves and opened the drawer of one of the nightstands. Spied sex toys and fur-trimmed handcuffs. Wrinkled her nose at the fleeting thought of Kamphuis cuffed to the brass bedstead. But no sign of children. Only an overwhelming sense of the house's owner.

Second bedroom was furnished as a guest room. Two single beds that hadn't been slept in, judging by the perfect, straight creases in the freshly ironed bedding. A thin film of dust on the scant furniture told George the cleaner didn't go in here unless she needed to.

Third box room empty but for some gym equipment. An exercise bike. A curved contraption that George felt sure was for working out abs.

Hope surged as they checked out the loft – surely an ideal space in which to conceal abductees. But it yielded no surprises beyond old suitcases, stuffed with outmoded clothes and photographs of a time when Dekker's face had been fuller and less orange.

Marie sighed, replacing the loft hatch carefully, crestfallen, with the drooping shoulders of the defeated, evident even though she was wearing a ski jacket. 'They're not here.' Her eyes appeared suddenly bloodshot, as though she'd had far more riding on finding the Deenen children than just a detective's job well done. Anger and disappointment strangling her voice. 'I really thought … Goddamn it! Shit, shit, shit!' Holstered her service weapon as an act of acceptance.

But the knot of apprehension in George's gut would not dissipate. She reached out to rub Marie's arm. Withdrew it. She thought about photos of Josh Deenen, wearing his big-boy nappies, despite him being old enough to be potty trained. Considered the tender two years of Lucy.

Wordlessly, she descended to the kitchen and located the bin. A person's rubbish was always revealing. Vague recollections of searching through her own rubbish when she had lived in The Cracked Pot Coffee Shop, looking for the contents of an emptied ashtray. Finding the souvenirs of a rough night for a good-time girl.

'What are you doing?' Marie asked. 'Give it up! There's nobody here, and if a neighbour spots us—'

George's breath came short as she spied the very thing she was looking for. Preceded by a foul smell of perfume and diarrhoea, she fished out a fat salmon-pink nappy sack, handles tied tight. Beneath it was another. Both stuffed with rolled up nappies and soiled wet-wipes, visible through the translucent plastic.

She held the first sack triumphantly in the air, swinging on the end of her gloved finger like a bio-hazard bauble. 'Phone Van den Bergen,' she said. 'Get forensics and a sniffer dog here.'

'But the place is empty,' Marie said, scratching at her hair.

Returning to the patio doors, George ventured out into the garden. Looked up at the back of the house. Pointed to a large window that faced onto the train line and trees beyond the fence. Obscured glazing, as though the glass had been etched or covered in special film.

'What was at the back of the master bedroom?' she asked, smiling at Marie. Blood coursing through her body with vigour. Senses on fire, carrying her on the rollercoaster up to the very top.

'Just fitted wardrobes,' Marie replied, scowling at the perplexing sight. 'Not a window.'

'It's a false front,' George said, her steaming breath coming short with adrenalin. 'There's a room behind those mirrored doors!'

The women raced back inside, George leading the way, intoxicated by her theory. Stopping short in front of the reflective bank of wardrobe fronts. Might a woman as vain as Carlien Dekker not have a walk-in dressing room?

Marie opening the narrow doors, only to find shelf after shelf of folded clothing. Pushing it onto the floor to see if something lay beyond.

'Nothing!'

'It's this one!' George said, prising the largest of the doors open, noticing tiny fingerprints much lower down on the glass, where the cleaner had missed them.

Beyond the door was a shallow void, but the cream carpet that ran throughout the house continued underneath a further door that appeared to be nothing more than the back of a wardrobe. Laminate. The colour of oak. Hinged at the wall with a tiny hollow that served as a handle. George prised it open. Heavier than a normal door. Thicker. Soundproofed.

The smell of shit caught her at the back of her throat.

'Hello,' she said to two small children who were sitting, legs akimbo on the floor. Faces covered in what appeared to be the dayglow orange remnants of cheesy puffs. Beakers of red juice lying with their lids off in red puddles. Empty food wrappers mixed in with Duplo blocks. Lucy and Josh Deenen, playing at a low plastic table with some kind of activity centre almost like an abacus made from twisted, brightly coloured metal and beads. The room, lit by daylight coming through the large window, covered, as George had suspected, with special film often used in bathrooms and toilets to give glass an etched appearance. Let light in. Keep prying eyes out. Clever.

Squealing then, suddenly, as the children realised two strangers were in their midst. Tears, streaming down their filthy faces.

Marie stepped forwards, scooping Lucy into her arms. The little girl kicked and punched against her with strong feet and fists.

'No, no, no!' the little girl screamed.

'It's okay, Lucy. I won't hurt you.' Marie had the singsong voice of a mother down pat.

But George didn't know what to say. Standing there, one hand on Josh's shoulder. Him, straining to get away from her.

'Carly! Carly Mummy!' Josh shouted. 'Where's Carly Mummy? Where's Daddy Olaf? Who are you?'

Heart thudding relentlessly against her ribs, George dialled Van den Bergen with her free hand. Gripping the boy as tight as she could, lest he tried to run away. He answered on the second ring.

'Van den Bergen. Speak.'

'I've found them, Paul! The Deenen kids! We've got them, safe and sound. They were right under our fucking noses all this time.'

CHAPTER 56

Zandvoort, Kennemer Golf & Country Club, later

Ending the call to George, Van den Bergen pinched the bridge of his nose, mentally pushing aside his emotional sandbags, letting the relief flood through him.

He turned to Elvis, grinning. A grin that made him feel whole again. He grabbed his protégé's arm and frog-marched him, mid-conversation, away from the manager of the golf club into the deserted car park.

'What is it?' Elvis asked, rubbing his arm.

'They're alive.' He started to chuckle, choking back unexpected tears.

'Who's alive, boss?' Elvis asked, smiling back at him but wearing a bewildered expression on his face.

'The Deenen kids. They've been stashed away at Kamphuis' mistress' place all this time. Would you bloody believe it?' The chemical cocktail that caused euphoria to pulsate through his body was the finest high he had experienced since Tamara's birth, shortly followed by the first time he had made love to George. Nagging doubt that his child was bringing her child into a withering world, not fit for human consumption, finally fading, now. On that sleet-washed, desolate car park, devoid of any other soul apart from them and the manager who had opened up the club house especially, Van den Bergen whooped.

'Boss,' Elvis said, staring at his red palm. 'Did you seriously just whoop and high-five me?'

'Can you blame me?' He unlocked his car, now on autopilot, climbing in, out of the path of the biting elements. 'Fucking Kamphuis. What the hell was he thinking? What on earth has he been doing with two toddlers for all these months? He's a disease!'

'He's evil,' Elvis said, eyes darting side to side as he processed the enormity of the news. 'Warped.'

Punching Piet Deenen's number into the phone, Van den Bergen gave the sun the moon and the stars back to a man who had lost his entire universe. He hung up, wiping a tear away surreptitiously from the corner of his eye.

'Hayfever,' he told Elvis, though in truth, just this once, he didn't care that the loyal detective was privy to the flint-faced Chief Inspector finally showing more complex emotion than displeasure or digestive discomfort.

Then, as abruptly as it had manifested itself, the euphoria left him. Tingling, optimistic warmth gave way to dread.

'Oh, shit,' he said. 'What the hell do I do now?'

'What do you mean?'

Elvis, chewed on the end of an unlit cigarette, obviously thinking he could take the piss just because of Van den Bergen's momentary show of weakness. Van den Bergen grabbed the cigarette, snapped it in half and threw it out of the car window.

'Hasselblad. The Chief of bloody Police is in bed with one of the biggest, most powerful and dangerous criminals on the continent. The untouchable Lord Bloom. Right? And how much actual evidence have we got against either of them? I mean, the sort of hard stuff that will stand up to scrutiny in court.'

'Nada.'

'Precisely. And Kamphuis – my boss; the damned Commissioner of the Netherlands Police; odious twat though he may be – has abducted two children and dumped them on one of the leading accountants in the country. Not a shred of concrete evidence against him either ... yet. I mean, how high up does this corruption go?' He looked up into the grey-white wintry sky and wondered when exactly God had left the celestial building. 'Is Kamphuis in bed with Gordon Bloom and Hasselblad? Piet Deenen said there were dignitaries involved.'

His breath was laboured. His fingertips grew numb. Pins and needles tingled down his arms. Was he having a heart attack? He could feel the panic settling in like inclement weather. He remembered the light fading on Ramsgate dockside some two years earlier. The anniversary of his father's death. The months of cognitive behavioural therapy that had ensued in a bid to quell his anxiety. Confessing his long-harboured innermost fears, whilst sitting in a chair that had given him terrible backache in a room that smelled of farts. Hadn't been much fucking use, after all.

Come on, you self-indulgent old bastard, he chastised himself.

He tried to conjure the therapist's earnest voice – *You have the wisdom to deal with this, Paul. Stop trying to impose order on chaos. You gain more control by letting go. Trust that it will all come good.*

Wise words reverberating uselessly around his head.

But what had been George's counsel? *Grow a pair, old man.* He felt suddenly bolstered by her mantra, far harsher than that of any €200-an-hour therapist.

'We need Kamphuis and Dekker behind bars before they can cover their tracks.'

'You going to get the uniforms to do it?' Elvis asked.

'No. They'll forewarn him. Kamphuis' arse-kissing brigade has infested the whole force like dry rot. Uniforms can pick Dekker up, but we'll get Kamphuis ourselves.'

'What about Hasselblad?'

Van den Bergen shrugged. 'We'll have to sit on that. Right now, everything Gordon Bloom said is no more than hearsay.

359

But Kamphuis…' He grinned, feeling the euphoria licking along his synapses again like a creeping, warming flame. 'Even if we don't have enough to convict him, we can make the bastard squirm. This will ruin him, whatever happens, and if I go down, for whatever reason, I'll make damn sure I take him with me for what he's done.'

CHAPTER 57

Maldives, North Male Atol, four hours ahead

In the crystal-clear water, twenty metres beneath the surface of the Indian Ocean, Gordon Bloom felt detached from the filth of life. Tropical fish darted to and fro around him as he clung to the reef. Oriental sweetlips – striped and spotted, monochrome, but for those flashes of yellow. Parrot fish in petrol colours. Bluefin tuna, darting in angry shoals like fat serrated blades through the water. Resisting the strong current that had tried to drag his diving party further out into the deep. Hadn't he always been swimming against the current? In life, as it was in the North Male Atol.

He laughed to himself. Bubbles rose from his breathing apparatus in a column of silver, an offering to the sea gods, heading upwards to the tropical glare of the surface. Turquoise waters here, so different to the brown swell of the North Sea that lapped against the disappointing shores of Margate – froth and pollution sitting on the surface like crocheted doilies on the occasional tables of that shit B&B Rufus had set up, frequented by those lesser souls who sought young flesh for comfort. But not here. None of that here.

A hand signal from the diving instructor. A fin on the forehead fashioned from his fingers. Four black-tipped reef sharks swam into view, each two- or three-metres long. It was a majestic sight. Built for speed. Built for violence. The perfect predators. Just like him.

When the wiry, dark-skinned crew on board the wooden dhoni had helped him to remove his oxygen tanks, once they were sailing back towards the island resort with sea spray spurting merrily up towards them, he popped his glass eye back into its socket. He seated himself on the platform at the prow, which curved skywards to a point like a wooden scimitar. Nice to be away from the noisy Italians and Germans who were on this dive with him. Enjoying the sun on his winter-white English skin. Checking the photos on his underwater camera. There were the sharks, grinning at him as though they recognized one of their own.

The signal returned to his phone as soon as the resort's long, wooden jetty stretched into view. An immediate call disturbed the paradise peace. The name on the screen told him this was Rufus' replacement. An educated voice belonging to a hungry young warrior, trained by Rufus in the subtle art of flying like a Son of the Eagle. As if Danny Spencer could ever have fulfilled that role and stepped into those hand-lasted boots. The fucking monosyllabic oik, still stinking of shit from the ghetto gutter!

'Ah, Calum,' Bloom said. '*Salaam aleikum*.'

'Having a good break, Lord Bloom?'

'Do call me Gordon, dear chap. Yes, the Maldives rather agrees with me. Now, did you manage to deal with those loose ends that have been bothering me so terribly?'

'I have a skilled professional who will remedy both problems by the end of the week. He has the job in hand.'

The line crackled but the implications were clear. Gordon Bloom ended the call. Waved the dhoni crew away, he remained seated on the paint-peeling bench, contemplating the myriad of plastic fins and life preservers at his feet. The warm breeze on his face. The salt tang in the air. Lazy palms waving to him from the strip of white sand at the opposite end of the jetty. If only he could suspend himself in this perfect moment, like Damian Hirst's shark, pickled in formaldehyde. *The Physical Impossibility of Death in the Mind of Someone Living*. But even Hirst's shark had started to rot after a while. Even those majestic creatures circling the Indian Ocean reef would become fish food one day. Change was inevitable. He thought about the changes his plans were about to effect. Ripples out at sea, becoming tsunamis on the shore…

CHAPTER 58

Amsterdam, police headquarters, later

'What the fuck do you mean you want to question me? Question me about what?' Kamphuis' face had quickly changed from its usual boiled-ham pink to the colour of young Gouda. Scattered across his desk were project plans, strategy documents and spreadsheets full of stats.

Van den Bergen looked down at the Commissioner: his nemesis for two decades. He couldn't quite believe this might be the beginning of the end. 'The Deenen children have been found.'

Insipid Gouda, quickly blanching further to the colour of zuurkool – a man made from pickled cabbage, cheese and cheap sausage in Van den Bergen's mind's eye. Stamppot gone rancid – the feast for the eyes portrait that surrealist Giuseppe Arcimboldo forgot to paint. Van den Bergen almost laughed at the thought. He decided he would give it a go once he got home and dug out his watercolour pad.

Kamphuis' forehead beaded with sweat. He reached for his naked lady statue and started to rub her breasts furiously. His eye, ticking like the indicator on an old car. 'Great,' he said, unconvincingly, the word seeming to strangle him. 'Where were they?'

'Oh, I think you know where they were, *Daddy Olaf*,' Van den

Bergen said, remembering George's description of the scene she and Marie had found.

'Just be glad we're not slapping cuffs on you in front of every cop in the building,' Elvis said at his side, clearly emboldened by the sight of a crumbling Commissioner.

Kamphuis gripped the tabletop of his desk. White knuckles. A quivering chin. Suddenly, the brass buttons on his jacket had lost their shine. 'I'll sue you for defamation of character,' he said, almost whispering, sounding like somebody had punched the air from his overinflated body.

'Yeah, sure you will,' Van den Bergen said, winking, knowing it would drive the morally bankrupt piece of shit mad, silently praying that Marianne de Koninck and her forensics team would find enough physical evidence of Kamphuis being party to the abduction to stop the snake from blaming it all on his mistress.

In the interview room, Kamphuis sat in silence for a full ten minutes, though the tape was rolling, perspiring with such intensity that the dry air quickly felt clammy. Once or twice, he opened his mouth, poised to speak. But when words came out, he simply demanded his solicitor. The moment that Van den Bergen had been dreading. The point at which he would have to confess that Marie had not had a warrant when she had broken into Dekker's house with George.

George. How would *she* deal with this? Understanding people's motivations. That's how she pieced together an accurate view of the world, triggering an avalanche of truth from the most reluctant witnesses. A criminologist, rather than a trained psychologist, but young Dr McKenzie had an innate grasp of how narcissists like Kamphuis were bolted together. *Think like George …*

'You know Hasselblad has been accused of consorting with transnational traffickers, don't you?' he said. 'Paedophile rings. Corrupt luminaries. The whole works.'

Wide eyes. Narrowed eyes. Suddenly leaning forward, head

cocked, as if this was welcome news. The hint of pink in Kamphuis' cheeks again. 'Hasselblad?' The hint of a smile, which was unexpected.

Van den Bergen nodded. He leaned back in the interview chair and bounced his right foot on his left knee. The bullet hole in his hip aching, but wanting to piss Kamphuis off made the pain worthwhile. 'Are you knee deep in the same mire as the Chief of Police, Olaf? Have you been renting out the Deenen children to every pervert in the Netherlands?' He deployed his best supercilious voice, normally reserved for talking to his son-in-law, Numbnuts. 'Maybe Belgium and Germany too, eh? That's a nice big house and an Audi Q7 you've got there. That's not your police issue car, is it?'

Kamphuis thumped the table. 'Hey! I'm no bloody paedophile, you lanky ball-sack!'

Van den Bergen slid his glasses onto the end of his nose and pretended to examine his notebook. School-teacher stern. Tut-tutting and shaking his head. 'Hmn. Two missing toddlers found sitting in their own filth in your mistress' house. Photographic evidence of you with Carlien Dekker. Clear links between you, Hasselblad, Jack Frost, dead paedos, a basement full of sexually abused Roma children, the Son of the Eagle ...'

Every time he referred to paedophiles or child abuse, Kamphuis winced. There was his Achilles heel.

'Shit sticks, Olaf. Especially when it comes from toddlers' nappies, eh?' He savoured every moment. Kamphuis started to pant heavily, nostrils flaring, as though the truth was trying to force its way out of his nose. 'Why did you take the Deenens' kids, Olaf? You can tell me, can't he, Elvis?' He turned to Elvis to evoke some kind of intimate, chummy triangle of trust. 'We're colleagues of old, here, aren't we? We've been through the good times and the bad, together.'

Elvis nodded. A lingering look told Van den Bergen that he understood the game they were playing.

'You shouldn't blame yourself if you've been bullied into supplying kids to politicians and celebrities, Commissioner.' Right then Elvis was the sincerest detective that ever lived. 'Even the strongest of characters would—'

'Fuck you!'

'I can understand the lure of the money,' Van den Bergen said. 'And peer pressure. When a person's weak, they're more susceptible to—'

Kamphuis was up and out of his chair like an overweight greyhound suffering from terminal optimism. 'I took the fucking children on purpose. Okay? It was my idea. I'm not weak!' Slapped himself on the chest. A self-saluting tyrant. 'I *knew* about Hasselblad, for Christ's sake! I've known for years that he was taking backhanders from that English ponce, Gordon Bloom, in return for keeping shtum. I'm *nothing* like Jaap goddamn Hasselblad. He's a bent cop!'

'And abducting two toddlers is the act of a straight cop?'

Kamphuis sat back down in his seat with a thud that signified surrender. He pulled on his bottom lip, tears welling in his eyes. 'This has taken a year of planning. A year! You have no idea.'

'Why?' Van den Bergen sat up straight in his chair, sombre like a priest, no judgemental edge to his voice, praying for a confession.

'Gordon Bloom is a murderer who pays other murderers to kill people like me and you if we so much as sneeze in his general direction. He had the protection of Hasselblad, for Christ's sake.'

'How did you find out?'

'Years ago at some drinks thing. We were out with a couple of politicians. Lads, you know? A couple of them started boasting about how they were beyond the law. One-upmanship. Jaap got blotto, snorted a load of confiscated coke he'd liberated from evidence. He'd blurted a couple of things that had jarred, so I started looking into his chummy golfing relationship with Bloom. When me and Carlien got it together – he'd treated her like shit, so she was looking for a way to settle the score … Anyway, Carlien had a tonne of dirt to dish, not least because she'd done Hasselblad's personal accounts. Offshore money, not to mention Hasselblad's missus being on the board of some of Bloom's subsidiaries. All laundered cash changing hands.'

'So, why steal children? I don't follow your thinking.' The headache that Van den Bergen had started the day with was clearing fast, the sun coming out behind storm clouds. Everything was being brought sharply into focus in perfect light.

Kamphuis examined his fingernails, chewed the inside of his cheek and fixed Van den Bergen with accusatory eyes. 'You. You with your cast-iron sense of right and wrong and your contrary ways and this stubborn-arsed feud between us. I knew if two perfect little Dutch kids went missing and if I forced you to investigate outlandish lines of enquiry, you'd start hunting for the nugget of truth wrapped in a pile of crap. The more I insisted it was the parents, the more I knew you'd defy me. You're predictable like a child! Do you know that?'

Willing himself not to respond, Van den Bergen settled for clearing his throat.

'And that tiring bitch McKenzie would definitely start looking at traffickers, because that's her thing. I hate your fucking guts, Van den Bergen, but I know you're a stubborn son of a bitch, and once you got the bit between your teeth, it wouldn't take long before you happened on Bloom and Hasselblad's seedy little goings-on. You were going to expose them for me. Do my dirty work. Worst-case scenario, you get bumped off by Bloom's people. Best-case scenario, there's a huge scandal in the national press, blowing the lid of this whole sick shebang. Bloom's taken out one way or another. Hasselblad gets arrested and goes to prison. I get to be the new Chief of Police with his scalp hanging from my belt.'

Elvis tugged at his quiff, frowning. 'I still don't understand why you chose the Deenens.'

Kamphuis chuckled mirthlessly. 'It was Carlien's suggestion. Piet Deenen had her do his accounts as a favour soon after they moved in. He didn't pay his bill. Big mistake. Then, Carly and me got talking late one night. I told her this crazy plan I had and that I was sick of being broke.' He looked up at Van den Bergen with watery eyes. 'I'm up to my neck in debt. Do you know how much more Hasselblad bloody earns than me?' He wiped his top lip, which glistened with snot, on his ceremonial jacket sleeve. 'But Carlien knew Gabi Deenen was a PR woman and would make a really big deal over it if her kids went missing. The family was dysfunctional with that Josh being such a head-banger and her being a fucking robot.' Head in hands, he leaned forwards and started to sob now.

'How would Gabi being in PR serve you, you demented prick?' Losing his temper now, Van den Bergen had the urge to slap Kamphuis across that bloated, idiotic face of his.

'The bigger the stir caused over the abduction ...'

'The bigger the plaudits if the case is solved on your watch,' Elvis finished. He gave a low whistle, shook his head, and raised his eyebrows at Van den Bergen. 'And if the Deenens had issues, it would make it easier to point the finger at them and get you haring off to conduct your own investigation on the side. Jesus, boss. Kamphuis was jerking you around like some kind of a puppet.'

But Van den Bergen was stroking the knuckles of his balled fist, biting his tongue. He wanted to rise above the testosterone impulses of an alpha male. Breathing deeply through his nose, he reminded himself that he was better than this arrogant, scheming fool on the other side of the interview table. He was a father. A soon-to-be-grandfather that he wanted his daughter to be proud of. In any case, the tape was running. This fucker had dug himself into a very deep hole.

'Did you hurt the children?'

Kamphuis shook his head. 'A bit of opulent neglect maybe.

Carly showered them in toys and snacks. But otherwise, they were looked after.'

Fuck it. Van den Bergen stood and punched his nemesis hard in the side of his head.

Kamphuis rubbed his red ear, wearing a wounded expression. 'Ow! What the hell was that for?'

Almost growling, Elvis had to drag Van den Bergen back into his seat.

'You call leaving two children under the age of five – one with Asperger's – leaving defenceless toddlers alone all day long *opulent neglect*? Do you?' Van den Bergen was yelling now, spit flying from his mouth, pointing, though really he just wanted to gouge Kamphuis' pissy eyes out with his long, vengeful fingers. 'Who was looking after them last night when you were boning Dekker in that motel? Eh?'

It was the first time Van den Bergen had ever seen Olaf Kamphuis looking properly contrite. Even when he had been caught on CCTV sexually harassing Marie, he had merely strutted around the HQ corridors, calling Marie a whore to anybody who would listen.

'You're a sociopath, Olaf,' Van den Bergen said, folding his arms in an act of self-restraint. 'Morally bankrupt. Can you imagine the anguish those poor bastards, Gabi and Piet Deenen, have been through?'

Tears drying already on his cheeks, Kamphuis sat back, staring Van den Bergen down. 'Anguish?' His voice was small but deadly. He took his jacket off carefully – his shirt was wet through – and hung it carefully on the back of his chair. 'Do you think I give a shit about their anguish, when taking down a transnational trafficking empire and a corrupt Chief of Police is at stake?' An askance look. 'They were collateral damage! Anyway, they're dead, aren't they? Why the fuck should I care about their sensibilities now?'

Van den Bergen stood, raising himself to his full six foot five, and barked like an angry dog. 'They're not dead. They're very much alive, you idiot! You think you're so fucking clever, but you didn't work out who your icicle-wielding serial killer might be?'

Kamphuis' mouth fell open, genuine surprise crawling across his face. 'I ordered you to get off the Deenens' case and get on the Jack Frost trail when potential key witnesses started being bumped off.' He swallowed audibly like a cartoon character. 'But I didn't think for a minute—' He shook his head. 'They were dead!'

Treating him to an unpleasant smile that he hoped would make the fat bastard squirm, Van den Bergen shook his head. '*Faked* suicides. You and Hasselblad botched the investigation so badly with your wild goose chases that the Deenens ended up turning vigilante. Well done, Einstein!'

'That chinless wonder Piet Deenen ruined everything I'd worked for?' Kamphuis glared at Elvis, eyebrows shooting into his hairline in indignation. A flush of hot pink had returned to his face.

Elvis touched his own chin and frowned. 'People will do anything for family,' he said.

'He didn't have it in him!' Kamphuis shouted, throwing his hands in the air. 'He's a streak of piss!'

Van den Bergen slammed his pencil onto his notepad with venom. 'You take a good man's children, don't be surprised if he turns into the Devil himself and lays your world to waste, Olaf.'

CHAPTER 59

A village South of Amsterdam, Carlien Dekker's house, then, Marie's office, police headquarters, later

Carrying the little girl to the car was a struggle. Marie clung on to her with difficulty, wincing as Lucy Deenen kicked and pummelled her.

'Where will they take them?' George asked, following behind.

The social worker was already strapping a surprisingly malleable Josh into a car seat.

Marie held Lucy's head carefully and manoeuvred her into the booster. Smiling, though the toddler's punches would surely come up in livid bruises.

'They'll go straight for medical assessment,' Marie said, straightening up. She slammed the door and waved at the bawling, angry girl, then opened and closed her hand wistfully at her brother. She exhaled heavily, a fat tear escaping from the corner of her eye. Remembering Nicolaas. Chubby and warm in her arms as she had fed him in the middle of the night. The suck, suck, sucking noise that babies make and coos of delight at almost anything, unless he was hungry. He had always been a hungry boy. *Still whingeing about cot death?* Kamphuis' words jabbed at the inside of her head, held there by the semi-permeable membrane of grief. No way out.

The car pulled away.

'Are you alright?' George asked.

Nodding, Marie blew her nose in a bid to conceal all traces of heartbreak. No need to stand there explaining to McKenzie. She would never grasp how deeply the loss of a child bit into the soul of a parent, devouring whole all the good that was left ... could never fully comprehend the suffering the Deenens must have endured, as Marie did. Though George had been supportive in her own strange way at the time of Nicolaas' passing – the gift of a USB stick containing Motown songs of love and loss; breaking into her apartment and cleaning it from top to bottom while Marie had been away; arranging Nicolaas' funeral – she hadn't yet grown a child inside her, let alone had one taken away.

Distract her. Don't let her see.

Marie peered down at her phone. Read a new text from a colleague.

'Dekker's been picked up by the uniforms,' she said, blinking hard, forcing a smile onto her face.

'I've had one from Van den Bergen,' George said, scrutinising her, as though she could read Marie's thoughts. But some thoughts, McKenzie couldn't read. Some thoughts, she must never read. 'They've got a confession from Kamphuis. He caved before his solicitor even got a sniff in!'

Marianne de Koninck marched smartly out of Dekker's house carrying samples, clad head to toe in a white jumpsuit.

'Hello, ladies!' she said, smiling with those dazzling white teeth of hers, one of those ageing beauties who always looked like she showered every single day. Marie had never once seen her without a hair out of place, apart from when she was in the ungainly jumpsuit. 'Damned good job!'

'Who'd have thought after all this time?' George said.

'At least they're safe,' Marianne said. Another bloody childless career woman. What did she know? 'Just a shame the parents won't be able to enjoy their return. So tragic.' She looked solemnly down at her overshoes. 'Will the kids be fostered out?'

Marie nodded. 'Hopefully adopted when the investigation's over.' The pathologist clearly didn't know about Van den Bergen's secret allotment squatters, then. Her cunning plan fermented quickly inside her, ideas mushrooming until they started to force their way out. 'By the way, did you ever pull any DNA from the Bijlmer man or the victims in Berlin and London?'

'Nothing at all.' A downturned mouth and a shake of the head from the pathologist told Marie everything she needed. 'Even if your lot had someone, there's not a shred of forensic evidence to get a ballpark match, let alone a conviction. Bit of a dead end, that case.'

As George climbed into the steamed up pool car to get out of the cold, Marie trailed Marianne to the forensics van. She watched her load the samples from Dekker's house. She smiled benignly as Marianne went round to the driver's seat for something, leaving the rear unattended. It took Marie only seconds to slide some unused samples bags and a pair of tweezers into her coat pocket.

Feeling distinctly that, despite the freshly falling sleet, today was looking up, Marie grinned. She was almost tempted to thank the BVM for divine inspiration. She knew exactly how to put things right.

Switching on the computer in the privacy of her office, Marie clicked on the Skype icon. She could see the call was going through. Would he pick up? Twenty seconds in, his face filled the screen.

'Franz!' she said.

'Marie!' he said.

Warm smiles on both sides. She was tempted to stroke the screen, but settled instead for toying with her earrings. He opened his mouth to speak. They both began at once.

'Thanks so much for the bank stuff,' she said.

'Did you nail your suspect?' he said.

There was some blushing. Some, 'you go on!' and 'no, you go on!' It was like being back at school but better, because Franz Dinkels was contained in a screen and couldn't hurt her. Then again, she had a plan, now. Maybe it was time to start taking risks again.

'I might be coming over to Berlin on business,' she said, biting her lip, praying that he wouldn't balk at the prospect and hastily end the call.

Chuckling. A look of undisguised delight on his face. 'Oh, really? When might you be coming?'

Marie checked her work diary. She knew Van den Bergen would require all hands on deck now that the Deenen case had been solved, with revelations on Jack Frost's murderous spree pending. She knew she could bag herself a free week with a bout of seasonal flu, though.

'Er, day after tomorrow?'

She dared to look up, hopeful that Franz's enthusiasm would still be present and correct. He was wearing a flowered shirt today. She liked it.

A glazed look. Busy hands as he clicked onto other screens, presumably checking his online diary. This was it. This was the bit where he would say he had back-to-back meetings all day and shrug and maybe say he was sorry to have missed her. She was already being pulled under by that sinking feeling.

'Are you around in the evening?' His face flushed pink.

'I have a meeting late afternoon, but yes. I am, as it happens.'

It was a sign. She had paid her penance and now it was finally time to be rewarded for a life, quietly lived, bringing sinners to their knees before God and a jury in a court of law.

Knowing that Kamphuis and Dekker were in custody, that Van den Bergen and Elvis were interviewing Kamphuis' wife, and that

George had gone back to the boss' flat to sort out 'parent shit', Marie cycled over to the Commissioner's grand house. She had been careful to conceal her identity – shoving her red hair beneath a black beanie hat; dressing in loose-fitting, androgynous clothing she had found at the back of her wardrobe – leftovers from her grieving period. She checked the coast was clear and snuck around to the back of the house.

'Smartarse McKenzie's not the only one with a skeleton key,' she whispered to the first stars to stud the midnight blue of the early evening sky. She clicked open the lock of Kamphuis' back door with ease, overshoes on her feet, blue, latex gloves already covering her hands. Sample sacks and tweezers were at the ready.

Within forty-two of the longest minutes of her life since Nicolaas' death, Marie had what she needed.

'Still whingeing about cot death?' *I'll give you something to whinge about, you fucking bastard.*

CHAPTER 60

Amsterdam, Sloterdijkermeer allotments, later

'I knew we'd find them,' Piet Deenen said, looking down at the photos of his grubby children on George's phone. Those precious little faces he had thought he would never see again, but which he had never stopped dreaming about. Praying that against the odds, they would be returned to him, safe and sound. Cherubic cheeks that he had willingly murdered for, in the hope that he would get to kiss them once more. Josh and Lucy. His beloved babies were back. He closed his eyes, momentarily. 'Thank you, God. Thank you.'

Tears spilled freely onto the screen and his lap. He didn't care what they thought of him. These were the most welcome tears he had ever cried, washing away months of torture in a seventh level of hell that seemed to have been created just for him ... punishment for being a weak husband and a lacking provider for his children. All over, at last! His worst nightmares had been just that – nightmares. Now he had only to contend with his conscience.

At his side, Gabi sat stiffly, still wrapped in her sleeping bag like a caterpillar, a glazed expression on her face. She had said nothing beyond, 'Oh!' since Van den Bergen and George had entered the cabin, bearing the sensational news. All emotion trapped inside behind a plug of disbelief, perhaps. Silently, Piet hoped that this was not symptomatic of her reverting to the Gabi she had been. The Gabi who had put up a front so unassailable that he had always struggled to get through to the woman behind. The Gabi whom the trolls had labelled 'monster' and 'machine'. Murder and physical suffering had seemed to be the only solvents to successfully breach that invulnerable veneer. Only time would tell.

He was transfixed again by the photos of his children.

'We don't think they've been interfered with,' the Chief Inspector said, 'which is great news. But the extent of any emotional damage will need to be assessed before they're placed with a foster family.'

'Foster family?' Gabi said. Her voice was cracked. Sudden ferocity, breaking her silence. 'Fucking foster family?'

She turned to George, pinning her to the cabin wall with an angry stare. Full of a mother's indignation, although Piet suspected that their actions were always going to have consequences. His tears felt like they were falling inside him, now; drip, drip, dropping into a deep well of sadness.

George, however, merely stood against the wall, arms folded in that mildewed, wooden prison amongst the frost-hardened allotments. She shrugged and seemed detached, as if she were elsewhere in the privacy of her own thoughts.

'Between you ...' Van den Bergen said, grunting as he crossed and uncrossed his legs, scowling at Gabi '... you've killed four men. This is the Netherlands. We're an open-minded society but we draw the line at letting serial killing couples go free so that they can play happy families.'

The enormity of the policeman's words registered with Piet. He had paid a father's penultimate sacrifice, stopping short of offering up the very breath in his body – he had relinquished his liberty to secure his children's safety. 'Jesus! What have we done?' he said.

'This is so unfair!' Gabi yelled, looking to George for solace.

'Life's unfair, Gabi,' George said, shrugging. 'Shit things happen to good people and utter bastards get away with ...' The bitter irony of her intended speech steamed above them in the freezing air.

'Get away with murder!' Piet said, softly. Stroking the forehead of Josh's image on George's phone.

Shrieking, tantruming, childlike outrage, as though, just like Josh and Lucy, it was the only way she could alleviate her frustration, Gabi lunged at Van den Bergen. Latching onto his shoulders. A very angry caterpillar. 'The Commissioner steals our children and then sabotages the investigation. Our lives ...' Naked fury in her eyes. 'Can you imagine the nightmare that our lives have become? Branded as shitty parents, at best. Kid-killers at worst! Imagining our son and our daughter lying in shallow graves, garrotted and forgotten. Violated! Having to fake our own deaths and be beaten up and pissed on by drunks and bullies on the street. Do you know how frequently men try to sexually assault female rough sleepers?' She held up her fist for Van den Bergen to see. Pink scarring on her knuckles. Purple shadows beneath her eyes that were the remnants of more than just late nights.

The Chief Inspector took her hands into his, looked apologetically down at them, then placed her hands back onto her lap. 'I'm so sorry, Gabi.'

'You promised you'd get the children back!' she said, a lioness' ferocity still there in tone, though the volume was dimmed.

'And I did. But I didn't promise I could keep you out of jail.'

'Kamphuis caused all this!' She thumped the table so that potting compost spewed from its fat sack onto the tabletop. 'And Hasselblad! They're the ones who should take the wrap for those dead perverts. Your Chief of Police let this all go on in the first place, if Bloom is to be believed. All we're guilty of is doing the world a favour in the course of trying to find our children!

Underwood, Lazami, Vlinders, those fucking German animals … All of them were evil bastards!'

Piet nodded. A glimmer of hope that they could somehow convince Van den Bergen to side with them. Be lenient. Cut them a deal. Wasn't that how the police dealt with informants in big cases? Didn't they almost qualify as super-grasses? 'She's right. Seems we've been fortunate with Josh and Lucy. From what you say, they've just been neglected for a few months by some heartless accountancy bitch with an axe to grind.' He offered a half-smile to his wife. 'I'm glad I didn't pay her bloody invoice! She must have been helping Kamphuis to cook up this terrible—'

'Underwood,' George said, bemused, her raised eyebrow saying she realised she had latched onto an unexpected detail.

Whoops. Feeling the heat in his cheeks, Piet attempted to steamroller over her moment of dawning realization. 'What about the children who are still out there, being groomed and abused? Eh? I set some of those kids free! And I uncovered a huge trafficking ring you might never have found if I hadn't gone on the rampage. It's a disgrace.' He shook his head, hoping he could dislodge her train of thought with every ninety-degree twist, as though he were an Allen key and she were a piece of flat-pack furniture he was trying to dissemble. 'You've got two corrupt policeman and a crime lord who are going to get away with the whole damn shebang. But that's fine, because we'll take the fall, like the idiots we are.'

'Woah!' George said, holding her hands in the air, taking a step towards him, rotating her index finger. 'Scroll back to the bit about Underwood. Are you talking about Trevor Underwood? The escaped paedophile? The man whose phone you brought to my Aunty's house?'

In the corner of the cabin, now pressed against the wall, Gabi blushed.

Van den Bergen cocked his head to the side, frowning. He

crossed those long legs of his, bouncing his right foot on his left knee. Agitated.

'What happened with Trevor Underwood?' George asked, gripping the Chief inspector by his shoulder. It was as though there was a silent, telepathic transfer of data between the two.

When Gabi started to examine her fingernails, bright red in the face, she hardly needed to explain what had happened. The caterpillar was out of the bag.

'He's in a carpet. In a skip. In fact, he's probably still frozen stiff and covered in snow. It was an accident. Self defence.'

'Jesus Christ, Gabi!' Van den Bergen shouted. 'And you want me to somehow pin your murders on somebody else or just let them drop? You've got to be fucking joking!'

'Please don't let us go to prison, Paul!' Gabi cried, tears welling in her eyes. Grabbing at the big policeman's arm. 'Invent a fictitious hit man. Pin it on whoever the fuck you like, but just let us go home to our children. Please!'

He stood, an impressive statue of a man, impervious to his wife's pleading. 'No, Gabi. I'm a cop. I'm a straight cop. The answer is absolutely not.'

CHAPTER 61

Amsterdam, Bijlmerbajes prison complex, 30 March

'How's my bail application going?' Kamphuis barked down the phone. 'And why the hell haven't you been in to see me? I'm climbing the sodding walls in here.'

His solicitor was on the other end, the slimy, overpaid bastard, coming back with some answer he could barely hear over the incessant chummer and wolf-whistling of the other prisoners – block-headed arseholes standing behind him in a disorderly queue. Tattoos of their names on their necks, as though they didn't have the mental capacity to remember what they were called. Scum. Here he was. Languishing at the bottom of the barrel. And there was Hasselblad, still safe in his Chief of Police's office. Fucking liberty.

'I'm going to struggle to get bail granted, Olaf,' his brief said down the crackling line. 'Carlien Dekker has told Van den Bergen everything in return for a reduced sentence.'

That much he heard alright. Resentment brewing inside. He wanted to slap his mistress – the fair-weather, disingenuous bitch. Too quick to spread her legs for any man she thought could profit her in some way. As if she needed it! Hasselblad's sloppy seconds. He should have known better than to go there. Old whore. Should have stuck to boning the office juniors in the archive store.

'Shit!' He thumped the phone receiver against the wall, hammering an even deeper hole into the plaster, pounding the earpiece in the same spot where many men before him had also taken out their frustration. His lip curled at the thought that he had anything in common with the bottom-feeders standing behind him.

'What about Hasselblad? He's standing up for me, right?'

'I'm afraid Jaap won't vouch—'

The phone cut out. Time's up. Kamphuis withdrew his phone card and stared at it in disbelief. Inserted it back into the slot. Took it out. Inserted it. Nothing. His balance registered as zero. Hasselblad wouldn't vouch for him. Jesus Christ! Had that fiend Van den Bergen told the Chief of Police that his very own deputy had been plotting a betrayal of biblical proportions all this while? That he had stolen the Deenen children ultimately to bring Hasselblad down? *No, no, no!*

He stared down at the phone card again, barely able to process the feelings of failure and rejection.

'Fuck off back to your cell, you fat bastard!' one of the brutes behind him shouted.

'That's enough, lads!' one of the prison officers said.

Kamphuis turned around, wrenching his thoughts away from the phonecard, Hasselblad, his solicitor and the Holy Grail of bail, and snapped back to focus on this grim place with its emulsioned walls and its harsh lighting and the smell of sweat and tobacco. These hostile, violent men, gathered before him. No longer any distinction between the Commissioner of the Dutch Police and these cockroaches. And yet …

'Pig!' one of the prisoners shouted. A man with a shaved head, a face entirely covered by tattoos with a broken nose as its centrepiece. Towering above the others in this queue for contact with the sane world outside. Staring straight at Kamphuis with manic eyes that said he'd smuggled amphetamines or coke in somehow. 'Fucking looks one. Smells like one. Nonce!'

Grunting and squealing from the others. Pack-mentality at its worst.

'I'm not a nonce!' Kamphuis shouted. 'I'm the opposite of a nonce. I'm … I'm—'

'That's enough, lads,' the prison officer said, taking Kamphuis by the elbow.

He could feel his knees giving way, sweat rolling down over his belly into his waistband. But he didn't want to show these animals that his world was caving in.

I'm the Commissioner. I'm Olaf Kamphuis. I'm going to beat this charge. That lanky prick Van den Bergen will get the evidence he needs against Hasselblad and Bloom. The judge will cut me a deal for bringing down an international trafficking ring. I can do this. I've always done this. Somehow, I'll make a silver lining out of this dark cloud.

The prison officer marched him past the derisory mob and he felt his legs almost buckle. Testosterone and hate thick on the air made it difficult to breathe in this den of iniquity. Back to his cell, where he would at least be left alone to savour thoughts of his elegant home, his magnificent car, his wife … comforting himself, as he pondered how he would feel when he eventually sold the rights to his true life story for a sum of money that would make a Chief of Police's salary seem like pocket change.

Eyes boring into him as he walked through the recreation area, though. Men playing cards, the tension between them palpable. Porcine grunting noises again, emitted in his direction.

Ignore them. Think of the future.

He may have scuppered his chances of taking Hasselblad's job, but he wouldn't be the first jailbird to sell a story about his rise and fall to Hollywood. All he needed was his solicitor to pull it out of the bag in court and a good agent to come knocking. *It's going to be fine.*

'You bearing up?' the prison officer asked as they neared his cell. A short man with the strength of an ox. No nonsense. Pincer-like grip on his upper arm.

Fleetingly, Kamphuis wondered what the prison officers thought of the Deenen case. Did they too hate him?

'Yes. Of course I'm bearing up,' he said. 'I'm the Commissioner, aren't I?' Pulling his arm free with a disdainful jerk. Best to show these uniforms who was really boss around here. *Act like a policing legend and you'll be treated like one.*

Cell door, open. Newspapers waiting for him on the bed. Every single front cover – broadsheets, red tops and magazines – plastered with the Deenens' faces.

COUPLE ADMITS TO FAKING DEATH.

DEENENS: BACK FROM THE DEAD.

FRAUD OR DEVOTED FATHER? WHO IS PIET DEENEN?

ROBO-MUM RETURNS – SHOULD GABI GET HER KIDS BACK?

'Did you put those there on purpose?' he asked the officer, grinding his teeth, eye ticking.

But the fire alarm was ringing suddenly. Resounding throughout the prison with lights flashing near the ceiling, as if to corroborate that this was, indeed, a red alert. Almost immediate mayhem, as the prisoners' cell doors were all unlocked. Men jeering. The pelting of feet on lino as inmates ran hither and thither towards muster points.

Bewildered, without his prison officer escort, Kamphuis found himself alone. He looked inside his cell. Without a lock it offered no sanctuary. But the alarm was ringing insistently, protesting, 'Fire! Fire!'

'Hello, darling. Fancy that. Me and you. Alone at last.'

It took Kamphuis a moment to register to whom the voice belonged. The giant of a man from the phone queue who had called him a pig. Those eyes … manic, staring, inside a head the size of an extra large bowling ball. The Dutch flag tattooed in amateurish fashion in red, white and blue on the man's right cheek. The Nazi iron cross in faded blue on his miserly forehead. A winged SS insignia on his neck. Now that he was only three feet away, Kamphuis could behold him in all his terrifying splendour. Skulls, adorning his skull. Sleeves of ink all the way to his wrist depicting hellish scenes of torture and pain. Bulbous arms that had been pumped up with steroids and a membership for life of the prison's gym. Yellowed, twisted teeth with the front incisor missing from the top that put him in mind of a nineteenth-century bare knuckle fighter.

'Oh. There's a fire,' Kamphuis said, smiling weakly. 'We need to, er …' It was as though his voice had given up on him. Like it knew something he was refusing to believe.

In a feeble attempt to square up to the advancing tattooed man, Kamphuis stuck out his paunch and stood on his tiptoes, still optimistic that he could somehow turn this confrontation around to suit him.

'I knew when I first saw you,' Kamphuis said, winking. Chummy. 'I thought to myself …'

But even if his voice hadn't faltered once more, bonding to the accompanying sound of the fire alarm was clearly not on the agenda for this painted beast.

The prisoner took out a length of what appeared to be thin gauge electrical wire.

'Oh,' Kamphuis said, pointing uselessly at the ligature, every sense on overdrive, fear so acute that it had paralysed his fight or flight impulses.

His attacker's movements were swift and practised. He moved in quickly for this last deadly tango, where he led and Kamphuis could only follow. Wire wrapped around his neck. Spinning him around somehow, so that the portly police Commissioner had his back to the tattooed man's chest. Fingers inside the workshop-garrotte. Desperately trying to fight the pressure, as his assailant squeezed tighter and tighter.

He tried to buck the man and kick out behind. Suddenly Kamphuis' bleeding fingers were free. He was gasping, gasping. Dizzy and disoriented. But the man had a fresh grip on him again. No fingers in the way this time. The pain was intense. Wire cutting into his neck. No better than a piece of Gouda on a cheese board. Desperately trying to kick his way free. Lights popping behind his eyes, as his vision blurred. Still, part of him was surprised that this was ending so badly. A fleeting moment, where he felt abject self-pity, already lamenting the passing of Olaf Kamphuis. Fading fast.

Why?

Perhaps a taker of life can hear the thoughts of the dying.

'The Duke says, "Hello," Commissioner. Says you should have kept your nose out of his fucking business.'

Kamphuis' last thought was one of regret that Van den Bergen would probably get his job now.

CHAPTER 62

Amsterdam, mortuary, 31 March

Standing beneath the harsh overhead lights in her scrubs, staring down at the saddening bulk of the grey corpse, Marianne de Koninck sighed heavily.

In Van den Bergen's peripheral vision, he realized she had turned towards him for a reaction, but he was unable to tear his own gaze away from the sight of his nemesis on the slab. Naked. Lifeless. A footnote in policing history.

'Who would ever have thought, eh?' she said. 'Olaf bloody Kamphuis. Dead.'

Van den Bergen closed his eyes and tried to identify how he felt. Bereft? Not really. Relieved? No. Triumphant? He wasn't the kind of man to gloat on the misfortune of even his enemies. He realised he felt nothing. Numb. The sight of a dead fat man with livid strangulation marks around his neck did not even inspire his old friend, health anxiety, in him. Glum resignation. Almost pH neutral, but not quite. A sense that the world was a shitty place and that he, like Olaf Kamphuis, was a fallible man.

'What have you got, Marianne?' he asked, turning away, focussing on the hollows in her cheeks that marked her out as a long-distance runner. So alive. So healthy. So unlike Kamphuis.

'I've made a preliminary examination and it's obvious he was garrotted with something thin and strong, like wire,' she said, leading the Chief Inspector into her office, where she had notes spread out on her desk and records up on her computer screen. 'Inmates can be violent bastards, I'm sure, but this was clean. Looks like the work of a professional.'

'Maybe someone he'd put away,' Van den Bergen said, contemplating how many convicted criminals inside that prison might have wanted a police commissioner dead. Especially one who had orchestrated the kidnapping of two toddlers. He tried to picture Kamphuis on the inside. So reviled, he had had to be escorted everywhere by his own dedicated prison officer – strangely absent during a fire drill. An alarm going off just as Kamphuis was neither in his cell nor in a public area.

How fortuitous it must have been for a man who had intended to strangle the life out of a heavily guarded inmate to have freedom of movement inside the prison. No guard. No witnesses.

Van den Bergen's numbness suddenly gave way to a delicious thrill of realisation. 'It was a hit. Somebody put out a hit on Kamphuis.'

An eyebrow shooting northwards said Marianne was surprised. 'You think? Why?'

'There was a motive behind Kamphuis abducting those Deenen kids, but I can't share the details. Not yet.'

'Oh?' She narrowed her eyes at him, clearly rattling through the possibilities in her head.

'It's sensitive.' He folded his arms high across his chest, and blinked hard at her, willing himself not to blurt Hasselblad's name. He felt it in every inch of scar tissue and his probably rheumatic bones that Bloom was behind Kamphuis' death.

Change the subject.

'So, I was bloody relieved when Elvis finally impounded Kamphuis' Audi last night,' he said. 'Parked on the wrong side of town, would you believe it? God knows what he'd been up to in that. Are you going to be able to take a look at some point today?'

Talking fast. A friendly tone. Hoping to distract this most intelligent and intuitive of forensic pathologists.

She was still frowning. Dissecting his expression, as she would soon be dissecting his opposite number's corpulent body. 'Strietman's already on it,' she said. 'Said they'd found a couple of mobile phones in the glove box, hidden beneath the casing.'

'Really?'

'Yes. Did Elvis not tell you?'

'Little bastard.' Van den Bergen watched Marianne move the mouse over the mouse pad, clicking. He wondered if Kamphuis had kept a phone for every woman he'd been screwing behind his wife's back.

'Talk of the devil. I've just had an email from Strietman,' she said, frowning, a look of alarm contorting her handsome features. There was a change in the timbre of her voice from idle interest to deep suspicion. 'Look at this.'

Leaning over her desk, Van den Bergen slid his glasses from their chain onto the end of his nose. She turned the screen around to meet him.

Marianne,
   Just switched on those mobile phones. No pin or password protection on them. The name Hauptmann rings a bell but not sure about Underwood. Any thoughts?
   Strietman.

Staring at the black words on the white screen, Van den Bergen's thought processes came to an abrupt halt. Scrambled neurons. Overcooked synapse spaghetti where separate strands glued themselves together. It made no sense.

'Hauptmann was one of Jack Frost's Berlin victims,' Marianne said. 'Well, Jack Frost or Krampus, or whatever the hell you want to call him. How on earth did Kamphuis come to have his phone? And who's Underwood?' She was glaring, now. Inching her face

390

closer to his, as though she could intimidate a response from him with an accusatory glance alone. 'Paul?'

'Trevor Underwood,' Van den Bergen said simply, remembering Gabi's confession that she had killed the escaped convict, leaving his body to freeze, wrapped in a rug, dumped in a builder's skip in London. 'A paedo.'

Spaghetti sticking together. A mess without substance or meaning.

Piet Deenen had admitted to killing Rufus Lazami, Tomas Vlinders... Gabi had admitted to killing Underwood in self-defence. He was certain that one or both of them had killed Hauptmann and Meyer in the zoo. All tied up. Wasn't it?

'We didn't have a shred of useful forensic evidence from those Jack Frost murders,' Marianne said. 'And now we've got two mobile phones in the Commissioner's car. What exactly have your investigations been throwing up, Paul? What's so sensitive you're not prepared to talk about? Was *Olaf* Jack Frost?' Incredulous voice and a wry, half-smile on her face.

'No. He wasn't. I'm absolutely certain of it. I *know* who Jack Frost is. I'm preparing the case.'

Marianne scratched her scalp beneath her cap and shrugged. 'Well, if you think—'

'Go through your evidence again, Marianne. Please. Every last sample. Something here's not right.'

CHAPTER 63

Amsterdam, The Cracked Pot Coffee Shop, at the same time, then, police headquarters, later

'What do you mean, why we packing up?' Aunty Sharon said, neatly folding Tinesha's clothes and stacking them inside the old suitcase. She turned to George, bags beneath her eyes said she hadn't been sleeping so well, sharing that lumpy old bed with her daughter; kept awake by the sound of Inneke downstairs, screwing her way to a paid utilities bill. 'I wanna go home. We all do.'

Frustrated, noticing that the heavy old curtains hadn't been pulled back sufficiently on the left hand side, George pressed her palms to her temples.

'This isn't over, Aunty Shaz. You're still in danger,' she said, eyes roving over the place, noticing the orange roses in a vase on the side. Photographs from Aunty Sharon's place. A plant. The place smelled clean, as it had done when George had lived there.

'If that cow, my sister can up sticks and leave, then so can we,' she said, wafting into the kitchenette to retrieve a cardigan, hung on one of the battered cabinet handles. 'My Patrice is missing school. Tin is down on her wages. They won't pay her for this little holiday.'

George sighed and sat down on the edge of the chaise longue. She could smell Patrice's feet. She stood abruptly and dizziness from days of worrying about her mother's whereabouts and nights of sleeplessness battered her until she felt like a woozy bare-knuckle fighter, taking too many punches.

'Van den Bergen will sort it.'

'What? Like he said he'd sort us a nice hotel?' Her Aunty closed the lid on Tinesha's case. Zipped up. Snapped the tiny padlock shut.

'He did!'

'Yeah.' Hand on hip. Raised eyebrows. The standard Williams-May response to an outlandish suggestion. Face arranged into an expression that said she was about to disparage the shit out of George's notion. 'Some shithole in the middle of nowhere? A train ride into town.' She sucked her teeth, long and low. 'If I'm going to have an enforced holiday in Holland, I'm going to make damn sure I'm where the action's at, if I can. We ain't no suburban types. But enough's enough now. I'm homesick for London and my house with my things. There's shit I can't get at the supermarkets, here. I can't do no baking in that crappy little oven, neither.' She pointed to her 'holiday wig' and then pulled it up to reveal her hairline beneath, even more dog-eared than usual. 'See that? I tried to put the oven on gas mark six the other day and singed my poor fucking barnet. It ain't dignified, George.'

But George had no space in her thoughts for idle chit-chat about the non-safety of Jan's cooker. Remembering the man that had broken into Aunty Sharon's house, just as the cussing band of refugees had exited through the back gate, George swallowed hard. Fear infecting her bones like the sickly ache of a virus. As though it had happened only yesterday.

Sharon grabbed her arm and pulled her into a bear hug, unexpectedly. 'You worrying about *her*? Don't worry about her. It ain't the first time she's gone missing, is it, darling? What was it she texted you? She wanted time to herself. Time to think?'

But her aunt's embrace did nothing to stem the advance of George's fear. 'It's not Letitia I'm bloody worried about! It's you! People are getting bumped off left right and centre. This place ...' she looked up at the cracks and cobwebs that marked the high, gabled ceiling out as old '... this seedy, crappy room seems to be a safe haven, whenever I need it. And we need it now! Danny is dead. Right? The Commissioner of the police force is dead! You need to stay here until me and Paul—'

'Sod Paul!' her Aunt said. 'He ain't gonna get me my job back from Dermot Robinson, is he? He ain't gonna pay for all that heating you mother's been using. My windows need cleaning, George! You know how it is. I don't want that bitch across the way pointing the finger.'

'Just stay put for another couple of days!'

'No!'

'Please!'

'*No ways!*'

'Paul, they're going to walk straight back into the lion's den!' Now, more than ever, she needed Chief Inspector Van den Bergen to sideline his investigation in favour of her. Be her lover, not a high-ranking policeman. Just for two minutes. Just long enough for him to pick up the phone and say something authoritative that would stop Sharon in her tracks. 'Paul! Are you listening?'

She leaned on the edge of his uncluttered desk top, trying to engage him, but he was in the tunnel, sifting through forensics reports with Marianne de Koninck's signature on the bottom, by the looks.

George slammed her hand down on the wood. His photo of Tamara fell over.

Finally, Van den Bergen looked up, his grey eyes seeming too large through the lenses of his reading glasses.

'What?'

'You've got to stop my stupid, boneheaded family from getting on the next flight back to London. Aunty Shaz is having a meltdown. And I still haven't heard from Letitia since that text,' George said. Even though they had agreed that the police HQ was not the place to show affection to one another she wanted more than anything for him to hold her.

'Someone's tampered with the evidence for the Jack Frost murders,' he said, taking the glasses from his nose and chewing on the arm.

She hated it when he did that. So unhygienic.

She glared at him. Hurt, fatigue and irritation reacted inside her – a chemical experiment that would end badly if he didn't pay attention. 'I'm talking to you about my family. My family. Remember? Living people who are in mortal fucking danger, Paul.'

He waved dismissively, wrinkling his nose. 'I'll make a call at lunchtime. They'll be fine. Stop worrying.' His hooded eyes widened, focussing back on the report, which he snatched up and waved in the air. 'Marianne went through the evidence again and lo! Some new samples have mysteriously showed up. Kamphuis' hair allegedly taken from Tomas Vlinders' body. *That* wasn't there before. I had a MET detective in London on the phone this morning, telling me Trevor Underwood's body has been found in a skip outside a derelict pub – details that only Gabi and Piet knew about, because they bloody well killed him. And yet, their forensics guys are saying there's one of Olaf Kamphuis' fingernails snagged on Underwood's clothing. Then, Elvis digs out two victims' mobile phones from Kamphuis' private car. One of them, Underwood's!' He rammed his glasses abruptly back onto his nose, scratching at the overgrown white and iron-filings stubble that betrayed over-long shifts, working the case, falling wordlessly into bed beside George at 2 a.m. 'This stinks.' His dark eyebrows gathered like storm clouds above those melancholy grey eyes. 'Someone's framing Kamphuis for those murders. We *know* the Deenens did it.'

'They confessed!' George perched on the corner of his desk. She longed for some physical contact to calm her mounting anxiety, feeling annoyed with herself for needing him.

'Yes. They confessed to us. In the confines of my super-shed. You know that counts for nothing. I wasn't wearing a wire.' He slapped himself in the forehead and winced. 'I thought when they agreed to come back to Amsterdam that they'd just hand themselves in if the children were found.'

'They stayed at the allotment all this time,' George said. 'You weren't to know any of this would kick off.'

'I certainly didn't think they'd start invoking their right to silence. And now, this, out of the blue. Nothing points to the Deenens. Everything points to a dead, disgraced policeman. Jesus, George! They're going to get away with serial murder.' Desperation etched into his face. A man who liked to tie up loose ends with the correct, regulation knots. Fastidious. Unimpeachable. Some of the things she loved about him.

'Could they have somehow paid someone to plant the evidence?' She knew it was shit theory but it was all she had.

'They were locked in that cabin the whole time until we carted them off to the station on fraud charges. I had the key! Only me. When the hell would they have had chance to do a deal?'

'Piet's had access to his mobile phone. Waiting for Bloom to make contact, wasn't he? For all you know, he could have called someone.'

Van den Bergen narrowed his eyes, pursed his lips, then shook his head. 'No. Whoever planted this new evidence knew about forensics procedures and investigation techniques. It's got to be an inside job.'

There was something about the way he looked at her then that George steadfastly, wholeheartedly, did not like.

'What?' she asked, standing tall, which wasn't tall at all, feeling like he was assessing her in the same way he sized up suspects in an interview room. 'Why you looking at *me* like that?'

'What was it between you and Gabi? Why did she keep coming to you and Sharon?'

CHAPTER 64

Amsterdam, prison services' family centre,
1 April

'Are you ready?' the social worker asked Piet and Gabi.

Gabi patted her hair, tied up in a tight chignon. She smoothed her jeans along her legs – so loose-fitting, after her stint on the streets, eating whatever scraps she could find in the bins behind sandwich shops and restaurants. She knew the lines of her face were that much sharper now. She prayed they would recognize her, despite the physical changes, and hoped they would still come running to her. Cleave to the very essence of her being, as the woman who had given them life. Chubby arms outstretched, just as she'd fantasized over and over in her mind's eye, sleeping outdoors under an unforgiving winter moon, giggling and gleeful that Mummy was back. Or would they smell murder on her, knowing instinctively that she had taken life? Snuffed it out willingly in a violent frenzy. They might reject her, and then, she would have failed. Failure on a biblical scale. Gabi didn't do failure. Now, her heart was thudding so hard and fast, her voice had its own vibrato. 'I've been ready for months,' she said.

Sitting next to Piet on the brightly coloured sofa, in that jaunty playroom where they conducted supervised visits, she wondered what sort of expression she should wear. A grin? Something more demure? Should she laugh when they came in?

'You okay?' her husband asked, taking her hand into his. Happiness in his eyes, though she could see it was diluted and polluted with the blood of those men. Always would be, now.

She nodded. A flicker of a smile. A sob accumulating inside her. *Stuff it down. You were always brilliant at that. Muscles have memories, Dad used to say.* 'Fine. Can't wait.'

Commotion in the corridor beyond the glazed door. Childish, squeaky voices, speaking in a mixture of Dutch and English. Gabi leaped to her feet, unable to contain those emotions. Today, her muscles only had memories of happy times, of holding her children, of wrapping her family in a protective wall of love, however stilted the outside world might perceive that to be.

A frumpy, middle-aged woman with short grey hair opened the door, looking behind her, beckoning her temporary charges forwards. No surprise when Josh pelted beneath the woman's arm into the room ahead of Lucy. Yelling. Pretending to be an aeroplane with arms outstretched. He made straight for Piet.

'Paps!' Headbutting his father's thighs. Piet swung him into the air, blowing a raspberry on his belly.

Through a waterfall of hot tears, Gabi spied Lucy, trotting in behind him, holding the social worker's hand. Reticent. Looking up at the woman for reassurance, a teddy tucked under her arm. Chewing coyly on the stuffed toy's ear. Teething, maybe. Flaming cheek on the left-hand side pointed in that direction. All those years when she had bitched about being kept up at night by teething toddlers, chomping amid tears on ice cool teething rings. Gabi could think of nothing better now.

She held her arms out, forcing a bright, sunshiny Mummy voice from behind the sorrow and loss and relief. 'Lucy! Come to Mummy.'

But Lucy was so much younger than her brother. A tiny girl, yet bigger than she had been at the time of the abduction, dressed in unfamiliar clothes that Gabi had not bought, wearing her hair in a style that Gabi had not determined. She looked startled by this unfamiliar visiting room, with its gaudy children's posters and colourful roadmap rugs. And still, she hadn't run to Gabi.

Sinking to her knees, Gabi simply waved at her daughter. 'Hello, Lulu,' she said, hoping the pet name would act as an immediate aide memoire.

'Lulu!' Lucy said, cocking her head to the side, examining her mother with the sparkling, razor-sharp curiosity of a two year old. 'Where's Carly Mummy?'

Sucking the sobs back into her body, Gabi fixed a smile on her face, willing herself not to show the hurt and rejection to her confused toddler. '*I'm* Mummy, Lulu. Remember? Come to Mummy for a snuggle.'

The girl smiled. 'Snuggles!' she said, cackling with delight. She approached her mother with a bouncy, rigid legged run, typical of her age and size, and buried her face in Gabi's chest and sniffed. 'Mummy.'

Sandwiched between her and Piet, Josh fidgeted and wriggled and even punched them in their bellies with impish delight. And though she had always excelled in self-containment – prided herself on her iron discipline and poise – in that visiting room in the foster home, with her children in her arms, Gabi let the joy and the grief and the regret flow forth in equal measure.

Remembering how it felt to be a family. Remembering the encouraging email from her solicitor that had said the fraud case against them would be thrown out. Remembering the wink from the red-headed police woman as she had slipped out of Van den Bergen's cabin, carrying Hauptmann's and Underwood's mobile phones.

The meek shall inherit the Earth, she had said, before locking them back in.

Today, Gabi's legacy was not the Earth, but a small slice of purity in a world gone bad.

CHAPTER 65

Amsterdam, Hasselblad's house, 2 April

'Gordon?!' Hasselblad said, opening the front door. A tentative smile on his bug-eyed face said an unscheduled visit from a criminal associate at eight in the morning was not welcome. 'You look well. Been away? Haven't seen you on the golf course for a few weeks.' He was babbling, fiddling with the buckle on his belt. Off guard. Good.

'Alone, are we?' Bloom pushed his way into the hall.

He had asked the question, though he already knew the answer.

The ambushed Chief of Police closed the heavy door behind him. 'Mieke's at the gym. Do you want a coffee?'

Bloom surveyed the familiar interior of Hasselblad's house as he walked through to the kitchen, all marble work surfaces and crystal chandeliers. Mieke's taste. He had fucked her up against the wine chiller only a month ago, making the Bollinger bottles rattle on their wire shelving with every thrust. The perverse thrill of banging another man's wife in his home and castle while that other man was out, pretending to solve crimes that he had a secret, sordid vested interest in. It was a poetry, of sorts.

'Go on. Make mine a strong one,' he said. 'I'm still jetlagged.'

Watching Hasselblad boil the kettle and prepare the pot, he realised the Dutchman was nervous. Frog-eyes darting from the kettle to the sink, clearly avoiding making eye contact with his uninvited guest.

'You know why I'm here, don't you?' Bloom asked, deliberately keeping it relaxed. For now.

'No. It's always nice to see a buddy, though. Nothing wrong, is there?' Hasselblad poured the black brew into dainty espresso cups. He pushed one towards Bloom, then checked his watch. 'I do have to go soon, mind you. I've got a press conference about Kamphuis. You know? My Commissioner. You met him once at some drinks thing.' A downcast expression that seemed rehearsed. Knowing Hasselblad, he'd been practising in the mirror ready for the cameras. 'He's dead.' He looked back up at Bloom. It was difficult to read him, then. Those bug eyes gave little away apart from the suggestion of thyroid eye disease. A flicker of satisfaction, perhaps, lurking behind a slick show of respectable, measured grief.

'I know,' Bloom said. Time to drop the bombshell. He tried to conceal the grin behind the espresso cup. 'I had him killed.'

His host slammed his cup down with such force that black liquid spurted all over Mieke's precious worktops.

'You did *what*?' Colour rose in this overweight, overinflated, overpromoted Chief of Police. 'You were behind that?'

Bloom nodded. Smiled. Fixed Hasselblad with his one good eye, savouring the man's obvious discomfort. Veins bulging in Hasselblad's wide, proletarian neck. His type were built for manual labour on the flat land, farming Friesian cows. Not the seats of power.

'Kamphuis was onto us, you fucking plum. Why do you think he took those kids? He was gunning for us. Everything I've built over decades. Every triumph. Every war I won. I'm not the Duke for nothing!' He stretched himself upwards, standing as tall as he possibly could, and puffed his chest out. 'He was lighting a fire beneath *my* tower. If I hadn't had him taken out, he'd have brought the whole bloody shebang down.' He poked Hasselblad in his gassy stomach. 'And you with him, you remedial arsehole.'

The surge of colour in Hasselblad's cheeks drained fast. He took a step backwards in his stockinged feet. Mouth flapping open and shut like a faulty letterbox as he tried to find the worlds. Lips, greying. 'Van den Bergen never mentioned any of this in our last briefing.' Blinking fast.

Bloom removed his coat and suit jacket. He threw the coat onto a leather sofa at the end of the kitchen island, then hung the jacket on the back of the ornate bar stool, weighted down on one side by the insurance policy in his breast pocket. He started to roll up his sleeves. 'Use your brain, Hasselblad. Why would Van den Bergen let slip that he was looking into rumours about your involvement with my illegitimate business empire?'

Hasselblad shook his head, mouth open, momentarily. 'Van den Bergen knows?'

'That bitch he's shagging … *she's* the one who took my eye! McKenzie's the only person outside my circle of trust who could ID me as the Duke. For two years, I've been praying I would never run into her ever again. She's the reason I had this work done.' He bared his filled incisor, pointing at his nose. 'One loose end I wish I'd had the sense to tie off when I had the chance. Except, she's got some pretty hard-core people in the British government watching out for her, for some reason. So, I decided to let sleeping dogs lie. You don't go looking for trouble when MI6 is involved. But there she was, in a railway arch in London. Me, McKenzie, the Deenens and one of my men. I had a gun pointed at my head, Jaap.' He poked at his temple. 'Deenen's a psychopath. He thought I'd taken his precious children. But it was Kamphuis, setting Van den Bergen and his whore on the trail like over-enthusiastic fucking sniffer dogs. I was going to die! I had to give you up to save my own skin.'

'Bastard!' Hasselblad lunged at him, then pushed him hard into the opposite bank of units, swinging a punch at him.

But Bloom was in better shape. Younger. Quicker on his feet.

He spun Hasselblad around and slammed him into the wine chiller, pinioning him to the glazed door using his forearm held against Hasselblad's neck. Hasselblad's eyes bulged even more than usual. A vein had risen in his forehead like a fork of green lightening.

'All this time, I've given you generous back-handers,' Bloom hissed. 'All these long years, Mieke's sat on various boards, coining it in. Fancy cars. Expenses through the nose. I looked after you. We were buddies. What did you have to do in return, eh?'

'Let me go, you nutcase!' Hasselblad sputtered, deep red colour surging to his rubbery lips as he strained against Bloom's arm.

'All you had to do was keep your trap shut. That was it! But I have ears and eyes everywhere, Jaap. I hear you've been mouthing off over drinkies with Kamphuis and some ministerial types. Boasting, like some schoolboy in a game of one-upmanship. You infernal cunt! He's a cop. Didn't you think he'd put two and two together? Did you think he'd let human trafficking and class A drugs and *paedo rings* slide? Did you?' He was screaming, now. Craving the thrill of ending a life. Only, the part of him that made cool business decisions was still running in the background like a small but crucial file on a computer's overloaded hard drive.

Should I just choke him to death and have done with? Do I need him? Maybe once Van den Bergen and the girl are gone, things can get back on an even keel. No. Kill him! You're top of the food chain. You're the Duke.

He deliberated for five seconds too long. Bloom had a good grip on Hasselblad, but his arm was tiring, the balls of his feet stinging. He shifted his position by an inch or two.

It was all Hasselblad needed. He pushed Bloom away with his bulk, and was suddenly on top of him on the floor, like a cuckolded lover engaging in revenge seduction.

'I'm going to knock that glass eye out of your head, you pompous English bastard!' Hasselblad yelled, punching Bloom repeatedly on the temple.

Though he felt the blows raining on him, one after the other, Bloom delighted in the fight. It made him feel vital. It made his blood race faster though his veins. He brought his knee up fast between Hasselblad's legs, hitting the sweet spot with force.

His opponent fell off him, buckled up, clutching his crotch with eyes squeezed tight.

Bloom lost no time in rounding on him. Hands around his neck. Pressing on his windpipe. Excited that death was in the room an erection made its presence felt in his trousers. He rubbed the swelling against Hasselblad's back.

'I fucked your wife a thousand times in this house. In this kitchen. In your bed! Bet you didn't know that, either, eh?'

Beneath him, Hasselblad made spluttering noises, trying to buck Bloom off. He started to ram him into one of the cupboard door handles to their right, rhythmically forcing the sharp metal into Bloom's kidneys: agony he couldn't afford to bear for long.

Bloom stood, staggering backwards. Hasselblad was back on his feet, fists raised like a drunken pugilist. But Bloom was fast, pulling a cook's knife from a wooden block on the island.

'Come on, then!'

Hasselblad's focus drifted down to Bloom's crotch. A look of disgust and disbelief on his face. 'Oh, you're demented. I never should have got involved with you. Do you fuck the children you steal and sell on?'

Bloom grinned. 'Who's the bad guy here, Jaap? I'm in the business of supply and demand. But you're a cop who should know better. I've got Daddy issues. What's your excuse, you fucking hypocrite?'

Panting from exertion, unsteady on his feet, Hasselblad reached for the bar stool but grasped Bloom's jacket instead. Stumbling. Pulling the jacket to the floor where it landed with a metallic thunk. Hasselblad frowned down at it, clearly puzzled.

'Leave it!' Bloom said. 'Leave it where it is, or I'll stick this knife in you, so help me God.'

Why didn't you keep your mouth shut, you bloody fool? Bloom chided himself. Eyes on the jacket, now knowing what was in the pocket.

But there was Hasselblad, snatching up the jacket too quickly, pulling out the hidden contents. His damned gun, of course. Pointing it at him.

'All this time, you had this on you?' Hasselblad said, smiling at the fortuitous turn of the tables in a game of deadly weapons top trumps. 'Why didn't you pull it on me straight away? If you wanted to kill me, I'd have been dead by now.'

Bloom held the knife up. Unflinching, though his kidney ached. This was going badly. 'I fancied a fight. I like fighting. Okay? Guns are too easy.'

Hasselblad clicked off the safety, grinning. 'Not for me, they're not.'

The doorbell rang shrilly, interrupting their standoff.

'Shit,' Hasselblad said. He glanced at the clock on the wall. 'It's my driver. He's early.'

Banging on the door, now, but it was too insistent and booming to be a brass knocker. More like a battering ram. One, two, three. The sound of splintering wood. Footsteps thundering towards them down the hall. An armed unit wearing full riot gear. Van den Bergen at the front, holding a pistol, wearing a Kevlar vest over his shitty Chief Inspector's clothes.

'Hands in the air,' he shouted. A towering menace. 'You're both under arrest.'

'It's all lies!' Hasselblad shouted. A dark stain seeped through the crotch of his trousers, betraying his fear. 'It's Bloom. He's a criminal.'

'I know he's a criminal, you donkey,' Van de Bergen said. 'And you're a corrupt piece of shit. That's why I'm arresting you both.'

Bloom swallowed hard. He saw in his flinty, angular face that Van den Bergen was not a man to bribe or reason with. He'd been too slow to have the big idiot bumped off. Too much coke. Too much confidence. Shit! He should have put the hit on him first; Kamphuis second. But at least the bitch of a girl would not get off so lightly. She'd be feeling the vengeful wrath of the Duke before he'd even made the call to his solicitor.

As the uniforms yanked his and Hasselblad's arms uncomfortably behind their backs, snapping on the cold, unyielding cuffs, Bloom scrolled back through the morning's events, trying to remember whether or not he had been followed to Hasselblad's place.

'How the hell did you know we were here?' he asked Van den Bergen.

A wry smile from this oddity of a man. With the longest fingers Bloom had ever seen, Van den Bergen pointed to the top of the kitchen cupboards, where scrolling cornicing obscured whatever lay behind. 'See that small black tube?'

Bloom scanned the woodwork with his good eye. 'No.'

'Kamphuis did his job properly, then.' A broad grin from the smug, white-haired son of a bitch.

'What do you mean?' Hasselblad asked, squinting up at the dusty tops of his cabinetry. Then, spotting whatever it was that Van den Bergen had referred to. He blanched suddenly. 'Oh.' He turned to his underling. 'Kamphuis installed cameras in my bloody house?'

Van den Bergen belched quietly, gun holstered now, those good teeth of his flashing like an annoying fluorescent strip light. He thumped his stomach and popped a pill from a blister pack. 'He was onto you, Jaap. Say that for the prick, he knew how to do surveillance. He had every room tapped and wired, feeding into a laptop in his en suite.'

'Is this some kind of sick joke?' Hasselblad yelled.

'Nothing like a bent cop to take down another bent cop, eh? I've got Marie and Elvis watching you from HQ, now. It's a live feed.' Van den Bergen waved to the camera, clearly euphoric at his own wit, the wanker. 'Say hello! They've been working 12-hour shifts apiece, bless their cotton socks. We've been praying for a moment like this. So was Kamphuis, evidently.' He winked at Bloom. 'And when you showed up at the door, we had a feeling our prayers were going to be answered.' He gazed up at the ceiling, hand over his heart, as if invoking heavenly spirits. 'Poor Olaf. Pity he didn't live to see his own finest moment as a documentary-maker.'

His phone rang.

'Ah, this is Elvis, now.' He listened attentively, those ugly hooded eyes sparkling with his own self-importance, and ended the call in a theatrical manner. 'Yep. We've got everything loud and clear on tape. And Kamphuis even had a warrant for this.' He gestured towards the camera with his phone. 'Kept that one quiet, didn't he? Clever, dead sod. You underestimated him, Jaap.' Another wink. Van den Bergen clapped the Chief of Police on the back.

Bloom emulated the policeman's swagger by winking back. 'If you think you've got this all neatly sewn up, I think you'll find you've underestimated me, my friend.'

CHAPTER 66

Amsterdam, Van den Bergen's apartment, then, Vinkeles restaurant, later, 4 April

'Do you want some toast then or not?' George asked, waving a blackened piece of bread at Van den Bergen. Wanting to slap him over the head with it. Or kiss him. Or both.

Van den Bergen looked up from his copy of *de Volkskrant*. Holding it aloft like a trophy. Mugshots of Kamphuis, Hasselblad and Bloom on the front page. Pan-European disgrace that had made it onto every TV station from the UK to Poland, according to the police's PR people. The headline, clearly the reason for her lover's chipper expression: Amsterdam's first son of law enforcement cleans up a continent.

'You basking in the glow of your triumph?' she asked, scraping the burnt outer layer of the toast into the sink, forcing herself to bear the heinous black mess in the shining stainless steel bowl she had scrubbed vigorously, because she knew the sound would set his teeth on edge.

His smile waned, giving way to a grimace. 'There's nothing to celebrate.' He folded the paper shut and flung it onto the kitchen table as though it was radioactive. 'This whole thing's an almighty cock-up.' He rose and approached the sink, enveloping her slowly from behind.

George revelled in his post-shower scent, the warmth of his torso pressed against her back. She felt certain he was going to rebuild the crumbling bridge between them.

'You brought down a transnational trafficking ring, for God's sake! That's hardly a cock-up.' He would definitely stoop to kiss her now. She was mad at him, but she needed this.

Abruptly he snatched the toast and knife out of her hands, edging her out of the way with his hip. 'Stop doing that, George! You know it goes right through me.' He threw the toast into the compost bin and washed the knife, putting fresh bread in the toaster. No kiss. No apology. No relief from the ill feeling that hung in the air, making his apartment a place where she felt suffocated, rather than safe.

'You still think I did it, don't you?' She pulled at his sleeve, trying to get him to look her in the eye. He focussed on her hair instead. 'You sleep next to me. You share a bed with me. But you think I framed Kamphuis because I felt sorry for the Deenens? You're a fucking arsehole of gigantic proportions!'

Just as he placed a hand on her upper arm, she pulled away and made for the living room, casting a penitent eye over the empty sofa.

'George!' Van den Bergen shouted after her. 'Don't run off!' He came to the door with a tea towel over his shoulder, contrition all over his handsome face, though she knew, as she flung her door keys into her bag, that it was bullshit.

'Forget it. I asked you to stop my family from getting on a plane, and you didn't! I asked you to look for my mother, and you haven't. It's all work, work, work.'

'That's not fair!' He advanced into the living room, leaning awkwardly against a bookshelf as though he wasn't entirely sure what to do with his long body. 'We've both been toiling away to solve not one, but two fucking cases! Letitia's a force of nature. She comes and goes in your life as she pleases, leaving a trail of devastation and cigarette butts behind her. I wasn't putting police resources into finding a woman who texted you to say she doesn't want to be found. And I tried to get Sharon to stay. What did she do?'

'Don't start laying into my Aunty Shaz, man. You're out of line. She's a good—'

'She threatened me with calling the British Consulate!'

'She was highly emotional,' George said, pulling her coat on. 'Her windows are overdue a clean. That's the way my family thinks. Small stuff is big stuff.' She lambasted him with ghetto-attitude measuring nine point five on the Richter scale. 'But you don't care, because you're a cynical workaholic, and your precious principles and dead people come first!'

Tears sprang to Van den Bergen's melancholy eyes. 'That's such a cruel …' he looked at his feet as if the words were embroidered into his black socks '… and unfair and *hypocritical* thing to say. You're every bit as bad as me, Georgina McKenzie.'

'Fuck you!' George said, thumbing through her emails. 'I'm off to the library, and then I'm going to meet my estranged father for a fancy lunch. Maybe *he* can fulfil my emotional bloody needs.'

So much to think about. Too much to think about. Heavy books testing the engineering resolve of an Albert Heijn shopping bag in one hand. A cigarette in another, almost as an act of rebellion against her contrary lover.

'Cantankerous old arsebiscuit,' George muttered, shouldering stubborn tourists and students out of the way, visualising Van den Bergen. The black ice that covered the Keizersgracht cobbles beneath her feet was as treacherous as he was. The falling fat snowflakes that hit the ground, only to melt within seconds, were as cold and fair-weather as he was. She was failing to get a grip, even in her best winter boots. 'Calling me a hypocrite! Fuck you very much, Paul!'

An elderly man stood aside to let her pass as she barrelled her way through a group of ambling pedestrians. He looked at her askance as she argued with fresh air.

'Cheer up, lovey!' he shouted after her.

George turned back. Rheumy eyes still on her. Bemused old gadge in a fur hat with floppy ears.

She smiled. Turned away. Said, 'Piss off!' too loud, knowing she was probably still within earshot.

Trouble was, George was struggling with the notion that she should be happy. The Deenens had their kids back. Brilliant. Kamphuis' name had been besmirched, while the Deenens walked free. Even better. The Deenens deserved a break and she had no regrets about having helped the beleaguered Gabi. And yet, in many ways, she had footed the bill for everybody else's happy ending. Van den Bergen's resulting lack of trust in her had turned her own relationship from a highroad to happiness into an overpass to nowhere. Riddled with concrete cancer. Doomed to collapse.

'Bastard!'

And Danny was dead. And Letitia had absconded with her pulmonaries. And Sharon, Patrice and Tin were back in South East London, risking life and limb for clean windows and better-stocked supermarkets.

'Idiots. Why do I come from a family of congenital twats?'

Her long scarf kept falling loose, getting wrapped around her thighs. Irritated, she tossed it over her shoulder. She felt like there was some kind of super gravity in the canal, pulling her towards its freezing deadly blackness, though she was not normally one for wallowing in self-pity.

I'm going back to Cambridge after this, she thought, gazing at the four-storey houses. Today they seemed to lean in towards her in an accusatory manner, windows bearing down on her, like a judgemental audience, clock-tower rooflines marking time before her happy house of cards with Van den Bergen came tumbling down. *I wish I didn't love the cruel, unfair, judgmental bastard.*

We're on. We're off. Make up your fucking mind! And that Letitia *can rot in whatever bolthole she's found for herself. I'm sick of it.* *Everyone puts their shit onto me. I'm so tired.*

But Vinkeles was within sight now; the prospect of her estranged father loomed like the mist that rose from the freezing canals when it wasn't snowing. One shithouse, displacing another.

'I can't believe I'm doing this,' she told the yellow plates of a Mini, parked diagonally to the inky river. 'I must be mental.'

A vision in her mind's eye of a battered photograph of her father that Letitia had kept in the old-photos-suitcase: an olive-skinned man with dark straight hair giving his Spanish origins away: a smile that had lit up her childhood; Daddy's strong, hairy arms, swinging her though the air; the graze of his stubble on her face when he had kissed her goodnight; the boom of his voice, his black eyebrows knitting together when he and Letitia had argued.

For the first time that day, her heart fluttered. The lightness of butterfly wings. She was buoyed towards the eaterie by optimism and curiosity. It felt good. The gravitational pull of the river lessened.

'I'm meeting someone here,' she said to the maître d': an elegant man in a sharp black suit. The place smelled of garlic, warmth and lilies. 'Michael Moreno. I think he's got a table reserved.'

'This way, mevrouw,' he said, deftly taking her coat and heavy plastic bag, then showing her to the window where a good length of Keizersgracht was there for her to admire. 'He has not arrived yet, but there is a package for you.'

'For me?' She started to unravel her scarf, then stopped and sat down, eying the small white box with bemusement. It looked like the sort of package chocolates might come in. Sitting on the pristine white tablecloth, it looked like expensive packaging.

Left alone with a menu and the promise of water – at her request containing only three ice cubes, in a clean glass with no lemon at all – George touched the box. She giggled nervously when it suddenly started to vibrate.

'What the hell?'

Music emanated from inside. Desmond Dekker signing *Israelites*. Getting up in the morning, slaving for bread, sir. Plinking bassline. Unmistakeably, her mother's ringtone.

Feeling the blood drain from her face, flashbacks to the Firestarter, flickering past in the microfiche archives of her memory, George gingerly opened the box. Gasped. There was Letitia's mobile phone.

'Excuse me!' she shouted, waving at the waiting staff that were facing the other way.

The phone was still ringing. Other diners looking at her, askance, as they put their cutlery down with a clink. One gesticulated that she should turn it off.

With her pulse racing, George took the phone out of the box. There was something wrapped in tissue beneath. A typed note with it.

Holding her breath, she read the five words.

An eye for an eye.

George unwrapped the tissue to see an enucleated bloodshot, brown eye staring back at her.

'Letitia,' she whispered hoarsely.

She opened her mouth to scream, but nothing came out.

Letitia's phone rang again and again. The Israelites, in their biblical struggle for survival. George trapped in a waking nightmare. She felt Amsterdam fading from view as she slid beneath the table, consciousness leaving her at the sight of that unseeing eye. And before she passed out, she realised what she had done.

For too long, she had walked in the shadows, believing she could always find her way back to the light. Paying little heed to the consequences. But all the shadows had yielded was evil: a cloying darkness that she couldn't shake off, that she could never leave behind. Infecting everyone around her. Nobly, foolishly, selfishly, George had crossed the Devil himself. Now, she was being made to pay.

Acknowledgements

The Girl Who Walked in the Shadows was a complicated book for me to write, tackling very difficult subject matter. In the main, it's a story about the relationships between parents and children, and if it has turned into something dark and raw, that's mainly because the period during which it was written has been a dark and raw time in my own life. When the going gets tricky, we rely on the supportive people around us. I certainly have and continue to do so. So, I'd like to thank the following folks:

Christian, for ably stepping into the parenting void on those occasions when my workload demanded and for ensuring a nice G&T was always on hand when I needed it most.

My children, Natalie and Adam for their constant cheerleading and inspiring gorgeousness.

My literary agent, Caspian Dennis for his ongoing encouragement, loyalty and guidance and his inimitable daft anecdotes that keep me smiling when I should be concentrating on more serious matters.

His colleague, Sandy Violette and their staff at Abner Stein for their professional excellence: namely Ben Fowler, Laura Baxendale and Felicity Amor.

The wonderful team at Avon, who continue to be so enormously supportive of me and enthusiastic about George and Van den Bergen, in particular, Oli Malcolm, Eli Dryden, Helen Huthwaite, Kate Ellis and Natasha Harding. I'll raise a glass to us really taking the crime fiction world by storm with this third George book, guys!

Dr. Rosemary Broad, criminologist extraordinaire at Manchester

University for her practical wisdom regarding George's career path.

My wonderful friends - in particular, my bez, Louise Owen and fellow writers, Steph Williams and Wendy Storer who are always full of wise words.

The success of the series has in no small part been down to the support of many book reviewers and bloggers, including the splendid Ann Giles, Steph Broadribb, Garrick Webster and Keith Nixon for Crime Fiction Lover, Gordon Mcghie, Victoria Goldman, Christine from Northern Crime, Kindle Ninja (I'll keep his identity a mystery), Julie Boon and Celeste McCreesh. There are more, and they are all utterly terrific people, but I've got to hand in a book by June, so... This thanks also extends to the wonderful people who run and participate in online book clubs. I'm proud to feel welcomed in circles of such avid, savvy readers.

Mark Edwards for his perfect quote for the cover of *The Girl Who Broke the Rules*.

Helen Smith for her amazing dedication to BritCrime, of which I'm proud to be a part.

A colossal thanks to the Cockblankets for their ongoing, daily support – they know who they are and I'll tell you now, they're fabulous fuckers with the finest brains, sharpest wits and most glorious looks of any fuckers I know.

Finally, the biggest thanks of all goes out to my readers. You are the bestest, most brilliantest readers in the world and I love you in a non-biblical way forever.

Enjoyed *The Girl Who* series? Get your hands on the fifth gripping thriller in the George McKenzie series.

Available now.

**Find out how it all began in *Born Bad*, the first in the gritty
Manchester crime series**

'A leading light in Mancunian noir' *Guardian*

How far would you go to protect your empire?

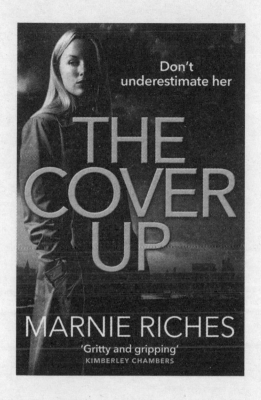

A heart-stopping read with a gritty edge, perfect
for fans of Martina Cole and Kimberley Chambers.